The

MAGIC MAN

The MAGIC MAN

The Olympic Peninsula series #3

Cat Treadgold

The Magic Man
ISBN: 979-8-9877363-3-3 (Trade Paperback)

Library of Congress Control Number: 2023915173

Any references to historical events, real people, or real places are used fictitiously. Names of restaurants and companies central to the plot are products of the author's imagination.

Cover design by Gemma Rakia
@gemmarakia
Interior design by Cat Treadgold
Anacortes, Washington
Cat@CatTreadgold.com
www.CatTreadgold.com

Printed in the United States of America

For my sister Laura
You are my rock!

I am so grateful for
your honest, always kind feedback and support and
your sharp editor's eye

THE OLYMPIC PENINSULA SERIES

The Silent Woodsman
The Guardsman
The Magic Man
The Changed Man
The Fallen Man

BEYOND THE OLYMPIC PENINSULA SERIES

Mister Movie Star
(Coming Soon)
Miz Country Goddess
Mister Heartbreaker

CONTENTS

PART I

CHAPTER 1

MADDIE FELT LIKE AN EXTRA who'd wandered onto the wrong movie set. In an attempt to look like she belonged, she feigned interest in the contents of the bookshelves. Loitering in the main parlor of the historic Manresa Hotel, she might as well be wearing a sign on her back saying FIFTH WHEEL. Once again, here she was, tagging along with her mother and her new fiancé. But hey, you didn't turn down an invitation to an intimate gathering hosted by a major country music star like Joe Bob Blade. Now retired from performing, Joe had gone back to using his real name—Joe O'Connell.

To make the situation still more intimidating, the rehearsal dinner had only fifteen guests, eighteen if you counted the nanny, May Allen, and Joe and Ali's identical twin daughters, who were only three months old and would be banished to the nursery when they got too cranky. From what Maddie had observed so far, that would be soon. Joe was one of five children, but his father had been dead for over ten years, and two of his brothers were on shaky ground with him and his sister Teresa, who would be married tomorrow. Shaky enough that they had better things to do than attend their only sister's wedding.

The groom was Joe's brother-in-law Liam. A grande dame like Carrie O'Connell couldn't be thrilled with her daughter's choice of husband. Liam was a first-class hunk of gorgeousness who could build a house on his own, outshoot Deadeye Dick, and throw knives like a circus performer. Skills that meant little to a society who valued status, money, and education above all else.

Maddie was only five feet two, and the O'Connells and the Ryans seemed to belong to another, superior species of human. They were all tall, especially Joe's older brother David, who had to be six-five. No wonder they'd named the family business Big Paul's Outfitters, after the mythical lumberjack Paul Bunyan. Every last one of them was larger than life and gifted with jaw-dropping beauty. Joe's father must have looked like Cary Grant; Joe and David both had a similarly eye-catching cleft chin. His mother Carrie was a famous beauty in the Grace Kelly mode and aging with all the "grace" money could buy.

"The party's downstairs," a bass-baritone voice boomed, making her jump. She looked up, way up, into the wide, merry, sea-green eyes of David O'Connell. The lyric "You get no sleep when you sleep with sheep" popped into her head. David was a dead ringer for the eldest brother in the movie version of *Seven Brides for Seven Brothers*, with his bold features and close-cropped bristly auburn hair and light dusting of beard.

"I was just scoping out some reading material," she said, straining for a valid excuse to avoid the cocktail hour.

David scratched his head. "You're staying at the compound, right? They don't have anything interesting on the bookshelves there?"

"I might be a guest here someday." Talk about digging the hole deeper. *Just admit you're escaping the party.* She didn't blush or cower, though inwardly she was doing both. Her acting training was even more useful offstage. *Never appear nervous unless the part calls for it.* With a wry smile, she admitted, "This is your family, not mine. You're all a little intimidating." She pointed at a book. "So, what's with all the *Reader's Digest* Condensed Books? Did someone sell off their entire collection?"

David's grin brought the adjective "piratical" to mind. "I imagine your average person isn't a fast enough reader to get through an unabridged novel during a three-day stay. What, you're too much of a snob for *Reader's Digest*?"

"Not at all. This shelf has led me to reevaluate my reading habits. I remember the plot of a book for a few months, but ultimately I only recall whether I liked it or not. Maybe I should stick to abridgments. Done well, they'd keep all the best parts. I could appear a lot more well-read."

He responded with a gratifying laugh, a rich, thrilling sound. With a decent ear, he'd have a wonderful singing voice.

"Besides," she went on, "you gotta admire the person with the cojones to condense *To Kill A Mockingbird*. That book is a masterpiece. Seems like sacrilege to cut anything."

"What about *The Way of All Flesh*? I've seen it in several of these anthologies."

"Have you read it?"

The suggestion seemed to amuse him. "No. Other than nonfiction and magazines, I read mostly thrillers. No 'classic' fiction that wasn't assigned to me in school."

"It's not erotica, you know. The 'way of all flesh' refers to death. It's an oldie but goodie. I liked it."

"But you don't remember what it was about."

"Nope."

They both laughed.

"There's a song called 'A Trip to the Library' in the musical *She Loves Me* that refers to that book. I was curious, so I read it."

"You were in the musical?"

"Yes." She decided not to elaborate. David didn't need to know she had played an ignorant good-time girl who meets a nerdy intellectual and gives up her slutty ways. David, though hardly nerdy, was super smart. You had to be brilliant to finish medical school by the age of twenty-four, one year younger than Maddie was now. Then he'd gone off to Africa, selflessly dedicating himself to helping the needy. Funny, he didn't look like a saint. She would have guessed the opposite.

"Come with me …." The way he beckoned wasn't reassuring. The man was just so formidable. She felt like a stray dog following an animal control officer into a trap. "We're nice when you get to know us, really."

"Even your mother?"

He considered the question a hair too long. "Her too. Recently she's had to rethink her goals in life. That can be painful. We need to cut her some slack."

As they walked through the hallway to the other side of the building, Maddie wondered why they'd chosen this venue for the rehearsal dinner. Manresa Castle was a nice enough Victorian hotel, but when you had the big bucks, why not go way fancier, like the Four Seasons in Seattle? Still, this place had great ambiance, and it wasn't as if Port Townsend offered anything equivalent to the Four Seasons. Occupying an entire block, the Manresa was a rich businessman's attempt to recreate a Prussian castle, with its cream-colored stucco and black mansard roof, turrets and all. It hadn't stayed a private residence for long. After the businessman died, the building remained vacant for a time, then served as a Jesuit seminary before being converted into a hotel. Maddie had no idea what the rooms were like. She was staying twenty minutes from town at the O'Connell Compound, four acres of beach-front property that centered around a graceful modern-colonial style mansion. The compound included guest houses, a separate gym, a recording studio, a fenced-in vegetable garden, and a large flagstone terrace with a killer view of the Strait of Juan de Fuca.

Manresa Castle displayed books in every common room, but the room they called "the library" had been rearranged to accommodate a long dining table. She stood at the entrance to take in the crystal chandeliers, velvet curtains, gleaming wood-paneled walls and ceilings, long Persian carpet, and portraits of the original owners—or were they people from that period whose portraits had ended up in curio shops? Maddie tugged up the bodice of her filmy little black dress with its nipped-in waist and low-cut neckline, hoping it wasn't too revealing. Due to her short stature, she was easily overwhelmed by too much fabric and never wore skirts longer than knee length. Dwarfed by David, she regretted her decision to wear flats.

"We are stepping back a hundred years in time," David said. "It's 1897, and we're terribly civilized and wonderfully naïve to the troubles of the world."

"You just returned from Africa, right?"

"Yes." Seeing how the question made him shut down, she didn't push it.

Ali was gently herding everyone to the table; the place cards told them where to sit. Joe's wife was every bit as kind as he was. No surprise, her origins being even humbler than Maddie's. She and the groom, Liam, were twins and former foster-children. Ali had met her birth father Duncan only two years ago, but she had been thrilled to find a blood relative and instantly embraced him. Then again, Duncan was hard to resist. Maddie couldn't believe he'd chosen her mother, who could talk an auctioneer under the table. Duncan was the coolest guy his age she'd ever met, and that included all the aging actors, a notoriously charming bunch. Duncan had their charm but also warmth and depth, qualities most actors had to fake. Spiky gray hair, an earring, a mellow Irish brogue, and the familiar features that marked him plainly as the father of Ali and Liam—the high cheekbones, the intense, cobalt-blue eyes, and the slightly crooked nose, though his skin was weathered by sun and hard living. Long and lean, about the same height as Liam, six feet two.

"Maddie," Ali said from across the table, "I'm going to seat you between Linc and Kilo. Linc is Joe's manager, and Kilo is the local yoga god." Kilo appeared taken aback by the introduction. Ali quickly added, "He and Teresa are old friends, and he's Liam's hiking buddy. He was once a featured dancer in the Groban Phillips Company." Maddie was duly impressed. Groban

Phillips had studied under Twyla Tharp and was now almost as famous as his mentor. She wondered at the "old friend" comment. Could a woman be simply a "friend" with a man as attractive and comfortable in his own skin as Kilo? Kilo was intriguing, but she'd rather sit next to David, who was seated across from them. On second thought, maybe not. David was flanked by his dauntingly aristocratic, expensively blonde mother Carrie, who scared her silly, and Ali's best friend Becca. Becca was an exotic, olive-skinned beauty, with a curvy figure, and long, curly black hair. When she spoke in her "New Yawk" accent, it was slightly jarring. Maddie had met Becca and her irrepressible French-Canadian chef husband Jean-Louis at Ali's birthday party a month back. They had an effortless, you might call it effervescent, chemistry together, with enough energy crackling between them to power the entire Manresa Hotel. Joe presided over the head of the table, next to Linc, and the two of them were engaged in a joking, teasing exchange. Linc's bushy gray hair and mustache and folksy manner would have made him a shoo-in to understudy Hal Holbrook in the play, *Mark Twain Tonight*. He was scary-tall, like David.

Kilo held out Maddie's chair, and she hid her surprise as he seated her. That never happened. She wondered how old he was, surely younger than thirty. Guys of her generation rarely did things like open doors for you, kiss your hand, or pull out your chair. Well, actors did. Charm was part of an actor's arsenal. They called it schmoozing. You were always kissing up to someone—agents, more established actors, directors, stagehands, costumers, fans, potential fans—in other words, everyone. You never knew who would recommend you for your next role or put itching powder in your costume if you crossed them.

Kilo's gentlemanly gesture inspired instant distrust.

"David," she heard Carrie say, "when is Sylvia coming to visit?"

David didn't reply immediately.

Who is Sylvia? Maddie thought.

Clearly disgruntled, David dragged his fingers through his short thatch of auburn hair. "She has a sister and brother-in-law in Portland, and she promised to spend Christmas with them. Her plan is to arrive in Port Townsend the day after and stay through New Year's."

Colleagues didn't spend the holidays with you unless they were *really* good friends. Dismayed, Maddie realized her glass was empty.

"Another?" Kilo asked, already pouring. She thanked him with a polite smile, one ear still cocked at David and Carrie.

She heard, "Mom, I have no idea where that relationship is going. I haven't ruled out marriage—if that's what you're getting at. You know why. Last we spoke, the ball was in her court."

She didn't catch Carrie's response because Kilo was vying for her attention. She'd heard enough, unfortunately. David was taken. With a disappointed sigh, she turned to Kilo. He did have beautiful dark eyes and really long eyelashes. Like many Eurasian men, he had a unique appeal. His skin appeared to be almost poreless, and there was that androgynous thing. Not that Kilo wasn't manly. He was a lot taller than she was, and she'd bet he looked fabulous naked.

"Ali says you're an actress," he said.

Ah. Her least favorite conversational opener, usually followed by *What have I seen you in?* "Not a successful one," she replied. "I got my Equity card last spring doing a Theater for Young Audiences tour."

"What was the play?"

"A one-hour adaptation of *Charlotte's Web* for kids. The musical score was kind of stupid, but the costumes were fun."

The way he zeroed in on her was flattering. Though she should know better. Most actors could do that super-attentive listener role convincingly for a short period before they switched the subject to themselves.

"I can't recall much of the story," he said, "though I don't see you as the pig."

She laughed. "I was the girl, Fern. I would have loved to be Charlotte the spider, but I seem to be typecast as a young girl or boy. My height, you know."

He gave her an appreciative sweep of his dark eyes. "I can see you as a beautiful boy." His gaze stopped at her breasts. "Almost."

"I bind them." Her blunt response made him blush, a reaction that surprised her. She self-consciously fingered her short blond curls. Her mother had dyed her hair the exact same color, as if they were in competition. "As a matter of fact, I'll be playing a boy in my next play, here in Port Townsend. Shakespeare's *A Midsummer Night's Dream.*"

There was something odd about his smile. "How great is that? Decent pay?"

"Not exactly," she said, fairly sure he was coming on to her. Maybe that was okay. "It's a Lort D Theater. Better than non-Equity but hardly a living wage."

He nodded. He didn't ask, so she didn't bother to explain that was the lowest paid of the union houses, with a mix of Equity and non-Equity actors.

"The show will run Thursday through Sunday for three weeks in

February. They'll extend the run if they can sell enough tickets. Rehearsals begin shortly after New Year's."

"And you're Puck? Heart-shaped faces look great in short hair. I can totally see you as Puck."

Interesting. A dancer who knew his Shakespeare. Maybe he'd seen one of the movie versions.

They were serving the main course, a choice of grilled salmon or chicken, since no one was vegan or, she gathered, vegetarian. Kilo and she both chose salmon. Wait, he was pouring her another glass. She vowed not to drink it. Wasn't this her third? That was about her limit.

That was when her mother butted in. "You teach yoga?"

"I own a studio on Lawrence Street," Kilo responded, making the distinction between mere instructor and owner for Maddie's benefit, no doubt. Maddie smiled to herself. She was warming to the idea of Kilo. Leave it to her mother to talk about types of yoga she'd tried, yoga injuries, hot yoga …. Kilo listened patiently and only chimed in when he couldn't avoid it. Reddening, Maddie cast a helpless look at Joe, whose eyes twinkled in sympathy. David and Carrie seemed oblivious, though David did catch her eye and held her gaze for a disconcertingly long moment. What was he trying to tell her? She applied herself to her salmon and tuned in to the other conversations within hearing distance.

"I have a view on a building at the edge of town," Jean-Louis said in his heavy Québécois accent. "If I can negotiate a good price, we'll begin renovations after New Year's."

"A building with a view?" Carrie asked, confused.

"It does have a nice view of Port Townsend Bay," Becca said, "but he means that he has his eye on it. Port Townsend already has a high-end French restaurant, but we're betting there's also room for one featuring wild game and seafood. Joe and Liam are investors."

"Another Lah Fetuh Sovajuh?" Linc said in a mangled French accent.

Jean-Louis' mobile features stilled, his expression blank with incomprehension. Realization finally dawned, and they were in motion again. "Ah, yes. Like the other two restaurants in North Bend and Bellevue, La Fête Sauvage. The Wild Feast in English. *Là, là*, our décor is becoming less … *vulgaire*. No more trips to Quartzsite."

"He means less … low brow," Becca said with an indulgent smile. "No more animal heads from flea markets in Arizona. Just artists' renditions of heads and fake racks of antlers."

Jean-Louis's thick eyebrows drew together and he glared. "*Becca* ... I told you I don't need a translator."

Ignoring his rebuke, his wife went on, "Lots of gilding and gold spray paint, though. The kitschy thing is Jean-Louis's trademark. And reproductions of Delacroix paintings, of course, or Delacroix-esque *hommages*." Becca's French was fluent, and she pronounced the word with an authentic flourish.

"Will you buy a house here?" Teresa asked.

Every time Maddie saw her, she looked different. She guessed it was the hair. Like her mother, Carrie, Teresa had rocked a society princess's sleek blonde chignon when they'd first met. Now it was short and curly like Maddie's, only hers was auburn with strawberry-blonde streaks. Teresa was still willowy and slender with a petite build, but her lovely face looked softer, her sky-blue eyes more luminous. If she'd been an actress, they might have competed for the same roles, though Teresa was a few inches taller. Maddie envied the way she and Liam gazed adoringly at each other. Despite the faint shrapnel scars on one side of his face, Ali's brother was gorgeous enough to be a movie star, and he only had eyes for Teresa. He had little to say, however, at least at this gathering. His silence added to his mystique.

"The place we are 'eyeing' "—Jean-Louis paused to glare at Becca— "has apartments above. We need to keep it simple, because we will divide our time between Port Townsend and North Bend, and we don't wnt too much maintenance."

"I told you," Ali said, "you are welcome to take one of the cabins."

Jean-Louis grew serious. "We would never abuse your hospitality."

Teresa pretended to pout. "Whose cabin is up for grabs?"

Ali gave her a stern look. "Not Liam's. You'll stay with him for the foreseeable future, right? But I can see your real concern. Where will you put all your clothes?" Teresa pretended to hang her head. "Don't worry, Liam will build you a special climate-controlled storage room."

Liam finally spoke. "I will?" His eyes glinted with mischief. "Oh, I definitely will. It may be an eyesore though. Just so you know."

"In the meantime," Ali said, dismissing him with a mock-stern glare, "I'll store them in the closet in the guest bedroom we rarely use. We hope you'll stay as long as you like. What would we do without the dogs?"

For a moment, no one spoke. This part was still up in the air. Maddie knew that the tiny Chihuahua/Jack Russell mix Coogan and giant German Shepherd/mastiff mix Harry—named after Clint Eastwood characters—were best friends and a key element of the compound's security against thieves and paparazzi. Though they loved everyone, they were particularly attached to Teresa and Liam.

"I hope there won't be a custody battle," Duncan remarked, deadpan.

An uneasy laugh rippled around the table. Dessert provided a timely interruption, and Laurie excused herself to go to the bathroom, releasing Kilo from her conversational web. With her mother out of earshot, Maddie apologized.

"She does like to talk," Kilo admitted, making a show of wiping his brow.

Maddie sighed. Loyalty demanded that she not badmouth her mother or acknowledge her social gaucheness.

Turning to Maddie, Linc said, "I hear you have an agent. Joe says you're quite a songbird." She couldn't place his accent. Not a Southern drawl, but sort of folksy. He'd grown up in Port Angeles, but most of his clients were based in Nashville.

"She's pretty good, I guess. This is my second agent. I'm lucky to have found someone more concerned with career building than instant results." Seeing the question on his face, she supplied her agent's name. "Lola Deters. So far she's only gotten me print work, but I've had a few callbacks for commercials and industrials. I'm told that if I want to get serious, I'll have to move to L.A. or New York."

"For TV and movies, maybe," Linc said. "Quality of life should also be considered. Seattle isn't the Podunk town it used to be. It has a vibrant theater community. Joe says you're doing a show in Port Townsend?"

"Yes, in February. Shakespeare's *A Midsummer Night's Dream*, with original music and choreography. The director was in my acting program at NYU."

She turned to Joe, eager to take the attention off herself. "Ali says you have enough material for a new album. I meant to ask about it when we rehearsed the song for the wedding yesterday."

Joe flashed her his killer smile. The whole family could do that, melt your heart with one easy grin. "I still have to record it. I can do that here in my studio once I locate a solid sound engineer. Preferably someone local. People do record their own stuff without outside help. I prefer to have another set of ears on it."

"Will you tour?" His features grew pinched, making Maddie wish she hadn't asked. Joe's career had hit the skids when vocal nodules had forced him to bow out of a tour. A few different tours, in fact. His speaking voice still sounded rough.

He recovered quickly. "Don't think so." He cleared his throat. "Even if my voice cleared up dramatically, I'd be reluctant to leave the girls. They might do something exciting while I'm gone, like speak in a language I can understand."

Carrie laughed, and Maddie was surprised to observe signs of thawing in the ageless ice goddess. "You and Jake used to do the twin-talk thing."

"So you claim," Joe said, patting his mother's hand.

In the silence, Jake's absence became more glaring. They promptly dropped the subject.

"How long will you be in town?" Kilo whispered in her ear.

She hadn't expected him to make his move so soon. She did feel his heat. "I'll see you at the wedding," she whispered back. "I don't have any other catering work until the weekend after, so I could stay till Monday. It depends on Duncan and my mom. They're my ride."

He slipped her a card under the table. "I wrote my cell number on it. I'd love to take you dancing."

Behind her, Laurie said, "Maddie, I'd like to show you something." She almost toppled her chair in her rush to stand. "Come with me?"

"Okay." She surreptitiously slipped Kilo's card into her purse. Eyeing her half-eaten dessert with regret, she said, "If the waiter comes, he can take away my plate." She wanted to finish the chocolate mousse, but she was about to be lectured, and it wouldn't look so appealing if and when she returned.

Out in the hallway, Laurie lowered her voice to say, "Do you have to pick up the yoga instructor in front of the whole family? You know, he used to be married to Teresa."

"*What?*" She did a mental readjustment.

"They were high school sweethearts," Laurie said, hands on hips. "They eloped. The family arranged for an annulment."

Really? Maddie thought. *What is he doing at Teresa's rehearsal dinner?*

"He's friends with Liam now," her mother explained as if hearing her thoughts.

"I wasn't 'picking him up,' " Maddie said wearily. "He's an inveterate charmer. I know the type. They can't help themselves. Was I supposed to make it clear to everyone that I spit on guys like him? We weren't exactly playing footsie under the table."

For once her mother was at a loss for words. "I'm only asking you to watch your step," she sputtered.

Maddie tried making light of the situation. "I didn't let him drag me into the garden so we could make out."

"I'm just saying … you've had a bit to drink."

"So have you. So have we all. It's not like I'm eyeing the lampshade as possible headgear."

"Not yet."

Duncan joined them in the hallway. "Shall we go back to the compound? Party's breaking up." He winked at Maddie. She loved his Irish brogue. Becca called him, "the coolest dad ever." No kidding. When Maddie was fourteen, her own father had run off with a neighbor and died a year later of cirrhosis. She hoped Laurie wouldn't blow it. She loved her mother, but she was a handful, and this was her first serious relationship in years.

In the garden, she caught sight of Kilo watching her from his car, a vintage Corvette. The streetlight made it appear midnight blue. Could he be any more obvious? She waved, and he blew her a kiss. *Hmm.* The guy was smooth. Too smooth. When she reached Duncan's sensible Toyota Camry station wagon, she stood by the door, waiting for it to be unlocked.

That was when she caught a glimpse of David, also watching her. He stood silhouetted in the shadows, so still he might have been a statue. She wished she could read his expression.

The two men set off a battle in her brain.

David's an adult, a little voice insisted. *Kilo will never grow up.*

David is too much of an adult for you, another voice argued. *And he's not available.*

That doesn't mean you have to date Kilo.

Most women would kill to date a guy like Kilo.

Can you even call that dating? That would be a fling, nothing else. You've had too many of those already.

Not that many.

She gave herself a little shake as she put on her seatbelt. *Stop that. Live for the moment. Your life is too up in the air for anything permanent. You'd break David's heart or destroy his relationship. Or he'd break your heart and derail your career.*

No one spoke during the twenty-minute car ride back to the compound. Not even her mother. Which gave the querulous voices in Maddie's head full rein.

* * *

David had retreated to the garden for a breath of fresh air—in other words, to escape his mother. At times like this he wished he were a smoker, a great excuse for others to give you a wide berth. Bless Joe and Ali for offering him a refuge in Port Townsend while he got his head straight. It seemed to have worked for Teresa and Liam. He loved seeing his sister so happy, and Liam was surprisingly down-to-earth for James Bond's better-looking brother.

Who was this Maddie? Other than every teenage boy's wet dream, with her Kewpie Doll face and Barbie Doll body. On the opposite end of the spectrum from Sylvia, certainly. He'd stopped short of telling Carrie and Joe there was no "David and Sylvia." His mom was already up in arms about his love child, Lorenzo. He could just imagine how she'd react when he confessed to having no interest in marrying the kid's mother. One sticky revelation at a time.

This Kilo guy, owner of the local yoga studio and Teresa's high-school folly …. Edward had chased them to California, and soon after, Carrie had the marriage annulled. You couldn't really blame Kilo for that—he'd only been eighteen. But what was he up to now? Even if he had been wet behind the ears ten years ago, Kilo was a studly hot-to-trot adult male now. A regular snake in the grass. And Maddie was the mouse. Was she going to fall for so obvious an act? David had thought she was interested in *him*, and he was plenty interested back. But the timing sucked. Sylvia's visit was a done deal. If he wanted any kind of access to little Lorenzo, he had no choice but to wriggle out of that marriage trap with extreme caution. He might have better luck escaping a straitjacket while underwater.

David heaved a heavy sigh. He would have to let Maddie slip through his fingers. Besides, what was she going to say when she discovered his big fat secret? "Oh, no problem, I'm totally up for a relationship with a freak of nature." He scowled as he watched Kilo ogle Maddie from his penis car. Then Maddie caught David's eye. *Damn*. Apparently invisibility wasn't one of his superpowers. He moved back into the shadows.

CHAPTER 2

———•———

Jesus, Mary, and Joseph, how I love this man, Teresa thought as she stood next to Liam at their makeshift altar. Her wedding was a far cry from the sun-drenched affair she had pictured. Not that Teresa had ever been one to obsess over her perfect wedding. In fact, her only wedding dreams had been nightmares where she found herself poised to marry the wrong man. She and Kilo had eloped, and that had been "made right" by her family. Then she'd been engaged to Paul, financially and socially ideal but morally bankrupt. With Liam, she had no doubts at all. She gazed up at him, so magnificent in Joe's tux. Joe and Liam were the same height. Joe wasn't as muscular as Liam—who was?—but Joe favored less fitted styles, and the tux might have been made for Liam.

She almost giggled. Who knew that her fierce guardsman could take on a persona appropriate to any scenario? Her first glimpse of him had been as a bank guard in Israel—he still hadn't elaborated on those three-plus years he'd been "missing, presumed dead." In their second encounter—a welcome-home dinner at her mother's—he'd looked like a European dandy. But mostly, Teresa knew him as the paragon of manhood who chopped wood, threw knives, and could build or fix anything. That was her favorite version of Liam—the glistening muscles framed in jeans, work boots, T-shirt, and flannel. He'd trimmed his straight, blue-black hair, but a lock still fell boyishly across this forehead, where faint shrapnel scars scored one side of his face. The scars were more pronounced on the right side of his chest and leg. He claimed not to recall the explosion or the days of healing when they'd induced a coma. Teresa had never met someone less concerned with his appearance. Of course, the scars only heightened the splendor of his face and form.

Jean-Louis, with his usual *joie de vivre*, was making the most of his second stint as wedding officiant, his license to marry obtained online. The burly, bearded descendant of indigenous Canadians and French fur traders turned master chef and restaurateur proclaimed every word of the abbreviated Catholic service with a flourish.

"Liam Lord Ryan, do you take this woman …."

There was an awful moment when Teresa thought the gathering would erupt into laughter. Liam's startled deep-blue eyes met hers. His middle name was "Lord"? There was still so much she didn't know about him. No matter. She knew what was important. That he loved her, would die to keep her safe.

Then it was Liam's turn to be amused as her expense: Jean-Louis referred to her as "Teresa Flora O'Connell." Not even Granny had been a fan of her given name.

The rain drummed harder on the canopy as Liam slipped the ring on her finger. He had no family heirlooms, but he did have a Swiss bank account, it turned out, and he certainly had taste. The ring was simple yet elegant, a perfect solitaire surrounded by smaller diamonds in a platinum setting. She still couldn't believe how Joe had transformed the weather disaster into a boon. The stormy seas of the Strait of Juan de Fuca presented a dramatic backdrop, and Joe, Liam, Linc, and Duncan had draped the canopy with moss, fir boughs, and ferns from the area they'd cleared for a hot tub, intertwined with gauzy fabric purchased in town. The forecast had been favorable, but anything could happen in mid-October on the Olympic Peninsula—even in Port Townsend, which was in the rain shadow.

Teresa and Liam remained at the altar, holding hands, as Maddie came to the forefront and Joe tuned his guitar. Teresa didn't know why anyone would want to subject themselves to the rigors and humiliations of an acting career. She supposed it required a particular temperament. Personally, she'd never craved the limelight; in fact, she could have done without this ceremony. Maddie, who glowed with dewy nubile beauty like an erotic fantasy of a woodland fairy, had a quiet confidence about her as she stood next to Joe and beamed at the audience, welcoming them into her warm circle.

Joe began to play the opening to "Our Love is Here to Stay," by George Gershwin. When Maddie opened her mouth, her voice rang out in the stillness.

"It's very clear, our love is here to stay. Not for a year, but ever and a day …."

Teresa wished she'd asked Maddie for tips on how to project. Maddie had a clear, mellow voice that bathed you in its purity. Teresa didn't know much about singing, but Maddie's gift seemed extraordinary. And the emotion behind the song moved her to tears.

Which was ironic, because judging from last night, Kilo and Maddie were going to be a thing. She hoped Maddie understood that no "love" with Kilo was here to stay. Teresa would give it two months, tops, since Maddie was special. Of course, Teresa's knowledge of Kilo's character dated back to high school, not just to the yoga classes she'd attended upon arriving in Port Townsend. One afternoon, before she and Liam had acknowledged their attraction, Kilo had lured her into his lair for a few minutes before they were interrupted. That brief encounter told her he hadn't changed. She suspected he didn't do monogamy, even serial monogamy. Maddie deserved better. Someone like David, who appeared entranced. At the rehearsal dinner, Teresa had detected chemistry between them. Only, David was involved with a fellow doctor. How involved? He hadn't divulged any details.

David. What had happened to him? Like all her brothers, he had a maddening habit of internalizing everything. The reasons for his return would have to be dragged out of him. Had one patient too many died? Once he'd been a bright light, full of joy. Even as a geeky, gangling kid, too brilliant for his own good and two years younger than his classmates. Now he just seemed … resigned. Teresa saw him looking at Kilo, whose gaze expressed … hunger. Could Maddie handle a Kilo? At eighteen—she couldn't vouch for earlier— he had already possessed an impressive understanding of the female body. He had been Teresa's first, the only man she'd slept with other than her former fiancé Paul and Liam. Paul had never measured up to Kilo, but Liam had spoiled her for all others.

She squeezed her new husband's hand, and he squeezed back.

Teresa had implored her brother Jake to attend, but he insisted his presence would put a damper on her "big day." Besides, he was off in Oakland, California, overseeing the new corporate offices of Big Paul's Outfitters, the family business. Granny didn't owe her fortune to Big Paul's. She'd made wise—or simply lucky—tech investments, a windfall they hadn't discovered until after her death. Nineteen then, Teresa was too devastated by her annulled marriage to appreciate her new address on Easy Street. She'd been almost fourteen when Da's death from lung cancer had ripped the family apart. He'd left his wife Carrie another fortune, earned through investments, patents, and in the last ten years of his life, the success of Big Paul's. The five siblings were set for life, but to Teresa, it had felt like blood money. She would have gladly given it all for another twenty years with her father.

Unaware that Joe and Jake were twins or even related, Ali had started dating Jake because of his resemblance to Joe, who she'd never expected to see again. When fate finally threw Joe in her path, she dropped Jake like a hot potato. At six feet, Jake was still tall but built more like a male model than the others, who had inherited their father's impressive physique. If only Jake wasn't so uptight and obsessed with money and status …. Joe's magic lay in his quiet charisma. Joe and Jake were estranged. Jake had initiated the rift, and he'd never told Teresa the cause. Was it jealousy or something Joe had done?

Then there was Edward, the eldest, the Catholic priest who had written them all off for some mysterious reason that might be as simple as a lack of piety. They exchanged the occasional email, card, or letter, but he never traveled West, and their mother was the only one who visited him at his parish in Philadelphia.

The song ended. The guests were so mesmerized, they applauded. Funny, at a wedding. She and Liam exchanged amused glances. Then, realizing their inappropriateness, the guests clapped louder, laughing and hooting. It was just the core group from last night. Teresa whispered, "I love you, my Lord."

Liam bristled, then his mouth quirked into a devious smile. "You'll pay for that. I didn't choose that stupid name, and I have a few choice words for the person who told Jean-Louis."

Teresa chuckled. Liam could handle a little teasing, though she didn't want to take it too far. The absurdity of that middle name was just too rich to ignore.

When the clapping died down, Ali's twin baby girls broke into a chorus of screams. Everyone but Ali and the nanny laughed. The two women carried the black-haired blue-eyed imps off to the house in short order, and the laughter died down enough for Joe to play the recessional. Odd as Mendelssohn's Wedding March from *A Midsummer Night's Dream* sounded on the acoustic guitar, Joe made it work. Wasn't that the play Maddie would be doing in February? People threw confetti, and Liam and Teresa exchanged another chaste kiss for their benefit. More hooting and hollering, especially from the men—her brothers, Ali's father, and Joe's manager Linc.

When they reached the end of the canopy, Liam whispered, "Will they forgive us if we disappear into the cabin now?"

She gave him a stern look. "Photos first, a few congratulations. You can handle it, my Lord." She waggled her brows. He sighed and shook his head before bracing to face the gauntlet.

Not much of a gauntlet, Teresa thought, though his attitude said as much.

She was particularly interested in the way he drew Carrie in for a hug. Her initial resistance was glaringly obvious. It didn't last long. Teresa's new husband was irresistible.

Back at the cabin, Liam wasted no time in lifting the cream chiffon sheath over her head. "I love this dress, but I love what's under it even more." He kissed her belly button, then his full lips descended from there, beneath her sheer panties. He eased her back onto the bed and she dissolved into a puddle of need, surrendering to his tongue. He was awfully good at this. They hadn't discussed his past sexual exploits, which could no doubt fill volumes. He'd matured freakishly early—they called that precocious puberty. She suspected his first time hadn't been fully consensual. Her sexual past couldn't fill a pamphlet, but the parts involving Kilo provided the highlights. That was why Liam had befriended Kilo, to de-fang him. It didn't seem fair somehow. Did she want to know? Definitely not.

She was already close to climax. At her moan, Liam drew back and slid his hands up her back. Then he slowly pressed her onto the bed, his glittering blue eyes boring into hers, his lips parted. She reached up to help him with his tux, though he was managing well on his own, shrugging it off like a snake sheds its skin.

How many women had he had—fifty, a hundred, more? *Don't think about that now.*

She sighed as he entered her at last and began to move, at first with agonizing slowness, circling, thrusting. His eyes, which never left hers, were glazed with lust.

She had no doubt that he loved her … at this moment.

* * *

Ali and Joe were lying together, sated, in their king-sized bed. Ali snuggled against him with a happy sigh. "That was … amazing. Maybe you were inspired by the day?"

He chuckled. "The air was thick with pheromones. Not just Liam and Teresa. I hope Maddie knows what she's doing with Kilo."

"He's hotter than a pepper sprout, all right."

Joe snorted. "Someone's been listening to Johnny Cash. You know, pepper sprouts aren't all that hot." He rolled back on top of her. "Maddie's far from naive. She can handle someone as obvious as Kilo. I just hope she makes him wear a condom."

"Joe!" Ali gave him a stern look. "Friends don't let friends fall for Kilo."

"Oh, relax." He silenced her with a lingering kiss.

17

Amazed, she felt him stir against her. "Was that …?"

"Oh, yeah."

When they were side by side again, their breathing returning to normal, she said, "Why not David?"

"Why not David what?"

"Why not Maddie and David? I sensed chemistry."

Joe gave her an odd look. "David's engaged. Or something like it."

"Then why didn't his fiancée come home with him?"

Joe folded his hands behind his head. "Good question. One of many I might ask my dear brother, were he open to talking. He isn't. But really? Maddie and David? He's six foot five and she's, what, five two? Their necks would have permanent cricks. They'd call that story, 'The Giant and the Fairy.' Plus, he's ten years older. It is simply too odd. Our little clan is already incestuous. Liam is my brother-in-law twice over. Teresa is your sister-in-law twice over. That is weird enough. We can't have my older brother marrying the stepdaughter of your birth father."

Ali glared. "Laurie and Duncan aren't married yet."

Joe drew lazy circles on her stomach. "Don't get your hopes up. I know she isn't your favorite person. Yeah, she talks too much. But her heart is in the right place. And she did *something* right. She raised Maddie."

Ali stared at the ceiling. "I hope Liam really has changed. The reformation is hard to swallow, considering his callous behavior toward all his past girlfriends—the ones I met before he disappeared, anyway."

"That was before he got blown up by Hamas and barely survived."

"You also went through something pretty traumatic," Ali said in a small voice.

"Hmm. You mean my traitorous vocal cords." He paused. "Hardly on a par with surviving a terrorist attack. If not for that, how would we have met? You were ambling around in the woods performing some voodoo ritual for your supposedly dead brother, and I was sulking in Linc's cabin because I was sworn to absolute silence."

She frowned at his unflattering description of her little ceremony in the woods, when she'd hoped to commune with Liam's spirit through the Navajo medicine bag his drama teacher had given him. She alone had believed he was still alive, that she could contact him through twin magic. Not as absurd as it sounded, given their psychic connection. She had heard his voice then, telling her to "soldier on," the way he always had when she was close to despair. But it was pure luck—or maybe fate—that had led her to that cabin in the woods, where she'd fallen for a rugged woodsman who turned out to be a famous country singer. He'd written a song about their meeting, and the rest was history.

"I don't worry about Liam," Joe said, interrupting her thoughts. "I *do* worry about the honeymoon Teresa planned as a surprise. He should have had a say in that. The trip to Jerusalem is his only experience with travel overseas, and look how that turned out?"

Ali closed her eyes. "We both grew up dreaming of Paris and exotic places. The reality was something of a disappointment for me." She recalled those dreary final months of her pregnancy in Paris. The gray skies, her ponderous body.

Already cradling her tenderly, Joe drew her in closer. "Don't blame Paris. You were pregnant with twins. We'll go back someday when the girls are older and you can appreciate it. We'll go in the spring. It's nicer then."

"If you say so. The Parisians can be awful snobs."

"You can find those anywhere, especially in big cities, among the rich and famous."

CHAPTER 3

———•———

AT THE WEDDING AND DINNER that evening, Maddie kept her contact with Kilo to a minimum. No need to ruffle her mother's feathers again. It wasn't anyone's business but hers if she decided to go out with Kilo.

Stealing a moment when she believed she was unobserved, she approached him at the buffet, a delicious array of cold meats and salmon, salads, and pickled and sauteed vegetables prepared in advance by Jean-Louis's newest restaurant in Bellevue. When she sidled up to Kilo and said hello, his face lit up. "I thought you weren't talking to me."

She kept her voice low and pretended to concentrate on the food. "I don't want my mother to get her panties in a twist. So, pay attention. You want to see me again?"

Matching her cool demeanor, Kilo said, "How about tomorrow night? Do you know Kelpies? I could pick you up."

"In that flashy Corvette? I don't think so. Meet you there at six?"

"Works for me."

"Tomorrow, then." She walked away as if they'd exchanged nothing more than innocuous small talk.

She'd gotten the ball rolling. Would she regret it? Kilos she understood, couldn't possibly fall in love with. Her life was too unsettled for Davids. They demanded things, wanted you to stay in one place, had complex psyches that sucked you in.

* * *

The morning after the wedding, David moved into the cabin Teresa had vacated weeks earlier. Carrie and Rostand had left at seven to drive Teresa and Liam back to Seattle so they could catch their flight to Paris from Sea-Tac Airport later that night. David could just imagine the discomfiture of that drive. Rostand, his mother's Algerian-born cook and factotum, seldom spoke except in response to questions or requests, though his British English was better than that of most Americans. Carrie still smarted from having to watch her only daughter marry beneath her, and now she had to tolerate a long car ride with the Neanderthal groom. Needless to say, she hadn't appreciated David's decision to stay behind.

Too bad. David was at his wits' end, sick to death of doing what was expected of him, what was noble. He wanted to go all caveman—toss Maddie over his shoulder and haul her back to his cabin. God knows he needed some outlet for the tension that threatened to crack him like an egg, showing everyone exactly how gooey and wishy-washy he'd become. He'd always been a doer. Presented with a problem, he acted, took a step toward making it right, no matter how small. But Sylvia was a force of nature. No point in planning or plotting; he could only react in the moment. To keep from going bonkers, he strove to put her out of his mind until the day of reckoning arrived.

At lunch they feasted on leftovers from the wedding. Ali and Joe still had a houseful of guests, which now included Becca and Jean-Louis.

The sun had returned, after abandoning them during the rain-soaked ceremony. But the evening was too cool to lounge around outside, even with heat lamps and a firepit. While the others sat at the dining room table, Joe led David into the living room, where they sat with plates of smoked pheasant, beet salad, and Crab Newburg.

David was still puzzling over Teresa's decorating choices. The art deco living room, for instance. Cream-colored walls, tiled floors, a grand piano, and intricate embellishments—the furniture upholstered in cream floral-chenille fabric with multiple scrolls in the wooden details. Joe and Ali would have favored knotty pine and bear-skin rugs. This room should be occupied by petite French people, the men donning vests and cravats and consulting their pocket watches, the bird-like women draped in sequined gowns with simple lines à la Coco Chanel. David felt like a lumberjack at a seven-year-old girl's tea party.

Joe cut to the chase. "You didn't kill anyone on the operating table, right? No one was slaughtered in front of you?"

David chuckled at Joe's attempts to keep it light. "Nothing like that.

The poverty and ignorance were intense, but we didn't stumble into any warzones or get kidnapped. We did a lot of vaccinating and education. With all the different dialects, most of the townsfolk know some English, if only to communicate with each other. We had a traveling clinic. I performed some surgeries on the spot, mostly appendectomies, wound treatment, bone setting. I could bore you with details. Spare us both and change the subject."

"In a moment," Joe said, holding up a finger, his smile a tad forced. "So, nothing dramatic sent you home."

"Not at all." *That's mostly true*, David thought. *One specific event, to be sure, but also a clusterfuck of tragedy and annoyance.* Aloud, he said, "Four years and three months was enough. They don't ask for more than a three-month commitment from surgeons because you're always on call. I'm no saint. I missed the US of A. Will you tell me about your album now?"

"Hold your horses. After you took a look at my vocal cords the other day, my voice was totally clear for the first time in years. Did you do anything?"

Ah, you noticed, David thought. He'd paid a steep price: a four-hour migraine. Knowing what was coming, he'd told them not to expect him for dinner. "Weird," he told Joe. "Perhaps your recent hoarseness was more psychosomatic?"

A silence loomed, then Joe said, "One last thing. How are things with Sylvia? I know she's going to visit us over the holidays. I don't want to step in anything while she's here by raising sensitive subjects."

"Sylvia." David put his plate aside and slumped against the unyielding couch. "If I could, I'd tell her not to come." Predictably, Joe raised his eyebrows. "It's gonna be awkward as hell. I wish I could spare you. The last thing I worry about is *you* being insensitive. I haven't made any decisions regarding Sylvia. For reasons that will become clear."

Joe got the message and steered the conversation back into calmer waters—his music, the twins, Teresa and Liam. David supposed he shouldn't be surprised by Joe's giving him the third degree. He had every right. But he sure had been leadfooted about it. David knew they were worried, that he wasn't his usual jolly self. It was possible that person was gone forever. Sylvia didn't seem to mind. Too bad he couldn't be as accepting of *her* flaws. In the field, she had been courageous, brilliant, and decisive. Also domineering, opinionated, and mercurial, though those qualities surfaced later. He sure as hell wasn't going to marry her. He probably wouldn't even sleep with her. The question was, if not, how would he get what he wanted? Not without a battle.

He hated battles. The verbal kind. He was fine with beating a guy to a pulp if he deserved it.

* * *

Maddie had unintentionally eavesdropped on Joe and David's conversation from a hidden corner of the alcove, but before she could hear David's response to Joe's Sylvia question, her mom's boyfriend Duncan sidled up beside her and said, "Are you having a good time?"

She cursed his timing. "Oh, ... yes." She began to veer toward the kitchen, hoping he hadn't alerted Joe and David to her presence. "I'd like to get a glass of water." As she poured from the pitcher, she said, "The wedding was so refreshingly intimate. Nothing like those spectacles I usually wait tables for."

"Your performance was a high point. Ever sing opera?"

"I was trained classically, and I did learn some arias and art songs. Not much call for them. People want to hear *Phantom of the Opera*, not *actual* opera. Even Puccini, the most easy-listening opera there is. 'Think of Me' is in my repertoire. Stupid song."

"Not my favorite show."

"*Hugely* popular," Maddie said with a sweeping gesture. "You and I are iconoclasts. However, I sing what I'm paid to sing and act the lines I'm paid to act. Even if they stink, I find a way to believe in them. Fortunately Christine is a lyric soprano who belts—not my best range." Maddie did a mental pivot, thinking she must be boring him. "What will you do now that you're retired? Will you and Mom move to Port Townsend too?"

"Laurie has her real estate gig and her volunteer work at the foodbank. Not that she couldn't do both here. I'm inclined to join the cult." He laughed to show her he was kidding. "I've caught the bug from Liam and Ali, who have connected with this area bigtime. Might write a memoir about my adventures deep-sea diving. Everyone's doing it. Memoirs, I mean."

"I will *never* write a memoir." Maddie spoke so emphatically that Duncan looked concerned.

"That sounds like *too* much to tell. You're only twenty-five."

"Actors grow up fast. It's an ugly business. Can be, anyway. But the growing up part began with my alcoholic father. Maybe I'm talking about loss of innocence, not maturity. My father didn't molest me," she rushed to reassure him. "I hated to witness his decline, that's all, and he used to embarrass us in public a lot. As for acting, it's just tiring—not the performing part. Most of it involves endless auditioning and a lot of rejection. Even the rehearsals can be tedious. I probably shouldn't have taken this local gig. It won't lead to anything. I thought it might be … restful. I didn't have to audition because I know the director and producer. Ali's invited me to stay here. Otherwise I'd be rooming with other actors."

"How will you get around?"

"I've got my eye on a Vespa with a for-sale sign. It's parked by one of the B and Bs." Duncan was frowning again, as if already assuming the role of father. "I know they can be dangerous, but I'll only be tooling around the area. Liam's been showing me how to ride his motorcycle so I can use it while he's gone."

"My God." The disapproving frown had been replaced by wide-eyed dismay. "Someone your size can ride a monster like that?"

She laughed. "With caution and a few tricks. Don't worry, it's a temporary measure."

"Even with the Vespa, I'd worry. Won't your rehearsals run late?"

"If it's late enough or the weather's bad, I'll stay over with a friend in town. Does that calm your fears?" She smiled reassuringly.

His answering smile was wry. "Here I am, acting like a mother hen. I'm not your dad. I'm thinking about what happened to Teresa. The accidents that weren't accidents."

"The bad guy's dead, right? They exposed the man who hired him, and he's no longer a threat. No one's targeting *me*. I'll be fine."

Ali and Becca joined them. "You're getting a Vespa?" Becca asked.

Maddie cocked her head. "How much did you hear?"

"I can totally see you on the Vespa," Becca hedged. "You're gonna break some hearts in Port Townsend, I can tell."

Ali turned to Becca. "You and Jean-Louis will be here over the holidays too, right? You all are family, you know. Duncan, Laurie, and Maddie too, of course. Did I tell you we're having another house built next to the hot tub? Not just a cabin, a *house*."

Becca gave her a sidelong look. "If you build it, they will come?"

"Huh?"

"Liam and Teresa. You're hoping they'll move in."

It was obvious to Maddie that Ali was used to having Becca read her mind. With a grin, she said, "A girl can hope."

Becca gave Maddie a friendly nudge. "You know, Maddie, just because your degree is in acting doesn't mean you have to do it for a living. My degree was in French literature."

"Mine was in comparative religion," Ali said, her eyes merry, "and

Teresa's was in creative writing. I don't give religion much thought these days, and Teresa's 'Bondi Blue' iMac just gathers dust."

The conversation was making Maddie uncomfortable. They'd overheard too much. "Uh, not to change the subject, but I won't be at dinner tonight." She tried to sound casual, keeping her voice low in case her mother was nearby.

"Ooh," Becca said, "I smell subterfuge. Maybe some incense. A yoga instructor? Would Teresa mind, do you think?" She directed the question at Ali.

"No," Ali said emphatically. "She'd worry *for* you, though. Kilo is addictive, and you might have to share him."

Duncan looked thoughtful. "Maddie can take care of herself. I worry more about Kilo."

CHAPTER 4

<MADDIE HAD CONVINCED LIAM TO leave his Harley in her care, with the understanding that she wouldn't take any foolish chances by venturing beyond Port Townsend. Her height made riding it tricky but not impossible. He lowered the seat and had her practice mounting it from the high side of the hill or a curb. If all else failed, she could hop on. Before handing over the keys, Liam made her practice mounting, dismounting, and walking the bike until he was satisfied she wouldn't be courting death.

Duncan had promised to back her story that she was going into town to hang out with friends and hear a band, so Maddie hadn't bothered with explanations as she headed out on her date with Kilo. She took off around five, planning to amble around Water Street first. She was dressed semi-casually in designer jeans and a tight velvet T-shirt with a sheer panel covering her cleavage. She'd snagged a pair of knee-high Frye boots at a consignment store for a fraction of the actual cost. The evening being on the cool side, she wore her puffy down jacket, green to match her eyes.

As she drove the giant Harley with extreme caution, she had to look anything but cool, more like a child riding a tractor. A Vespa would suit her perfectly, if only she could cough up the cash. After parking on a side street a block away from Kelpies, she browsed the antiquarian bookshop on the first floor. She did *not* want to arrive first. She paged through an illustrated hardcover copy of *The Secret Garden*, recalling how much she'd loved that story of a spoiled girl orphaned by cholera who is taken in by an initially indifferent relative and befriends a sickly boy. She could only recount the story because she'd seen several film versions, and she'd studied songs from the musical, although there was no obvious part for her unless they cast her as the girl. This book was meant to be kept and treasured, and she had no place in her life for precious possessions. Or keeper men, like David. She put the book back on the shelf and checked her watch. Ten after six. Perfect.

She scampered up the long staircase leading to Kelpies. Once she reached the landing, she slowed her gait to a stroll—or maybe a saunter—as she made her way down the long hallway. Kilo was hanging out at the bar as if the stool was his second home. The female bartender leaned toward him, laughing at something he'd said, thrusting her mostly exposed breasts in his face. "You might have to share him," Ali had said. *As long as you don't give me any STDs*, she told him silently.

She stood at the entrance, waiting for him to take notice. Only a few seconds ticked by before his head turned, along with several others. She should be used to male attention, but it never failed to throw her. Most of the men were old enough that it didn't go to her head. She gave Kilo the megawatt smile that worked reliably for photographs. He didn't bother to disguise his excitement as she approached the bar. She'd once complained to her mother about being constantly leered at by strangers who weren't shy about telling her what they'd like to do to her. Her mother's response was, "Enjoy it while you can. At some point, it just stops."

After her father's early, ignominious exit from the world, she craved male companionship and respect but mistrusted purely sexual attention, writing off the guys who slobbered over her and preferring to cultivate gay colleagues. A lot of gay actors passed as straight because their agents basically forced them to. As for heterosexual men, she was more likely to respond positively to indifference or the pretense of aloofness. David was the exception. He took her seriously and seemed to genuinely like her. *Stop it. David isn't here tonight. Kilo is.*

"Hey there," she said to Kilo, sliding onto the stool next to him.

He leaned over to kiss her cheek, where his lips lingered, and breathed her in as if she were a freshly baked pie. He smelled pretty wonderful himself, a subtle cologne that enhanced his natural scent. Some essential oil they sold at the yoga studio's gift shop? In frayed jeans, an open dress shirt, and a leather jacket, he was more in his element than he had been during the wedding festivities. She admired the boy-idol features—warm brown eyes, smooth golden skin, and puffy lips. Tousled, blue-black hair. Like Liam's half-brother with an Asian mother.

He drew away as if resisting a magnetic pull. "How's it going?"

"I'm good," she said as she ordered a glass of chardonnay from the bartender, who, while not unfriendly, was sizing her up. Had she slept with Kilo? Were they friends with benefits?

"Enjoying your stint on *Lifestyles of the Rich and Famous*? If that show hadn't gone off the air, they'd have eventually gotten around to Ali and Joe."

"Really? I don't think so. They aren't at all ostentatious." Maddie resisted the urge to brush the errant lock of hair from his forehead. Maybe she just wanted an excuse to touch him. He could have passed for a teenager, though his actual age was twenty-eight, only three years her senior.

The bartender handed her a generous pour of white wine. *Uh-oh. Pace yourself.*

"Take that living room," Kilo scoffed. "It's like something out of a Colette novel."

Maddie felt duty bound to defend her hosts. "Teresa's responsible for the décor. Joe and Ali were in Paris at the time. If they'd been paying attention, they'd have gone for something simpler and more comfortable. Ski resort or Southwestern style. Lots of stonework, rugged wood siding, exposed beams. You know, earthier."

"Teresa." He shook his head with regret.

Was he indiscreet? Would he blab about Maddie to future conquests? Better to find out now.

"You were married," she prompted, giving him the rope to hang himself.

A rare bitterness crinkled his eyes. "We were kids, and she was … a princess. In the nicest sense. Not spoiled, just utterly … lovely, innocent. I had a dance scholarship at Cornish. I'd been making money on the side by dating older women. Not a gigolo, exactly …. Okay, a gigolo. It was a short-term, unfortunate career choice. I'd been selling pot to get by, and at the time, sleeping with rich women seemed less risky." He stared off into the distance. "I'm not proud of it, and I always used condoms. I truly loved Teresa. God, how I loved her. But I didn't deserve her. Liam's fabulous. He's a real friend now. I wish them well."

The perfect response. Maddie was impressed. As he no doubt intended her to be. "So, what's a kelpie?" she asked.

He pointed to the logo of half-horse, half-fish. "Your guess is as good as mine. Looks like a water spirit of some kind."

The bartender overheard them. "A water spirit who likes to drown people."

"Huh," Maddie said, taken aback by the relish in the woman's voice.

A band was setting up on the small stage. "Do you want to move to the dining room?" Kilo asked. "It might get loud in here."

A sautéed calamari appetizer arrived. He told the waitress they were moving to a table in the other room. Distressed wood tables with glass tops, pockmarked fir floors, wicker furniture, smoky-blue walls, and mirrors with gilded frames. Their table near the window overlooked the bay and the docks.

Kilo ordered more wine to accompany the calamari, and they agreed to split a burger. She asked him about his years with the dance company.

"Endless miles on the bus. The runs were short and intense, with too many matinees. U.S. cities in winter, Europe in May and June. In July and August, that's when the Italians and the French go on vacation. So, on to Edinburgh, Copenhagen, and London. On our rare days off, we recovered as best we could. The dropout rate was high—injuries and broken hearts, you know—that meant fresh blood from the feeder companies." His gaze turned inward, and she wondered what anecdotes he'd thought better of sharing.

She laughed. "So … much like touring with a show. Little time for sightseeing. A lot of messing around."

There was something odd about his smile. "That could be fun. But you had to be careful, because when things went bad, people got fired."

"You?"

"Not me."

Though there was an entire saga implied in those two words, she didn't press him. He wasn't one to overshare on a first date. Not as indiscreet as she would have guessed. That was good, she supposed.

"Do you dance?" he asked as the band started up shortly after seven.

"Kind of a small space for dancing."

"Yeah, but people do."

"I'm just a singer who moves well," she confessed. "Not a real dancer like you."

He raised an eyebrow and touched her hand, briefly. "I do like your moves."

She clicked her tongue. "You know what I mean. I can pick up a combination quickly but I'm hardly a natural. I do take jazz classes whenever I can."

He handed the waiter a credit card. "Even if you had two left feet, I could make you look good."

She laughed. "I don't doubt it."

The waiter returned and he signed the credit card receipt, leaving a generous cash tip. "Come on." He pulled her to her feet. "I can't sit still for long." Back in the bar area, the song was just ending. There were no open seats, and a few other couples stood on the dance floor waiting for the music to begin, so they joined them, holding both hands and facing each other as if about to say their wedding vows or sing a love duet. It was an Irish band, and the last number had been something like a jig. The next song was "Red Red Wine," the version with a mellow reggae beat.

She was in his arms, letting him call the shots. It was a slow swing dance, and he kept his eyes locked with hers, except when he twirled her. The two generous glasses of wine allowed her to go with the flow even more than usual, and she enjoyed being tossed about in slow motion. At the end he twirled her into a tight coil, their bodies pressed together. The heat rippled through them and she gasped, feeling him harden against her leg. Was she really going to sleep with him on their first date? That just wasn't cool. But she ached to lose control. For weeks now she'd been letting her mother lead her around by the nose while exposed to the overactive pheromones of others. Joe and Ali, Liam and Teresa, Becca and Jean-Louis. Even Duncan and her mother. She hadn't had sex in ages. Well, not since her last show. After this weekend, she'd be back in Seattle, and when she returned to Port Townsend, she'd be busy with the play. Could she indulge herself just this once? But in between came the holidays, and Kilo would be invited. If things got weird and Kilo didn't want to see her then, he'd find some excuse, wouldn't he? The compound was more her turf than his.

The next number was livelier, and when it ended, everyone clapped for her and Kilo. She was suddenly self-conscious, wondering if she'd embarrassed herself by responding to him too obviously. He whispered in her ear, "Let's give someone else the floor," and led her toward the exit, his hand resting at the small of her back.

When they reached the landing of the long flight of stairs, he said, "How did you get here?" His voice was breathy, but not from exertion.

"Liam's Harley."

He gave her a blank stare then burst out laughing. "You rode it all by yourself? This I gotta see. Give me a ride home? I walked."

They climbed onto the bike, and she said, "You live above the yoga studio on Lawrence Street, right?" She handed him Liam's helmet and put on the smaller one he kept for Teresa.

"Yeah." He wrapped his arms around her waist, the contact throwing her hormones into a tailspin. "What's wrong?" he whispered in her ear.

"I'm new at this," she said in a shaky voice.

"Are you? I promise to be gentle."

She snickered. "At riding motorcycles. And this one is a big-ass mofo."

At the studio, he reluctantly released her and slid off the bike. "Your waist is what—twenty inches?" His hand traveled up and down her back, and she pulled away, ticklish.

"What are you doing?"

"Looking for your keyhole. I thought you might be a wind-up doll."

She wrinkled her nose. "Does that line work?"

"You tell me." He sounded sincere. "I've never met a woman with such a perfect hourglass shape."

She resisted the urge to contradict him. Personally, she wished her breasts and ass were smaller and her legs longer. She didn't look forward to binding her breasts to play Puck.

Parking next to the curb, she swung her leg over the bike and dismounted. Kilo trailed behind, steering her toward the entrance to his apartment. "I hope you're not allergic to cats," he said as they mounted the stairs, his hand caressing her ass.

As he closed the door behind them, they were greeted by a talkative orange tabby. "This is Swami." He lifted the cat into his arms and nuzzled it. "I dare you not to fall in love with him."

Swami rubbed against Kilo's legs as he opened a can of cat food, dished it onto a small plate, and put it on the tile floor next to the circling kitty, whose loud purr ended in a meow. "Purrrrow!"

The décor was minimalist and masculine. Maddie guessed it would have good feng shui, though she was no expert. The barstools were made of wrought-iron and wood to match the glass-topped coffee table. The couch and chairs were black leather. Otherwise, she observed a streamlined fireplace and a midsize TV and stereo in a no-frills black cabinet. The hardwood floors were covered with Persian rugs. Very expensive and masculine but with surprisingly little character. Like Kilo himself?

Kilo rinsed out the cat-food can and tossed it in the container under the sink. This man was not one to leave his bed unmade or his dishes unwashed. The only gewgaw, a statue of the many-armed goddess. No Buddhist altars. She had several actor friends who chanted at an altar, sometimes several times a day. It was a thing. One of them had tried to explain its purpose, that you chanted for what you hoped to achieve. She didn't see how that would make you a better actor.

Kilo poured two glasses of wine. "Here's to you," he said, and she dutifully took a sip.

"Nice," she said, surprised. "Way better than what I'm used to."

He shrugged. "I belong to a wine club. Following their recommendations has served me well. At restaurants, I just order the most expensive bottle or go with the sommelier's advice. Shall we sit down?" He indicated the couch.

She sat, wondering how this was going to go. He'd surprised her several times—pleasantly, so far. Maybe he'd do something completely unexpected like send her home unseduced. Was it still seduction if you wanted it?

"Finish off your glass," he said, as if it were medicine. He was awfully bossy. In her experience, a home this clean and uncluttered usually belonged to a control freak. Another reason this—whatever *this* was—could never be more than sex.

Kilo put their empty glasses aside and stood. She rose too, wondering if the evening was about to end. She was intrigued by the unpredictability.

He took her in his arms, dipping her over the couch as if on a dance floor.

She heard herself say in an odd voice, "I'm not *that* much of a pushover."

"No?" He gave her a little push and she fell back onto the couch. He'd maneuvered her perfectly so that she sank comfortably into the cushions. "We'll see about that."

His mouth was on hers, and his nimble fingers made fast work of her clothing. He tasted as good as he smelled. There had to be a vast parade of sexual conquests in his past. The tune to "I love a Parade" came into her head. How many men in her own sexual past? She'd stayed a virgin until she reached eighteen, then lost count. There would be one more, because she wasn't stopping now.

He pulled away, breathing hard.

"Too fast for you?" he asked in a husky voice. "I don't usually ...." His eyes raked over her naked body and he licked his lips. "You're just so ... perfect." Closing his eyes, he cupped her breasts reverently as if weighing melons for ripeness. He took a nipple in his mouth.

His hand was on her stomach, stroking, inching downward. She closed her eyes, thinking of ... David. His fingers expertly probed and plunged, and she strained against him, wanting release. Why was he still dressed?

She reached for his fly to open the buttons, though his complete immersion in the exploration of her body made that difficult. When she finally succeeded, he pulled down his jeans and briefs himself and practically ripped off his T-shirt. He produced a condom—from where?—and slipped it on. She was okay with a quickie. She wanted to feel him inside her *now*. She guided him in, and he thrust with an incoherent cry. She climaxed first, and he must have been waiting for her, because he finished a split second later.

He collapsed on top of her, and they lay still. She wasn't sure what had just happened. Brief as the encounter had been, she wasn't disappointed. His smooth, golden body was exactly as she'd imagined it. In the film version of *Cupid and Psyche*, Kilo would be ideal as the god too beautiful to be seen in daylight. Unlike the mythical Psyche, Maddie had slept with a fair number of male beauties, and those Cupid stand-ins often proved to be elegantly wrapped packages with nothing but a bunch of tissue paper inside. She had to hand it to Kilo, he was a trip and a half.

He seemed almost as dazed as she. "Um …" he began, "that isn't my … I don't. I'm usually …. God, I sound like an idiot. I'm sorry, that's all." He stood up, magnificently naked and unselfconscious, and looked down at her. "I wasn't expecting you to be so … flawless. Your body, my God. It's a little overwhelming. I wanted to take my time with you, and then I saw you naked." His normally dry laugh had an edge of hysteria. "I couldn't wait."

She smiled up at him. "Did I ask you to?" The way his eyes skidded over her, almost worshipful, was starting to make her feel ridiculous. "It was good, believe me. Do you have a towel?" She looked around, as if one might materialize as magically as the condom.

"In the cabinet next to the bathroom. I'll bring you one."

"No need." Gathering her clothes, she went to clean herself up. Swami appeared, swishing his tail ominously. He sat, staring, and uttered a demanding, "Meow!" as if scolding her for abandoning his owner.

"Go ask Kilo," she told him. "I'm sure he speaks cat. I don't know where your food is."

"Meow!!"

"It's no use. If anything, I'm a dog person."

As if to put the lie to her statement, Swami started purring and rubbing against her legs. "Purrow!" he exclaimed.

"See?" Kilo said. "Swami wants you to stay over too."

She headed for the door. Kilo put up a hand to stop her. "If you stay, I'll take my time, I promise. Don't go."

She kissed him lightly on the lips. "That's tempting, but I'm going to head back to the compound now. We can do this again sometime."

He pointed to the clock. "It's only nine." He was still naked, and his erection was weighing in.

Tempted as she was, if she left now, no one would even suspect that her date had ended with a … uh … *bang*. "On Liam's motorcycle, I'm a road hazard. No one would hire me to play Barb Wire. Once I have a Vespa, I'll feel more comfortable staying out late."

"I could drive you home."

"I can't leave the Harley here. If something happened to it, Liam would have my head on a platter."

"When do you return to Seattle?"

"Monday morning."

His expression turned petulant. "That leaves only Saturday and Sunday."

God, she didn't want to argue. She wished he'd accept her decision with good grace. "I can't just move in with you for two days, not with my mother tracking my whereabouts. You have to teach tomorrow, and Ali and Joe will have activities planned. I don't want to seem ungrateful."

"I have a break from one to four tomorrow. Can you get away?"

If she made it home alive tonight, she didn't want to tempt fate by taking the Harley out again tomorrow. She could ask to borrow Teresa's bicycle. "I'll try. I'll leave you a message if it doesn't work out. Are you okay with things being vague?"

He didn't look okay with it.

The ride home was scary, but Maddie made it to the compound by ten, still in one piece. Everyone was still awake, sitting around the living room twiddling their thumbs like a bunch of nervous parents waiting for their daughter to return from the prom.

"Hey, Maddie," Duncan said too cheerily, "you're just in time for a nightcap."

Her smile was tight. "I'll pass. Herbal tea would be nice."

Ali jumped to her feet. "We do have that." They all looked far too relieved.

Joe helped her off with her puffy jacket. "Did you have a good time?"

"Yes, it was fun." Maddie took a seat on the couch. "An Irish band at Kelpies." She looked around the room, noting their expressions. Becca and Jean-Louis exchanged an amused glance. She hadn't fooled anyone, except possibly her mother, though she did appear tense. David …. These O'Connell men were hard to read. He leaned back in his chair, relaxed, speculative.

"We were worried about you riding the Harley," Joe confessed in the silence.

She gave a helpless shrug. "Yeah, I won't do that again. That thing's a beast, more than I can handle. Exciting, though. I need something more my size, like a Vespa." She couldn't stop her brain from comparing the Harley with David, the Vespa with Kilo. Kilo she could handle. But it would be more exciting if he weren't quite so much of a sure thing.

CHAPTER 5

AFTER LUNCH THE NEXT DAY, Maddie asked Ali if she could borrow Teresa's bike. "Sure," Ali said. "Honestly, I can't remember the last time she used it."

"That's great," Maddie told her. "Don't worry about me. I might be gone a few hours."

"I won't worry," Ali said. "Not with you on a regular bike in daylight. But riding on these gravel roads can be tricky after dark. Jean-Louis is cooking dinner. We hope you'll be home by then."

"No problem," Maddie said.

She arrived at Kilo's almost at one on the dot. No need to play coy, not now that they both knew what this was. Her body was fully awake, her nerve endings on fire, and her sex pulsing with need. She shouldn't have awakened the sleeping beast. Much as she loved a good adrenaline rush, it was bad for her. Her private life should be more anchored if she was going to stay sane. She already suspected she was borderline manic depressive. But she liked sex, and marriage was not in the cards. That would mean following a husband's bliss, not her own. Actors had to go where the work was. Someone like, say, David, would never stand for that.

The buzz of the intercom was still reverberating when the lock released. Kilo didn't bother to confirm her identity. Waiting at the top of the stairs, he pulled her into his apartment as soon as she was in arm's reach then locked and deadbolted the door behind her.

Barefoot, he still wore yoga clothing—white cotton pants tied at the waist and a tight T-shirt with the studio logo on it. The scent of soap combined with some kind of essential oil emanated from him enticingly.

"How … are you?" He yanked off her jacket and threw it aside, already working at the zipper of her jeans. Tempting as it was to slap his hands away and tell him to slow down, she was caught up in his urgency. She was vaguely disturbed by his earlier comment that she was doll-like, and he seemed to be treating her like one now. He was gentle enough, if more forceful than she was used to. He pivoted her around so that he was behind her, pulling down her jeans as he pressed her against the wall. She kicked them off, along with her tennis shoes. He ran his hands up her bare waist and sides as he skimmed off her T-shirt, unhooking her bra as he went. In no time, she wore nothing but bikini panties.

"What about *your* clothes?" she gasped, her cheek pressed against the wall. She'd managed to untie his pants, but they were only partway down; otherwise he was still dressed.

Keeping her pinned against the wall, he thrust inside, one hand spanning her breasts and the other fingering her sex. Once again she felt as if she were being attended to by an expert rather than engaging in an act of mutual lovemaking. She hadn't been aware of him putting on a condom, but she assumed he had and let him have his way with her. Deliciously helpless, she climaxed in a series of intense pulses and rushes, collapsing against the wall as he pulled out and guided her slow descent to the floor. She'd barely caught a glimpse of his face. Talk about animalistic. She was limp and sated—also unsettled. Kilo made love as if pouring his entire lifeforce into it, and yet, she felt more like an elaborate bong than a person. A delivery device for his drug of choice. It was disconcerting, to say the least.

Finally, chuckling, he pulled her to her feet, still reeling. "Good?" he said, needlessly. He knew it had been mind-blowing. "We're just getting started."

An hour and a half later, he carried her into the shower, where he made love to her again, then washed her thoroughly with the soap infused with essential oils. Now she smelled like him. He hoisted her up so that her legs were wrapped around his hips, and she gripped a metal bar in the stall strong enough to bear her weight as he filled her and brought her to climax once more.

Utterly drained, she wondered how she'd manage to bike all the way home. *Damn, there are a lot of hills.*

After the shower, he wrapped her in his robe and carried her to the couch, where he arranged her in a sitting position. Emerging from a sensual haze, she tried to wrap her brain around the past few hours.

When he was sitting next to her, his own clothes back in place, she said, "Um, don't take this the wrong way. You really like to be in control."

He chuckled, pleased with himself. "You didn't seem to mind."

He pulled aside the robe to reveal one breast. She covered it again. "Don't you like having things done to you?"

"There will be time for that."

"Not this trip. Tomorrow is an excursion to Sol Duc Hot Springs. I won't be back in Port Townsend until Christmas."

A confusion of emotions flashed across his face: surprise, annoyance, disappointment. "Was this afternoon too much?" he said in an even voice. "I didn't sense one iota of reluctance. I know enjoyment when I see it."

She couldn't deny it. But it had been like something out of a porn movie, and in her career she was surrounded by too much decadence already. Suddenly what Joe and Ali had sounded awfully good. Even Liam and Teresa's relationship seemed pure in comparison. Maddie had thought Kilo genuinely liked her. Once you opted for this route, did you ever stop to smell the flowers? She didn't think so. It wasn't that she wanted a real connection with Kilo, but she preferred to be treated as something more than a sex toy. Now she understood why this man was so dangerous. She'd believed she could handle him. Heroin addicts felt the same way in the beginning.

"Can't you come back on your own?" he finally said. "Stay with me for a week, two weeks. As long as you like." No pleading, rather a caress. A seduction. He was touching her all the while, running his fingers under the robe, stealing her will yet again.

"Unlike my hosts, I have to make money." She pushed him firmly away as she stood, straightened the robe, and stepped back, out of reach. "The busy season for catering is about to begin—Thanksgiving, the Christmas parties." Why was she relieved to have an excuse?

She grabbed her clothes and started putting them on under the robe, turning her back to him. Swami, looking like he'd slept through the whole thing, appeared from the bedroom and sat, watching her, unimpressed. "Meow?" he said softly, cocking is head. It probably meant, "You think you're special?" She glanced over at Kilo, who remained on the couch, body languid, eyes hooded with desire. Once dressed, she went into the bathroom to check her appearance. She didn't wear much makeup anyway when she wasn't on stage, but her hair, which he had washed but not blow-dried, was a mass of wild curls. If only it had been raining, she could claim to have been caught in the rain. A bike helmet would have helped. Could she sneak past all the O'Connells without their noticing her dishevelment?

Her cheeks were glowing, and her lips were swollen. *Ugh.* She had *not* thought this through.

"Purr—ow, purr—ow, purr—ow …." Swami was suddenly a feline motor mouth. The cat had demands too. She had to get out of both their clutches.

Kilo tailed her like an eager puppy. "Think about what I said. Come stay with me. Anytime. During the week if that's all you can manage. I'll get a sub." He kissed her neck, but she succeeded in detaching herself.

"Bye, Kilo," was all she said.

* * *

Sol Duc Hot Springs closed for the winter at the end of October. It was Ali's favorite side trip, and only now did she feel comfortable leaving the twins, knowing they were in the capable hands of May Allen the nanny.

Once Ali and Liam aged out of the foster-care system, until that fateful trip to Israel where Liam disappeared, the twins had reserved the same campsite at Sol Duc for a few days each summer. The best and most accessible hike in the immediate area led to the falls, a five-mile loop of flat trail—a walk in the park for serious hikers. Still, they both liked the cozy campground, and you could soak in the hot spring-fed pools in back of the main lodge for an extra fee. She'd always wanted to stay in the cabins, but Liam assured her they were little more than basic and didn't warrant the exorbitant rates.

Ali, Joe, Jean-Louis, and Becca traveled in one car, Duncan, Laurie, David, and Maddie in the other. You drove seventy minutes to Port Angeles and then a short stretch on 101 before you came to the turnoff to Sol Duc, a slow-moving fifteen miles. All in all, a two-hour trip.

Ali and Becca sat in the back. It didn't take long for Becca to say, "So, when does sex qualify as a class-one drug? Is it time for an intervention?"

"You're talking about Maddie," Ali said, thrumming her fingers on the seat beside her. "Not intervening there. Thank God Laurie is so clueless."

"I almost lost it when she came in yesterday," Becca said. "She looked like she'd been held captive by Casanova himself. Of course she is a major hottie. I'm not sure she realizes it. She's so self-effacing when it comes to her looks and her talent. I wish we could have spared her Kilo."

Ali gave her a long, hard look. "We? How is it our business? I'm sure you had a few Kilos in your time."

Becca snickered. "A few. However, at Maddie's age—or should I say *stage* of romantic discovery, sex is all there is. You don't understand how much a real connection enhances things."

"She's only three years younger than we are."

"We can hear you!" Joe called from the front seat. "And it's not fair that we can't hear you better."

"She reminds me of a female Liam," Jean-Louis remarked. "A female Liam," he repeated, louder, when Ali insisted she couldn't hear. "Everybody has to speak up if we're going to *bavarder*, ah, how do you say it, *gossip* about Maddie and Kilo."

"I think there's a real age and a sexual age," Becca said. "You men should butt out, because only a woman would understand. You all are just ready for anything as soon as you discover *Playboy* magazine and start hogging the bathroom."

"Or *Hustler*," Jean-Louis remarked to Joe.

"Really?" Joe made a face. "My dad subscribed to *Penthouse*. He kept them in a box in the basement labeled 'Taxes.' Edward pointed out that he couldn't keep all his tax stuff from every year in the same box."

"That must have been before his calling as a priest," Jean-Louis said.

"Yeah, he was a wild one. Hard to buy that he's totally celibate now. Catholic priests make a vow, right? Anyway, he was kind enough to alert the rest of us to his treasure trove. Not Teresa, naturally."

Becca leaned over the seat and smacked Jean-Louis on the shoulder. "This isn't about you and your sordid coming of age, emphasis on *coming*. We're talking about Maddie."

"She has too much temptation," Ali said. "It must be super confusing to have a body like Mitzi Gaynor in *South Pacific* and be in all those shows alongside such charismatic and gorgeous men. She's so guileless and easy to talk to. That must make her even more of a target."

"I hear she's been through some major shit," Becca said. "Her father died when she was fifteen of cirrhosis. I can just imagine the lead-up to that. Then, in New York, while she was getting her BFA, there was another shit-show. Laurie implied as much. With a teacher."

"That woman talks too much," Ali grumbled.

"Maybe Kilo will be her burning bush," Becca said.

Joe laughed and hit the steering wheel. "She said 'bush'!"

Ali swatted Joe on the shoulder. "Get your mind out of the gutter."

"Perhaps she is *Kilo's* burning bush, did you ever think of that?" Jean-Louis said, waggling his eyebrows at Becca. "It is the more anatomically correct metaphor."

Ali turned to Becca. "Explain."

"In the Bible, it's the light-bulb moment for Moses. Kilo is the embodiment of pure sex devoid of substance. Maybe Maddie can move on to a good guy now. She didn't look like a woman glowing with love when she came in yesterday. More like a racehorse ridden to the brink."

"Becca, ew!" Ali scrunched up her face.

"I understood your reasoning the first time," Jean-Louis said smugly. "Kilo may have found his match in Maddie. It is more likely she will hurt him than the other way around."

Ali thought of Ulla, the nanny who had resembled a Nordic supermodel. She'd told them she had a female partner, then made passes at both Liam and Joe. Maddie wasn't a flirt, which made her less threatening to women. She was a sweet kid with major talent, sex appeal, and stage presence. As far as Ali could tell, all she lacked was ambition. She didn't need public adulation to prove her own self-worth the way most actors did. She might succeed anyway. From what Ali had observed and what Laurie had told her, Maddie was *that* good.

"Do you think David and Maddie could ever work?" Ali asked. "I've seen sparks between them."

"If so," Joe said, "it's spectacularly bad timing. David is involved with Sylvia, who we'll meet at Christmas. Maddie swims with the tide, and right now it's taking her out to sea."

Ali hated the sound of that, but Joe's words rang true. "David still hasn't come clean about what brought him home," she said. "It must have been awful."

"He claims not," Joe said. "He'll tell us in his own good time. No point in pushing it. In case you haven't noticed, the O'Connell men tend to brood. David has always been the exception. He was a nerdy, scary-smart kid who endured some pretty brutal teasing from his peers, and yet, he had the sunniest disposition of us all."

Not anymore, Ali thought.

CHAPTER 6

———◦———

MADDIE COULDN'T BELIEVE SHE WAS sitting in the backseat of Duncan's station wagon next to David. Laurie was talking a blue streak in the front seat, making the silence between her and David deafening. For a long time, she went with it, staring out at the ocean, the passing trees, the surprisingly varied types of chainsaw art. Now they were catching glimpses of Lake Crescent, a spectacularly beautiful turquoise-blue crater lake, protected from developers and motorboats. David seemed lost in thought.

Finally Maddie couldn't take it anymore. "Are you enjoying your stay with Joe and Ali?"

He started, as if jettisoned from some particularly vivid memory. "Oh, uh, yeah. The décor is a little weird, isn't it? More Teresa than Joe and Ali."

"I thought so too," she said with a smile. "Teresa must be reincarnated from some early-twentieth-century French pianist."

"Do you believe in that kind of thing?" he asked with no hint of condescension.

"It's a nice idea," she said, "though personally, I'd just as soon not be reborn. I want to be a free-floating spirit, able to go anywhere, see anything, attend every Broadway play, hang out in the rain forest."

He appeared to give her vision of the afterlife serious thought. "So, we still get to appreciate all the beautiful things in the world, enjoy them as ghosts, who take up no physical space, so there's room for all the dead people who want to see, uh, the musical *Rent*, for instance." She made a face. "Not your choice?"

"Overrated. It's a rip-off of Puccini's *La Bohème*, with only one good song."

"I dunno," he said, "you can't argue with success. It's *hugely* popular."

"Have you heard the soundtrack?"

"No." He grinned, that signature O'Connell smile that just knocked your socks off. "What would your spirit be seeing this season?"

"The revival of *Candide*, definitely."

"Bernstein," he said, surprising her. "Might be a hard sell outside of New York City."

"You mean because it demands something of the audience," she said.

"Could you sing Cunegonde?"

"It's a part for a coloratura soprano. I'm a mezzo but I can sing soprano roles if they don't go above an A. I can vocalize higher, but it's not the best part of my voice, and the tessitura would kill me. I'd hate to get hired for a role outside my vocal comfort zone. I'd dread pulling off a miracle night after night."

"You must understand how it was for Joe, then."

Sobered, she said, "Yes, certainly. He's handled that awfully well."

David cleared his throat as if hoarse himself. "On the outside. We O'Connells are a grin-and-bear-it tribe. Thank God for Ali. I wish I could have been here for him. But I was off in the jungle, fulfilling my life's mission."

He might as well have said, *I was off in Hawaii surfing.* Like he was kicking up his heels while his brother suffered.

"I don't think you need to apologize for saving people while the rest of us pursue frivolous professions."

His smile was indulgent, as if to say, *I don't expect you, of all people, to understand.*

"So, back to the décor," she said. "Your dream living room. What does it look like?"

"That's easy," he said, surprising her yet again. "Colonial Africa. Back before industry and greed and drugs took Africa's innocence and slaughtered its animals for trophies and alternative medicine. Of course the Europeans weren't welcome and they started the downfall of Africa, but it's my fantasy, so I don't have to defend it. Like your version of paradise. Do you know the movie, *King Solomon's Mines*?"

It was her turn to grin. "*Love* that movie. Stewart Granger and Deborah Kerr."

"What, not Richard Chamberlain and Sharon Stone?"

She pretended to gag. "That movie was a joke."

David laughed. "Didn't see it, thank God. Although my mother liked those *Doctor Kildare* reruns, and I thought Richard Chamberlain was pretty good in that. She liked all those medical shows. *Marcus Welby, M.D.* No wonder I wanted to be a doctor. On TV, they were so romantic. Anyway, I wanted to *be* Allan Quatermain—the Stewart Granger version. To me, Africa was romance." He shook his head. "Turns out the movie was mostly filmed in New Mexico and California. Okay, some of it was filmed in Kenya and Congo. Still, a misleading story for an impressionable young man."

She touched his arm lightly. "Not to mention that Allan Quatermain is not your most realistic role model."

He looked down to where her hand had been and said, "Saving lives seemed like a superpower to me."

"To me, too." She tried to picture interior scenes from the movie. "Uh, your ideal living room? A tent? 'Cause I don't recall many indoor scenes in that movie."

"Oh, yeah. I've got my films mixed up. As a kid I pretty much saw every movie that took place, or supposedly took place, in Africa. *Out of Africa, The African Queen, Mogambo.* Africa was the backdrop of all my fantasy adventures. I have no idea what kind of interior would fit that. Whatever it is, I didn't see much of it while I was actually there."

"I think I can picture the room," Maddie said. "Dark wood. Tribal masks. Statuettes of animals or primitive people made of stone or clay. Colorful prints."

David rolled his eyes. "Someone must have told Ali. You could be describing my cabin. Without the masks or statuettes. You?"

"My ideal décor? I can't afford to be picky. I've been crashing with friends rather than accepting Mom's hospitality, so … anywhere the furniture isn't at war with the wallpaper. Where all the elements work together, and the atmosphere is cozy and safe."

"I get it," David said. "Like the Oscar Wilde quote: 'This wallpaper will be the death of me.' "

"Yes," she said with a rueful smile. "I've contemplated many a lethal wallpaper."

"Do you mind if we return to the subject of your fantasy afterlife?" he asked. She shrugged, and he went on, "In your version of paradise, are you allowed to avoid the bad stuff? You like the Hoh Rain Forest, and so do I. Could we just float around there, ignoring the part where loggers destroy habitat or poachers kill helpless animals or a bald eagle kills a baby bunny?"

He clearly didn't understand how to savor a good fantasy. "Um, I didn't say I actually believed that's what will happen after I die. It's what I, personally, consider paradise."

"No, I like it. Can we agree that the villains get to see only the bad stuff, like Jacob Marley in *A Christmas Carol*?"

She nodded, relieved that he had entered the spirit of the game. "They have to sit through the really bad Broadway plays. They must endure all the endless showcases staged by desperate actors in hopes that someone other than their friends will attend—an agent, a casting director, a manager." She leaned toward him and whispered as if revealing a secret, "Never happens."

"Been to a few of those, have you?"

"Also acted in more than a few, sad to say. The worst are written by people with deep pockets and no clue. They hire talented performers to realize their half-baked visions"—she made a helpless gesture—"to no avail. As an actor, you're too embarrassed to invite anyone you know."

"Why would you agree to be in something like that?"

"For the money, of course." She didn't know why she bothered. These O'Connells couldn't imagine doing *anything* just for the money. Not like her … or Kilo. She flashed back to the day before and felt her face heat up. She was totally conflicted. It had been both thrilling and shameful. As much as she craved an encore, she dreaded it. She and Kilo had too much in common. It couldn't end well. She'd have to join Sex Addicts Anonymous.

"I'm sorry," he said, watching her curiously, "I don't know what it means to struggle financially. I went to Africa to atone for my upper-middle-class privilege and in search of adventure. It serves me right."

He'd misinterpreted her silence, and now he sounded disgusted with himself.

"What is *it*?" she asked. At his puzzled expression, she explained, "You said, '*It* serves me right.' What happened to you over there?" She'd heard the whispering. Had anyone other than Joe asked him outright? David hadn't given Joe a straight answer. Trapped in the car with a virtual stranger, perhaps he could come clean.

David shot her a look of annoyance. "It wasn't any one thing, just an all-around shit show. We were always short of supplies, so we had to improvise. Then militia members would break in and steal what supplies we had. People would die of bizarre illnesses I've never seen and wouldn't have known how to treat if I had. The hunger and poverty and disease had damaged them beyond recovery before we arrived. Far too often, there was nothing we could do."

Nodding, she said, "Interesting. You know, if someone asked me to write dialogue for a doctor helping poor people in Africa, and I wasn't allowed to read any individual accounts or do any other research, that is the speech I'd write for you. Because all that seems like a given. You'd know that going in."

He appeared nonplussed, as if realizing he'd been called on his BS. But then he said, "Thinking you're psychologically prepared for something and actually experiencing it are totally different kettles of fish."

"So," she went on, already worried she was pushing it, "I'm just going to assume that something awful happened to you, personally, while you were there that you aren't ready to talk about. A life crisis of some kind. You must know that when you don't tell people things, they just fill in the blanks with stuff that's worse than the reality."

That was when they pulled into the parking lot.

* * *

David gave Maddie a sharp look as they came to a stop. She wasn't far off, but she was crazy if she thought he was going to confide in *her*. Nothing she could imagine could come close to what had actually happened—not because it was so horrible, just impossible to believe. She'd think he was nuts for sure. Had it been a mistake to retreat to the compound? Were they all going to keep prodding him until he spilled his guts? What then?

He thought of the way Maddie had looked when she came in yesterday evening—like she'd survived an epic Roman orgy—and itched to strangle Kilo. What a hound. In the afterlife he'd concocted for Kilo, he would be condemned to an eternity of celibacy and forced to sit through the full-length version of Rossini's *William Tell*, all four hours of it, over and over again.

CHAPTER 7

———◆———

THE CARAVAN HAD KEPT PACE, and Duncan's car pulled up next to them in the main parking lot. Ali would love to have known what had been said in the backseat, but she doubted Laurie had stopped talking long enough for Duncan to have overheard anything.

The Sol Duc Hot Springs Lodge appeared old, but the original—a grand lodge ten times the size of the present resort—had burned down in 1916 after only three years in operation. Updated in the 1980s, the present model looked convincing enough—a cozy colonial-style main lodge with dark-stained wood siding and a cedar-shingle roof. The main building housed the corporate offices, restaurant, and gift shop. The guests stayed in cabins.

The day was cloudy and cool, almost cold. That wouldn't matter once they were soaking in the pools. The breeze carried the faint rotten-egg scent of sulfur from the hot springs. To Ali, the smell was a pleasant reminder of those halcyon days alone with her brother, before harsh experience stole the remainder of his innocence.

Ali heard Maddie say to David, "What do you think, David? Would Allan Quatermain be comfortable here?"

He laughed and shook his head.

Ali was pleased to see that they'd regained some of their earlier rapport. She wished David could have been spared the spectacle of Maddie directly after her hookup. At least Kilo hadn't given her visible hickeys.

"Lunch, anyone?" Joe asked. He got no argument, it being one o'clock. They proceeded directly past the gift shop into the unassuming Spring Room with a view of the pools. After getting a general idea of what everyone wanted, Joe ordered an assortment of dishes and a few bottles of wine, beer for the men. Ali hadn't stopped marveling at what it meant to be so wealthy. Certain aspects of life were so much easier. No agonizing over how to split the check. Joe was paying, and he wouldn't have it any other way. He had reserved a large table by the window. She noted the curious stares of the other diners, but if anyone recognized Joe, they didn't approach.

After lunch, they went to the changing rooms to put on their suits.

"Ugh," Ali said to Becca as she stood before the mirror trying to suck in her tummy. "I am never getting my waist back."

"Honey, you look *good*," Becca assured her. "Maybe better than ever."

Ali had always been a beanpole, in contrast to Becca's lush curves. She envied the firmness of her friend's body in her red bikini, a James Bond girl in the flesh. Ali had filled out, and she couldn't get used to it. "Oh well. Joe doesn't seem to mind."

Becca put her hands on her hips. "You bet he doesn't."

They turned as Maddie emerged from her dressing room. And tried not to stare. Maddie was wearing a modest one piece—modest on any other woman. But her body was so spectacular. The lime-green suit with little flowers revealed a generous portion of the flawless globes of her breasts, and her prominent nipples attested to a lack of padding. Her waist had to be twenty inches, if that, which made her slim hips look fuller. For a petite woman, she had long legs. The kind of fashion-doll body everyone assumed didn't exist without surgical intervention. Ali wondered how often she had been directed to shed her clothing in plays. It seemed to be a thing nowadays, nudity on stage, even at Seattle Rep and Intiman. Ali always felt sorry for the actors. With a body like that, she would have been acutely self-conscious, but Maddie appeared to be oblivious.

"I'll meet you guys outside," Maddie told Becca and Ali, who had to work hard to keep from gawking. The men's eyes were going to pop out of their heads.

"Wow," Becca said, after Maddie went outside. "I have *never* seen a body like that. Laurie's the long, lean type, like you. Must be from her father's side."

Ali blew out a long breath. "I'm not sure looking like that is a good thing in her profession. She's obviously not an exhibitionist. No wonder she likes playing boys. No nude scenes."

Becca rolled her eyes. "I hope the guys can keep a lid on it."

Ali dragged her by the arm. "Let's go. This, I gotta see."

The men, along with Laurie, had congregated along the side of the hottest pool, and Maddie was dipping her toe in the water across from them, leaning down and trying to adjust to the temperature. The men wore hilariously blank expressions, their energy laser-focused on not reacting to the sight of her; only Duncan managed to avert his eyes. Laurie seemed unaware of the effect her daughter had on men.

Becca settled in next to Jean-Louis and whispered, "Shut your mouth. You're drooling."

He blew out a puff of air. "*Là, là!* Can you blame me?"

"Nope," she said with laughter in her voice.

Ali floated in next to Becca, with Joe on her other side. That left space next to David, who was almost reeling, as if recovering from a blow to the head. Maddie came over to fill the space, her breasts glistening above the surface of the water. "Are you all right?" she said. "You're the doctor, but water this hot is bad for some conditions." Could she really be clueless about her effect on men?

"I'm fine," he said in a slightly strangled voice.

Ali and Joe exchanged glances, lips twitching. "Some conditions do require cold water," he whispered to her.

She slapped the water, splashing him in the face. "Behave!" Maddie appeared not to have heard the rude comment.

Maddie gave David a curious glance, then lay back against the edge of the round soaking pool, breasts bobbing at the surface. "I'm hearing a lot of Russian, or some other Eastern bloc language," she said, watching a sealion of an older woman flap her arms as she doused her ponderous upper body with water.

"They love Sol Duc," said Joe, who, Ali was glad to see, had recovered his equilibrium. "Their countries of origin are cold, with a lot of geothermal activity. This place reminds them of home."

"Your family has been coming here a long time?" Maddie asked.

The question seemed directed at David, who took way too long to answer. Eyes averted from her breasts, he said, "We visited Sol Duc every summer growing up, but we stayed at Lake Crescent Lodge. We just came here for the day. It's evolved quite a bit. They keep doing different things with the pools. When we were kids, it was just one big cold pool and one hot pool. It almost went out of business. They had to solve a bunch of technical issues when the source seemed to dry up."

"The cabins are nothing special," Joe said.

"Liam and I reserved a campsite for several years in a row," Ali said.

"We liked staying here. Are we going to hike afterward?"

"Everyone up for a hike?" Joe asked. "It's a five-mile loop, and Sol Duc Falls is the midway point. They're spectacular."

"Shouldn't we have hiked first, soaked later?" Becca said.

Joe shrugged. "Probably. It's a flat hike, not difficult. We could soak after, too."

"Well, I'm pruney," Maddie said, showing them her fingers. "I'm not much of a soaking girl. I'll meet you all in the gift shop." She swam to the edge and clambered out.

"She even has a perfect ass," Becca said in a disbelieving whisper.

"Becca!" Laurie remonstrated.

Becca looked hurt. "It's not an insult. I'm just saying what everyone else is thinking."

"Her body is a little … exaggerated," Maddie's mother said. "She would be more versatile as an actress if she looked more like you, Ali."

Becca laughed. "I'm sure she does just fine with what she's got."

When they returned from the hike, it was dinnertime, so they skipped the additional soak and ate at the resort's restaurant again. During the hike, Ali and Becca had fallen behind, distracted by a grouse attempting to lead them away from its nest, a large black beetle, a particularly gnarly bigleaf maple, a bird they couldn't identify, and a hawk soaring overhead. Jean-Louis, Duncan, David, and Joe had formed a tight group at the front, laughing and joking the whole way. They started a game where Joe sang little snippets of songs, the winner being the one who could identify the singer or the song first. Ali was surprised they hadn't frightened away every wild creature within hearing distance. Laurie and Maddie mostly formed their own unit, but at one point Ali heard Laurie say, "You're not going to date that Kilo fellow, are you? He seems like trouble to me."

"Don't worry, Mom," Maddie replied. "I have no plans to see Kilo again."

* * *

Maddie was exhausted. The session with Kilo, a restless night following, an intense soak in too hot water, and now a brisk hike. Maddie wasn't a seasoned Olympic Peninsula traveler like the rest of them. She was still blown away by it all. Mosses formed a thick carpet on the rocks and nurse logs and clung to the giant trees. Other types of greenery—lichen, maybe?— were draped over the branches like green tinsel. She stood on the bridge overlooking the falls and sighed from sheer happiness, wanting to linger as long as possible. But Joe pointed out that if they left now, they still wouldn't eat until after seven.

Seated next to David in the car again, she didn't even try to engage him in more conversation. They all thought she hadn't noticed the way they'd ogled her in her bathing suit. What was she supposed to do, call them on it? Easier to pretend it wasn't happening. Her weird body embarrassed her—it always had, ever since her breasts had sprouted at age twelve and no boy ever looked her in the eye again. Acting classes had taught her to block out the unwanted attention, and she had a sixth sense for when a particular man's attention might lead to an actual assault so she could head it off. With the teachers, it had been trickier. She had shoved those incidents to the farthest reaches of her mind.

She closed her eyes and relaxed into the car seat. She was flying above the rain forest, and David was flying with her. They were disembodied spirits, but she could hold his hand and feel his flesh. They flew downward and descended amid the trees, landing on a patch of emerald-green moss. The sun streamed down as David reached over and touched her face, kissing her lightly on the lips. The moss was as soft as any featherbed, and they rolled about on it, naked. He was gazing into her eyes and touching her hair, kissing her cheeks, her eyelids ….

An excerpt from a song weaved into her dream: "To be the kind of girl designed to be kissed upon the eyes …." "Much More," from *The Fantasticks*, a song sung by the girl Luisa about the longing to escape her narrow confines and experience life. Maddie was suddenly on stage, naked, singing "Much More," aware that she'd have to tackle the finale, which demanded a high C, and knowing she couldn't pull it off. Where had David gone? Why was she still naked? This was a family musical!

She woke with a start and found that she'd been dozing against David's shoulder. He hadn't shied away.

"You okay?" he asked. "It seemed like you were having a bad dream."

She scooted away from him so she was practically pressed against the window. "Sorry! I guess I was more tired than I thought. I have anxiety dreams about acting sometimes. A while ago I was called back for *The Fantasticks* off-Broadway—you know, the one that has been running forever at the Sullivan Street Playhouse. I was doing summer stock in Idaho at the time. My agent wanted me to fly back to New York for the callback, but I knew I couldn't sing that role, night after night, because of the conspicuous high C in the finale. Not to mention that I couldn't afford the airfare. So, my agent dropped me."

"That was the nightmare?"

"No, the reality. In the dream I'm on stage singing 'Much More,' which I can handle, no problem, knowing that when the finale comes, everyone will see that the role is beyond me." She didn't mention that she was naked in the dream, or that it had started with their spirits making love. Acting teachers drummed into your head the need to be emotionally naked on stage as well as unafraid to bare all physically. Anything less was holding back. Baring her breasts had been bad enough. Her one full nude scene had been the hardest thing she'd ever done. As Ophelia in *Hamlet*, she'd performed the mad scene naked. Although the director hadn't forced himself on her, he'd wanted to, and every night of the run she'd felt violated by his hungry eyes as she exited the stage. Being involved with the man who played Hamlet that summer kept the director in check but screwed with her head in other ways. Andrew—Hamlet—was in his early thirties. She was eighteen. Looking back, she could see he wasn't going anywhere as an actor. He didn't lack the talent or the looks, just the drive. Heavy drinking was chipping away at his face. She hadn't kept track of him, but she'd bet good money he was still waiting tables in between poorly paid gigs. *Like you*, she added ruthlessly.

"Where did you go just now?" David said, and she realized she'd drifted back to that summer in Maine then indulged in another bout of self-flagellation. "Must be an unpleasant memory."

"Not particularly," she said with a tight smile.

Why this fascination with David? Was it because he was an enigma and committed to someone else? If he were to pursue her actively, would she lose interest? After all the narcissistic men Maddie had been involved with, it was refreshing to meet someone who lived for others. Only, what price had he paid?

We all pay a price for our choices, she thought. *For some of us, the return is meager.*

CHAPTER 8

---◆---

Teresa and Liam's honeymoon began with five days in Paris. They hadn't planned on staying even that long. Teresa had assumed Liam would hate the snobbery of the City of Light. It turned out the house they had rented in Ménerbes wasn't immediately available. It also turned out that Liam loved Paris.

His only other experience with travel outside of Washington State had been to Israel, and that had ended badly. Presumed dead in a terrorist attack, he had lived out an unlikely scenario—awakened from a coma to find he'd been claimed by a mother from a powerful family whose own son had died in the explosion. Liam had resided in Teresa's imagination initially as an abstract: Ali's deceased twin brother whose death her new sister-in-law would not accept. Then Joe's detective had located him working as a security guard under an assumed name, proving that Ali had been right all along. Teresa, on a Church tour of Jerusalem, had been the one to find him and convince him to return home.

After the first-class plane trip to Paris where Liam hardly slept because he wanted to enjoy all the amenities, they headed directly to their luxury hotel, the Pavillon de la Reine, overlooking the Place des Vosges in the Marais. On the taxi ride, Liam chatted nonstop in his rusty but game French with the gregarious Algerian driver about politics, Americans, and aristocrats. Teresa left the talking to him. She couldn't stop smiling at Liam's ebullience.

The hotel was a seventeenth-century palace covered with ivy, and the staff was surprisingly friendly, thanks to Liam's irresistible charm, which inspired everyone he met to spontaneous acts of generosity. An extra-nice bottle of wine in the room, a box of Swiss chocolates, elaborate pastries topped with a thick layer of wild strawberries. Maybe everyone received this star treatment, but Teresa didn't think so.

Liam had big plans for each day, and when, late at night, they were alone in the comfortable attic room with its quirky slanted ceilings, he always wanted to make love. Teresa didn't know how he managed to get by on so little sleep and still look bright-eyed and bushytailed. He was particularly enchanted by the Musée d'Orsay, the old train station converted into a museum that housed most of the art from the previous century. Teresa had visited there many times during previous stays. It was fun seeing all her favorites through his eyes, but after that initial visit, she let him go back on his own while she read or shopped. Otherwise they strolled endlessly, visiting parks and especially the cemeteries, finding the resting places of their idols. Teresa was especially interested in the poet and author Guillaume Apollinaire. Liam wanted to visit Jim Morrison, also at the Père Lachaise. Both wanted to give their regards to Claude Debussy, buried in the Passy Cemetery. They loved reading the gravestones of random dead people and speculating on the origins of the sculptures: a man waking up next to his wife and watching over her eternal sleep, a beautiful naked woman crying over the body of a young man. One day they picnicked on wine, cheese, sausage, and a baguette and were excoriated by a huffy young *gendarme*, who informed them that picnicking in the cemeteries was illegal. When it was time to take the train to Avignon, Liam wanted to extend their stay, but they were committed to a week in Ménerbes.

Now they sat by the saltwater pool at their rental, gazing at the Luberon Valley. The stone house was over two hundred years old and situated three miles from the medieval town, built as a military stronghold on a hilltop in the Luberon Mountains. They had three small patios where they could sit in the sun or shade, depending on the time of day, including the area by the pool, but Liam preferred hanging out in town. On one of his runs, he befriended a gay couple who owned a coffeeshop. Now he was helping them fix their plumbing. Teresa had hoped they'd spend more time lazing around, but "lazy" wasn't in Liam's vocabulary. She'd bought *Memoirs of a Geisha* at the airport and finished it too quickly. Soon she'd be rummaging through the German owners' bookshelves trying to find something appealing. Liam had assembled a stack of slender Ian Fleming novels.

"What do you suppose they're up to at home?" she asked her new husband, who'd just prepared a delicious lunch of sausage and greens served with a local red wine she didn't particularly care for. Not that she'd complain to Liam, who clearly enjoyed it. This was yet another novel version of Liam, dressed like a Parisian man of leisure in white linen slacks and a short-sleeved burgundy linen shirt, unbuttoned to reveal an expanse of sleekly muscled chest. It wasn't the first time she'd admired her husband's chameleon-like ability to blend in wherever he went. He'd purchased the clothing in Paris when she'd thought he was at the Louvre.

"Do you miss them?" he asked, efficiently dispatching a fly with the *International Herald Tribune*.

"Not really, but I *am* curious."

He threw back his head and let loose that full-throated laugh she heard so frequently now. No more brooding Liam. "You're curious about how the Kilo-Maddie-David triangle is progressing."

She tried to look offended but couldn't carry it off. "Okay, well, yes."

"I'll tell you," Liam said. "Kilo has made a big play for Maddie, and I'd bet good money that she went for it. He's damn compelling, and she's at loose ends. As for David, if he could get his head out of his ass, he'd realize Maddie would choose him over Kilo in a New York minute. Unfortunately for him, Maddie's not the type to wait around for someone who's stuck in a muck of self-pity."

Teresa stood up and kissed him on the cheek. "Thank you, Nostradamus," she said lightly. "Now we can stay here indefinitely." She sat back down again, so close that their legs touched.

"I'm sure Ali will fill you in when we get back." A pat on the knee turned into a hand roving along her thigh and under her sundress. "You're not jealous, are you? Still have feelings for Kilo?"

"Absolutely not," she purred, already responding to his clever fingers. "Are we going to *faire la sieste*?"

"We might take a nap … eventually. Don't you want to hear what's happening in the world?"

"Not particularly."

His fingers teased at the edges of her panties. In a seductive voice, he said, "Israel and Palestine signed a modest peace agreement, the government is trying to break up Microsoft, and the Republicans still want to impeach Clinton for lying and obstruction of justice." He chuckled wickedly. "Need I go on?"

"Oh, go on, definitely, but please shut up. It's like nothing ever changes. These same headlines will probably be reappearing years from now with a different cast of characters."

"I'm going to ravish you," he said in a cartoonish, snarly voice. He rose to his feet, walked purposely to the far end of the pool, then swiveled and attempted a menacing stance. He rubbed his hands together and crouched, preparing to stalk her.

Struggling to keep a straight face, Teresa propped her legs up on the table and spread them so that he could see her pink lace panties. "Ravishing requires me to be unwilling."

"Can't you pretend, just this once?" In a funny French accent, he added, "*Moi, je suis* un medieval conqueror, and you have fear of me."

"You sound like Pepé Le Pew."

"I can do that." Starting at her wrist, he kissed his way up her arm. "Ah, my leetle, er, stroganoff of *boeuf*, my leetle pie of pumpkin!"

Giggling, she said, "Um, I'm glad we just ate lunch. I think I prefer the medieval conqueror."

He released her arm and struck a new pose, legs spread, chest puffed out, hands in fists.

She fell to one knee and clasped her hands, pleading, "Oh, *monsieur*, I am innocent! Do not take my maidenhead."

He crossed his arms, unimpressed. "The mocking tone doesn't do it for me."

"Right. Like you're so serious?"

"Noted. Okay, from here on out, deadly serious. I'm coming for you right now."

With a devilish "Ha, ha!" he lifted her into his arms and draped her over his shoulder, Viking style. Or what she imagined Viking style to be. "Sack of potatoes" was the first cliché to come to mind.

She pounded his back and cried out, "No, no! You evil man."

He kept up his deranged cackling as he carried her inside and tossed her on the bed. Not exactly "tossed," more like gently lowered. Then he unbuttoned his slacks just enough to free his male magnificence, pulled up her dress and pulled down her panties. "I am taking you *now*. I, Vladimir Lord Ryan, do not bother with preliminaries."

A few giggles escaped as she wriggled against him provocatively, uttering little sighs and cries of "Ah, no! What shall become of me?"

Contrary to his words, he probed to see if she was ready for him. "You want me," he whispered in her ear. His deft fingers already had her close to climax. In his hokey French accent, he added, "Which eez why I make you wait."

"I don't vant you, I don't!" she cried out unconvincingly. Now she sounded like a bad imitation of Bullwinkle's archnemesis Natasha.

"I don't believe you," he whispered, and she quivered to feel his hot, sweet breath on her neck. She luxuriated in his essence of Liam, a little different now that he didn't have his herbal soap but still recognizable and just as enticing. Would she ever get enough of him?

She reached for his beautiful, fully aroused cock, wanting him inside her *now*, but he hovered over her teasingly. "I told you, I make you wait," he growled in that silly French accent. "Only," he added in his own voice, husky with desire, "*I* can't wait any longer."

Taking his own sweet time, he eased inside her, and they both sighed extravagantly with the pleasure of it, this melding together that seemed so organic. Hovering above her, he began his inexorable rhythm, circling and pumping, filling her, his eyes brimming with love. Then his lips descended on hers once more, teasing, tasting, nipping, then retreating, causing her to strain upward, wanting more.

* * *

"Have you talked to Teresa lately?" Ali asked Joe. She would have loved to get a firsthand scoop on her sister-in-law but figured Teresa would rather keep the details of her first getaway with Liam to herself.

May Allen had the afternoon off, and they were sitting on the living room floor playing with Josie and Caryn, now three-and-a-half months old. They'd spread out a blanket, and Joe was helping Caryn stand up. She could almost do it. Josie lay on her back, kicking her arms and legs. Both were giving them gummy smiles. They were good-natured babies but dauntingly energetic.

"Not since they arrived in Ménerbes," Joe said. "She sounded deliriously happy. Liam adored Paris." He made googly eyes at Caryn and said in his funny baby voice, "Yes'm, in no time you're going to be running us ragged, I can tell. Yes you are, yes you are!"

"I'm worried they are going to toddle right through the back door and over the cliff," Ali said. Caryn let out a high squeal.

"Shh, don't give them any ideas. Okay, I know what you mean, but they're a long way from walking, aren't they? When do babies start crawling, anyway?"

"Between six and ten months. They're teething, though. Look at that." She pointed out Caryn's emerging tooth.

"Hmm. That's why they've been fussing so much."

"May knows what to do. They seem okay at the moment. Can we let the dogs in?"

As usual, the dogs were peering through the window, tongues lolling, as if shut out of paradise. Coogan had to sit on a chair, but Harry was big enough that he could look in by standing on his hind legs. Ali couldn't help but pity them, knowing how they craved human company.

"We've been through this," Joe said. "They have each other. And Liam is their master, not us. We can't undo his training. They're *dogs*. It's not even cold out, and they have a nice warm garage to sleep in. They're fine."

Ali sighed. "All right. Maybe once Liam and Teresa take them away, we'll get a sweet little lapdog." He made a face but didn't repeat his favorite rant about "real" dogs versus the toy kind. "It's kind of nice to have the house to ourselves," Ali went on. "But when May returns, we could go to the empty cabin and pretend we just met." She batted her eyes at him.

Joe was making faces at Josie. In his baby voice, he said, "That sounds like an excellent idea. Wouldn't you like your mommy and daddy to make wild, passionate love in a place where no one will bother them?"

"That voice is pretty goofy," Ali said. "Here, let me take Josie. I think she's hungry. You take Caryn."

Joe kept up the silly voice. "I do like to watch that. Can you feed them at the same time? That is an incredible turn-on."

She rolled her eyes. "What is it with men and breasts? All right, then." She arranged the special pillow and laid them side by side so they could both suckle at once.

Joe propped himself up on his elbow, watching. "I have the most incredible hard-on right now."

"Down, boy. You'll have to keep it in your pants until May gets home."

The door opened, and David came striding in. "Oh, shit!" he said, covering his eyes.

"It's okay," Ali said. "You're a doctor, right? Relax."

"It's still embarrassing if it's your sister-in-law," he said, taking a chair and continuing to shield his eyes.

"How was the interview?" Joe asked. "Are you hired?"

"Yeah," he said, unenthusiastic. "It's not the greatest job, but it might be the only opening in the area for a doctor right now. I won't be doing anything but seeing patients at the clinic. At least the hours are regular, and it will give me breathing space. Nothing too harrowing, I hope. UTIs, sore throats, and minor injuries."

Aiming for casual, Ali asked, "Will you get a place in Sequim?"

"Do you want me to?"

"No," Joe said bluntly. "We want you to stay. It's an easy commute."

He sat forward in his chair, elbows on his knees. "Don't you need your privacy?"

They both snorted, then pointed at each other and laughed. Buttoning her blouse, Ali said, "Privacy is a foreign concept until these two are in kindergarten. We're always in search of adult conversation—not that we don't enjoy each other's company. Joe spends so much time alone in the studio. He's missed having Liam here, and who knows how long Liam and Teresa will stick around once they return from their honeymoon?"

"When do you expect them back?" David asked.

"Not sure," Joe said as he laid a towel over his shoulder and gently thumped Caryn on the back. In a few seconds she made a faint "urp" sound. "Teresa says Liam is having the time of his life. They might go on to London and see a few plays."

"That sounds nice," David chuckled. "We should join them. I don't start work until January. That's when the doctor I'm replacing goes on maternity leave."

"Aw, wish we could," Joe said. "Traveling with the twins would be a nightmare. And we can't leave them alone with May at this early stage. You should go." He paused, then added wickedly, "Take Maddie, she'd love to go to the theater in London."

David gave him a dirty look. "Don't even joke about that. Not that I wouldn't be tempted if …."

Ali rose to her knees, all ears. "If what?"

"If things were resolved with Sylvia. And if she weren't seeing that Kilo jerk."

"Hmm," Joe said. "Calling it 'seeing' is giving it too much importance." He set a gurgling Caryn down on her stomach.

"That man is a cobra," David grumbled. "And what does it say about Maddie?"

Ali felt vaguely offended by his judgmental tone. "You think it was slutty of her? She's just a modern woman, taking her opportunities where she finds them. Kilo's hard to resist. She wouldn't have given him a second glance if you'd been available."

"Okay, okay, but it bothers me," David admitted. "I couldn't date someone like that. I'd make Othello look like a proponent of open marriage."

"If you'd spent as much time on the road as I did, you'd understand," Joe said. "Performers don't look at the world the same way. Everything's fleeting. You're lonely and stressed, and you reach for whatever offers itself, especially when it comes in a nice package."

Ali didn't enjoy the picture he was painting. Joe's singing voice was almost back to normal, and she feared another tour was in the planning stage. They hadn't discussed it.

"It's not so different in my line of work," David said. "Those hospital shows only exaggerate a little."

"I'm looking forward to meeting this Sylvia," Ali said in an artificially bright voice, trying to change the subject.

"Humph," David said, still grumpy. "Will Maddie also be here at Christmas?"

David was even more maddening than his brother, divulging as little as possible, avoiding a question by asking another. " 'Fraid so," Ali said. "I hope you're okay with that."

"*Kilo's* invited?" Now David seemed angry.

"Not necessarily," Ali was quick to say. "I'm sure he's got family somewhere, or friends, or another place to go. He's been in Port Townsend a few years now. We didn't adopt him. Right, Joe? He may be Liam's only friend here other than Joe and Peter, the guy he helps out at Fort Worden, but my brother will understand."

Joe nodded vigorously. "Right. Family first."

The back door opened, and seconds later, the nanny strode in and immediately took charge of the twins. Ali loved May Allen's no-nonsense, brisk but friendly manner—and the fact that she looked like one of the Golden Girls rather than a Nordic supermodel.

"Uh, David?" Joe said, steering Ali out the door. "Ali has something she needs to show me in the empty cabin. Can you entertain yourself for a few hours?"

David's bass-baritone laugh reverberated throughout the house. Though Ali didn't appreciate the humor being at her and Joe's expense, she was glad to hear such a merry outburst from Joe's irritable brother.

CHAPTER 9

———•———

As Ali bounced Josie in her arms, she passed by the calendar displaying scenes from the Pacific Northwest and stopped to appreciate the December photo. She longed for the day she and Joe could travel to those spectacular areas without worrying too much about the girls. The picture of Mount Rainier in all its snowy glory made her imagine the twins starting an avalanche. Hurricane Ridge was almost as impressive and hazardous, and it was right next door. Still, the twins could get into all sorts of trouble right here at home. Once they were mobile, anyway.

She kissed the top of Josie's head and said, "You wouldn't do that, would you, sweetie? Start an avalanche, I mean." Josie gurgled, as if delighted by the suggestion. At five and a half months old, the girls had a luminous beauty, with their bright, long-lashed blue eyes and masses of curly black hair. There were no baby pictures of her and Liam. The only photographs of their formative years were staged ones from high school and a few candid shots taken by Becca. Nothing before they'd gone to live with their final foster parents, Emily and George, at age eight.

It was Wednesday, December twenty-third, two days before Christmas. Thank God Teresa and Liam had finally returned from their impromptu reenactment of *Around the World in 80 Days* to help out. Most of their guests had arrived yesterday. Becca and Jean-Louis would spend the holiday with Becca's large family, joining Ali and Joe December twenty-seventh. Hannukah had ended December fifteenth, but Becca's family were non-practicing Jews and made an even bigger deal out of Christmas. They'd graciously agreed to pick up Sylvia at a luxury hotel in downtown Seattle and drive her the rest of the way.

The twins had started fussing at six this morning, so Ali got up to feed them, hoping to spare Joe. As usual, he slept soundly—or pretended to. May Allen would have attended to them once the crying began, but Ali was still the main source of their nourishment. They were eating some solid food, mostly cereal, and formula mixed with her breast milk. Tomorrow, Christmas Eve, she would drink a glass of wine, maybe two. The girls were nearly old enough to be weaned. Her conscience was still going to bother her for not nursing longer, but she'd had enough of watching others make merry while she drank sparkling water.

The three main cabins were occupied by Teresa and Liam, David, and Laurie and Duncan. While Teresa and Liam enjoyed their extended honeymoon, a crew had built two more cabins to accommodate Carrie and Becca and Jean-Louis. Maddie would stay at the house until after the holidays; then they'd move her to a cabin for the run of her play. Carrie's manservant Rostand remained behind in Seattle. May Allen's widowed sister Susan from Cincinnati was sharing her room next to the nursery, and they were paying Susan to help out wherever she could. They'd told the FOSSP kids to take the holidays off. Nervous about Sylvia, Ali didn't want witnesses to what might turn into a family melodrama. Liam had convinced Kilo to make other plans. Ali doubted that he had given up on Maddie.

The new log-cabin-style home under construction was still a few months from completion. More and more, Ali was hoping she and Joe would move in there and leave the main house—an eclectic mix of styles dominated by Modern Greek Revival with its widow's walk, columns, and covered porch—to Liam and Teresa. The new place was farther from the cliffs, and a tall fence would keep the twins out of danger. After all, what they now jokingly referred to as "The Sea Captain's House"—it had been built by a successful studio musician in 1990—contained Teresa's piano and reflected *her* decorating preferences. Ali had finally realized she *did* care about the décor. She wanted *American Bungalow*, not *House Beautiful*. Only problem was, she suspected Liam did too. She didn't want to introduce friction into their young marriage. Ali had already braced herself for a rocky adjustment. Teresa always got her way, and so did Liam. Their "ways" were bound to diverge more often than not. *Enough. I'm not going to worry about that—or Joe's pending tour—until after the holidays.*

Deprived of childhood Christmas traditions, Ali and Liam weren't emotionally invested in a holiday everyone else seemed to anticipate all year long. But Ali was game. She wanted the twins to grow up believing in Christmas magic. The Christmas tree, its crowning star one scant inch from the twelve-foot ceiling, was dense with white lights and Victorian-replica ornaments collected from shops in town. When Carrie had offered the family's traditional decorations, Ali had Joe buy another tree from a farm—she didn't approve of chopping down noble firs from the forest. The original tree graced the rec room downstairs, which was equipped with a foosball table, a dining table with eight chairs, overstuffed couches and chairs facing a giant TV, and multiple shelves of boardgames and puzzles. With the cooler weather, Joe and Ali spent most evenings there. Its humble knotty-pine walls and silk-and-wool-blend carpeting made it the friendlier retreat. Ali loved to picture the twins playing with their cousins in the rec room. Any day now they would be crawling. The child-proof doors were in place, but the girls were so rambunctious and clever, Ali feared they'd outsmart them. Josie's first word had been "Mama" and Caryn's "Dada," which settled that particular bet in the nicest way possible. So far, nothing else was intelligible. They still communicated with each other in babbles that almost made sense. Like watching an Ingmar Bergman movie.

May Allen and her sister Susan breezed in, gave her a cheery greeting, and took charge of the twins. Upstairs, Ali found Teresa in the kitchen.

"You're up early," Ali said as she stood at the espresso machine.

"Still confused about the hour," Teresa confessed, looking at her watch. "I was hoping to beat Mom to the breakfast table so you and I could grab a moment alone."

"You're going to have to speak fast," Ali said. "That's a lot of ground to cover. You really flew to Egypt and India?"

Teresa helped herself to a glass of water. "It was wild. I've never been so spontaneous. Cairo is perfect in October. Highs in the eighties, lows in the sixties. We saw the pyramids and rode camels. We saw the Al-Azhar Mosque and a bunch of other stuff. I have a million slides, and I promise to bore you to tears with my travelogue at some point. But right now, I want to sit here in this kitchen and hear what's going on with you. Joe told me you've finished another website?"

Ali placed a double latte in front of Teresa. "Not a new one, just a redesign. You know our organization, Foster Splash Pad, that helps young people who've aged out of foster homes. We're expanding into Port Angeles. I'm hoping Liam will get involved."

Teresa held her latte reverently, as if gifted with ambrosia. "Try and stop him."

"Do you think the name works?" Ali asked. "Susan didn't know what a splash pad is."

"That's weird. To me it's clear: like they have at water parks."

Ali helped herself to an Americano. "It's way harder to come up with an original name than you might think. Joe gave me the idea when he said that small clubs were splash pools for old rockstars. I thought 'splash pad' was less confusing. There are a lot of organizations like ours, only not in this area. I've hired some new employees and therapists and expanded our housing." She led Teresa to the computer in the kitchen and navigated to the website. "What do you think?"

Teresa started clicking through. "I love it! Very professional. I'll see what Liam is up for, and I'll give it some thought too. I'm sure Becca and Jean-Louis will find ways to contribute, once the Port Townsend Fête Sauvage is open."

"Okay, enough about me. The twins are both saying Mama and Dada now, and 'No!' I'm fairly sure I heard 'Mine!' from Josie the other day. Any day now they're going to start crawling."

Teresa rubbed her hands together. "Oh good, I didn't miss much."

"You and Liam? Still happy?" She sipped her own Americano and sighed in contentment.

Teresa pointed at the cup. "Did you wean the girls?"

"Almost. I'm reintroducing coffee and wine to my own diet as of today."

"Well, go easy. You'll need your calm once Mom starts weighing in on everything."

Ali joined her at the counter. "Liam?" she prompted.

"*Happy* doesn't begin to describe it. We had the time of our lives, and Liam left a trail of broken hearts, starting with Rolfe and Adam in Ménerbes. Liam upgraded their plumbing, so they insisted we stay with them a few days when the rental on our house was up. I'm pretty sure they wouldn't recognize me if I ran into them at a grocery store, but they will never forget Liam."

Joe ambled in. "T-Girl!" He gave her a big hug. "You look radiant."

"Thanks, JJ," she said. "I guess I've made peace with the new look."

Ali couldn't get over Teresa's transformation. No longer the clone of Carrie, with her Hollywood blonde chignon and rail-thin figure, this new Teresa was a lightly tanned, healthier girl, a few new pounds filling her out in all the right places. Her strawberry blonde curls were almost shoulder-length. In her boiled-wool sweater, fitted trousers, and knee-high boots, she reminded Ali of old photos of Amelia Earhart. She looked fierce, like Liam.

Ali never would have guessed that her formerly feral brother would have such a liberating influence on Teresa.

A moment of silence pulsed with all the things Joe and Ali really wanted to ask. Was Teresa pregnant? Would she and Liam stay for a while? What were their plans? But Joe and Ali had agreed not to overwhelm their siblings-*cum*-in-laws.

"Okay," Teresa said, "you're not fooling me. You have a million questions. One, I'm not pregnant, hard as we tried. Liam and I have no idea what comes next, so I can't answer you there either. Until then, we'd like to stay. Does that about cover it?"

Ali nodded. "Pretty much. You know we hate to pry."

"I don't know anything of the kind," Teresa said with a smile. "Speaking of prying, how's David? Is Maddie still seeing Kilo?"

Joe answered, "David got a job at a day clinic in Sequim. He's not too thrilled about it so no need to drum up enthusiasm, should the subject arise. He starts in January. Maddie just arrived, but we already promised David that Kilo wouldn't be part of our Christmas. We're pretty sure that's what Maddie wants, too. If you'd seen her after she spent an afternoon with him, you'd understand."

"Oh," Teresa said with a sympathetic grimace. "He must have overwhelmed her." She looked around for Liam before adding, "I'm sure he gave her the full treatment. He knew what he was doing ten years ago. I can imagine how much, er, expertise he's picked up since then. Still, he might have overplayed his hand. Maddie's special. I'm guessing most of his women aren't."

"Could be," Ali said. "Maddie didn't act like a woman in love, more like a fawn who barely escaped a cougar. She'll be spending a lot of time with us, since rehearsals on her show begin after New Year's. At some point I'll get her to open up."

Joe snorted. "Poor Maddie. Does she know she's starring in a soap opera for our private amusement?"

"Don't be a spoilsport," Teresa pouted. "We're rooting for David."

"David might be too much of a prude for Maddie," Joe said. "I'm not sure he can get past her fling with Kilo."

Ali plunked down a platter of bacon in the center of the table and a plate of toast. "Eat," she said. "All bets are off until we meet Sylvia. First we'll get to know this paragon who captured David's heart. Then we'll dispatch her." Seeing Joe's look of mock horror, she said, "I didn't say *kill* her. Just send her packing."

"Wash her out of his hair, so to speak," Teresa said wryly. She said to Joe, "You're welcome. I know you like a good earworm in the morning."

Joe was already singing, "I'm Gonna Wash That Man Right Outa My Hair" with a bump and grind dance that might have seriously messed with *South Pacific's* G-rating.

Uh-oh. Maddie was standing at the door, watching. They should have been more careful. After all, she was staying at the house. You couldn't see her coming like the guests using the cabins. Ali wondered how much she'd overheard. She had a knack for silent hovering.

Seeing that she had been noticed, Maddie said, "Nice," in a deadpan voice. "You missed your calling, Joe. Your choreography is an improvement over the production I was in. Any coffee?" She wandered over to the espresso machine, and Ali hopped up to help her make a latte. "It's nice to see you, Teresa. I hear you did a little unscheduled globetrotting."

Her tone was friendly enough, though the words struck Ali as snarky. Who would blame Maddie for being envious? Ali herself would have loved to embark on such an adventure. If only they'd done more traveling while they could. But the twins had been conceived a few weeks before their wedding, and once she'd started to show, they'd settled in Paris. Traipsing around Europe while suffering from morning sickness hadn't appealed. The call telling them Liam was coming home had given them an excuse to go back to Seattle a few months before the birth.

Perhaps out of sensitivity, Teresa didn't launch into another pocket description of her travels. "You played the Mitzi Gaynor role?"

"Yes," Maddie said, taking a seat and helping herself to a piece of toast. "A non-Equity production."

"You look a little like Mitzi Gaynor," Teresa said. "I mean your—"

"Body," Maddie finished for her. "I know, I'm a freak show. I see people staring. It's okay. If I had two heads, you'd stare too."

"It's spectacular," Ali said. "You don't seem to agree."

"If you say so. My breasts are too large for the rest of me, and men don't …. Let's just say being taken seriously isn't easy. I'd rather look like either of you. You're both gorgeous, and your bodies are on the beautiful side of normal." Her expression turned to panic. "That sounded so … condescending. I didn't mean it that way at all. I want to wow people with my talent, not my freakish assets."

"You're the furthest thing from a freak," Ali said, mystified that she'd think otherwise. Maddie's wide, shining green eyes with their forest-green limbal rings, thick golden-blonde curls, pert nose, and heart-shaped face alone would have made most men gaga.

Maddie gave her a helpless shrug. "I'm cute enough. But if I were tall and long-limbed, I'd be more versatile as an actress."

She's parroting her mother, Ali thought. The more she saw of other people's mothers in action, the more she realized her emotionally distant foster mother Emily hadn't been so bad.

"A lot of actors are short, right?" Teresa offered. "Tom Cruise, for instance. He wouldn't have to stand on a box with you."

"Yes, it might be useful when I become a movie star," Maddie said with a grin to show that she was kidding. "For stage work, it's a liability. Listen, I know I'm the stranger, so I'm fair game, but you're bound to be disappointed if you think David is going to fall for me. I already blew it there. And for your information, the fling with Kilo is over too. I was an idiot to fall for his shtick."

Ali couldn't believe how straightforward and clear-headed Maddie seemed to be.

As if in response to Ali's thoughts, Maddie added, "No one pussyfoots around in this business. Especially on the East Coast. I'm aware of my faults and my strengths. Typecasting is a reality everywhere except in high school and amateur productions." She looked around at them. "Did I totally turn you off? I certainly managed to kill the conversation." She gave a little wave. "The Maddie Show is over. We now return control of your television set to you." She waited. "Sorry, obscure reference. You never saw *The Outer Limits*?"

Joe leaned back in his chair, grinning. "You're a trip, Maddie."

Ali and Teresa exchanged amused glances. "Maddie, we love you," Ali said. "Don't hold back for our sakes." Seeing how she eyed the bacon, she told her, "Eat as much as you like, though you might have to wrestle David for it."

Teresa pointed out the window. "David and Liam are coming down the hill, trailed by adoring dogs. What a pair. Do you think they'd stage a woodchopping contest for our enjoyment? Shirtless, of course."

"Hey," Joe said, feigning hurt. "What about me?"

Ali patted him on the leg. "I hope you can forgive your sister for not appreciating how magnificent you look shirtless."

"What about David? Why does *she* want to see him *shirtless*?" Joe teased.

Teresa gave him a broad wink. "For Maddie's sake," she said in a stage whisper.

The men entered amid a burst of fresh air. Ignoring Maddie, David made a point of greeting all the family first. "You look good, D.O.," she said. "The air here must agree with you."

"D.O.?" Ali said, looking to Joe for an explanation.

Joe chuckled. "Orson. David Orson. We all have crosses to bear in the form of oddball middle names."

David gave his brother a flinty stare. Then, as if only now noticing her, he said to Maddie, "Nice to see you, Maddie."

"And you," she said with a gracious smile.

Nice try, Ali thought. *You* so *noticed her first*.

CHAPTER 10

———◦———

MADDIE HAD OVERHEARD MOST OF what they'd said about her, including how she'd blown it with David, but she knew that already. They were all way too interested in her business. Understandably so, and they hadn't said anything unkind. She was glad to have cleared the air. David was being weird—also understandable. Though still dreaming of him, Maddie had given up on having him in her waking life. She resolved not to treat him any differently than the others. He simply wasn't a prospect for her, never had been. She knew exactly one person in the cast of *A Midsummer Night's Dream*, Jeremy Fairewell, out and proud but content to play straight on stage. She looked forward to catching up.

Kilo didn't know how to contact her. She'd made sure of that. Oh, she felt a wave of lust while recalling those few intense days, a testament to his skill. That didn't change the fact that he scared her. She was done with being consumed by lust. She'd been there and done that, and it had never ended well. No different from going on a drunken binge, she supposed. It felt really good until it didn't, and the regret went on and on. She wanted the O'Connell clan to like her and the play to be a fun experience. That meant no major distractions. Kilo was really into control, a quality she'd learned to fear when it came to men. No sexual escapade was worth derailing her already precarious career.

Maddie, Teresa, and Ali were supposed to help Susan pull together Christmas Eve dinner while Laurie and Carrie—who seemed to have little in common other than both being mothers—went into town to shop and see a movie. At breakfast, Joe, David, Liam, and Duncan had shared their grand scheme for turning the house into something that could summon Batman—no matter that Commissioner Gordon had used a spotlight. Liam had drawn up what looked like architectural plans. By late morning, they were scrambling up and down ladders, draping strings of white lights on every available surface, hanging icicle lights from the eaves and wreaths on the doors, and arranging incense cedar boughs and red electric candles on the windowsills.

Around eleven, Maddie walked back into the kitchen, where Ali and Teresa were each feeding a twin with a bottle while May Allen the nanny and her sister Susan stood by. Ali and Teresa wore besotted expressions. *That's what babies do to you*, Maddie thought, *rob you of your brain and ambitions*. The smiling girls, with their curly black hair and electric blue eyes, were so irresistible it might be worth feeling lobotomized.

"Um, Susan?" Ali said. "You're looking at that craggy cliff of a roast as if you're afraid it might come to life and attack you."

Ali had set the enormous slab of prime rib on the counter, but no one was making a move to do anything about it.

Susan drew herself up to her full height and put her hands on her hips. "I didn't realize I was here as a cook." She was a solid, no-nonsense woman in her mid-fifties. To Maddie, everyone seemed tall, but at six feet or more, Susan topped even Ali. Her hairstyle was one of those permed bubbles many older women affected. She resembled May Allen, plain faced and friendly, only taller and with muscular arms. She lifted the meat as if it were a plastic stage prop.

"Are you a weight lifter?" Maddie asked.

Everyone laughed, but Susan replied, "Yep. I've placed in some contests."

"She's really strong," May confirmed.

Maddie thought someone should acknowledge this compliment, and everyone else was standing around with their mouths open, so she said, "Nice."

"But not a cook," Teresa said, returning their attention to the immediate problem at hand.

"Nope, not my forte."

The women set the gurgling babies in their pram and starting milling about the kitchen as if waiting for inspiration or Godot. "Where's Jean-Louis when you need him?" Ali groaned, gesturing to the ceiling as if God might be listening. "I tried cooking classes in Paris, and Joe tolerated my efforts, but we're cooking for a whole houseful today. I've done a bunch of fussy dishes but never dealt with large chunks of meat."

"Liam always cooks for me," Teresa confessed. "My skills are even more rudimentary than yours. Is this why Mom agreed to accompany Laurie? She must *really* hate cooking. Oh, sorry, Maddie."

"Think nothing of it," Maddie said, hoping they'd all stop tiptoeing around the topic of her mother in her presence. "They're seeing a movie. Not even my mom talks during movies. And shopping doesn't require much interaction."

"Which movie?" Ali asked.

"*The Man in the Iron Mask.*"

Ali cocked her head. "Does your mother like historical dramas and swashbuckling?"

Maddie laughed. "Not usually."

"It was either that or *Fear and Loathing in Las Vegas*," Teresa said.

Maddie grinned. "Johnny Depp plays Hunter S. Thompson. Perfect. I love Johnny Depp."

Ali gave her a friendly nudge. "I'm not sure you'd like him in this role. He's not his usual scrumptious self. Right now, we need to concentrate on dinner."

It was time for Maddie to step up. "Um, besides prime rib, what's for dinner?"

"Potatoes, vegetables?" Ali said, as if improvising.

"You have cookbooks, right?" Teresa asked. "We can figure this out."

Maddie pushed up the sleeves of her sweater. "No need. It's simple enough. Let's start with the meat. It should have been marinating for a while, but that's not essential. Okay if I take over?" She reached for the garlic container and crushed a clove with the flat of her knife so that the skin fell right off before chopping it up. "I'll need several heads of garlic."

Ali produced a garlic press.

"That'll make it quicker," Maddie said, "but you should still take the skin off first."

"We have fresh herbs," Ali said, indicating the row of pots hanging outside the window. Joe had caged the area to keep out deer. "What do you need?"

Maddie combined fresh thyme and rosemary, garlic, sea salt, and ground pepper into a mash. While the others watched, she washed her hands thoroughly and coated the roast with olive oil, herbs and spices and covered it with foil. "We'll let it sit at room temperature. It will cook for about two hours. What else?" At their blank faces, she started rummaging around in the two refrigerators and the freezer. "Who shopped?"

"Liam," Teresa answered. "He was gonna cook, but the other guys enlisted his help with the lights, and he assumed Susan could do it." Susan squirmed and hunched her shoulders as if trying to make herself smaller. "He was wrong to assume anything," Teresa told her. "People, uh, like us, usually have a cook on staff. It's not like we asked for your résumé."

"You were so kind to let me visit May," Susan sniffled. The sisters exchanged hangdog looks.

Ali waved her off. "Really, it's okay. In fact, if you don't mind cleaning up later, why don't you visit with your sister now? Josie and Caryn seem to be on best behavior. Can the two of you take them to the rec room and watch them roll around on a blanket? Put on a movie. There are too many cooks in this kitchen already."

Susan and May didn't need to be told twice. Thanking Ali profusely, they backed out of the room.

"Now we can get crazy," Teresa said, swiveling on the kitchen stool.

Maddie had placed everything she had foraged on the kitchen island. Onions, mushrooms, and new potatoes. "Are we making Yorkshire pudding? Because if so, I'm going to prepare the batter now. It has to sit." They helped her locate the ingredients then stood by as she worked. In ten minutes, it was done. Meanwhile, Ali made a pot of herbal tea, and Teresa went off to fix a fingernail. "What's for dessert, figgy pudding?" Maddie asked Ali. "Just kidding. You're supposed to age it for something like a year."

"I have no idea what Liam had in mind," Ali said, "and I don't feel like asking him. The dinner is our responsibility now, darn him."

"What about cookies?" Maddie said. "I know a good recipe. It's basically a white cookie with nutmeg. We can decorate them."

Teresa was back. "I could go ask Liam," she said, but Maddie was already making the dough.

After putting the dough in the refrigerator to chill, she chopped up onions, cubed potatoes, turnips, and carrots, then sliced up sweet peppers. "We'll lay the roast on a bed of vegetables, which will take on the flavor of the seasonings. We'll also douse them with olive oil. What are we doing for salad?"

They exchanged blank looks.

In no time, Ali, Teresa, and Maddie were driving to the local co-op to buy the remaining ingredients.

"Is it okay that I took control?" Maddie asked. "My mom never liked cooking, and I've needed a variety of survival skills to get by. Cooking is one of them."

Ali pulled into the packed parking lot, where someone was just leaving. "Are you kidding? You're a lifesaver."

As they drove back to the compound, Ali said, "You know, I think we have a lot in common. I mean, what we put up with as children."

"Ah," Maddie said. "You had an alcoholic father? No, don't answer that. You did have some tough crap to deal with."

Ali's brow creased. "But …?"

"You had a brother and some pretty decent foster parents. My father was a drunk, and my mom was in denial. Sometimes I think I raised myself. Anyway, my story does not end happily. I am on my own." They had arrived at the compound.

"Your story could still have a happy ending," Teresa said, her husky voice ridiculously chipper.

Maddie wished they'd stop trying so hard. She picked up a sack of groceries. "Listen, I'm not given to self-pity, and right now I'd say a lot of people would envy me. But … Christmas is weird when the tree is dead before you can decorate it, no one can find the ornaments, your dad hates Christmas carols, and he can't sober up long enough to play Santa."

Ali grimaced. "Tell me about it. Christmas with George and Emily made the Cratchit family celebration look like that Christmas party in *The Great Gatsby*. I figure I'm catching up on lost time. You can too. You're free to create your own traditions now."

Maddie smiled gamely, certain as she was that *Christmas at the O'Connell House* would not be on next year's calendar. By then they'd have adopted some new strays, or she'd be doing the theatrical version of *A Christmas Carol*, where she was typically double cast in the minor roles of Belle and Mrs. Filch. This year she'd turned down both *A Christmas Carol* and the alto part in one of the Dickens Carolers quartets that roamed Seattle and entertained at various events in authentic Victorian costumes. The money was decent by amateur standards, but catering paid more, and she'd wanted to breathe deep of the O'Connell's rarefied air, just this once. A year from now, Duncan would have surely kicked her mom to the curb.

As they walked down the hill toward the main house, they observed the men buzzing around with the efficiency and organization of a hive of drones as they strung lights and repositioned ladders. "Of course I'm not surprised by Liam," Ali said, "but David and Joe are awfully self-sufficient for rich guys."

"We had a do-it-yourselfer father," Teresa said. "There's nothing like setting a good example."

Maddie stared wistfully at the rambunctious work party. She didn't blame Teresa and Ali. They couldn't help saying stuff that reminded her of her own father's glaring defects. No good example to follow there. It was just as well she didn't have a brother.

"You're awfully quiet, Teresa," Ali said as Maddie pressed out the dough for the cookies and started arranging reindeer and snowman shapes on the cookie sheets for them to decorate.

"I'm afraid I have a history of pretty fabulous Christmases," Teresa said, as if confessing to a past life as the Grinch's secret helper. "Christmas at our house was quite the extravaganza. *Tastefully* extravagant, naturally."

Ali laughed. "I can only imagine."

"Given free rein, our father would have thrown taste out the window. That's why Joe and David want the house to explode with light like a ballfield."

Ali cocked her head. "The white lights are tasteful."

"They'll be adding red lights somewhere," Teresa predicted, "a whole constellation of them. To goad Mom. She never fails to complain that red lights make the house look like a brothel."

"So, Maddie …" Ali began. "Before the others invade our three-person coffee klatch, I'd like to try something, if you're okay with it. I'll start. A little trip into the dark side of Christmases past. Nothing too bleak, though you can go there if you like." She paused to consider her reindeer before pressing chocolate bits into its horns and red sprinkles into its saddle. "One Christmas, there was a big present under the tree for me. I dared to get excited. It was a frying pan. I was only eleven, but my foster mother Emily thought I should be building up my kitchen for when I was on my own."

"Awww …" Teresa hugged her arm. "I hope it was a nice one."

Ali raised her eyebrows. "I think she bought it at Sears. Nothing special. One of those pans that needs to be seasoned. Almost too heavy for me to lift."

"Cast iron," Maddie said. "I prefer them now, but yikes …."

"Do you still have it?" Teresa asked Ali.

"I couldn't get rid of it as long as we lived with George and Emily. As you all probably know, they died a few years back, in a motorcycle accident in Botswana. I gave it to Liam, who was more interested in cooking. I bought a small, nonstick frying pan. I bet the guys he shared a house with in Renton still have that cast-iron clunker." Having finished decorating her sheet, she put it in the oven and set the timer. She tapped Teresa on the shoulder. "Your turn."

Teresa nodded. "Much as I love my brothers, they could be mean. One Christmas Eve, when we had even less supervision than usual, David tried to stuff me down the laundry chute. When he suggested the idea, I thought it might be fun. Fortunately, my shoulders were too wide. I didn't get stuck, but for a moment there I thought David was going to find a way to make me fit and I started crying. Mom heard me, and David caught hell for it. There was other stuff like that. They left me behind a lot. One time we all went bike riding and they got so far ahead that I lost them completely. I just sat and cried until some stranger found me and phoned the house."

"Ugh," Ali said. "Good thing it was a friendly stranger and not some child molester. Liam was the opposite kind of brother. *So* opposite. I never got left behind. I *wanted* to be left behind. He was very worried about my safety because of that first foster family." She corrected herself, "Foster *mother*. No family. One of her boyfriends came into my room with a knife. Liam almost killed him. With his bare hands. We were only eight, but Liam matured freakishly early. He was already five feet eight with a man's muscles by then."

Maddie felt the heat suffuse her face, and she never blushed. How dare she assume her past was worse than Ali's. "Oh man, that is bad," she said. "Did Liam go to juvie?"

"Not that night," Ali said lightly, as if speaking of a scene from a movie. "Until the whole story came out, no one knew what to do with him. If he should be praised, punished, or reformed, and how to do that. It helped that our foster mom's boyfriend had a criminal record. For a while there, it looked as if we'd spend the rest of our childhoods in an orphanage. Until George and Emily came along, no one wanted us. The social worker convinced them Liam wasn't violent, just loved his sister. Of course George and Emily never went so far as to adopt us." She paused. "Maddie, you don't have to contribute. I just wanted you to know you're in good company."

"No, I'll give it a go," Maddie said, as she slid the last sheet of cookies into the oven. "I love your stars," she told Ali. "They have personalities." Their hostess had given them distinctive faces. "This one with the beetle brows reminds me of my PE teacher." Seeing that her audience grew restless, Maddie stopped stalling. "All right then, I confess, even though Mom was tone-deaf when it came to Christmas magic, the holiday was okay until I was thirteen. Mom worked full-time, but she did try to compensate for Dad's lackadaisical parenting. In those days, he was hardly the only disengaged father. Until a year before he left us, he was a secret drinker. The Christmas Eve of my thirteenth year, he got visibly drunk. My mom's childhood best friend lived down the street, and she and her husband and daughter always joined us for Christmas Eve. That night the husband had the flu and stayed home in bed. Lisa was also thirteen, and we were friends because we'd both, uh, *blossomed* early. In other words, we had breasts. Lisa was a lot taller and looked older. She could pass for sixteen—eighteen, with enough makeup." Maddie took a deep breath and wiped away a tear. She envied Ali's ability to disassociate from the bad stuff in her past. Rather than repress bad memories, actors were trained to channel them into a character's emotional center. Blocking out the concern on the two women's faces, she continued, "My dad had a certain smarmy charm that got gross once he'd had a few too many. He started flirting with Lisa. Stuff like, 'You're a big girl now, aren't you? I bet you could have any boy you want.' Our mothers were visibly alarmed, but Lisa kind of liked it. She was already playing Spin the Bottle at those parties my mom forbade me to go to. They left early, and my parents had a horrendous shouting match. She threatened divorce, and he called her a ballbreaker and other terrible things. I shut myself in the basement and watched the Alistair Sim *Christmas Carol*. Merry Christmas to me! By the next morning, they seemed to have called a truce. Christmas morning was … tense."

Ali came over to lay a sympathetic hand on her shoulder. "I'm almost afraid to ask how that ended, though Laurie has told us the salient points. We know he left home when you were fourteen and died when you were fifteen."

Maddie nodded. "In August, he ran away with another of Mom's friends he'd been having an affair with. I'm hazy on the details because we had no contact with him after that. It's not like he was ever a candidate for Father of the Year. He was gone most of the time—he sold medical equipment, was on the road a lot—and when he was home, he shut himself in his den or hid behind the newspaper. I'm not sure why Mom didn't leave him a lot earlier. Despite Women's Lib, women still put up with a lot to avoid being divorcées." She hastened to add, "At least he didn't molest me. Some of my friends have stories like that." Maddie reached for a tissue and blew her nose.

Ali inclined her head toward Teresa. "You know, Teresa lost her father when she was thirteen."

"Almost fourteen," Teresa corrected.

Maddie gasped. "You were even younger than me."

"My father liked to drink too," Teresa said. "Smoking was what killed him—lung cancer. But he was a helluva nice guy. My brothers have told me a lot of stories. I do wish I'd had him around while I was in high school. Your situation was worse. Money doesn't buy happiness, but it sure helps."

Maddie's eyes stung with tears, and Teresa was also glassy eyed.

"I'm so sorry, guys," Ali said in obvious distress. "Wow, I did not intend for this to be like a visit to Scrooge's Christmas Past."

Maddie laughed through her tears. "You know what? It's totally cool. I haven't talked about this stuff for a long time. It feels cathartic. Don't apologize. So you can see, my mom's been through some crap too. She's different when she's alone with Duncan and me. I hope she'll calm down with your family eventually."

"I believe you," Teresa said. "My mom is also different when it's just core family. She's too prickly when it comes to Liam and Ali. She envisioned different futures for us. The four boys would follow in Dad's footsteps and help run Big Paul's Outfitters, and I'd carry on with her causes and wow her social circle with my sophistication and chicness. Doesn't everyone secretly long for children who walk in their footsteps? But she's softened a little. Right, Ali?"

Ali took too long to answer. "Uh ... she's great with the twins."

"I think some parents are better with babies and some are better once they become little people," Teresa said. "Mom was the first kind of parent. Dad was better with us later on. If you want a sad Christmas memory, I'll tell you about the Christmas after he died. He died on Thanksgiving, only a month after being diagnosed with lung cancer." She looked at each of them in turn and laughed. "Not going there. From now on, it's all visions of sugarplums."

The timer went off. "Last batch is done!" Maddie said brightly, relieved that the conversation wouldn't keep swirling down the drain. She didn't want to think of her own father's death, either. Alone, full of regrets, begging to be visited one last time in hospice.

Teresa checked her watch. "Wow, it's four already. We skipped lunch. If you don't count all the broken cookies. The men never came in. Should we check to see if they were electrocuted?"

Ali laughed. "They must have gone to Kelpies for lunch. When we left to go to the store, Joe's car was missing."

Teresa pretended to pout. "They didn't invite us."

"They had manly stuff to discuss," Ali said.

"What do they talk about, do you think?" Teresa wondered.

Maddie smirked. "Not their feelings, that's for sure. And you can bet they weren't recalling any sad memories, either." She sprang to her feet.

"Prime rib needs to go in the oven. When it's resting, we'll do the Yorkshire Puddings."

After the roast was in the oven, they descended to the basement to watch *Christmas in Connecticut*, Teresa's favorite Christmas movie. "Ah," Ali said once it was well underway, "I get the appeal. Barbara Stanwyck is you. Beautiful, can't cook, clever wit, wants a real man, not a corporate tool."

"Who's a corporate tool?" Liam walked in, holding half a cookie. "I can smell dinner, but no one seems to be minding the store."

"That's why you felt free to raid it?" Teresa said. "You're eating one of Ali's star people. I hope you took the time to appreciate the artistry that went into it."

Stricken, Liam looked down at the fragment of cookie. "It tastes good," he said, apologetically. "Oh, oh yeah, I see the mouth and the silver-ball teeth. Very creative." He patted Ali on the head, and she pulled away, feigning hurt.

"Nice save," Teresa said. "Your sister may find it in her heart to forgive you."

Maddie checked her watch. "Will you turn down the oven to three twenty-five? Otherwise, we're on track."

Teresa patted the space next to her on the couch. "Come, sit, watch the movie with us. It's really good."

"Can't," Liam said, already backing away toward the stairs. "I have to turn down the oven. Besides, I've seen this one, and yeah, it's good, but we're not quite finished. We'll be expecting some major oohing and aahing."

"No injuries yet?" Ali said.

"Nope, safety first." A shout came from outside. "Uh, I better see what that's about." Seeing Ali jump up in alarm, he pointed at the couch. "Sit. That did not sound like a cry of pain. Frustration, maybe. If there's a problem, we'll fetch you." He mounted the stairs, two by two.

Maddie followed him. "I don't trust him to turn down the oven," she explained over her shoulder.

After the movie was over—while the prime rib was resting and the Yorkshire Puddings were in the oven—Ali went to check on the twins. Then they ventured outside to admire the men's handiwork. Coogan and Harry nosed their legs, looking for love.

"Ooh-ee," Ali said. "Have the dogs kept you company all day? They didn't get underfoot?"

"They're such good boys," Liam said to Coogan, who gave a little yip of delight. The giant dog Harry also barked once, a deep "Ruff!"

"You too," Teresa said to Harry. "You're *such* a good boy!" As she rubbed his back, she gave Liam a sly look. "You've made the house so bright, we can't see the stars."

He moved behind her and enfolded her in his arms. "Ah, but the stars can see us."

Joe also held Ali, making Maddie doubly aware of David, who stood alone, pretending to focus on the sea of lights. Seeing that the dogs were looking for love, she did her best to take up the slack, murmuring endearments as she scratched behind their ears.

"Where are Mom and Laurie?" Joe said. "It's nearly seven."

A few minutes later, Carrie's Cadillac drove up, and Carrie and Laurie descended the hill on the lighted pathway.

"What are you all looking at?" Carrie said. "Were you worried about us?"

"A little," Joe said. "Also, we can't admire our Christmas lighting without your usual comments about the red lights turning the place into a brothel."

Carrie laughed. Maddie was astounded to see the women looking so relaxed. "I don't have to say it now that you've pointed it out. I could say it looks as if the Sugarplum Fairy regurgitated on the house."

"*Mom*," David remonstrated, "that's disgusting."

"I think it's beautiful," Laurie said. She raised her fist. "All for one and one for all!" That triggered a gale of laughter from the two women.

"Looks like the two of you had a fine time," Duncan said. "How was *Man in the Iron Mask*?"

"It wasn't true to the book," Carrie sniffed and seemed to hold her clutch closer to her chest. "We're supposed to believe that the prisoner could just take over for his twin brother the king with no one the wiser? All those years in prison, and yet he is educated and has impeccable manners."

"Carrie!" Laurie butted in. "Who cares? That Leonardo Capricorn is some cutie."

"DiCaprio," Carrie corrected. "He's easy on the eyes, it's true, if you're into dewy adolescents. Jeremy Irons is more my speed."

To Duncan, Laurie said, "You boys have to see it in the theater for the fight scenes alone."

"Maybe we will." Duncan put an arm around her waist and gave her a squeeze. "Sounds like the perfect boys' night out."

Inside, wood was crackling in the fireplace, the tree, bookcases, and crèches were glowing with white lights, and the aromas of roast meat, garlic, and cookies hung in the air.

Carrie paused at the threshold and made a show of breathing it all in. "Lovely. Rostand himself couldn't have done it better."

Teresa took Maddie's arm. "You can thank Maddie. It turns out May Allen's sister Susan can't cook. Ali and I could have managed, but Maddie is an *artiste* in the kitchen. If not for her, dinner would have probably been at nine, and the prime rib would have been burnt to a crisp … or at the very least, well done."

Carrie shuddered, as if the prospect of overcooked meat was simply too terrible to contemplate.

May and Susan had contributed as best they could by setting the dining room table.

"Don't worry," Ali said. "We will be so grateful to Susan once we can leave the cleanup to her. Right, Liam? On Christmas Eve, Emily and George always had a crowd of their Peace Corps buddies over. They owned a set of vintage Fiestaware plates, bowls, and serving dishes that they only used on special occasions. Liam and I were tasked with putting away the leftovers and handwashing everything while they watched a movie. What a heartwarming holiday tradition that was."

Liam laughed and ruffled her hair. "We kept each other entertained. Just be glad they only used those on special occasions, or we might have gotten lead poisoning. Let's not bum everyone out with our bleak Christmas memories."

Maddie wondered what he'd think of their earlier conversation. Sharing emotional pain obviously wasn't Liam's thing.

Christmas magic did seem to have infected the little group. At past meals Maddie had shared with the O'Connells, Carrie and Laurie had kept everyone on their toes. The general focus was on trying to mitigate some cutting comment from Carrie or draw the attention away from Laurie's diarrhea of the mouth. None of that tonight. In fact, far from leading the conversation, her mother deferred to everyone else. And Carrie seemed unaccountably good-humored. They lavished praise on Maddie, even though she insisted, truthfully, that the preparation had been basic. The meat was pink, tasty, and tender, the Yorkshire Puddings golden brown, the vegetables flavorful, and the dressing on the green salad not too vinegary. Wine flowed. Even Ali enjoyed a glass or two.

Maddie and David sat at opposite ends of the table—much to Maddie's relief. She preferred to pretend he wasn't there. Judging by the way he studiously ignored her, the feeling was mutual. The women debated who was hotter, Hugh Grant or Leonardo DiCaprio. Teresa and Ali were pro-Hugh, and everyone else voted for Leo. Part of the reason for this topic was to goad the men, who kept trying to talk about what trails you could hike this time of year, their goals for the property, or the merits of one wine choice over another. Maddie loved the teasing-yet-affectionate tone of it all and tried not to feel sad that she would never truly belong here.

After dinner, they moved to the living room for Christmas carols. Teresa played the piano, and Joe and David sang a killer duet of "O Holy Night." David had a deep bass singing voice surprisingly similar to Joe's, other than the timbre. Less polished, since his voice was untrained. She'd noticed the similarities in their speaking voices. Perhaps his height and heavier frame accounted for the difference in range, like a tuba versus a French horn. Joe's voice was free of the gruffness that had plagued him over the past year, and he was contemplating another tour. Ali was good at hiding her feelings, but the subject of Joe's tour was clearly unwelcome, much as she rejoiced that he could sing again.

Maddie sang, "Have Yourself a Merry Little Christmas" and was surprised to see the women tear up, especially Carrie.

"I love *Meet Me in St. Louis*," Teresa exclaimed. "Judy Garland has nothing on you."

"Don't mind us," Carrie said. "We're old softies."

For the first time that evening, Maddie caught David watching her. He looked away before she could even begin to read his expression.

Joe brought out his guitar and sang "White Christmas," then accompanied David as he sang, "I'll Be Home for Christmas," the saddest rendition Maddie had ever heard. She wondered how many lonely Christmases he'd spent in Africa. Interesting that he felt comfortable conveying emotion in his singing voice. During their short acquaintance, she'd had precious few peeks behind the pleasant, guarded façade.

The wine continued to flow, but as Susan and May put the kitchen back in order and ran the dishwasher a second time, the guests began to disperse. Duncan and Laurie first, David next, then Teresa and Liam. Finally, only Ali, Joe, and Maddie remained. It being ten o'clock, Maddie wasn't sleepy, but she could see that Joe and Ali were exhausted.

"Do you mind if I stay in the rec room for a while?" Maddie asked. "I'll work a bit more on the puzzle."

"No problem," Joe said, helping Ali off the couch. "We're toast. Merry Christmas! See you in the morning."

"Uh, is there a plan?" Maddie asked.

"We agreed on no gifts," Ali said, "and the twins, who don't care about gifts yet—thank God—are not getting any either. That means Christmas morning will be an artery-clogging breakfast Liam has volunteered to cook as long as we don't care if it is offered at eight or eleven."

"We have several more puzzles to tackle," Joe said. "Some of us may make a pilgrimage to downtown or Fort Worden. Laziness is also encouraged."

She saw Joe pat Ali's bottom, and they disappeared down the hallway.

CHAPTER 11

---◆---

Maddie soon lost interest in the puzzle, an artist's rendering of Notre-Dame Cathedral. She'd never been to Paris or anywhere outside the United States. She thought of Teresa, who had circled the globe many times and now had a husband straight out of *Christmas in Connecticut*. Some girls had all the luck …. Although she'd drunk a fair amount of wine, Maddie was too wired to go to bed. She put on her parka, gloves, wool cap, and scarf and walked slowly up the hill. The night was still, with a nearly full moon, and the house glowed as if about to burst into flames. The storage shed, dense with red lights, didn't strike her as looking like a brothel, exactly. *Welcome to Hell*, more like it. She was surprised no one had extinguished them for the night.

She walked over to the bluff to gaze out at the ocean, but it was too dark to see anything except the lights of a passing barge. She hoped all the seamen on the barge were singing Christmas carols and partying, but for working people, Christmas Present wasn't quite as relentlessly jolly as what the ghost had shown to Scrooge. Although, to give him credit, the ghost had chosen the best examples of holiday spirit. The elation of the evening had subsided, but Maddie wasn't depressed, exactly. She was hardly the only single one. Carrie was alone, had been since her husband died. Why was that? She was still so beautiful and elegant. Maybe relationships were too messy for Carrie. She must have had a decent sex life with the O'Connell patriarch, who sounded like a life-of-the-party type. They'd had *five* children. At least Maddie wasn't truly alone, sitting in a dingy apartment somewhere, watching reruns or movies that made her long for what she couldn't have. She was surrounded by, if not loved ones, nice people. Tonight had left her feeling closer to everyone. Except David.

The prospect of her next gig cheered her. A new beginning, a new theater family—for two months, anyway. She'd stayed in touch with at least one person from almost every show she'd done. Generally, they just exchanged Christmas cards and made vague plans to see each other again. Every so often they'd end up in the same play or a show nearby, and then they could visit. Learning a new role was a wonderful escape from reality; each one offered transformation to an unexplored alternate self. She wasn't Maddie when she recited Puck's lines, she was Puck. Fortunately, a fun character. Playing the villain or simply an unlikeable character could be brutal. The rest of the cast might start treating you accordingly.

Ever since she'd arrived, she'd been silently reviewing her lines in her room, not wanting to disturb the household by reciting them out loud. If she'd bothered to explain, they might have given her a cabin. She'd get one after the Christmas visitors left—not soon enough. Rehearsals would begin the first week of January. Until then, Maddie could go outside to practice. Sort of like outdoor theater. She looked up at the treetops, spread her arms, and declaimed part of her final monologue as Puck:

> If we shadows have offended,
> Think but this, and all is mended:
> That you have but slumbered here
> While these visions did appear.

She heard a stirring in the bushes, presumably a deer. The dogs would reveal themselves. She was somewhat disoriented. You couldn't miss the electrified house, and that made her aware of how close she was to the cabins. Everyone must be asleep or attempting to sleep. With the full moon and the Christmas lights, Maddie could see well enough, but the path was dimmer here among the trees. She reluctantly decided now was not the time to rehearse and headed down the hill. Then she heard a branch crack. Recalling the family's stalker and paparazzi woes, she whirled around to confront whoever was there, lost her balance, and hid the ground with a thud.

"Shit!" she cried out, feeling a sharp sting in her hip.

David emerged from the trees, crouched down, and shined a flashlight on her. "Are you okay?"

She shielded her eyes. "You're blinding me. What are you doing here?"

"I could ask you the same."

"I was *trying* to rehearse," Maddie said, sounding grumpy. "I can't do it in the house or I'll disturb everyone. Sorry if I woke you." She rolled to her knees but found she couldn't rise to her feet. Groaning, she crumpled against the pain.

"What is it? You're injured …."

"It can't be too bad." The fact remained that she couldn't do more than kneel and was favoring one side.

"Where does it hurt?"

"My hip." Maddie turned it toward him, and he moved in closer.

"It's bleeding," he said. "Can you walk?"

It looked like he was about to pick her up, and as much as she might enjoy that, she thought it unwise.

"Lean against me," he offered. "Come to my cabin so I can take a look."

Not a good idea, she thought. Damn it, this was her favorite pair of jeans. The only ones that actually fit her bizarre body. If they were bloody, she wanted to wash them out immediately. And what if the wound was bad? It hurt like hell. If she didn't let David treat it, she'd have to rouse the household. He was already propelling her toward his cabin, his solid, warm body distracting her from the pain.

She'd been inside Laurie and Duncan's cabin. This one had the same layout and curtains, but the colors of the bedspread, towels, and runners gracing the furniture were more vibrant African prints, as if designed with David—and Sylvia—in mind. The walls were bright too, a warm orange.

"Ali decorated it just for you," she said as they entered the cabin.

"She's like that, isn't she? Joe's a lucky guy. Teresa thinks *she's* the decorator, but Ali creates websites. She has a nice visual sense."

"She can draw too. Wait till you see her sketches."

He looked surprised. "Truly, I hardly know her." He opened his doctor's bag. "Let's take a look." His voice was neutral, as if she were any ol' patient. "I'll have to remove your jeans. Is that okay with you?"

* * *

David wanted to bay at the moon. Could this situation—rife with temptation and reeking of forbidden fruit—have been avoided? He'd been getting a breath of fresh air when he heard Maddie's vibrant voice and heeded what might as well have been the call of the fairies. He should have run as if pursued by the hounds of hell. Now that she was injured—his fault—what choice did he have but to treat her wounds?

They had to be thinking the same thing, that Sylvia would arrive the day after Christmas, that Maddie could leave no trace in David's cabin. He brought the towels out of the bathroom and laid them on the bed. "These will be easier to clean. I'll have to use washcloths to cleanse the wound."

She turned her back to him and muttered, "Ow, ow, ow" as he helped her pull down her jeans.

For a moment he was paralyzed by the sight of her perfect ass in thong panties. She might as well be naked. *Jesus*. Maddie in a bathing suit had been devastating enough. David struggled to regain his equilibrium. *Just do your job*, he told himself. Thank God he was standing behind her so she couldn't see his face—or his hard-on. "It's just a wicked scrape," he said, choking a bit on the words. "It should heal quickly. It's not going to be easy to, uh, dress." He blotted at it with the warm, wet washcloth. "I think it's mostly stopped bleeding. If I bandage the deepest parts, that should be enough. He worked in silence, glad that she didn't feel compelled to fill it with nervous chatter. He needed to concentrate. After he finished dressing the wound, he closed his eyes and rested one hand on her hip. He felt the familiar heat suffuse the wound, which was far worse than he'd let on. Maddie didn't move or speak. She had to be freaked out. Hands didn't just heat up like electric coils. Normal hands, anyway. *Stop there*, he told himself. *That's enough. She's already going to be suspicious.*

"Uh, Maddie?" Her eyes flew open and he saw the desire there along with a huge question mark. "Do you want to try to put your jeans back on?"

She held them up to reveal a tear at the site of the wound. "Oh … phooey. It's my favorite pair."

"I don't think they're ruined," David said. "It's a clean rip. I can mend them for you. But first, I'll have to rinse them out. Here." He passed her one of the towels. "Wrap that around your waist." He went into the bathroom— glad for a moment to compose himself—and scrubbed the blood from her jeans, drying them with the blow dryer hanging from a hook on the wall. Back at her side, he reached into his bag and found some thread. Sitting on the bed, he expertly threaded a needle.

"Is that for suturing?" Maddie asked.

He laughed. "Nope. I keep regular thread in there as well. You should see what I can do with a sewing machine. It's amazing the skills you acquire when you're far from civilization." When he was done, he showed her his handywork. "Not bad, huh?"

She stood before him, arms at her sides, close enough to touch. She could have easily stepped out of reach. The towel tucked at her waist was too small to cover much of her shapely thighs.

She examined the mended spot up close. "That's amazing. Your work is so neat, it's almost like a decorative seam."

When she moved to step into the jeans, David reached out to stop her. He was sitting forward on the bed. She started at the contact, and he realized his hand was clamped around her arm like a steel trap. Ashamed of his brute strength, he released her and nodded at the clock on the wall. "It's eleven. Did anyone see you go out?"

"Just Susan and May Allen. They were cleaning up in the kitchen."

"They won't say anything," he mumbled, as if speaking to himself. Then they locked eyes. "If you go now, we can recount this funny story and it will still be the truth."

"Or ...?"

Shit, was he possessed by demons? Possibly. Maybe she'd be the voice of reason and turn him down.

"Or, you can stay for a few hours," he went on, calmly, reasonably, watching her face for clues. Was she shocked? Tempted? He thought so. He could feel it in the way her body vibrated. "And when you tell the story, you won't have to tell the *whole* story."

She gulped. Was she feeling trapped? Lord, he didn't want that.

Oh shit. She was going to agree.

"Um, what about Sylvia?" She hadn't said no.

With horror, he saw his own hand reaching for her breast as if taking on a life of its own, then tremble as he took control and drew it away. "If you, uh, stay, no one will be the wiser. Sylvia and I .... We're not going to get married. I just didn't want Carrie to be weird about her sharing my cabin. Now I wish I'd insisted she sleep in one of the other guest rooms." *God*, he was a babbling idiot. "Only," he continued, "it'll be a full house, and Sylvia would be furious if I put her up in a hotel. There's some other, um, stuff that needs to be resolved between us, and I have to stay on her good side. It ... suits my purposes to call her my fiancée. I'm, uh, not looking for a relationship. For ... so many reasons. You aren't either, right?" He didn't wait for her to answer. "Your lifestyle is itinerant. As long as it's understood that I'm not interested in, uh, permanence." He was so distracted, he could hardly put a sentence together, but that didn't stop him from trying. Justifying himself. It was sickening. If it weren't his cabin, he'd leave. But it was, so she had to be the one to go, and by God he wasn't going to suggest it. His physical need for her had claimed his entire body. He'd never felt anything like it, not even with Sylvia, whose sexual power had walloped him hard when they first met. Meanwhile, Maddie just stared at him, open-mouthed, as if he were a snake and she, a mouse.

"I get it," she said. He heard the ice in her voice and flinched. She might as well have said, *You just want to fuck me and then pretend it never happened.*

* * *

Maddie wanted David too. Badly. She guessed that wasn't going to happen if she pointed out the obvious, that he respected her so little that all he'd consider was a one-night stand.

She breathed in his warm, masculine scent—with a hint of nautical aftershave as if he had just breezed in from a sea voyage—and felt her resistance dissolve. He looked like he wanted to devour her.

In a husky voice, David said, "Forgive me, Maddie. Right now I want you so badly, I can't think straight. If you know what's good for you, you'll go."

Neither of them moved. Their breathing was ragged. Oh, great, he was leaving the decision up to her. "But … we have to co-exist in this compound together for the next few m-months," she stammered.

"Even if you leave right now," he said, "the weirdness is inevitable. I can't take it back."

"What makes you think I'm so easily forgotten?" Maddie said in thready voice.

"I don't care. At this moment, I don't care. You're here, and I'm here, and …"

She gave the towel a tug and it fell to the floor.

His hands flew to clasp her waist, and he drew her toward him as if manipulating a doll—shades of Kilo. Crouching down, he kissed her breasts through her sweater. Then his lips caught hers in a light, teasing kiss. He pulled away, and his liquid green eyes glittered with satisfaction as he took her mouth again, harder, exploring with his tongue.

They fell onto the bed, and she surrendered to the large, capable hands that skimmed under her sweater, traveled to her waist, and finally cupped her breasts. As he heaved a shuddering sigh, those long fingers began to move again, lightly scoring her nipples and the curve of her breasts with his nails, massaging and circling as if memorizing their contours. He rolled her onto her back, and she felt him press his palm against her sex. He was a fantastic kisser, knowing the exact right amount of pressure to make her respond with equal enthusiasm.

Again, he pulled away, eliciting a soft moan of protest. Had he come to his senses? God, she hoped not. She was boneless, a puddle of raging need. But no, he was undressing, urgently, even popping a button on his shirt. He pulled off his T-shirt, revealing a gleaming, muscled chest—did he shave it?—then stood and pulled down his jeans. He was getting off on her watching him strip from her helpless position on the bed—naked, robbed of will. When he was naked, too, she gasped. My God, he was huge. She gulped, and he chuckled, guessing her thoughts.

"I'll take it slow," he whispered, on top of her again. "Are you on birth control?"

"Yes," she whispered. "An IUD."

He unwrapped a condom. Had to be extra-large. "Put it on for me?"

She fumbled with the condom, first licking him and taking a part of him in her mouth. He took the condom and put it on himself.

His fingers teased her sex again, bringing her almost to the brink, watching her the entire time so he knew when to stop. He didn't want her to come yet. Then, finally, he was at her entrance, moving a millimeter at a time, gradually filling her completely. She was so ready for him that he had no difficulty.

"Give me a moment," he whispered. And stopped. Something was wrong. "Don't move," he groaned when she wriggled against him, and then he couldn't help himself. With a louder groan, he fell against her.

An owl hooted outside in the stillness. David took off the condom and lay beside her on his back, his eyes closed. She wondered what he was thinking. He hadn't let her come, and now he was finished. Rather disappointing. Was he filled with regret? Was she? At least she'd confirmed that he wasn't the all-time greatest. Kilo was arguably more skilled, but Kilo wasn't the one she wanted. There, she'd admitted it.

She decided to reassemble the scattered shards of her dignity. After she found her panties and bra, she turned to him, surprised to see that his features had twisted into a rictus of pain. His entire body seemed racked with it. What was happening? "What's wrong?" she whispered in horror.

He was breathing hard. "I'll be okay. It's a … migraine." Unable to explain further, he held the sides of his head and moaned.

She panicked. "Should I get someone? Call 911?"

"No," he managed to say. "It will pass."

"Is there a pill I can get you?"

"No. You should go." Between long breaths, he said, "Promise … I'll be … okay."

"Are you having a seizure?" If so, he might swallow his tongue.

"No," he said harshly. "Go."

She dressed quickly, then went to the bathroom and found a washcloth, which she saturated with cold water and wrung out. She laid it on his brow and covered him with a blanket. Should she stay? She was torn. *He* was the doctor. If he were in real danger, wouldn't he admit it? He obviously didn't want her to witness his ordeal. She had no experience with migraines. They didn't kill you, did they? If she left, he'd probably go to sleep, and the headache would subside. "Are you sure I can't get you anything? Ibuprofen?"

"No," he said through gritted teeth, pressing the washcloth to his forehead.

She wanted to stay, to help him feel better. But really, hadn't they been saved by the bell? If she left now, she could tell herself he was a substandard lover. She was alarmed by his health issues. What if he had a brain tumor? What about her career? He wasn't her problem. He had disrespected her.

You owe him nothing.

Grabbing her parka, gloves, hat, and scarf, she shut the door behind her.

CHAPTER 12

——•——

"Wʜᴀᴛ ᴛɪᴍᴇ ɪs ɪᴛ?" Tᴇʀᴇsᴀ whispered to Liam, realizing that he was awake too. "I hear someone outside."

He listened. "Huh. The dogs would alert us to any real threat. It's probably just someone who can't sleep. I hope they have a flashlight. As you well know, with all the roots and rocks, it's easy to trip and fall when you're not on the path."

"Hah," she said. "I haven't injured myself in a long time."

He planted a light kiss on her lips. "You wouldn't have fallen if that photographer hadn't shown up."

"I was such a wreck for a while there. My hair, my cheek …."

"I'm a sucker for a good fixer upper." His fingers roamed lightly over her breasts and down her flat stomach. "Just checking to make sure everything's in order. Ah, there it is."

She laughed, and they didn't speak for a while as she rolled on top and took control. Not that he put up much resistance.

"Merry Christmas," she whispered. "Oops. I opened your package early. But I can see it's the gift that keeps on giving."

"You're the saucy little package," he whispered back.

"I'm glad no one can hear us," she said, taking him in her hand and receiving a gratifying response. "That's enough corny puns for one day."

"I'm just getting started." He trailed kisses downward, starting at her navel.

"Liam! We're going to be exhausted tomorrow, I mean, later today. You're cooking breakfast, remember?"

He looked up. "I told them sometime between eight and eleven."

"They assumed you were joking. We can't keep everyone waiting just because we can't keep our hands off each other."

In a muffled voice, he said, "I'm not using my hands."

Despite their early morning exertions, Teresa was awake by six thirty. Liam slept soundly. In sleep, he looked so boyishly beautiful …. She traced the subtle shrapnel scars on the side of his face, knowing they were deeper beneath his thick hair, wounds severe enough at the time of impact to make the doctors wonder if he'd ever wake. They were also more pronounced along the side of his body from armpit to hip, but none of them seemed to bother him. He claimed not to remember the explosion or even the morning before it happened. Then he'd lain for weeks in an induced coma, recovering from a brain injury. He had been so lucky not to lose any of his faculties.

Liam opened one eye. "You're spying on me. Go back to sleep, or I'm going to have to ravish you again."

"I wish," she said, "but we are going to be responsible adults and make breakfast. Besides, I'm hungry." He threw off the covers and stretched, largely for her benefit. "Very nice," she said, patting his erection. "Tell him to come back later."

His sigh was comically inflated. "You win, or rather, you lose." He wandered to the bathroom, scratching his firm backside, and she heard the shower running. She dressed quickly in her jeans, sweater, and boots so he wouldn't make another assault on her willpower when he emerged, freshly showered.

Maddie joined Liam and Teresa in the kitchen at eight, and Teresa made her a double latte before she could ask. Maddie was pale and wan, as if she'd slept badly. Was she losing sleep over the upcoming show?

Teresa handed her the mug. "Merry Christmas."

"Oh, thanks!" It might have been a lifeline.

"Was that you I heard outside around midnight?" Teresa said without thinking. At Maddie's guilty flush, she wished she'd kept her mouth shut.

"We thought we heard someone communing with the night spirits," Liam joked, still unaware that they'd stumbled into quicksand.

"I, uh, couldn't sleep and was practicing my lines. I didn't realize anyone could hear me."

"Don't worry," Teresa jumped in, to give her an out, although she was curious as hell. "Liam and I are light sleepers, and we heard rustling, that's all. Did you have a flashlight with you?"

Maddie shook her head as if admitting to something far worse. "No, no flashlight."

Liam reached into a drawer for a small flashlight, switching it on and off. "This is more powerful than it looks. Keep it handy for the next time you feel the urge to wander the grounds at midnight."

"Okay, thanks." Leaving her coffee, Maddie took the flashlight back to her room.

While she was gone, Teresa said in a low voice, "What was she really doing up there ... visiting David?"

"You think so?" Liam's eyes were wide as he brushed oil on the waffle iron. "That's interesting."

Maddie came back in.

"Bacon and sausage are warming in the oven," Teresa said. "Liam is making quiche. In the meantime, you might want to see what Santa brought you."

Maddie perked up. "What? I thought we said no gifts."

"*We* said no gifts. That doesn't include your mom. On the hill, in back of Duncan and Laurie's cabin."

Rather than jumping up to claim her present, Maddie stood at the window and scoured the area for activity. Finally she said, "I'll be right back."

After she was gone, Liam said, "Wouldn't Duncan want to show her? It's from him and Laurie."

"He mentioned it to me last night," Teresa said. "Said he hoped she'd find it by accident."

Liam gave her an affectionate nudge. "I don't think you pointing it out to her counts."

Snatching a piece of bacon from the plate in the oven, Teresa said, "She needed a distraction."

* * *

Maddie kept one eye on David's cabin as she trudged up the hill. No signs of life. In the cold light of day, regret weighed heavily on her. What had possessed them? The more she thought about it, the more his words and actions pissed her off. He saw her as just some wild girl he could fuck while waiting for his fiancée. He had spelled out the rules in advance. In acting class, you were taught to react to insults in the moment, not to let them fester. Women, especially waspy ones, did that—let insults roll over them to avoid a scene. But she'd wanted him as badly as he had wanted her. Really, she knew better than to believe that earth-shattering sex could convince a man to choose you over a rival, in this case the mysterious Sylvia. And then he'd been gripped by that horrible migraine. *Lord*, what if he was dead?

She rounded the corner and gasped at the sight of the white Vespa with a large red ribbon on the handlebars. It had been polished to look like new. She wouldn't be trapped here in the evenings anymore. She thought about Kilo's open invitation. Perhaps they could come to an understanding? *Kilo, we can only do this if you keep it light. I don't want some heavy affair.* God, that sounded like David. Some people showed you their warning labels upfront, and you ignored them at your peril. She couldn't fault David for making false promises. *As long as that's understood ....*

She was standing there, staring at the Vespa and lost in thought, when Duncan's voice snapped her out of it.

"I see you found your present," he called out. "Oh, sorry, didn't mean to startle you."

She ran over and gave him a huge hug. "I love it! Now I'll have my own transportation. Thank you *so* much!"

"It's from your ma, too." She wiped away a tear. "I hope those are tears of joy."

"Oh, they are," she lied. Or partially lied. She'd just had a vision of the weeks ahead, and it was *not* pretty.

It was the day after Christmas, late afternoon, and Maddie was riding the Vespa around the neighborhood. The cold cut through her several layers of clothing, and she welcomed the discomfort. She wished she could just keep riding all the way home to Seattle. Leave David and Sylvia far, far behind.

Christmas itself had been wonderful. David joined them at nine. Other than the hollows beneath his eyes, he looked well. After Liam's bountiful brunch, they'd convened in the game room, where a fire crackled in the fireplace. They'd started a new puzzle of Klimt's *Tree of Life* in a thousand pieces. When she needed a break, she played with the twins, who were in their playpen, gurgling happily to each other. May Allen and her sister Susan had the day off, so they all took turns—even David, a natural with babies. He would pick one up and coo at her, and she would reach for his short red beard, mesmerized. Maddie couldn't tell them apart. Caryn had a mole next to her ear, but you had to search for it.

The mood was convivial, and David made it a point to treat her as he always had—as he had since her fling with Kilo, anyway. Distant but friendly.

Maddie had been amazed when she took the bandages off her "wound" Christmas morning. She'd never had a good look at it, but it must have been way more superficial than she'd believed from the amount of pain and blood involved. No one healed this quickly.

David had told them nothing about Sylvia, at least not in her presence, so the woman was even more of a shock than Maddie had expected. She arrived after lunch the following day, along with Becca and Jean-Louis. Sylvia Conti was Italian, with a pronounced accent and an aristocratic air. Artfully arranged dark-brown curls fell past her shoulders, and she had bold features—tilted dark eyes, pronounced cheekbones, a long face, and smooth olive skin. The kind of dramatic makeup Maddie associated with black and white photo shoots. Arresting, more handsome than beautiful. She was taller than Maddie—most people were—but her chunky high heels made her even taller than Ali. Everything she wore, down to her watch and earrings, looked expensive. Her exaggerated curves reminded Maddie of Sophia Loren. Obviously David was into breasts. Sylvia made it a point to greet everyone individually and learn their names. When she got around to Maddie—dead last—she said, "Ah, Maddalena, is it? You are so ... cute, like a doll. What is that sweet little doll with big eyes?" She snapped her fingers. "A Kewpie doll! I hear you are an actress."

A Kewpie doll? How insulting was that? Maddie pictured the naked baby doll, with its blond topknot and googly eyes. Why had Sylvia singled out Maddie for belittlement? Well, *she* looked like a good-looking man in drag. *Easy, girl*, she told herself. *Don't stoop to her level.*

"It's Madeleine, but please, call me Maddie," she said, turning on the formal charm she used with unpleasant people in the acting business she couldn't afford to alienate.

"Maddie," Sylvia repeated. Maybe it was the woman's accent, but her tone implied that she thought it was a silly name.

Soon after Sylvia had arrived, she and David retired to the cabin and were still sequestered there when Maddie left the compound.

A half-hour into her ride, she was too chilled to continue. It was getting dark, and besides, the scenery on the paved main road was underwhelming. The deciduous trees were bare. Just the occasional lake or meadow and glimpse of the ocean.

After she parked the Vespa, Maddie saw David and Sylvia emerge from their cabin and ducked behind a tree. Sylvia, long hair pulled into a loose ponytail, had changed into a more casual outfit that still looked expensive—a black leather jacket, linen trousers, and knee-high boots with two-inch heels.

She took David's hand, not the other way around. Before coming down the hill herself, Maddie waited for them to shut the front door behind them.

The house smelled deliciously of turkey. Liam had put it in the oven early that morning, but now Jean-Louis had taken over, which meant they were in for a treat. Maddie steeled herself before going inside, accepting five minutes of doggy affection from Coogan and Harry and feeling the better for it.

This too will pass, she told herself.

CHAPTER 13

ALI HAD NEVER BEEN SO glad to see anyone as she had her best friend Becca and her teddy bear of a husband, Jean-Louis. Christmas had been fun … until the tension between Maddie and David seemed to escalate. Now there was another fly in the ointment, Sylvia. From the get-go, Ali could see she was trouble. One of those volatile, insecure yet arrogant, carefully put-together women who got what they wanted through sheer force of will. Rina Bakersfield, Joe's ex-girlfriend and a country music star in her own right, had been like that. Ali gnashed her teeth just thinking of Rina. If Joe gave in to Linc's pleas and agreed to an abbreviated tour, who would be his opening act? A man or another Rina, younger and more beautiful than the original? Who would have thought that Joe's getting his voice back would impact their lives negatively? They'd been happier as a couple after he'd given up performing and resigned himself to composing songs for others. Ali was ashamed of such selfish thoughts. Joe's voice meant everything to him.

Laurie and Carrie had driven to Fort Warden for a stroll and Maddie had taken off on her Vespa. Jean-Louis was whistling while he prepared dinner in the kitchen, Sylvia and David were sequestered in his cabin, and Joe, Liam, and Duncan were completing the area around the new hot tub—building a privacy fence, putting in a brick patio. For them, the work was fun. This was how men bonded, not over intimate conversation. Becca, Teresa, and Ali had, blessedly, been left to themselves. After working out together in the separate gym and showering, they retreated to the rec room. The dogs, who'd been sleeping in their beds in the corner, lifted their heads and wagged their tails.

Ali went over to greet them. "It's okay, boys. You stay where you are." To Becca and Teresa, she said, "Be right back."

Having checked on the napping twins and reassuring herself that the baby monitor was working, Ali returned with a bowl of popcorn and a pot of tea and shut the door. Teresa was sitting on the floor between the dogs so she could pet them both.

"Since when do the dogs get to come inside?" Becca asked from the couch. "I thought Liam was dead set against it."

"I'm not sure you noticed, but Ali had a doggy door installed," Teresa said. "Liam trained them so well that they know this is the one room they can enter. We wore him down, didn't we?" she said to Coogan, who responded with a little whine.

Ali remained by the door, her hand on the deadbolt. "I'm tempted to lock it," she confessed.

"Ooh, a secret meeting of the nasty girls' club," Becca said. "Where's Maddie?"

"Riding her Christmas present," Ali said, reluctantly leaving the door unlocked. "Laurie and Duncan bought her a used Vespa."

Becca kicked off her boots and propped her feet up on an ottoman. "Cool. I'm glad she won't be taking out Liam's Harley anymore."

"I think she wanted to escape Sylvia," Ali said.

Becca blew out a raspberry. "Who wouldn't? She was pouring on the charm with Jean-Louis and me in the car, but we weren't fooled. She is one stuck-up broad. Plus, she directed almost everything she said to Jean-Louis. Safe bet she doesn't have a lot of girlfriends. She can go plant her flag somewhere else. I do *not* see her with David. Way too pushy."

"Maybe she was trying too hard with you," Teresa said. "She seems okay to me. A little overbearing, maybe, but she's a strong woman who clawed her way to the top of a man's profession—a surgeon, like David. How *does* she manage, away from civilization? The nails, the hair … I don't see her roughing it."

"I can see her playing a doctor on *ER*," Ali said. "An evil one."

They all laughed, and Teresa tossed a kernel of popcorn at Ali. "You just want David to fall for Maddie."

Becca pedaled her stockinged feet in the air. "Tell me, tell me!"

Ali laid another log on the fire and poked around with the fire iron. "On Christmas Eve, Maddie went out at ten and came in at midnight. That means she was in someone's cabin, because it was too cold to be wandering out there for so long."

"She wasn't in ours," Teresa said, hugging her knees to her chest, "and Liam and I heard her too. Around midnight, a door shut and there were footsteps. It was a quiet night, almost no wind, and every sound echoed throughout the compound."

"She could have been visiting Laurie and Duncan, I suppose," Ali said, taking the easy chair next to the couch, where Teresa had moved to pour tea.

Becca tapped her chin. "Yeah … no. The weird part is, I don't see David and Maddie sneaking around like that for sex."

Teresa took a thoughtful sip of tea. "They are awkward as hell together, and it doesn't feel like an act. I can't imagine either coming on to the other, so if something happened, it must have started by accident. Maybe Maddie mistook his cabin for her parents', then they both decided to bury the, uh, hatchet."

They shared a hearty laugh over Teresa's theory, but no one could come up with anything more plausible.

Ali clapped her hands to her cheeks. "I wish Sylvia wasn't here."

Becca patted her on the knee. "Don't worry. David will take her sightseeing and out on the town. We won't have to put up with her … much."

Ali shook her head. "Just when Laurie was starting to calm down. She and Carrie have been getting on surprisingly well. Ever since they saw *The Man in the Iron Mask* together."

Becca's eyes widened. "Really? I can't picture that."

Teresa chuckled. "It was pretty amusing. They liked it, believe it or not. And they've been spending time together ever since. It makes our lives easier."

A knock on the door, and a voice they recognized as Joe's said, "Hey, in there! You all decent?" He opened the door. "Damn, thought I'd catch you in your underwear or something. Just kidding," he said to Teresa, who was giving him the hairy eyeball. "We're having cocktails upstairs, and I need you all to, uh, dilute the impact of Sylvia. She's in paroxysms of pleasure over the living room, and frankly, Teresa, you're the only one who can wax poetic on that subject."

Teresa groaned. "Where's Mom? She can play one-upmanship with the best of them. She even enjoys it."

"She and Laurie haven't returned yet. Maybe they stopped for tea and scones. Or a few belts at the bar. Who knows? I'm not looking a gift horse in the mouth. It's good to have Mom occupied." He tapped his foot. "So, you coming?"

Exchanging long-suffering looks, they trudged upward as if in the final stretch of the world's longest staircase that led to nothing good.

Becca made a face. "Huh. Does this mean we can't hang out in the rec room while Sylvia's here? Is she too classy for knotty pine?"

The dogs each barked once, knowing it was forbidden but absolutely needing to weigh in.

"Shh," Ali giggled, aiming her admonition at both the dogs and Becca. "She's gonna hear you."

Ali blessed her sister-in-law for being such a trouper. Teresa sat next to Sylvia and described, in depth, her "process" in designing the art deco living room—the places where she'd purchased the artwork and the furniture and the origin of the overall concept. The conversation turned to Paris and Michelin-starred restaurants. "How do you manage in Africa?" Teresa asked, all innocence. "You look like a city girl to me."

"I do all right," Sylvia said with an airy wave of her hand. "I do not dress like this."

"Sylvia would look chic in overalls," David joked.

"But I would never wear them," she said, as if the very idea were unthinkable. She sipped her wine. "Very nice," she said to Joe. "How did you stock your cellar?"

Joe played along, giving Sylvia the conversation she craved. Ali wondered if the other doctors Sylvia worked with enjoyed talk of art deco style, the great cities of Europe, and fine wine. Why had David fallen for her? She had to be great in bed. And yet, she could swear Sylvia embarrassed him, that he'd rather be anywhere but here. Was he trying to drum up the courage to break it off? Would he really marry the woman? At that precise moment, Maddie came in looking flushed and lovely from her ride, her curly blonde bob fetchingly tousled. The green of her hoodie matched her luminous eyes. With her naturally pink lips and long lashes, Maddie was gorgeous without makeup. The phrase "gilding the lily" came to mind. Sylvia appeared to be sizing her up, speculating what she was to David.

"Sorry to be late," Maddie said, taking in Sylvia's pencil skirt, lavender silk blouse—unbuttoned to show an impressive amount of cleavage—and Louboutin boots. She looked down at her own jeans and tennis shoes. It wasn't hard to read her mind. The rest of them had changed for dinner in Sylvia's honor after David warned them of his fiancée's expectations.

"Maddie, come with me," Ali said. "I want to show you something." Once they were out of earshot, she said, "Do you have anything dressy with you?"

"Uh, better jeans, boots, a cashmere sweater?"

"How about slacks or a skirt?"

Maddie shook her head, apologetic.

"I bet you'd fit Teresa's clothes. She's not that much taller than you. Wait here." Ali went back into the living room and returned with Teresa. "Do you have something Maddie can borrow? We're always so casual here. She wasn't prepared for a guest like Sylvia."

Teresa's smile was twisted. "None of us were. Come with me." Maddie noted the gleam of conspiracy in her eye.

"Do I dare come with you?" Ali said. "Joe's not going to be happy."

"We won't be gone long," Teresa insisted. "Come on. We'll be quick like bunnies."

They trotted up the hill toward the cabins, where Teresa selected one of her designer dresses for Maddie. "This one's too short for me, anyway, so it should work on you. Our coloring is similar."

Indeed, Ali reflected, Maddie looked amazing in that dress. It was a lacy leaf-green number with a sweetheart bodice that displayed just a hint of Maddie's creamy cleavage and flared out at the bottom in a sassy ruffle. Maddie was a few bra sizes larger than Teresa, which made the fit snug. Oh, this was gonna be fun ....

The only problem was the shoes. Maddie's feet were a size six, and Teresa's were seven and a half. "You wear the same shoe size as Mom," Teresa said. None of the cabins were locked, and they found a pair of cream-colored kitten heels in Carrie's cabin that worked with the cream details on the dress.

When they reentered the living room, Joe raised his eyebrows, letting her know he was on to her. But he looked amused. Meanwhile, Carrie and Laurie had joined the group. Carrie took one look at Maddie's feet and said, "Those shoes ..."

"... look amazing on Maddie, don't they? She says she's never worn them before."

Joe took Ali's arm. "Sweetie, why don't you help me select another bottle of wine?"

Like I'm so good at that, she thought, knowing he was going to give her a hard time. Once they were in the temperature-controlled wine cellar, Joe said, "What are you up to? Those are Carrie's shoes, and if I'm not mistaken, that's Teresa's dress. I know you're on Team Maddie, but turning Sylvia against us will only make David's life a misery."

"I know, but she's such a—"

"I don't like her either," Joe broke in. "Believe it or not, even Mom seems put off. Maybe it's because I'm famous, and Sylvia was nervous about making a good impression. I'm going to give her the benefit of the doubt. Now, instead of rubbing Maddie's charms in David's face, can you help me try to put Sylvia at ease, so we have a ghost of a chance of discovering what David sees in her?"

Ali felt like a teenager being chastised by her father. "I'm sorry, sweetie. I promise to behave."

He grabbed two bottles at random and they headed up the stairs. At her questioning look, he said, "It's all good, right? If Sylvia isn't impressed, she's not going to let on. I'd like to see her try it." He gave Ali's bottom a playful spank as they reached the landing, and she squealed.

Carrie was gamely name-dropping with Sylvia, mentioning "friends" they might have in common from the minor aristocracy of Europe, of which Sylvia was one. Since Sylvia made frequent visits to Rome, Carrie asked her what restaurants she'd enjoyed most and why. Jean-Louis jumped in with his own knowledge of Michelin Guide-sanctioned restaurants, making it a four-way conversation. Liam had escaped to the kitchen to deal with the gravy and mashed potatoes. Ali was suddenly panicked about serving such an ordinary meal. Until she reminded herself that she didn't care if Sylvia approved. David was wiping sweat from his brow as if he might be coming down with the flu. It was sixty-eight degrees in the house, and he wasn't overdressed, so it had to be flop sweat.

"Dinner is served," Liam announced with amusing grandeur, a cloth draped over his arm as if he were a headwaiter at Maxim's, and Ali directed them to their places at the dining room table.

Ali had taken care to seat Maddie and David at opposite ends of the table, but she saw the way his eyes kept returning to her, as if he couldn't believe the transformation. Ali couldn't quite, either. Maddie was almost as much of a chameleon as Liam. Here she was, chicly dressed but with no makeup, like a Jane Austen heroine who didn't even need to pinch her cheeks for color. She looked like a fairy creature. And then there was Sylvia, a painted lady, and not the butterfly kind.

The turkey was moist and done to perfection, and the oyster dressing delicious. Everyone—including Sylvia—praised Jean-Louis and Liam for their efforts. If Sylvia had been expecting something more *haute cuisine*, she didn't let on. The long table didn't lend itself to one common conversation, thank goodness, and Ali could leave Sylvia to Teresa and Carrie. The men discussed landscaping for the hot tub and what still needed to be done to assure privacy and keep out the deer. David, seated across from Sylvia and next to Duncan, was mostly quiet, but Ali saw his glances of longing at the other men, then the way his eyes strayed to Maddie, who was encouraging Jean-Louis and Becca to talk about their plans for the new restaurant. When Sylvia excused herself to go the "powder room," they heaved a collective sigh.

Carrie spoke in a low, urgent voice. "Really, David? No, no, no. I can see that she's smart and comes from a good, dare I say *aristocratic* family, but no."

"Mom," he whispered urgently, "she'll be back any minute. This is a conversation for later."

"Don't think we won't have it," Carrie said. "And soon. I know you have a child together. But there must be a way …. Wait …. You haven't told them?"

The words "have a child together" hung in the air, like smoke from a burning refuse pile.

As Ali struggled to recover, she noticed the others reeling too. Maddie's face was almost as green as her dress.

"All right, everyone, shake it off," Joe said. "Dinner is over, right?" He indicated the mostly empty plates. "Let's retire to the living room. I wish we could go outside. We could all use some fresh air." He looked at David. "As a matter of fact, that's an excellent idea. David and I will get some air. The rest of you, entertain Sylvia. And don't let on that you know anything."

The men grabbed their coats and gloves and went outside. Ali heard the dogs greet them with a single bark each and the four of them headed toward the hot tub area.

Sylvia took her time in the bathroom. When she returned, half of them were in the kitchen, helping Susan to put away leftovers and load the dishwasher, and the others were attending to coffee and dessert.

"Sylvia," Ali said brightly, "would you like coffee? Joe wanted to show David their progress with the hot tub."

"Do you have espresso?"

"Of course." It wasn't really an "of course" situation, but Joe had recently purchased a fancy new machine. If there was anything the former barista knew how to do well, it was make fancy coffee drinks. "Latte?"

"No." Sylvia made a face, as if Ali had asked if she wanted her coffee flavored with arsenic. Too late, Ali recalled that the Italians and the French only drank coffee with milk in the mornings. She couldn't cover her gaffe now.

"What are your plans for tomorrow?" she asked.

"David is taking me to lunch, then to Fort Worden," Sylvia said, as if dreading both prospects.

"When will you return to Africa?" Ali tried to make the question sound casual. She wanted to ask when she was going to leave *here*, though the real question was "how." Becca and Jean-Louis planned to stay till after New Year's, and Ali thought she might go ballistic on Sylvia if she had to tolerate her company that long.

"I will not return," Sylvia replied mysteriously.

The conversation hit a lull, and Becca came to the rescue. Sylvia was sipping her espresso, frowning, as if it didn't measure up. "What about a video?" Becca asked. "I see you have *Dances with Wolves*. I've always wanted to see that."

"Sure," Ali said. "Great idea. Sylvia, have you seen *Dances with Wolves*? I don't know how accurate it is, but it's an interesting story about the Wild West and fun for history buffs."

"And fans of Kevin Costner," Becca added.

"Kevin Costner makes me swoon," Jean-Louis said in a falsetto voice.

Becca giggled. "Just for that, I'm going to make you watch the whole movie. And if you fall asleep, I'll wake you up."

Comically dismayed, he slapped his face playfully. "*Ayoille!*"

As Becca started to drag him out of the kitchen, she said, "You coming?"

"Of course. Sylvia?"

"I will wait for David."

Of course you will, Ali thought.

CHAPTER 14

JOE JOINED THEM DOWNSTAIRS FIFTEEN minutes later. Ali paused the movie. "Where's David?"

"With Sylvia. I'll explain later."

"We're all friends here," Ali said.

Becca jumped up. "I'm going up to see if the coast is clear. If they've returned to the cabin, we can talk freely." She zipped up and down the stairs. "All clear."

"I'll start with the good news," Joe said. "She's leaving day after tomorrow."

Ali sighed with relief.

"Now the bad news. When he first arrived in Africa, David fell hard for Sylvia. She's a skilled surgeon, and believe it or not, she has a way with the locals. She speaks several languages and had picked up enough of the local dialects to communicate. In other words, she was in her element. I asked about the hair and makeup, and he said she can do without. She did take frequent trips to Rome to unwind."

"Where is the child?" Ali asked. "Boy or girl?"

"Boy. His name's Lorenzo. He's in Portland with her sister Chiara, who's married to a Nike executive. They live in a townhome in the Alphabet District and have no children of their own. Sylvia wants David to marry her so they can raise Lorenzo together."

Ali felt a headache coming on.

"Where?" Carrie said, looking a little green herself. "In Africa?"

"He's not returning to Africa," Joe said, "and he's not gonna marry her. Not that he's told her yet. He hasn't even met the child. And it's her way or the highway. She's been hired as an ER doctor by a large Catholic hospital in Chicago."

"Can he ask for a paternity test?" Carrie persisted.

"That's what I advised," Joe said. He stopped her with a raised palm. "Don't get your hopes up. David's seen pictures, and the boy looks an awful lot like him."

"How old is he?" Carrie said, calmer than Ali might have expected.

"Three and a half," Joe said.

"Could David get partial custody?" Ali asked. "If so, we could bring him here. The more the merrier."

"To be determined," Joe said wearily. "Anyway, I'm toast. Y'all gonna finish this movie? I've seen it."

"Me too," Becca said. "It was an excuse not to entertain Sylvia anymore. Although I do like the part where he dances with the wolves. Lordy, I hope that child takes after David."

* * *

Maddie, Teresa, and Liam walked up the hill so Maddie could return the dress and the shoes and retrieve her own clothes. "You rock that dress," Teresa told her. "As far as I'm concerned, it's yours." She looked down at her feet. "The shoes, however, need to go back to Mom, pronto. I'm already going to get chewed out."

"She was pretty fabulous," Liam said. "Caught on really fast. I'm impressed. I think she's finally adjusting to all the radical changes in her life."

"We just keep 'em coming, don't we?" Teresa said. "This new one is a doozy."

Maddie emerged from the cabin, flashlight in hand, having refused Liam's offer to escort her back. Halfway to the house, she heard voices. David and Sylvia, Sylvia bundled up in a fur coat, were standing outside their cabin, arguing in Italian. Maddie extinguished her flashlight, stepped off the lighted path, and froze, praying that the darkness would keep her concealed. She'd studied Italian her first year in college, back when she was flirting with the idea of singing opera, but her Italian wasn't up to Sylvia's rapid-fire delivery. David spoke slower, which meant she caught more of what he said.

From Sylvia, she caught *puttana*—whore—and the words for "borrowed dress." She was pretty sure the woman was talking about her, and the gist was, "They dressed up the whore in a borrowed dress to make me angry. Why would they do that? They hate me. Who is that woman to you?"

What really killed her was his answer. "She's nothing. She's sleeping with the local yoga instructor and God knows who else. She's just an actress. A minor one." David held Sylvia at arm's length and forced her to look at him. In English, he said, "Did you have to compare her to a Kewpie doll? Why insult her in front of the others like that?"

Sylvia batted his arms away and spat out, "You are the one for confusing messages. It is you who compared her to that doll when I first arrived. I didn't realize it was an insult. Until you described one, I didn't even know what a Kewpie doll looks like."

Maddie closed her eyes and felt the tears run down her cheeks. Until now, she hadn't understood the extent of David's disdain for her. None of the others judged her that way. They wanted David to like her. Although they'd never mentioned it, they seemed to know something had happened with Kilo and they didn't give a hoot. Why was David so judgmental?

Still arguing, David and Sylvia went back inside. *They deserve each other*, Maddie thought angrily.

When she came into the kitchen, Joe and Ali were sitting at the counter drinking tea. They looked up, faces filled with concern.

"Maddie, what's wrong?" Ali asked.

Should she say anything? No, she shouldn't, but everything was too raw, and they looked so … kind. "I overheard a conversation."

"Hmm," Joe mumbled. "Do you want to tell us?"

"Yes, I do." Maddie sat down at the counter. "I'm not sure I should."

Ali set a mug of tea in front of her. "It's chamomile. Please, you can trust us."

Maddie rubbed her temples. "Let me see …. Sylvia called me a whore, and David said I was nothing, just a minor actress who was sleeping with the entire male population of Port Townsend."

Ali laughed, then stopped herself. "Sorry. But that's funny. What did he say, exactly?"

"That I was sleeping with the yoga instructor and God knows who else."

"Ouch," Joe said. "How did he get to be such a prude?"

"They were speaking Italian," Maddie said, "so it's possible I missed some nuance."

Joe perked up, impressed. "You speak Italian?"

"I studied Italian my first year of college, enough to understand. I studied French, too, in high school. Italian is way easier."

"Let's say you did understand them correctly," Joe said, gesturing with his spoon. "David spoke in the heat of the moment. You can't take what you overhear at face value. He's obviously, uh, interested in you, but he's highly motivated to placate Sylvia. Until they come to an agreement about Lorenzo."

To Ali, Maddie said, "If you overheard something like that, could you get past it?"

Ali cleared her throat. "All I know is, David's a good guy who's been through some truly stressful stuff. And this business with Sylvia isn't helping."

Joe added, "We love you, Maddie. Even if you do decide to sleep with all of Port Townsend."

Ali gave him a playful smack.

"It might be a more difficult job than you bargained on," he joked. "Most of the male population would probably need Viagra. But seriously, I had my share of women when I was on the road. I know how it works. I'm the last person to pass judgment. Ali wishes she'd had a wild period."

Ali smacked him again, but he grabbed her hand and kissed her. "Oh, relax, darlin'."

Later that night, as Maddie tossed and turned, she resolved never to be alone with David again. Too bad they were about to become next-door neighbors.

* * *

Wide awake with worry, David lay next to a snoring Sylvia. He sat up in the darkness and opened the window a crack to better appreciate the storm—the howling of the wind and the crashing of the waves, the tang of salty sea air. Sylvia was so out of place here, like a cactus in the rain forest—a hearty plant in its own environment that wouldn't thrive in the cold and wet. She was prickly like a cactus too. In Africa, they'd traveled where they were needed, starting in Ethiopia, and she'd always been able to adapt. David wasn't used to seeing her so off balance and insecure as she'd been with his family, so flagrantly cruel as she'd been with Maddie. After all that needless drama, here she was, sound asleep, as if unleashing her inner storm on him had brought her the catharsis she needed.

His plan had been to make her realize she'd be better off without him and break it off herself. It had to be working. Why else would she pull out all the stops to alienate his family? In Africa, she'd been respected, liked even, though famous for her strong opinions and hot temper.

When they'd fallen into bed this evening, he'd felt the echoes of their old passion, turned off his brain, and given her what she wanted … sort of. Sex had been a difficult balancing act, as he tried to satisfy her physically without giving her the reassurance she craved, letting her know by his very aloofness that their intense bond, formed through mutual danger and commitment to a mission, was irretrievably broken.

This must be how an escort felt. He had provided raw sex and the illusion of couple status in exchange for … not money, but access to his son. He blamed himself for the way Sylvia had dumped on Maddie. If he'd managed to hide his hard-on for her, Sylvia wouldn't have used her for target practice. And now he'd have to grit his teeth and "escort" Sylvia to Portland, where he'd repeat the charade for her family, and where, if he were lucky, Sylvia's pride would force her to set him and their son free.

Lorenzo had been conceived during David's first month in Africa, thanks to a broken condom. A staunch Catholic, Sylvia wouldn't hear of an abortion. After her three-month commitment was up—that was all they asked of surgeons, who were expected to work grueling hours—she'd returned to the States, rejoining their group three months later. When David had quizzed her about the child, she'd said her sister Chiara had agreed to raise him, giving him no say in the matter. Then she told him he wasn't her only lover, that there were at least four other candidates for "sperm donor." He'd been vastly relieved to hear the child wasn't his. Theirs was a randy group. They'd continued their affair, only it was an open relationship.

Then came the car accident that changed everything. Sylvia started to hint that they might make a life together—the three of them—in the States. Right before they'd traveled home—she to Portland, he to Seattle—she'd shown him a photograph of long-limbed, redhaired Lorenzo. It might have been a photo of David as a baby. None of the male nurses and doctors Sylvia had hooked up with was tall and auburn-haired.

David hadn't meant to insult Maddie. He'd needed to defuse Sylvia's jealousy quickly. Unlike Sylvia, he didn't look down his nose at the acting profession, and he didn't think of Maddie as a whore, a slut, or even a good-time girl. He was the last person to make such judgments, considering the revolving door of hookups in his otherwise dedicated group of medical professionals. He winced as he recalled the whispers about his "magic" cock that all the women and some of the men wanted to experience, overshadowing, fortunately, the rumors of his "magic" hands. Those rumors were much more dangerous because they might have made him the target of kidnapping—already a risk for any doctor or nurse in their position. Remembering those wild days when it seemed that life was going to be too brutish and short to worry about the wisdom of gathering ye rosebuds while ye may, David hoped he wouldn't be confronted with more illegitimate children in the future.

As for Maddie, he hoped to hit the reset button when she returned to Port Townsend to do the play. If he hadn't already blown his chance with that fiasco in his cabin …. He should have known the migraine was coming. Healing always came at a cost, and weirdly, the more minor the healing, the worse the headache. No pain killers touched the feeling that his brains were slamming against his skull as if determined to escape, so he didn't bother. Maddie probably thought he had a serious health condition or a secret brain tumor. Maybe he did. Pain like that might inflict lasting damage. He knew better than to use his gift so carelessly. God, the things he'd said …. Why? Was he afraid of letting her get too close, afraid of being hurt himself, afraid she might see him too clearly? Really, he should leave her alone. He was too screwed up.

Sylvia rolled over in her sleep, her arm curling around his chest. She didn't wake when he removed the possessive arm.

He still believed that the wild beauty of the Olympic Peninsula might bring him clarity, given time. Enough clarity that he might allow himself to be a decent father to Lorenzo, fall for someone kind. Maybe that person could be Maddie.

But first, he had to extricate Sylvia from his life without leaving her hellbent on revenge.

PART II

CHAPTER 15

———◆———

MADDIE SAT BY HERSELF IN the audience of the Theatre by the Marina, located a few blocks from the Point Hudson Marina on Washington Street. Another plain but homey colonial-style building, a red Saltbox playhouse—as the name implied, a large square-shaped building, with rows of uniformly sized windows and a seating capacity of about three hundred.

It was seven o'clock. Tonight wasn't a rehearsal, just a meet-up. Because the non-Equity cast members would be minimally paid—if at all, no one had told her the arrangement—most of them had day jobs. Rehearsals were scheduled for evenings and weekends. A theater of this size was allowed to hire a maximum of three Equity performers. For all she knew, she and Jeremy were the only ones. Which would be weird for the others. Although Puck was a major part, it was, arguably, not the lead. One of the deciding factors might have been her singing voice. The fairies were dancers, not singers, and when they "sang" for Titania, it would really be a solo for Maddie, double cast as a fairy when singing was required. During Titania and Oberon's dance at the end, she would act as one of the instruments, singing long syllabic phrases on "ah." She assumed Jeremy would be Oberon.

"Well, butter my biscuits and call me baked!"

Maddie was almost catapulted out of her seat. "My God, way to give a girl a heart attack."

"Madeleine Leftwood, as I live and breathe."

"Jeremy Fairewell, you are a sight for sore eyes." She gave the human Adonis a warm hug. He was blond, blue-eyed, six feet one, classic-featured, smooth-skinned, and slender as an adolescent. Too beautiful to be straight.

He plopped down beside her. "Frank told me you were Puck." Frank was the director. Maddie looked around the group, which had assembled while she was woolgathering.

"He's not here yet," Jeremy confirmed. "I am just thrilled to see a friendly face. I figured on being bored to tears in this tiny town."

She was glad to see him too. Jeremy worked hard to amuse, and his efforts had been much appreciated during a production of *The Threepenny Opera* so tedious the cast dubbed it *The Trepanning Opera*: the director's dark concept made watching it on a par with having a hole drilled in your head. As Mack the Knife, Jeremy had been totally convincing as the epitome of manly womanizer. Maddie been Polly Peachum, one of the three main women competing for Mack's affection. The other casting choices had been less felicitous.

"You're … what … Oberon?" Maddie asked.

"Titania." Grinning, he waited for her reaction.

"No, *really*?" In Shakespeare's time, all the roles—male and female— had been played by men because the Puritans had banned women from the stage, so it wasn't surprising that directors liked to play with gender ambiguity. Frank was notorious for his odd casting choices.

"Once makeup gets done with me, you won't even know I'm a man," he said in a convincing falsetto.

Maddie looked around, wondering who had been cast as Oberon. If there was a third union actor, that would be the one. Small theaters looked to cast their leading roles with actors whose creds could be touted in press releases that would swell audiences. That included Jeremy, who'd spent a few years on a soap until his character was killed off, despite being a fan favorite. Jeremy confessed to having slept with the wrong person. He'd never said who that person was—someone with major clout, clearly. Since the soap, he'd had small but memorable parts in several big studio movies without ever managing to snag a breakout role.

"What made you decide to do this show?" she asked. "It's awfully small-time for you."

"Like you, I count Frank as one of my most reliable old friends, and I have relatives in the area." He grimaced. "My sister and I are close, and she has a new baby. It was an opportunity to help out and get a break from the rat race."

"Are you a New Yorker now?"

"Nope, I'm an Angeleno."

She nodded. "Makes sense. I guess you *have* to be in L.A. All those roles in movies and TV shows."

"All those *bit parts*, you mean." He pointed. "Hey, there's Oberon. He's a local celeb. Used to dance with the Groban Phillips Company. What a dish. Straight, though, more's the pity."

No, it couldn't be. It was. "Good God," Maddie groaned. *Talk about your worst nightmare,* she thought. Puck and Oberon had multiple scenes together. "I know him," she blurted out in a horrified whisper. "He's a dancer, not a Shakespearean actor."

Jeremy's eyes widened. "He's been in lots of Shakespeare. He attended a prestigious training program in London. They cast him here all the time because he fills the seats. The other Equity actor. I hear he's good. Some history there, I gather."

"Uh, yeah," she said. "He used to, uh, date someone I know."

Jeremy let loose a rich, stagy laugh. "From what I hear, he doesn't really 'date.' Your *friend* is just one in a long line of lucky women."

No fool Jeremy. How dare Kilo do this to her? He'd never so much as hinted at being cast in the same play. Not that they'd done much *talking*, except on their one getting-to-know-you dinner date. Had he been a last-minute replacement? Not likely, in that he had one of the three coveted Equity salaries.

Frank arrived, a short, burly, middle-aged gay man with a full head of hair. He and the producer/composer, Will—tall, gangling, and bald—were a longtime couple who reminded her a bit of Laurel and Hardy.

Kilo gave her an airy wave and a grin as if nothing were more normal than their current situation. She followed suit. *Two can play at this game.*

Frank hugged several of the actors, including her, as he made his way down the aisle toward the stage. It was a fairly large cast: eight leads, two supporting players, eleven featured parts, plus several extras, including additional fairies. She scanned the faces of her fellow actors, knowing how much the ensemble members appreciated it when you called them by name. She was terrible with names.

She tried to take notes as everyone introduced themselves, but she knew she'd have limited success making sense of it all later.

Frank started talking about the production. "As you know, we'll rehearse any scene involving featured players and ensemble on evenings and weekends. I've given you a form to write down your availability. I'd prefer to rehearse leads during the day when possible."

Maddie checked the box for "All of the above."

Frank continued, "About the concept. Given our budget and costume resources, we are going with Deep South in 1915, maybe Alabama." Seeing the puzzled faces, he said, "Don't ask. As you know, like every other director, I like to spice up Shakespeare when the opportunity arises, which is why Jeremy is playing Titania. I want the fairies to be as oddball as possible. You will all have Southern accents. There is a dialect coach for those who can't pick up the accent easily and"—he held up a cassette—"I've made copies of a dialect tape. Puck is being played by a woman, Madeleine Leftwood. Puck is traditionally a non-singing role, but Maddie, who has an amazing set of pipes, will be doubling as a fairy to sing the lullaby and accompany Oberon and Titania's dance at the end. Puck is often played as a mischievous gnome, but I thought it would be more fun to make him a cute boy who Oberon has a thing for." He raised mischievous eyebrows at Maddie, who bared her teeth in a semblance of a smile.

As if the situation weren't bad enough already.

"You'll want to be subtle, guys." He winked at both Maddie and Kilo, as if these two crazy kids might just go gaga with lust if left to their own devices.

Did he know about her and Kilo? Surely not. He was just being funny. *Ha, ha.* Kilo appeared to enjoy the joke, goddamn him.

"The Southern accent is said to be closer to a British accent than any other American dialect," Frank went on. "It's quite contagious. I think you'll enjoy it. In a nutshell, you change diphthongs into single vowels and single vowels into diphthongs. What most of us think of as a 'Southern accent' has a lot of variations. I don't care if you all sound as if you come from the same region, or even if you sound particularly authentic. Have fun with it."

In the readthrough that followed, they all attempted Southern accents, most with some degree of success. Maddie had no trouble, having played Maggie in *Cat on a Hot Tin Roof* when she was in college. She thought it was kind of fun. Frank put her next to Kilo, who enjoyed the whole sexual innuendo aspect of their relationship way too much. Frank had to tell him to tone it down. In response to her glare, Kilo waggled a finger at her as if she were only feigning outrage. Her wish that he'd turn out to be a terrible actor was not granted.

They wrapped it up at ten thirty, and Kilo followed her out to her Vespa.

"No more motorcycle," he commented. "Did you wreck Liam's?"

"Ha, ha," she said as she put on her helmet. "Christmas present from Duncan and Mom."

She wasted no time climbing on.

"I guess a nightcap is out?" Kilo said with a touch of snark. "Since we have to work together, I hope you're going to drop the attitude."

She gave him a long look. "Yeah, about that. How did you fail to mention you would be in the cast?"

"If you'd checked out the website, you would have known. You'd also have seen that I've been in several of their productions."

"You might have mentioned it."

"Oh yeah. Well, sorry. Sin of omission. See you at rehearsal." He blew her a kiss and strode off.

Maddie rubbed her clenched jaw.

Back at the compound, she almost regretted having her own cabin. She really wanted to talk to Ali or Teresa. At almost eleven, everyone would be in bed. She'd have to catch them at breakfast. Her first rehearsal with Kilo was tomorrow at three—to accommodate his yoga studio schedule. At least she'd be home in time for dinner.

CHAPTER 16

———•———

"I WISH YOU'D LET *ME* pay occasionally," Liam grumbled. He was driving Teresa home from Port Angeles in the new truck Teresa had bought him for Christmas, a red Ford pickup he'd been coveting. "Why are you so rich, anyway? I realize the family business is successful—I love Big Paul's stuff as much as anyone in the Pacific Northwest—but why would a percentage come to you instead of back into the business?"

Liam was in a grumpy mood. He'd been grumpy a lot lately. It wasn't just the fact that Teresa had passed her credit card to the waitress while he was in the bathroom at lunch. They hadn't ever discussed her finances, only his. His Israeli "mother" had left him over two million dollars when she died—partly out of affection and partly as payment for rescuing her daughter from kidnappers. Teresa's net worth was easily four times that. Seeing that Liam expected an answer, she said, "It's not from the family business. My grandmother—Da's mom—invested well."

"I'm listening."

"She divided her wealth between us when she died, nine years ago, a few years after my father passed. The family was already prosperous by then, thanks to Big Paul's and Da's patents, but her fortune dwarfed that. We weren't expecting it. No one realized how rich she was. She was an early investor in tech stocks." Liam was drilling her with his scary blue gaze. "Please keep your eyes on the road."

"Why didn't you make me sign a prenup? *Someone* should have. Joe, for instance."

"See? We were totally right to trust you."

Liam blew out a harsh breath. "In some ways, you hardly know me."

"Liam, I hardly knew ye," she sang in a thin little voice, knowing her sarcastic reference to the song "Johnny I hardly knew ye" wouldn't go down well.

They drove in silence for a time. Liam seemed to be digesting her news, and it wasn't sitting well. All her brothers and her mother had urged her to make him sign a prenup, especially Jake. One of the reasons Jake wasn't talking to her now. It didn't take much to alienate Jake, apparently. That man had serious anger issues, all bottled up inside. He hadn't spoken to Joe in ages. Some weird one-sided rivalry Jake just couldn't get past. Joe had confessed to wronging Jake in college—something about a woman. She wondered if David were in contact with Jake.

Post-Africa David was this giant enigma. Teresa couldn't stand that Maddie seemed to have become a long, sharp thorn in his side. When she wasn't present, David relaxed and acted almost like his old self. Funny, effortlessly charming, joking around with his twin brother and new brother-in-law. After Sylvia's mercifully short visit, David had driven her all the way to Portland to spend time with her family and meet his son. During his absence, they'd all worried. He'd assured them that Sylvia behaved much better when they were alone together, that she was just too Italian and aristocratic to adjust to the laidback atmosphere of the Pacific Northwest. He'd returned to Port Townsend a day after New Year's, and although he'd debriefed Joe, Teresa had only the barest of details. The engagement was off, and David would stay in Port Townsend for now. He was "requesting" shared custody of Lorenzo. How would that work if Sylvia took her son to Chicago? David seemed to have no backbone when it came to Sylvia.

"Are you going to buy the school?" Liam said, interrupting her thoughts.

Another touchy subject. Why was he raring for a fight? The realtor's tour of the empty music school had been the main reason for their trip to Port Angeles. The place was shabby and neglected. Major renovations would be required just to bring it up to code. The building's poor condition was only one reason Liam opposed buying the school. Before they were married, he'd encouraged all her hopes and dreams. Now he was a pragmatist, telling her he had enough on his plate and didn't need to oversee a fixer-upper in a town over an hour's commute away.

Liam was still helping Peter at Fort Worden and lately had been overseeing the renovation of Joe and Ali's temporary residences for former foster children. Most had aged out of the system, but some were teenage runaways. Ali and Liam also offered informal counseling for the residents, lending a sympathetic ear and helping them figure out what came next. They'd try to smooth the way by directing them toward internships or scholarships. Sometimes they gave them money. Joe cautioned his family against getting too involved emotionally because some people were too damaged and just couldn't be saved. Liam didn't discuss individual cases with Teresa, but she noticed when a particular meeting weighed him down. She missed the playful Liam of their honeymoon.

"You've never taught piano before," he argued. "How do you know you're going to like it or even be good at it? Playing the piano beautifully is one thing, teaching another." He regarded her sullenly, as if unable to get over how dense she was. More and more these days, he made her feel like a spoiled child, ignorant of cold, hard reality. "You'll be dealing with children, most of them bratty and forced by their parents to study piano. They won't love it like you do. They won't practice. If you're lucky, you might have one good student who practices regularly and has real talent. Then again, you might end up with a bunch of students, kids and adults, who want to study piano only because they have a crush on you. What happens when you get tired of it? You can't just walk away."

He was relentless, repeating the same old arguments that made too much sense.

"You sound like Reynard," she said without thinking, raising the specter of the handsome and celebrated pianist and composer she had dated briefly before she and Liam had finally gotten together. A sore subject for Liam.

"Well, score one for Reynard," Liam muttered.

What was happening to them? They were caught in a vicious loop, always circling back to the same sticking points: the music school, her wealth, her admiration for creativity and education—qualities he was sure he didn't possess and she must wish for in a man. Liam was endlessly creative and as hungry for knowledge as anyone Teresa knew. No amount of reassurance could convince him of her high opinion.

"I know it's a major commitment, and I realize that getting other instructors won't be easy," she said, acknowledging the hard truths they'd all been giving her. "The music teachers at the community college have their hands full, after all."

"Yes, that's what we've been saying. Because it's true."

She sighed.

"I know this is a sensitive subject." His voice was calmer now. "If you don't mind, I'd like to make a suggestion."

She tried to wipe the pout off her face. Liam had a right to speak his mind. It's just that she'd spent all her life doing what other people wanted her to do, and now, apparently, she had to answer to her husband.

He glanced over at her. He could read her so well. "You don't need my permission, as you well know." She didn't reply, so he went on, "What if you bought a piano for the FOSSP residence in Port Townsend? You could build a studio in the backyard—there's lots of room." She couldn't help but roll her eyes. "What?"

The suggestion made sense but didn't appeal. The FOSSP kids were adults. Loving the art of the piano usually meant starting as a child, while your brain was still malleable. She shifted to a related subject. "Speaking of the FOSSP residence, I think they're building that new house on the estate for us. I can just imagine what it took to get the permits."

"No doubt the local government is grateful for all the philanthropic work they've been doing in the community."

"Teaching adults piano is way harder than teaching children," she said. "In fact, I'd venture to say it's too late. They'll never get beyond a certain level, and that's assuming they hang in there long enough to make any progress at all."

"There's a Boys and Girls Club in Sequim," he said. "Buy them a piano and teach there. Start with one or two students. You could even carpool with David once in a while." He paused. "That wouldn't work. You'd be stranded there all day."

Sick of the subject, she replied, "Actually, it's a good idea. Not the carpooling, although I'd like a chance to find out what makes David tick now. He's been so weird lately."

Liam snorted. "You might be weird too if you were dealing with so much change. A volatile ex-fiancée who's the mother of a son you just met for the first time, a career in limbo. We still don't know what made him hightail it home from Africa."

"I figured it was Sylvia."

"No, Sylvia had decided to move to Chicago before he threw in the towel. He says she was tired of roughing it, and I believe it."

They both laughed, helping to restore their rapport, which had been missing too often lately.

"What about Ali's drawings?" Liam asked. "Doesn't she still need someone to write the story?"

Teresa blinked. "To tell the truth, I'd forgotten about the drawings." She'd pored over the sketchbook of whimsical rain-forest creatures way back when she'd been angsting about Liam and needed something to take her mind off what she believed was an unrequited crush. Ali thought Teresa could pull the drawings together in a story. Her undergrad degree had been in Creative Writing, but she'd lost interest after writing the semi-autobiographical novel that was her final project. The highly romanticized version of her elopement with Kilo had ended with the lovers being killed in a car accident after being chased by her furious brother the priest. Accident or suicide? You decide. The memory was mortifying. Edward hadn't even been a priest back then. The manuscript had been pronounced "promising," but she'd never attempted to get it published, for obvious reasons.

"And ...." Liam was waiting to see what she thought of his new suggestion.

"Oh!" She snapped out of her reverie. "I'll take another look."

He wisely changed the subject. "How's Maddie doing? We haven't seen much of her since David returned."

"If I tell you, please don't pass it on to David. She swore Ali and me to secrecy."

He chuckled. "Like you could ever keep anything about that poor woman a secret." Liam's tone was teasing, indulgent.

"You're right, of course," she said with a frown. "Ali has her websites to work on, her drawings, and the twins, but I think she's getting cabin fever. And you and I don't know what we're going to do with our lives."

"You mean, should we stay on the compound," Liam said as they drove onto the property. "I like the new house, don't you?"

"Ali's decorating it," Teresa said.

"I have a theory about that." He shut off the engine. "They're building it for themselves."

"Huh?"

"They want us to live in the Sea Captain's House. You decorated it, after all. Now Joe's building *his* dream house."

Teresa felt her face flush. "Oh man, at the time she claimed not to care about the décor. I just forged ahead with my own taste, assuming it would work for everyone."

"If it helps, I like it well enough," Liam said. "The Sea Captain's house is too close to the bluff. They're worried about the twins' safety ... once they start walking. You may have noticed that the new house has an eight-foot-high fence."

Teresa smiled. "I thought that was about the deer." She paused. "Maybe we should offer to buy the Sea Captain's House from Joe? Because if we move, there's going to be a custody battle over the dogs."

They both laughed, a little uncomfortably.

She went on, "Joe will be on tour soon, and we can't leave Ali all alone here with just May Allen and the twins. She'll need our support as the inevitable rumors start flying. This tour is big news in the country music world, and a lot of that news is going to involve Joe and his rep as a chick magnet."

"That's over," Liam said. "He wouldn't dare."

"We know that, but does Ali believe it in a fundamental way? She could join him for part of the tour if she knows we're here to watch the twins."

A loud bark told them Harry was outside the door of the truck, and the giant dog was done waiting for them to come out. His bark was echoed by a single yip from Coogan.

"The natives are restless," Teresa said.

"I'm not letting you off the hook so easily," Liam said, preventing her from opening the door.

"Huh?"

"I'm talking about Maddie," he said. "How are rehearsals going?"

"Oh, okay. Except that Kilo is in the cast."

Anger flashed in Liam's dark blue eyes. "No. He would have told me."

"When was the last time you saw him?"

"Before Christmas, I guess." He blew out a sharp breath. "That snake! He must have known about this for months. He didn't so much as mention it in passing."

"Not to Maddie either," Teresa said. "And when Kilo and I were catching up before you and I got together, he omitted the part where he studied Shakespearean acting in London."

"*Catching up*," Liam repeated with a glower. "Did anything happen between you? Don't lie. That guy could charm the skin off a snake."

She *had* been about to lie, but Liam could read her too well. "Okay, we kissed some, and we went upstairs to his place." Seeing his stony expression, she rushed to add, "His receptionist was in his bed, waiting for him."

A short yelp of laughter. "What?"

"He'd asked her to feed his cat. She thought that was some kind of code. I got out of there as quickly as I could."

Liam continued to regard her with hooded eyes, understanding that if not for Kilo's uninvited guest, the outcome would have been very different.

"Can we change the subject? There was nothing going on between you and me then. Besides, you underestimate me. I was going to stop it. You're right about one thing though. Kilo's a charmer. Not as much as you. Like any man who's used to getting his way, he loves a challenge."

"The more Maddie resists, the more he's going to want her," Liam said grimly. "It's time Kilo and I had a little talk."

Teresa grabbed him by the arm. "Stay out of it. Maddie's a big girl. Whatever happens, she'll be fine. Kilo's not going to rape her, and she's not going to marry him. Those are the only two outcomes that could spell disaster. Everything else is just life."

CHAPTER 17

———◆———

THE HOT TUB LOOKED LARGE enough to accommodate a football team, but Ali kept thinking of some tough cowboy in a dime-store Western saying, "This town ain't big enough for the two of us."

The "two of us" being Maddie and David.

Then there was the bathing suit/no bathing suit debate. Joe argued that bathing suits retained soap residue from the washing machine, and that mucked up the water. Ali said she didn't feel comfortable being naked in front of anyone but him and the other women. So, they'd developed a silly system of bird feathers found on the property—one had belonged to a seagull, another to a crow, an owl, a hawk, some other seabird. Everyone had chosen a feather to represent them. First, of course, there had to be a spirited debate about which feather best suited whose personality. Liam chose the crow, Joe, the owl, and David, the hawk. That left Teresa and Maddie, less willing to assert themselves, as unidentified seabirds. Ali graciously let them saddle her with the seagull feather—everyone's least favorite bird. When using the hot tub, you stuck a feather in a board nailed on the entrance gate. Ali didn't want to contemplate what these silly feather assignments said about their family's power dynamic.

Ali, Teresa, and Maddie had first dibs in the tub after dinner. Afterward, they'd go in to watch a chick flick or hang out together while the men soaked. Ali supposed the novelty would wear off soon enough, and the need for the scheduling/feather system would subside. Or Maddie and David would give them all a break and surrender to whatever was roiling between them.

Once they were naked, Ali couldn't help but notice the faint redness on Maddie's side. "When did that happen?" she said, all concern.

"Christmas Eve," Maddie said nonchalantly. "Ah, this feels wonderful."

"Yes, it does," Teresa sighed, leaning against a jet. "And Ali, I know you're upset over the no-clothing rule, but it does give us a break from the men."

"I just think it's stupid," Ali said. "I don't want to see my brother or brother-in-law naked. Anyway, Maddie, you were about to tell us the story behind that scrape on your side. Are you sure it doesn't date back earlier? It's almost completely healed."

"I know. Weird, huh? It was nothing. I went outside to get some air and run a few lines, and I tripped."

"Then didn't come back in for two hours," Ali said. "Oops, did I say that out loud? I heard you go out and I heard you come back in. I was worried you'd fallen off the bluff."

"Liam and I heard you too," Teresa confessed.

Maddie had the panicked stillness of a trapped animal.

"It's none of our business. Although … if it's the reason you and David avoid each other …."

Maddie let out the breath she'd been holding. "It was so stupid. I was wide awake, and I wanted to try saying my lines out loud. I didn't realize I was so close to the cabins. David came out to investigate. He startled me, and I slipped and fell. Then, of course, he had to patch me up, as he would any wounded animal."

"Hmm, no bad blood there, I see," Teresa said.

An owl hooted overhead. The men had dismantled the Christmas lights, and the stars shone brightly. It was such a romantic setting. But Ali and Joe hadn't used it alone yet. "Uh, we can imagine the rest," she said, "unless we're imagining wrong."

"You're not," Maddie said, dejected. "I think we both believed it would clear the air."

Teresa rolled her eyes. "Like *that* works. 'The course of true love never did run smooth.' Isn't that line from your play? Someday Ali and I will tell you the stories of how we got together with Joe and Liam. Anything but smooth. Those men were determined to resist us every step of the way."

"True love?" Maddie wrinkled her nose. "I don't even like him."

"He's not very likable at the moment," Teresa admitted. "Though your attitude isn't helping. You treat him like some disagreeable relative you're forced to tolerate. You might be unhappy too if you had his problems. Not to mention that he isn't crazy about his job. He's a gifted surgeon, and he's stuck in the middle of nowhere treating broken bones and scrapes, prescribing antibiotics for infections and UTIs."

"He's great when you're not around," Ali told Maddie, "which just proves he's got it bad."

Maddie gave her head a brain-rattling shake. "The current situation is only going to make it worse. Kilo is in my face at every single rehearsal. The physical chemistry between us is echoed by our characters. Puck wants to hang out with Oberon; he adores him. At least in our version. And Oberon has the hots for Puck. That is terribly confusing. I always do this, become too caught up in my roles. I can't tell you the number of times I've fallen for a character then ended up with a man. A nauseatingly self-absorbed man who has nothing on his mind but sex and his own career."

"Do you have feelings for Kilo?" Teresa said. "That would be fine, too. He's basically a good guy, and he's genuinely talented. You could do worse."

"He's slept with every woman in our age range in Port Townsend," Maddie said.

"Isn't that what David accused you of?" Ali asked. "If you don't want David to judge you by your sexual past, you can't judge Kilo that way either. Don't think I wasn't bothered by Joe's reputation with women."

"Or Liam's," Teresa chimed in.

"Some people need to go a little wild," Ali went on. "Becca did. Her past brought her to Jean-Louis, the kind of nice, solid guy she never would have dated in college. Charming as he is, he can count his ex-girlfriends on one hand."

Maddie looked chastened. "I guess I'm judging Kilo by the same double standard. I don't think it's his past that bothers me so much as his … intensity. He seems obsessed with me. You should see the way Helena and Hermia— um, I keep forgetting their real names—come on to him. Every time he flirts with them, he checks out my reaction. This is a different issue, but I have only one friend in that cast, and that's Titania, I mean, Jeremy. Because he's a union actor. The others resent my meager monthly paycheck. They think their roles are just as big—that it's not fair. But they don't have my résumé. I've paid my dues."

Teresa nodded in sympathy. "That must be rough. I always figured sex with Kilo would be a lighthearted thing."

"Yeah," Ali said, "we had no idea."

"Not that it ever was between Kilo and me," Teresa amended. "Lighthearted, I mean. But I was seventeen then. If love wasn't intense, it wasn't love. Now I think the ideal relationship includes a lot of joking around. It does for me and Liam, anyway."

Ali nodded. "And for Joe and me." She paused to gather up loose tendrils of hair into her high ponytail. "Less so lately."

"The tour," Teresa said. She caught her sister-in-law's bemused expression. Ali had noted the rifts in her and Liam's gauzy romantic façade too, but she wasn't going to be the one to raise the subject.

To Teresa's question, she replied, "Yes, the tour. I can tell he's worried about his voice, though it's holding up fine for now. I'm more concerned about the groupies. Talking about it wouldn't help."

"Who is he touring with, do you have any idea?" Teresa asked.

Ali pictured the grizzled older singer. "Charlie 'Beau' Pullman. At least Joe won't be sleeping with him."

They all laughed. "Beau might be sleeping when he shouldn't be, though," Teresa said. "How old is he, eighty-five?"

"Only seventy," Ali said. "And he doesn't look a day over fifty. An odd-looking fifty. A lot of plastic surgery." She made a face. "Why do they do that?"

Teresa gave her a wry look. "My question is, rather, why do they *over*do that? In show business, who wouldn't try to look younger? In any business. Look at my mom. She's got the best doc in town."

"She does look fantastic," Maddie said.

"Wouldn't someone like Beau seek out the very best plastic surgeon?" Ali asked.

"Sure," Teresa said. "But they don't really see themselves as others see them anymore. They start with a little, then they want more. Think that if they keep going, they'll make it back to age twenty-five. Or in Michael Jackson's case, twelve." After the laughter died down, she added, "If one surgeon doesn't agree to do the procedure that's one too many, they find another who will."

"Maybe I should get a breast reduction," Maddie said.

Ali couldn't help it. She stared at Maddie's full, flawless breasts. Teresa did the same. "What are you, a D-cup? My God, your breasts are perfect. Don't you dare let anyone touch them." Ali smiled. "With a knife, I mean."

"Hey!" Joe called to them from outside. "The second shift is about to begin. Aren't you girls all pruney by now? We're comin' in." He rattled the gate, causing considerable squealing. "We promise to close our eyes."

"Hold your horses!" Ali yelled, scrambling to put on her robe. To Teresa and Maddie, she said, "If you guys want to put up with three naked stallions, be my guest." They were already reaching for their towels and robes.

On the way out, Ali couldn't help but notice the way David's eyes smoldered when they fixed on Maddie. *What a mess*, she thought.

Later that night, as Ali and Joe were lying in bed, reading, Ali said, "David and Maddie had sex."

He put down his book and removed his reading glasses. "You mean on Christmas Eve?" He didn't look surprised. "We already suspected it, then David admitted it when he told me how things went down with Sylvia. He said they had a knock-down drag-out fight. Sylvia found the missing button on his shirt and assumed correctly how it came loose."

"Did you tell him Maddie heard them fighting?"

"Yeah."

"That she knows Italian?"

"That surprised him," Joe said. "He was embarrassed and really sorry. Knew his words must have hurt her. Claimed he was trying to calm Sylvia down by telling her what she wanted to hear."

"Plausible, I guess," Ali said as she dragged her fingers lightly up and down his furry chest.

Joe closed his eyes and started to breathe a little faster. "He wants to apologize, but Maddie won't give him the time of day."

Ali's fingertips slid lower. "Funny. Kilo loves Maddie, who loves David but thinks he doesn't respect her. David loves Maddie and is too stubborn to hold out an olive branch. David thinks Maddie sleeps around too much, and Maddie thinks the same of Kilo. Sounds like *A Midsummer Night's Dream*, 1999."

"*Love*," Joe repeated, as if he had a bad taste in his mouth. "Strong word and maybe the wrong one for this situation." Joe smiled as Ali's hand settled on his erection. "Only there's no one for Kilo."

"Maybe there are too many for Kilo. All Maddie has to do is respond to him, and he'll lose interest."

Joe arched an eyebrow. He was on his side, enjoying her deft fingers. "You think so? Could be he's really hooked this time."

He rolled on top of her, ending the conversation.

* * *

It was six thirty in the evening. Maddie had just come from her costume fitting and was grabbing a hotdog from a nearby stand before the seven-o'clock rehearsal. They were dressing her in short-shorts with suspenders and a short-sleeved button-down shirt. The director had said not to bother binding her breasts—he wanted to play up the gender-bending thing and even give her a little bulge. She thought she looked really silly, like an exotic dancer for an unusually perverse clientele who fantasized about screwing elves. From what she'd seen of the other costumes, dignity would be in short supply all around. The fairies would wear skin-colored body suits and gauzy, transparent swaths of fabric. Unfortunately, when she sang the lullaby, she would also be a fairy, a complicated quick change that would happen in front of the rest of the cast. At least she wouldn't be naked onstage.

Kilo had the coolest costume, all black with thigh-high boots. Like Zorro without the mask. Maddie had seen the sketches. They obviously weren't sticking very close to the period—circa 1915—but then, fairies were basically timeless.

They were rehearsing Act Three, Scene Two, which was between Oberon and Puck but leading into a scene with Lysander and Helena. As she said her lines,

> Captain of our fairy band,
> Helena is here at hand;
> And the youth, mistook by me,
> Pleading for a lover's fee.
> Shall we their fond pageant see?
> Lord, what fools these mortals be!

David was never far from her mind. They were acting foolish, all of them. Every time Kilo was on stage with her, he oozed sexuality and undressed her with his eyes, though he stopped short of touching her. Maddie had to pretend to like it, and in so doing became hopelessly confused, responded in spite of herself. Needless to say, the director loved it and wanted more.

The next part of the scene was between the four confused lovers; Oberon and Puck were only observers. Everything was mixed up. Thanks to Puck's shenanigans, the formerly scorned Helena was now the object of desire. The four actors were perfectly cast, and she found herself enjoying the long sequence. She and Kilo were "hidden" above, with only their upper bodies visible to the audience. She felt his hand clamp onto her bottom, and there was nothing she could do about it. His face, naturally, revealed nothing, and after shooting him a lightning-quick stink-eye, she stayed riveted on the scene, her forcibly animated expression one of merry mischief.

The director stopped the scene to adjust the blocking, then he said to

Maddie and Kilo, "Maddie, I want you to stand in front of Kilo. Kilo, put your hands on her shoulders. You're tall enough that the audience will still see you. Puck is your protégé."

Back to the beginning of the scene. This time, as they watched the confused lovers, Kilo stood close enough that she could feel his erection. Though his hands were on her shoulders, their touch felt far too intimate. Even if Kilo had behaved inappropriately, she couldn't have reported him, but this kind of thing happened all the time in theater, and actors were expected to deal with it. After Oberon's exit, Maddie struggled to get her head back in the game. For her character, this was the most complicated scene, because Puck had to enjoy his role as puppet master of the despairing lovers, and the choreography was a bitch to remember. Once or twice, she worried that the director was going to stop everything and ask her why she was so distracted. He blew up at Helena a few times, but never at her.

She checked her watch; they were supposed to break at ten, and it was nine forty-five, thank God. The stage manager, who had just returned from a bathroom break, signaled to the director that he needed a moment.

"Oh no," Frank said after they conferred. To the cast, he said, "It's snowing. What a pain. Most of you can walk home, but Maddie, it's trickier for you. Tim says it's sticking to the roads. Can you crash with someone in town?"

Maddie looked around. She couldn't very well admit to Frank how little this cast liked her. She would look like a bad colleague.

"Sure!" Kilo said brightly. "I have a couch. That will work for you, right, Maddie?"

Maddie was in a panic. She couldn't impose on the O'Connell household by having one of them make a dangerous trip to pick her up. And she couldn't afford a hotel.

When she didn't speak, Frank said, "According to Tim, there's black ice. The temperature just dropped. Nothing like this was in the forecast. Maddie?"

"Yeah, of course," she said. "I can crash with Kilo." She was not imagining the poison darts Helena and Hermia sent her way.

Just then her cellphone rang. It was Ali. "Maddie, it's bad out there. Can you stay over with someone in town? Better yet, check into a hotel. We'll pay."

She didn't want to admit she didn't have credit cards with her. "Thanks, Ali, that's really nice, but I'll be fine. See you in the morning."

She hung up, her heart beating too fast. *Maybe you want to spend the night with Kilo*, a voice in her head goaded her.

CHAPTER 18

"Damn!" Ali cried as she put down the phone.

"What?" Joe said. He was standing at the window, looking out at the snow.

"You have to rescue Maddie." All sorts of wild scenarios were going through Ali's head. What she wasn't picturing was Maddie checking into a hotel, as Ali had expressly asked her to do.

Joe blew out a breath. "Why? Because you think Maddie's going to use the snow as an excuse to bed down with Kilo?"

David was standing next to Joe, and Ali fancied she could see his hackles rise.

Joe held Ali by the shoulders and looked her straight in the eye. "No one in this family is going to risk their own lives in order to 'rescue' Maddie. She doesn't need rescuing." He turned to David. "Don't even think about it. You are giving that poor girl *so many* mixed signals. Not so mixed lately. The message is basically, 'You're beneath my notice.'"

"What do you expect?" David huffed. "I want to apologize but she treats me like a leper. It's not easy living in the same house with her."

"Because you fucked her?"

Everyone, including Teresa and Liam, who were sitting together on the couch, gasped. David was speechless.

"How clueless are you?" Joe went on. Ali's normally easygoing husband was snarling. Maybe it was the pressure of the upcoming tour. "We all understand what you're going through. Lorenzo, Sylvia, Africa, and whatever it did to you. And now Maddie. She's a super-nice kid, and she is—well, *was*—really into you. I know it's not fair, but you're going to have to find a way to get through to her. It's too hard on the rest of us. Raise a white flag, already. And if she *is* sleeping with Kilo, you'll have to accept that too and not judge."

Ali held her breath. David's face was ruddy with pent-up anger, and his fingers were flexing. He looked like he might punch Joe or have a stroke. They stared each other down.

"Uh … guys?" Liam rose to his feet. "There's been some weirdness, yeah, but this isn't helping. David, can I make a suggestion?" David turned his feral gaze on Liam. "Just be nice to Maddie. Stop looking at her like she's one of Tennessee Williams' maneaters. Get to know her, no agenda. Act as if she's a visiting niece. Then maybe we can all relax a little."

Joe had calmed down. "I know she's driving you crazy. All we ask is, keep it to yourself. In a few months, she'll go back to Seattle. She's wrestling with her own demons."

Teresa headed for the kitchen. "Who wants a hot toddy? I have a batch ready."

David shook his head, and without bidding anyone good night, stalked out of the house and up the hill to his cabin.

Liam raked his hands through his shock of blue-black hair. "He is royally pissed off."

Joe collapsed on the couch. "I don't care. He needed some sense knocked into him."

Ali still stood by the window, staring at the ghostly drifts of driven snow. "I'm worried about Maddie."

Teresa handed her a steaming mug. "Join the crowd. Here, have a hot toddy."

* * *

Feeling both dread and anticipation—a little like she did opening nights—Maddie led the way up the hill toward Lawrence Street. It wasn't an easy trudge in the snow and ice, and every time she slipped, Kilo was there to steady her. They didn't speak. Her feet began to numb in her stylish, unlined boots. Other than that, she was dressed warmly enough. If she hadn't been so confused, she might have better appreciated the beauty of the night, everything blanketed in snow that glistened in the Victorian streetlights. So still in the absence of car engines, like a scene out of *Christmas in Connecticut*. The Pacific Northwest was never prepared for weather like this—even the people who owned four-wheel-drive vehicles had little experience driving in it—so when snow fell and began to accumulate, most of the cars stayed off the roads, allowing for hours of pristine winter wonderland. The snow was still falling as they arrived at Kilo's building. He unlocked the door and invited her to mount the stairs first. Though unable to see his face, buried in a scarf and hat, Maddie assumed he was gloating at his victory. He didn't touch her as she made her way up to his apartment.

Inside, he led her over to the couch then grabbed the remote and turned on the gas fireplace. As Swami the cat performed a soliloquy of differently pitched meows, Kilo retrieved a bottle of chardonnay from the refrigerator and filled two large glasses. After handing one to Maddie, he opened a can for Swami. Giving it a disdainful sniff, the cat uttered one outraged "Meow!"

"Oh no you don't," Kilo told him. "You love salmon." To Maddie, he said, "It's not even cat food. It's wild sockeye salmon."

Swami upped the volume. "Meow!"

Hands on hips, Kilo said, "You calling me a liar?"

Swami started looping around his legs with a purr so loud, even Maddie could hear it.

Kilo wagged a finger at him. "You little rotter." He picked up the protesting cat and the plate of salmon, put them in the bathroom, and shut the door. Joining Maddie on the couch, he said, "Sorry. Swami doesn't like playing second fiddle."

Maddie was laughing so hard that she had to hold her stomach, which made Kilo laugh too.

Still chuckling, he unzipped her boots and rubbed her cold feet. Other than that, he didn't touch her. No one was laughing now. Maddie tucked her legs beneath her on the couch and sipped the wine, waiting to see how long it took for Kilo to make his move.

Now that he had her alone, Kilo seemed to be at a loss. He drained half his glass.

"Better?" he asked.

"Better than what?"

"You acted as if staying over with me might be worse than a night in jail."

She stared him down.

"I've been a jerk."

"Ya think?"

"You weren't so nice, either." He paused. "I thought we were having a good time after the wedding. I guess I was wrong. Then you just… disappeared. And my invitation to spend the holidays at the O'Connells' place was rescinded."

Maddie had wondered why he wasn't there, hadn't known about the invitation. "I'm sorry. I wasn't consulted." She didn't like the thought that he'd had nowhere else to go. He and Liam were friends, enough to attend his wedding and even the rehearsal dinner.

"Then it was David."

That made sense. She hadn't considered it before.

"He's been through some difficult times," she explained, though it didn't excuse his behavior. She couldn't shrug off what he'd said to Sylvia. Easy to see how Kilo might feel used and discarded. With David, she was the used and discarded one.

She stared into her empty glass, which Kilo promptly refilled along with his own. He inched a little closer. "You're looking at me like I'm the Marquis de Sade reincarnated," he said, keeping a tiny bit of distance between them.

"Are you?"

"Only if you want me to be."

She thought about his behavior during rehearsals and wondered if he'd ever played that role in Peter Weiss's *Marat/Sade*. He'd be perfect.

"You know, I could have anyone in that cast, even Jeremy. I want you."

"Only because I'm not interested."

"Aren't you?" He brushed a knuckle across her cheek.

While avoiding his insistent gaze, she didn't pull away.

Instead, he did. "It's late. I'm going to brush my teeth and take a shower. The bed is like sleeping on a cloud, and the couch is like a bed of nails. One that is too small. I recommend joining me. I won't touch you unless you want me to. And if you do, no marathons. Promise. Just sweet and simple sex. Better than a sleeping pill."

She snorted. "Nothing is simple with you."

"Try me. And no one's going to cast you as Tammy."

She batted her lashes at him. "I play innocents all the time."

"Of course you do. You're a first-rate actress." He patted her knee. "I'll be out of the bathroom in the blink of an eye." He went into his bedroom, and when he came out, he tossed her a terrycloth robe. "I don't expect you to roam about naked for my pleasure."

Ten minutes later he emerged from the bathroom wearing only a towel, golden skin glowing, hair damp. "I left a new toothbrush for you by the sink and a fresh towel." He shot her an enticing look, then disappeared into the bedroom, leaving the door open.

As promised, a toothbrush, still in its package, sat on the shelf above the sink. A folded towel was draped over the sliding door of the luxury walk-in shower. She showered, brushed her teeth, then stood at the door of his bathroom, paralyzed by indecision.

"Meow." Swami, released from his prison, seemed to be saying, "What are you waiting for?" With a swish of his tail, he sauntered over to the window and jumped up on the sill to stare out at the snow.

All Maddie had to do was take one step to the left and turn around. Should she be insulted? He'd basically called her a skank while praising her acting skills. But he hadn't used that horrible word. Not being innocent wasn't such a bad thing, unless you were a prig. What about David? He'd barely said two words to her since returning from Portland. Yep, that was promising.

Her legs made the decision for her, transporting her to the doorway of Kilo's bedroom. The window shades were up, and the room glowed in the soft illumination of snow, streetlamps, and moonlight. On the other side of the king-sized bed, Kilo was lying on his side, facing her, covers pulled up to his chin, eyes closed. His lashes fluttered as she let the robe fall to the ground and crawled in beside him. Silently, he inched over so that they were almost touching. Her move. She lay on her back, so close she could feel his body heat, waiting to see what he would do. She breathed in his freshly showered, vaguely exotic, enticing Kilo-ness. His hand moved and hovered over her breast. It didn't land until her chest rose to meet it. The rest of her resistance melted away.

As promised, what followed was entirely different from their previous encounter. The restorative-yoga version of sex. His hands roamed lightly over every inch of her body until she squirmed with need. Then he kissed her—gentle, tasting kisses—as he shifted into position and slid into her, already sheathed with a condom, and began his slow, languorous movements, bringing her to the edge of orgasm with his fingers, withdrawing, bringing her to the edge again. They were both on their sides, fully relaxed, and the weird effortlessness of it all was unsettling. By the time he finally let her come, she shattered, only vaguely aware of his own low moan of release.

She slept so soundly that upon waking she was completely disoriented. For a moment she tried to make sense of the unfamiliar room, with its warm brown walls and sparse décor. A brass lamp on each nightstand, an oil painting of Hurricane Ridge, an etching of a naked woman playing the cello. Then she saw Kilo standing in the doorway, robe open to reveal his smooth, hard chest and silk briefs, two cups of coffee in hand.

"It's a beautiful day," he said, cheerily, as he placed a cup of coffee on each of the coasters on the nightstands.

She propped herself up in bed, instinctively covering her breasts.

"Oh, please," he said, gently moving her hands to her sides. "Don't. You are a work of art. I didn't know what my bedroom was missing until now."

He has coasters on his nightstands, Maddie thought, imagining this scenario repeated over and over ad infinitum. She eyed the comforter, wondering when it had been last cleaned.

He narrowed his eyes. "Okay, let's talk." His voice had lost the underlying purr of seduction. "I have a pretty good idea what's on your mind. You, like everyone else, think I do this every night. If that were true, how could I run a business in such a small town?"

"You have coasters on both your nightstands."

"So? They're mahogany. I have coffee in bed by myself a lot, and I sleep on both sides. If I have sex with someone from this town, I have to think long and hard about the consequences. It's enough to make a guy want to settle down." Correctly reading the apprehension on her face, he laughed. "I'm not asking you to marry me. But by God, after last night, I almost would." He took her hand and gave it a little shake. "Don't worry so much. I know I'm not your final destination. But you and I have a lot more in common than you realize. More than you and David, for instance."

He laughed again in his light, husky baritone, so different from David's deep bass. "See the way you just closed down? I know there's some weird, unhealthy shit going on between the two of you. If I were a woman or gay, I might go for that too. People like us, we welcome a challenge." He paused, sneered. "You don't like being lumped into the same category as me." He shook his head with a hint of annoyance. "Drink your coffee before it gets cold. I have an espresso machine. It's a latte with whole milk, just how you like it."

Wondering how he could possibly know that, she reached for the coffee and took a sip. *Perfect*. "Don't you think it's going to be weird now?" she asked. "In rehearsals, I mean."

His smile was indulgent. "Weirder than it has been?"

"That was you."

"Don't be so sure. And I see what's happening with the rest of the cast. I see you trying to make nice, them putting you off. Don't take it personally.

I've done enough stuff with this company to know that's how it is. They're at different points in their careers. They don't even know what it means to be professionals yet. They think it's all about talent. The only reason they kiss up to me is because they all want to fuck me. Yes, even the men."

That surprised her. "*Both* Lysander and Demetrius are gay?"

"Yep. That's working against you too. Vanity, thy name is actor. I've been in similar situations. It's just a job, right? Better not to bond too much with the cast. I bet it happened less often in the non-Equity productions you've been in because everyone was more or less on equal footing. It's worse when your character is a troublemaker like Puck. A troublemaker as beautiful as you."

She glanced out the window. "How are the streets?"

"Mostly clear now, at least the main ones. It's going to be in the forties today. You might want to wait until afternoon to ride your Vespa. We have a rehearsal at two anyway. Choreography for the final dance, which, it may not surprise you to learn, I'm in charge of. You can stay here as long as you like."

Swami entered at that moment, "Purrow!"

"See?" Kilo said. "He gave one of his signature purrows. That means you're in."

"I don't have my rehearsal dance clothes with me."

"I'll clothe you from my giftshop. My treat."

Suddenly, going back to the compound didn't seem like a great option. If David had been weird before, he was going to be even weirder now. Or was that possible? What would the others think?

"They're not going to care," Kilo said, sipping his own coffee.

"What?"

"You're wondering what your hosts will think of you. They're all cool. Not David, but you knew that already."

Kilo crawled back in beside her and kissed first one nipple, then the other. "Good morning to you too," he told her breasts. "I think you've missed me."

CHAPTER 19

MADDIE WAS SITTING BETWEEN JEREMY and Kilo at the makeup table that ran along the lighted mirror. She looked even less like a boy than Jeremy resembled a woman. When you played a man, you still needed makeup, but it was mostly contour, a more natural shade for the lips, eyeliner but no mascara. They wanted her lips pink and her cheeks rosy. Cherubic, not goblin-esque, as Shakespeare had apparently intended. Poor Shakespeare, no one did his plays as he'd intended anymore. On the other hand, who knew what Shakespeare had wanted? Shakespeare wasn't allowed to cast women. If indeed "Shakespeare," the man most history books described, had even existed.

Maddie figured everyone knew Kilo and she were an item, just as she knew that Jeremy was involved with Lysander and Helena was hooking up with one of the fairies, a dancer Kilo had brought in from Port Angeles, barely legal. Everything had fallen into place once she stopped resisting Kilo. The consummate professional, he didn't exhaust her with his attentions, and thanks to him, the rest of the cast had grudgingly accepted her. Jeremy was his usual jovial self.

As was common on opening nights, the cast members and the director gifted each other little tokens for luck. Treats, tiny toys, cards. Maddie had given everyone cards that opened to play a tinny version of the Everly Brothers' "All I Have to Do Is Dream." She'd expended more effort on Jeremy and Kilo, buying them both charm-bracelet figurines: Jeremy a fairy of indeterminate sex, and Kilo, a tiny, jewel-encrusted crown. Both gifts had set her back more than she could realistically afford. Jeremy's gift to her was a troll doll, no doubt to remind her that most Pucks didn't get to be so glamorous, and Kilo's, an antique cameo on a gold chain with a tiny version of his professional headshot inside. He pointed out that the profile on the cameo resembled her, though she couldn't see it. A more intimate gift than she was comfortable with.

"Baby doll, you're nothing like any boy I ever saw," Jeremy told her. He'd taken to calling her "Baby doll" after the Tennessee Williams's movie about a sensual but childlike bride. His nicknames for her changed frequently, and she didn't mind. "You look like something out of a rococo fresco. I still don't understand the 1915 thing and the Southern accents, but I guess it adds to the lazy, hazy summer-night atmosphere."

"Don't let Frank hear you say that," Kilo told him.

Maddie retreated to the other room to put on her costume. Not that anyone in the makeup room would have cared. Most of the other men were gay, and Kilo had seen every inch of her naked. There were two additional makeup rooms, and other than the three Equity members, the leads consisted of just the two young couples. When she came out, Kilo whistled.

" 'Who wears short shorts,' " he sang in a soft voice.

"Shh," she told him. "Keep it in your pants. Besides, you saw my silly costume at the dress rehearsal."

"What, no binding?" He winked.

"You saw that last night too—and at the rehearsal. Damn sexual ambiguity thing."

"No ambiguity there," Kilo said, giving her an appreciative once-over.

Jeremy, who'd also been changing into his costume, came back into the room and posed next to the door like a Hollywood vamp, head thrown back. "Oh, Oberon …" he gushed. He sauntered over and pressed his fake breasts on either side of Kilo's head. "Give me some head!"

"*Tit*-ania …" Kilo said in a mock-threatening voice as he pulled away and formed a cross with his fingers.

No one seemed particularly nervous about opening night. They were solid with their lines, and three weeks was longer than most fully professional companies got. In summer stock, Maddie had once pulled together a show in a week. The tech and dress rehearsals had gone smoothly, maybe too smoothly if you were superstitious, which most actors were. Maddie had seen plenty go wrong in performances. The lower the budget, the more likely it was that a set piece would malfunction or an actor would show up drunk or stoned and miss a cue. She couldn't see that happening with this group. For one thing, the set was simple, just three levels, and the tech crew appeared more than competent. The "magic" in the atmosphere relied on gauzy backdrops, whimsical costumes, fairy lights, an oversized full moon, and colored gels.

Maddie knew from experience that her own stage fright would disappear the minute she treaded the boards. Her nerves had less to do with flop sweat than the presence of her mother, Duncan, and the entire O'Connell crew—including David—in the audience. Becca and Jean-Louis, in town to oversee the progress of the newest La Fête Sauvage, were there too. They all knew about Kilo and seemed to accept the relationship as inevitable. No one had questioned her wisdom … to her face. Even David seemed calmer and—*gasp*—friendlier. Perhaps her declaring for Kilo had cleared the air. No question of Maddie and David hooking up now.

Did she love Kilo? No. She liked him, liked making love to him. She hoped he felt the same. It was enough for now. Their arrangement hadn't changed the way she felt about David.

* * *

Teresa had purchased a block of tickets for their group, choosing seats several rows back and to the side so they wouldn't be right in Maddie's face.

When Maddie finally made her appearance in Act Two, Scene One, Teresa was initially shocked by the sight of her in booty shorts, two crescents of firm butt cheek showing, and suspenders. Her short-sleeved cotton shirt was unbuttoned to reveal an expanse of cleavage. She moved like a boy and had a boy's rough energy, but she looked like Sally Bowles in *Cabaret*. Still, it wasn't long before Maddie disappeared so thoroughly into her role that Teresa no longer fixated on the costume. Then came the other big—no, *huge*—adjustment. Oberon and Titania's entrance. Kilo looked like a dark knight out of an Arthurian legend. Despite the presence of Liam at her side, she felt a pang for what might have been. Who knew that Kilo could do Shakespeare? His natural grace worked perfectly in the role, and the man playing Titania was almost his equal. Somehow it all worked—sexual ambiguity, Southern accents, and all.

Teresa wondered how David was taking all this. He sat in front of her, and the back of his lion's head wasn't giving up any secrets. Ever since they'd all confronted him that snowy night, his attitude—outwardly—had changed. He'd begun to treat Maddie more like a kid sister. Maddie confessed to Teresa and Ali that she'd spent the last two nights with Kilo. She hoped they were okay with that. "As long as you are," they'd told her, though disappointed for David's sake. Joe was right. It was a case of spectacularly bad timing.

In Act Two, Scene Two, Maddie appeared as a fairy and sang Titania to

139

sleep. She wore a flesh-colored leotard—no underwear lines—under some gauze, leaving little to the imagination. Teresa shuddered at the prospect of exposing herself like that, yet Maddie seemed free of self-consciousness and sang like an angel, no surprise. How did she change her costume so quickly? In no time she was back as Puck.

The rest of the performance flowed easily, and Teresa wanted to look away during the final dance between Titania and Oberon. She wondered if you ever totally got over your first love. When Liam glanced her way, his expression opaque, she squeezed his hand reassuringly.

* * *

After the show, Maddie and Kilo greeted their group together, and she couldn't shake the feeling that they were "coming out" as a couple. Kilo didn't have to glue himself to her side this way. Clearly, he wanted back in with the family. Who could blame him, an only child raised by a mother who'd died young? Everyone was gracious, even David. If only Maddie could let them know how it really was between her and Kilo—a temporary arrangement dictated by circumstances.

She hadn't expected her agent to show up. Lola Deters kissed her on both cheeks, Continental style, explaining that she'd always wanted to visit Port Townsend, and this way she could write off the trip. Leave it to Lola to offer too much information, coming off as both honest and insulting. In her reedy voice, she asked, "Maddie, have you considered my suggestion to go to L.A. for the second half of pilot season? I can also line up a few auditions with casting agents in case the right movie role comes up."

Recalling her dwindling savings, Maddie sighed inwardly. She hated asking Laurie for money. As if reading her mind, Lola said, "Maybe I can arrange some preliminary screentests in Seattle. That way it would be more of a calculated risk and less a crapshoot."

"That would be great," Maddie said, summoning the expected degree of enthusiasm.

"Will you introduce me to your Oberon?" Lola peered over at Kilo as if starstruck. Did Lola want a professional introduction or a date? The woman had to be in her mid-thirties, if not older.

"Of course."

Kilo, who'd been eavesdropping, was at her side in an instant, overwhelming a simpering Lola with his charm.

Maddie decided to leave them to it. "Lola, you'll call me about the screentests? Now that the show is open, the run is Thursday through Sunday.

I could pop back to Seattle on dark days. Tuesday would be the best, but in a pinch I could do Monday afternoon or Wednesday morning. The show closes in three weeks, on February twenty-eighth."

Knowing she'd lost Lola's attention entirely, she gave up. She'd confirm later by email. The O'Connell group was headed out the door, so she rushed over to say goodbye.

"You're not coming home with us?" Ali said, almost wistfully.

Maddie avoided her eyes. "Oh, I'm sorry, not tonight."

"We want to have a party for you," Becca said. "How about after the Sunday matinee? Jean-Louis will cook."

"That would be great!" Maddie said, then caught the sharp look Jean-Louis gave Becca. No one had asked him. He recovered quickly.

Maddie didn't ask whether Kilo was invited. *She* wouldn't mention it. If Liam asked him, then fine. Right now, Kilo was fully occupied with Lola.

Back at Kilo's place, he said, "Your agent made a pass at me."

He was laughing so hard that Swami struggled out of his arms and dashed into the bedroom.

Maddie was less amused. "Ah. I thought she wanted to sign you."

"That too. I don't think she realizes you and I are an item."

"You didn't enlighten her?"

They were sitting together on Kilo's black leather couch, limbs casually entwined. He didn't answer her question. Instead he said, "She told me about a reboot of *Hawaiian Eye*. You remember that old TV show from the sixties?"

"Nope."

"It ran from 1959 to 1963. I guess I only knew about it because I spent my childhood in Hawaii, and we were proud of every show supposedly set there. The part she has in mind for me is Tom Lopaka, who's supposed to be half-Hawaiian, although Robert Conrad played the role, and that guy is one-hundred-percent European. You know, James West in *The Wild Wild West*?"

"I remember *that* show." Maddie wished Lola showed half the enthusiasm for her career as she did for Kilo's, but then, his type was a lot less common than hers—beautiful, exotic, smart, talented heterosexual actors. Come to think of it, he might be the only one who hadn't been discovered yet.

"God, you were wonderful tonight," he whispered in her ear. "I'm glad your agent could see it." He slid his hands under her T-shirt.

She didn't want to talk about her career, his career, *anyone's* career. Thank God opening night was over. That was when any critics attended. For the rest of the run, the audience would be mostly strangers, and the play, just a fun job. "I had no idea you were so ambitious," she said, closing her eyes as he fondled her bare breasts.

His voice had turned husky. "I didn't know I was." He unzipped her jeans and pulled them off, straddling her on the couch. "After the Groban Phillips tour and the training program in London, I was burned out. I thought I was ready to hang it all up. Should I stop?"

"No," she moaned as his hands plundered her.

"Do you want me inside you?" he whispered.

"Yes," she managed to eke out.

"How bad?"

She opened her eyes to see the mischief in his. As usual, she was naked, and he was still wearing his jeans. He did love to be in control. She reached for his fly and fumbled with the buttons, but he didn't help her. Finally, she lay back in frustration and went limp, as if falling asleep.

"Oh, no you don't," he laughed, finally taking off his own jeans and thrusting inside her.

When they were both panting and spent, her thoughts drifted back to their previous conversation. He'd never answered the question about her agent. Lola was pushy, but she was a good-looking woman if you liked the New York Italian type, a budget version of Sylvia. They had never discussed fidelity, and why would they? This was just a fling, wasn't it?

CHAPTER 20

———◆———

AFTER THE SUNDAY MATINEE, MADDIE told Kilo she was going back to the compound, neglecting to mention the celebratory dinner. She felt particularly bad because next week they'd be flying to L.A. together for a few days. The producers of the reboot of *Hawaiian Eye* were putting Kilo up in a hotel, so her only expense would have been the plane flight—if he hadn't paid for her ticket himself. She'd also be meeting with casting directors, but with no specific project in mind. The fact that he'd invited her along meant that, for now at least, Kilo had no plans to sleep with Lola.

As she rolled in on her Vespa, Maddie felt the same profound feeling of peace she experienced whenever she arrived at the O'Connell compound. It was as if they were all caught in some odd holding pattern while residing in a fantasy land of love and comfort. Like Hollywood's vision of Mount Olympus in those B-movies featuring gods and goddesses. Until the twins were in kindergarten, Ali wouldn't consider any work outside the home, Joe was preparing for the tour no one wanted to talk about, Teresa was deciding whether to buy the music school no one wanted her to buy, and Liam was casting about for his next vocation, keeping busy working on other people's handyman projects. Becca and Jean-Louis were overseeing the renovation of the building that would house the newest location of La Fête Sauvage, and both worried that a gourmet wild-game restaurant wouldn't fly in Port Townsend. Even David, though employed as a doctor, was on hold, working a job that required a fraction of his talents. Only Duncan and Laurie seemed to be enjoying themselves. He was officially retired, and she was toying with the idea of selling real estate in Port Townsend.

They were all celebrating Maddie's success, but the way she saw it, she was in a temporary job and a temporary relationship, hoping that whatever life offered her next would allow her to rent her own apartment. As she walked down the hill toward the main house, she had a sudden longing to join the souls in this pleasant purgatory and let the rest of the world, including the acting community, be damned.

The party was already in full swing. A roaring fire warmed and illuminated the living room. Everyone hugged her, repeated their congratulations, and Jean-Louis rushed to fill her glass to the brim.

Ali pulled her aside. "Is Kilo coming?"

"Uh, no. Is that okay? I didn't invite him."

"Totally understandable," Ali said, looking relieved. To the rest of them, she said, "Maddie is flying solo tonight."

Dinner was cedar-planked salmon with green salad, a choice of sauces. Nothing fancy. May Allen's sister Susan, a permanent fixture now, did all the clean-up.

At dinner, Maddie told them about the trip to L.A. They acted as if Spielberg had already offered her a part in his next blockbuster, despite her clear-eyed assessment of her chances. It was all about Kilo, even though she had a few appointments—or Lola said she would by next week.

She heard everyone's updates, which drove home the glacial pace of life here. Maddie came out of the bathroom to find David mixing cocktails. It was the first time they'd been alone since the night they'd messed around. If not for David's headache, what might have happened?

"Hey," he said, as if they were good buddies, "we all loved your performance. Sometimes I forget how entertaining Shakespeare can be when it's done by actors who understand the language."

"Thanks for that," she said. "My training wasn't specifically for Shakespeare, at least not the way Kilo's was." She bit her tongue. *Can it with the Kilo talk*, she told herself.

"He's good, no question," David said, "but no better than you."

"The production isn't too oddball?"

David laughed. "Pretty out there. At first it was a little shocking. Once I got used to Shakespeare in an alternate universe—maybe Transsexual Transylvania—it was a lot of fun."

She sat on a stool next to him. The ice in the drinks was melting, and she hoped he wouldn't seize that excuse to cut their conversation short. "*The Rocky Horror Picture Show*. Do you like that movie?"

He sat down on the stool next to hers. "Love it. I used to have a Frank-N-Furter costume. I wonder what happened to it?"

She chuckled. "My God, I can't picture it."

"Don't try," he said dryly. "It wasn't pretty. Although I was much younger then, it's true." He passed her one of the cocktails. "Vodka tonic. The others have had enough anyway. I can make more."

She'd had enough too, but she sipped it to be polite and prolong the moment.

"I've missed this place," she said. "It's like this haven from the world. When I'm here, I'm safe. The rest of it doesn't exist."

"That's exciting about L.A.," he prompted.

"Yes, I suppose. Frankly, it scares me. Kilo is way more psychologically equipped to handle it than I am."

"How so?"

"For instance, my agent vamped him, and it doesn't bother him at all. That kind of thing freaks me out, all the people on the business end willing to exploit their power. If it were truly about talent, I could handle it a lot better."

He regarded her gravely. "What really worries you?"

He seemed so genuinely concerned that she answered truthfully. "I don't want to get pulled into parts that require a lot of nudity. So far the only full nude scene I've done is on stage, and it sort of worked in the context of the play. But once you start doing nudity on film, it's a permanent record. If I'm offered something like that, how do I say no? I'm a nobody, with no screen credits."

"Have you discussed it with your agent? Can't you include a no nudity clause in your contracts?"

She made a face. "I suppose. Doing nude scenes hasn't hurt other actresses' careers if it's the right part. Look at Annette Bening in *The Grifters*. She's a respected actress."

"Hmm," he said, absentmindedly scratching his stubble. "I'm guessing a part like that doesn't come along too often. Can't you tell from the script if it's exploitive?"

She shrugged. "I suppose. Acting careers in Hollywood are such crapshoots. One false move and bam, it's over." Realizing the conversation was turning into "All About Me," she said, "What about you? Is the job too terrible? I'm almost afraid to ask about Sylvia and your son."

For a moment, Maddie thought he wasn't going to answer, that he might just flee and join the others with no further ado. He shifted uncomfortably on his chair. "The job is just okay. I'm looking into other options in the area, but

I might have to go back to Seattle. Like you, I'm finding myself strangely stuck here. Stuck in a good way. Ali and Joe, Teresa and Liam—all of them, really—are so supportive. Communal living at its finest." He paused. "Sylvia has moved to Chicago, where she's an ER surgeon. Her sister Chiara and her husband have raised Lorenzo up to this point. They want to adopt him, and Chiara obviously adores him. Sometimes I think he'd be better off with them. I'm hardly in a position to raise a child."

"Marrying Sylvia isn't an option?"

He met her eyes, and they both laughed. "She's not so bad," he said. "I don't know what got into her during that visit. I guess she assumed our crowd would better appreciate her particular brand of sophistication. She's not used to our laidback type of celebrity and wealth. I've seen her perform heroic feats and rough it with the best of them. But I gather she's done with all that. Like me, burned out, ready to move on." He shook his head, sipped his drink. "She admits to having no maternal instincts."

"What's Lorenzo like?" She smiled. "It's a big name for a small child."

He grinned back. "He'll grow into it. He's too reserved for a three-and-a-half-year-old. A little too well behaved. I mean, he talks, don't get me wrong. Maybe it's only that he's shy around me. He's kind of an old soul. I don't want him to grow up hating me because he thinks I didn't want to be part of his life. I haven't figured it out yet. We're talking about him coming here for a short period, maybe while Joe is touring."

"I'd like to meet him," Maddie said, thinking that she'd be back in Seattle by then, or in New York or Los Angeles. All three possibilities depressed her.

"You're enjoying the show, right?"

"Yes. Why?"

"Because you seemed so sad just now. From where I'm sitting, you have the world by the tail."

"Funny expression. Like I'm wrestling an alligator. Most of the time it's more like, 'Stop the world, I want to get off.' "

"That's a musical, right?"

"An obscure one. Only a few memorable songs and a sad plot. The guy hates his life and becomes a major womanizer but in the end realizes he should have just valued the love of his wife, who then dies. He offers himself to Death in place of his sick grandson."

David gave her a strange look. "Who would pay to see that? Just hearing about it makes me want to shoot myself."

Maddie laughed. "It's all in the presentation. The main character keeps breaking the fourth wall to tell us, 'Stop the World.' It's very Theater of the

Absurd. I think the distancing makes the plot more palatable. It's true that the revival was a flop."

Joe came into the room and pointed at the drinks. "I was wondering what happened." He looked from one to the other, making Maddie blush. "We're about to call it a night."

"No one mentioned your tour," Maddie said, thinking the subject might be less verboten with Ali out of earshot. "Is it still on?"

Joe sat down heavily on one of the stools. "Yep." As if needing to defend himself, he said, "It's only three months, and there'll be breaks long enough that I can come home in between stops. We had the recording engineers here last week to complete the new album. Ali's not happy about the tour, but I owe it to Linc to promote the album. I've been absent from the scene too long, and it's been a while since I was named CMA Entertainer of the Year. I can't fill stadiums anymore, which means I'm stuck with medium-sized venues, a few casinos, some festivals, a rodeo here and there. Ali, May, and the twins will join us for a few dates. They could come along for the whole thing if she wanted, though I think she'd be bored out of her mind."

"I think she's treasured the lack of attention from the press," David said. "You've been doing a lot of interviews lately."

"I know, I know," Joe said wearily, dragging his fingers through his thick chestnut-brown curls. "She thought I was done with all that. But it kills me to give my best stuff away to other singers, who'll just turn it into something overproduced or cheesy."

"Can't you control who covers your songs?" Maddie asked.

"Not as long as I'm paid royalties. Even if I could, I wouldn't say no to a big star. As long as I'm also performing it myself, at least people know how it's meant to be sung."

He stopped talking at the sound of footsteps on the stairs. Ali and Teresa each held a baby. "Boy, you have to watch them every second," Ali said. "They are moving super-fast. Aren't you, you little rascal? Yes you are!"

"Dadadadadada!" the baby said, reaching out with both arms. Ali handed her over to Joe while Teresa passed the other baby to Ali.

"We're headed to bed," Joe said. " 'Night, all."

More goodbyes and hugs followed as Teresa, Liam, and the rest of the crew retired to their cabins. Laurie and Duncan had gone home Saturday after having brunch with Maddie.

Maddie and David were alone again.

"Can I escort you up the hill?"

As they walked slowly, side by side, Maddie said, "It's been nice catching up. Things have been … weird between us."

"I'm sorry," David said. "I've had some time to beat myself up about what you overheard me say to Sylvia. I didn't mean it. She was just so jealous, and I needed her to calm the hell down."

"I get that."

He cleared his throat. "I guess I'm jealous."

"Don't be," she told him. She didn't dare elaborate. She wanted to say, *Kilo will move on soon, and so will I. I'll still feel the same about you. Not that it will matter. I'll be back in Seattle.*

They arrived at her cabin. He didn't close the distance between them. "I hope you find what you're looking for," he told her. "Goodnight."

As he walked away, she almost called him back. But that wouldn't be fair to Kilo or to David, who was even more of a lost soul than she. He was too good for her, really. Unlike Kilo, he'd have the power to break her heart. And whatever decisions she made about her career had to come from her, not from a man too unsettled himself to commit to any one person or place. Maddie couldn't handle another furtive, rushed, guilty make-out session like their last one, even less a slow, languorous one.

More and more, when Kilo made love to her, she'd close her eyes and think of David.

* * *

After David shut the door to his cabin, he stood leaning against it for a long moment, eyes closed, breathing hard. His acting performance tonight should have earned him some kind of major award. The way he'd managed to keep from storming the stage on opening night and shaking that slimy man-slut Kilo until his teeth rattled. The guy was just so obvious. Why couldn't women see it?

What had she meant, don't be jealous? Who was she kidding? Still, he was proud to have stayed cool, kept his suffering under wraps. Thank God she didn't know how he burned for her every goddamned night. On stage she was so achingly beautiful and vulnerable and alive. David had no doubt she could be a movie star if that was what she wanted. That left no place in her life for him. He supposed that someday the memory of her and her performance would dim, and he'd be able to settle for an ordinary woman. Right now, that didn't seem possible.

He reached for the bottle of single malt Scotch on top of the minifridge and poured himself a stiff drink. He knew he shouldn't drink alone, and he guessed that Liam and Joe were in similar mind spaces. Especially Liam. Between rehearsing and recording, Joe couldn't afford to do any hard drinking, but he could use a respite from Ali's discontent. David had seen the way Teresa looked at Kilo during the play, and Liam couldn't have missed it either. Sure, the honeymoon had to end sometime, but he thought they were good together, just needed space. Anyway, David had no doubt his brother-in-law would welcome a drinking partner. Too bad he couldn't go over to their cabin and ask if Liam could play, like some kid looking for a game of catch. He settled back into the easy chair with his drink and opened the beat-up paperback copy of *Lucky Jim* someone had left on the shelf. Kingsley Amis was a clever writer, and the hangover scene was hilarious, but Jim was too much of a fuck-up. At least David could hold his liquor. Thank God Maddie would be back in Seattle soon. Because if David had to endure the agony of seeing her with that scumbag Kilo too much longer, he was going to give in and drink as much as it took for him to expunge her from his heart and soul.

There wasn't enough Scotch in Port Townsend for that.

CHAPTER 21

———•———

NOT SURPRISINGLY, KNOWING PEOPLE WITH deep pockets and primo connections made the dreaded trip to Los Angeles infinitely easier. Maddie didn't want to think how much it had cost Joe to charter the flight from Port Angeles to Seattle. It helped that Joe's manager Linc knew a pilot who made frequent trips. That short flight had saved them a long car ride, possible complications at the Hood Canal Bridge—which sometimes remained open for several hours to let government submarines pass through—a ferry ride, then the gauntlet of downtown Seattle traffic. They would still have to endure the commercial flight to Los Angeles and the snarled freeways.

By Wednesday night, Kilo had been offered the part of Tom Lopaka in *Hawaiian Eye*. It was just the pilot, and who knew whether that would be picked up. Only a small percentage made it. Successful pilot or not, there had been major buzz about Kilo's future in TV and film. They'd loved his screentest, and he'd done readings with the rest of the cast and hit it off with everyone. The producers had agreed to work around his schedule. The day after *A Midsummer Night's Dream* closed, Kilo would be off to Oahu for at least two weeks.

"What will you do with your yoga studio if the pilot gets picked up?" Maddie asked when the offer came in Wednesday evening. She was sitting on the plush couch in their luxury suite while Kilo roamed about the room like a caged panther. The producers had spared no expense. It was as if they had known Kilo was their man before they even saw him, before he so much

150

as opened his mouth. Lola must be a better agent than Maddie thought—for Kilo, anyway.

"I'll cross that bridge when I come to it." He was practically bouncing off the walls. The studio had sent over a bottle of Cristal and two champagne flutes. They shared an exuberant toast.

"To your career," Maddie said. "May it be as magnificent as you deserve!"

"Are we allowed to toast yours too?"

"Uh, no, this is about you." She pasted on a smile and clinked his glass. "It's okay, Kilo. You've had a wonderful two days, and we're allowed to celebrate that, even if it didn't work out as well for me." Though far from thrilled with her own L.A. experience, Maddie was determined not to step on Kilo's wagging tail. If she kept the attention on him, he wouldn't delve too deeply into how her meetings and auditions had gone. "I'm excited for you."

His mood had fizzled slightly. "Are you?" He put down his flute. "I'm not an insensitive lout. You seem depressed."

"I'm not, really," she lied, "just tired. We haven't slept much lately, and I don't have a big adrenaline rush of success to energize me."

"Tell me what happened in your appointments. You keep putting me off."

"Huh. You really want to know?" *Because I really don't want to tell you,* she thought.

"Yeah, of course," he said, less certain.

She sighed. "One casting director told me to get veneers."

Kilo nodded. "I have them. Most actors do. Your natural teeth are pretty nice, though. And veneers are an investment, almost as expensive as buying a luxury car."

"Someone else filmed me doing a monologue. That went okay. Then I had to do it again, topless."

"Oh." Kilo put down his glass. "God. I'm sorry."

She sighed again. "Such is the life of an actress with big boobs. Don't worry, I came through. I didn't have to strip entirely. They did want to see me in booty shorts, however. I obliged." She paused. "Then I met the Makos Brothers. Big producers. They asked me to strip. At least they didn't film it."

Kilo was quickly sobering up.

"Did anyone ask you to parade around naked?"

"I took my shirt off," he admitted. "I don't know if you ever saw the original show, but Robert Conrad was always taking off his shirt. And yeah, they wanted to see me in my underwear. I know, not quite the same thing."

He was trying to lighten the mood, and she smiled obligingly. "At least no one tried to cop a feel."

He gave her a heartfelt hug. "Oh, man, sweetie, I had no idea."

"It's okay," she said, patting his back as if to comfort him. "It's over. We're going home tomorrow. I doubt anything will come of it, for me, and do you know what? That's fine. Something else will come up. Another show." *Another catering gig*, she added silently.

"Stick with me, kid, and all will be well."

She'd said enough. She wasn't going to commit to a limited future as Kilo's arm candy, his date at awards shows. "I'm sure you're right," she said finally.

Now, mostly in silence, Maddie and Kilo were driving the final seventy-minute stretch from Port Angeles to Port Townsend. They were cutting it close. As long as no freak traffic jams materialized, they'd arrive just in time to get into makeup for the Thursday night performance. Maddie was exhausted, but once onstage, she'd rally; she always did. Kilo was high on life. Their experiences had been vastly different. Not that she had struck out. It was just that he'd received first-class treatment all the way, and she'd spent long hours in waiting rooms along with many other women who looked eerily like her, only taller and with perfect teeth. Maybe it *was* time to spring for veneers. *Ah, more debt*, she thought.

* * *

Teresa was indulging in the only therapy she allowed herself, retail therapy. If only the high weren't so fleeting. Lately she'd felt so miserable that she'd almost considered real therapy. Yoga had helped, at least in Seattle. Here it would just confuse her more. Unless she could find another studio, and she was very picky. She wanted Vinyasa Yoga with medium flow. Almost all the teachers were too hard or too easy. Teresa was the Goldilocks of yoga aficionados, and only Kilo's studio would do. Not that she'd run into Kilo there. He'd hired two teachers to replace him, and no one knew if they were temporary.

Then, as if summoned by her wayward thoughts like some wily demon on the alert for souls, Kilo stood before her. He was so energized, he practically glowed.

"Hey, stranger," he said.

"Hey yourself." She felt her cheeks heat up and hoped he'd assume the flush was from the cold. She'd been nursing guilty thoughts about him ever since the night of the play. She'd known it would be unwise to attend. She didn't want to admit Kilo was still on her radar.

"How are you?" he asked as if genuinely concerned.

152

"Oh, I'm fine, just dandy." *Uh-oh, too sarcastic?* She ordered her shoulders to relax. "I hear you're on the cusp of superstardom."

He laughed in that dry, sexy way of his. "Uh, not exactly, but I have a shot at something. Join me for a drink?" He pointed toward the window. They happened to be standing next to a hotel with a bar.

She looked at her watch. Four o'clock. Liam and the others wouldn't be expecting her until dinnertime. She didn't see the harm. Wasn't he hot and heavy with Maddie? They were old friends, catching up. *Right.* Her conscience told her to run, but her legs led her to the bar. "Just a quick one."

"New outfit?" He pointed at the bag.

"Uh, yeah," she said, embarrassed. Her wardrobe was yet another sticking point between her and Liam. Especially when she bought expensive designer clothing she had no occasion to wear. He thought it was wasteful and meant she was missing her old life. She just wished some fancy event might present itself. She'd dressed to the nines for the play, and everyone else had been casual. *Pitiful.*

"Can I see?" Kilo didn't wait for an answer. He grabbed the bag and pulled out the cocktail dress. "Ooh … I'd love to see you in this. Are you planning a trip back to Seattle or someplace where they actually dress up?"

"Uh, no."

"Bumps in the road of true love?" No flippancy there.

"Why do you say that?" she snapped.

He took her hand and gave it a little shake. "Sorry. Sensitive subject, I can see that. I always wondered whether it would actually work with you and Liam. You're the proverbial Uptown Girl, and frankly, he's not exactly Billy Joel. Better looking, of course, but not a musician or artist of any kind. Helluva nice guy." He was silent for a moment as he sipped his wine. "Teresa, do you ever wonder whether we could have stayed married?"

She felt the blood drain from her face. "What?"

"If your family hadn't staged an intervention, I mean. It might have worked. You could have toured with me, kept me centered. You would have enjoyed the scene. Seeing various cities, hobnobbing with artists and patrons."

She tried to joke, "Watching you get hit on by your fellow dancers and random women from the audience."

"So what? If you'd been with me, I wouldn't have needed anyone else. Too bad you can't come with me to Oahu. I'd be the envy of the entire cast."

She did not like the way this conversation was going. "What about Maddie?" she asked.

"Listen, I like Maddie a lot, but when it comes to her career, she's conflicted. She could be a big star, if only she were willing to do what it takes to make that happen."

"I hear that's a big price to pay," Teresa said primly, thinking of Maddie's stories of casting couches and nude scenes. "I thought you two were serious."

"I could be serious," he admitted, "but her head is elsewhere. Besides, I've always felt that I'd drop anything and anyone for you. But by the time we met again, you were already fixated on Liam. That day I invited you up, you thought that was just some casual thing?"

Teresa nodded, took another sip of her drink, aspirated some of it.

When she returned from the bathroom after her coughing fit, Kilo acted as if nothing had happened. He took her hand and examined the tasteful diamond ring. "Just say the word. I'm still here for you."

She pulled her hand away. "Kilo, I'm fully committed to Liam. I'm so happy you have this amazing opportunity. You deserve it. The last thing you need is to drag some tarnished old love into your shiny new life."

Kilo chuckled, finished off his drink. "Nice speech. You sound as if you're trying to convince yourself, not me. We could have a blast, Teresa. You'd love L.A. You could be the hostess with the mostest."

She laughed. "Do people still say stuff like that? I can't be a professional hostess. I still need to figure out what I want to do with my life."

"Not if you're the wife of a famous actor. You could become famous for your salons, like in fin-de-siècle Paris. Play the piano for your guests. We could go dancing."

"So now you're a *famous* actor," she tried to joke.

No hint of a smile. "Wait and see."

She finished off her glass. "Don't you have a show tonight?"

"Nope. It's Tuesday. We're Thursday through Sunday only." He threw down a twenty and stood up. "Give it some thought, Teresa. I've never gotten over you." He kissed his fingertips then touched her cheek. "Good luck with everything." He started to walk away, then stopped and turned around. "I know my track record isn't great when it comes to women. But who knows? With you, my love may last forever. Life is so brief."

And he was gone.

CHAPTER 22

"Do we have plans for Saturday night?" Ali asked Teresa, as they walked the twins around the rec room. They still had to hold their arms and balance them, but both girls were amazingly mobile. "Joe and I were planning a belated Valentine's Day party." Joe had been wrapping things up in the studio, promising her a celebration when they could manage it.

Teresa lay down next to Caryn and put on a goofy smile. In a silly voice, she said, "Did you have a restaurant in mind?"

"We hardly ever go into town," Ali said. "With all the recent publicity, it might not be the best time to begin. Joe's going to have to start wearing those ridiculous disguises again."

May Allen came in and sat on the couch. "I thought you ladies had lunch plans with Becca."

"Mama!" Caryn said, reaching for May. Ali winced.

"No, dear, it's May-May," the older woman explained patiently. To Ali, she said, "Don't you worry. They know who their real mama is."

Ali wasn't so sure. On the other hand, taking over the twins full-time was not in the cards. She was barely holding it together as it was.

"Where's Liam today?" Ali asked Teresa.

"He's helping Joe with the new house," Teresa said. "He seems to think the plumbers fuc—, uh, messed things up."

Once they were in the car, headed for the site of the third Fête Sauvage, Teresa said, "Are you and Joe planning to live in the new house?"

Ali kept her eyes on the road. "To be honest, I'm not sure what we'll do. Joe seems reluctant to make too many plans right now."

"You married a retired country music idol, who then decided he wasn't so retired."

" 'The course of true love ne'er did run smooth' and all that," Ali said with a halfhearted laugh. They'd been quoting the play a lot. Ali and Becca had seen it three times now. After opening night, Teresa had passed on further performances, for obvious reasons. It couldn't be easy to see Kilo in all his glory. She hoped Teresa didn't regret letting that ship sail without her. In Ali's eyes, Liam was twice the man, twice the person, Kilo was. No, Kilo was a talented flea, and Liam was a lion. Or an ox. She couldn't recall the details, but there was an Aesop's fable in there somewhere. Did Teresa understand how special Liam was in a fundamental way? The truth was, they had married in haste. So had she and Joe. She certainly wasn't repenting at leisure, as the old adage went. Was Joe? Was Teresa? She and Liam had been arguing more than usual, and that was just in front of Joe and Ali. It had to be worse when they were alone. How could he help but notice how riveted Teresa had been during *A Midsummer Night's Dream*? Then there was the music academy, which Liam was dead set against. And the decision on where they would live. If Teresa bought the school, logic dictated that they settle in Port Angeles. Liam thought Port Angeles was too conservative; he liked the relaxed liberal vibe of Port Townsend. In the meantime, they all just drifted along. Joe no longer raised the subject of the tour unless she asked him directly.

Maddie often entertained them with stories of the various hookups among her cast members. "That always seems to happen," she said. "After about two weeks, the rest of the world just disappears, and you reach for the nearest companion. Especially if they are mounting a charm offensive, and your character is attracted to theirs. People you'd never expect to cheat give in to the temptation. It seems safe, somehow, because you know it will end with the show, and then you'll get back to real life. Not really like cheating." The most recent one had been forty-year-old Theseus and twenty-year-old Hermia, a born-again Christian, both married to other people. If that wasn't proof that *anyone* could cheat, she didn't know what was.

"Uh, Ali, I think we missed our turnoff," Teresa said.

"Oh! Sorry. We'll go the long way." Ali turned right on Washington Street. The new restaurant was a short drive from town, near Manresa Castle.

She parked in front, and they stood outside for a few minutes to assess the progress. It was another huge Victorian, though not centrally located and off the main road, which meant it had less potential as a private house or B&B. It had required major renovations—a new roof, new paint, new plumbing, and of course a modern professional kitchen. A money pit, Joe had confessed. He wasn't worried about his investment, he assured her. For a restaurateur, Jean-Louis was a savvy businessman. He told her not to worry about Liam, either, but she did. Liam's "fortune" was hardly that. Not much more than two million dollars—a drop in the bucket compared to Joe's or even Teresa's assets. They'd set an opening date of May first, which seemed overly optimistic. Ali and Teresa walked in to find Becca sitting at a card table, the only furniture so far, aside from folding chairs. In the already completed kitchen, Jean-Louis was whipping up chicken crepes.

After they exchanged enthusiastic greetings all around, Becca disappeared and returned with a bottle of Pinot Gris. She covered the card table with a simple white tablecloth, and they opened up two more folding chairs. "I hope you don't mind roughing it. At least the heat works now."

Teresa made an "oh please" gesture, waving her away. "With central heating, Jean-Louis's cooking, and a bottle of wine, we won't suffer. The folding chairs even have cushions." She made a show of settling in with a contented sigh. "Quite comfy!"

For a time, Becca enumerated the various setbacks, and much as she made light of everything, Ali saw that the process had been hard on her friend.

"Will you still open on time?" she asked.

"That depends on the décor and the artist who's creating the sign. We're doing replicas of Victorian furniture, which are a lot more durable than the real thing. Tables, chairs, barstools. In the offices, we have boxes of gilded fake antlers waiting to go up when the rest is in place, and more *hommage-to-Delacroix* paintings. Also, the artisans who are installing the bar are running late on their current project. It'll get done somehow." She spoke with determination, needing to convince herself.

"*Mesdames,*" Jean-Louis called out, juggling three plates with all the elan of a former headwaiter, "*le déjeuner est servi!*" He apologized for the absence of a first course. "I must make haste, I'm afraid," he continued, holding Becca's cheeks and giving her a smacking kiss on the forehead. "*Ma blonde,* I'll see you in a few hours."

After his sweeping exit, Teresa said, "All he needs is a cape."

They all stared at her.

"You know, like in Victorian melodramas. When they exit? Never mind."

Becca rolled her eyes. "Everything has to be done with fanfare, even a simple errand. I married a French-Canadian Snagglepuss. You know, 'Exit, stage left!' I wish he'd mellow out occasionally."

The conversation came to a halt as the image of Jean-Louis as Snagglepuss registered.

"Oh well," Teresa said as they wiped away tears of laughter. "I hope the honeymoon's not entirely over."

"It's an adjustment," Becca confessed. "I adore him. Getting the second restaurant off the ground was so exciting. You'd think this one would be too, but I'm wondering if we haven't bitten off more than we can chew, so to speak. So far it's been one really tough cut of wild game."

Ali rubbed her back. "I'm sorry, sweetie."

"Enough about me," Becca said, relaxing at her ministrations. "I appreciate the chance to vent, but now I'm just sick of the sound of my own voice. One of you next."

Ali could tell Teresa was bursting with secrets she wasn't proud of. "You first," she said quickly.

"Oh well, it's winter," Teresa said, as if that explained everything. "We had so much fun on that weirdly spontaneous honeymoon. Reality was bound to be a letdown."

"With Liam?" Becca looked taken aback. "If you throw that fish back, you're going to have women drowning each other to get to him first."

"I didn't say anything about throwing him back," Teresa said, shocked. She took a bite. "Oh my God, don't let these crepes get cold. They are to die for. The sauce has wild mushrooms and bacon in it."

They dug into their lunch for several minutes, making sounds of appreciation as they savored every bite. "Eating this well must go a long way toward keeping the spice in a marriage," Teresa said.

"Yeah, like he cooks for me and him at all." Becca blew out a disgusted puff of air. "He says he enjoys it, but it's been a while. He does bring dishes home from the restaurant, but all too often I find myself eating alone. Sure, I could go in and eat with him and the staff anytime I want. I occasionally do that. He hires almost all men, and they drink a lot and get crude. At least the staff is ethnically diverse. All are eye candy, which is another kind of prejudice. And of course, they don't eat until the kitchen is closed, and that's too late for me. Now, with three restaurants, two of them a day trip away …." She cleared her throat. "We see more of each other here. You'd think that would help. Maybe once the new place is on its feet …."

"I wish you guys would move back in with us," Ali broke in, knowing she sounded too needy. "There's plenty of room. Joe is out all hours working on the album, and now that it's done, he's busy with publicity and rehearsals. The rest of his band is renting a house nearby. He insisted he didn't want to invade our privacy by having them stay with us. I think it's more that they're a wild bunch. He's worried about them damaging things or falling off the cliff after a night of heavy drinking. I wonder how much of the 'rehearsing' involves hanging out at Kelpies. The twins will forget who he is."

"Won't that change once the tour's over?" Teresa asked. "I know it's a lot to ask, but if you can just look at this period as a temporary hurdle, I bet you'll get the old Joe back when it's all over in June."

Ali threw up her hands. "That's just it. It will never be 'all over' again, not unless Joe's voice conks out again, and Lord knows I don't want that. Also, Joe is keen to have another child." Seeing Teresa's stricken face, she laid a hand on her arm. "Oh Teresa, I'm sorry. I know you're trying to get pregnant. I'm so tired all the time, it's like I have narcolepsy. I can fall asleep anywhere. The first pregnancy was hard on my body. I need a few years before I do it again. Joe says let's do it now while we're still young and have energy, then the children will be close in age and the diapers thing will be out of the way."

"Easy for him to say," Becca sniffed. "It's not like much effort is required on his part. Are you using birth control?"

"Yes, a diaphragm. He won't use condoms. It's a constant bone of contention."

"A boner of contention?" Becca offered. Trust her to see the light side. They all laughed.

"It might help my relationship with Liam if I got pregnant," Teresa said. "At least the decision of what to do about the music school would get kicked down the road."

They all shook their heads, and suddenly Becca burst into laughter and slapped her knee. "It's a goddamn pity party. I order you to drink your wine. Eat, drink, and be merry! I'll open another bottle."

"Who's going to drive us home?" Ali asked.

Becca waved her beautifully manicured hand in an airy, devil-may-care gesture. "Oh, we'll figure it out. Jean-Louis will grumble, but he can drive you in your car. Then Joe can drive him back here. I don't care how busy he is."

Becca disappeared into the kitchen and returned with another bottle. "You know, if I might insert a note of reality here …. We are three of the luckiest women on the entire planet."

"If you want to feel sorry for someone, feel sorry for Maddie and David," Ali said.

"What, collectively?" Becca said, frowning at her empty glass before she refilled it. "*Is* there a Maddie and David?"

"I didn't mean to mention them in one breath," Ali explained. "No, there is no collective Maddie and David. I just think their lives are a lot rougher than ours right now, that's all."

"Wasn't Maddie just in L.A.?" Becca asked, looking at Teresa.

Teresa looked at Ali. "You're better informed than I am. I thought she gave you the lowdown."

"She needs someone to confide in," Ali admitted. "Her mom wouldn't understand, and besides, she's not here. No mom wants to hear that you're sleeping with a co-star just to make life easier. She's only with Kilo because the show was going to be torture unless she gave in. He was driving her nuts, whispering stuff, ogling, looming over her."

"That's unprofessional as hell," Becca huffed.

Ali shrugged. "More like business as usual. At least that's what Maddie tells me."

"But Kilo…" Teresa began, then bit her lip.

"…is irresistible?" Ali finished for her. "Becca and I have been wondering if you're feeling just a teensy bit of regret over that one. Yes, watching him on stage is a trip. The entire audience looks like it needs to be hosed down whenever he appears. But Maddie knows the scoop. Kilo is over the moon to finally have his moment in the sun. He can hardly talk about anything else. She feels like such an also-ran in comparison." Ali paused, took another drink. "I know how she feels. I am so afraid that once Joe is on the road, he'll get caught up in that lifestyle again. Even if he doesn't give in and have a fling with some backup singer, he might not be so content to stay at home with his family anymore."

"Oh, Ali," Teresa said, "give him more credit. The road was never his thing, even when he was younger."

"If you say so. There were plenty of wild stories, and he never denied them."

"I want to hear more about Maddie," Becca said, stacking their empty dishes and heading toward the kitchen. "She's better than a romance novel." From the kitchen she called out, "You better tell me she's headed for a happy ending."

Ali stood up and stretched. "Can we take a walk? I know there isn't much to see in the immediate area, but I need to clear my head."

"There are some miniparks with trails tucked here and there," Becca said. "Not many sidewalks, but the streets are wide."

They piled on their winter clothing and headed away from the main road without any particular plan. "What's the temperature out here, thirty-eight?" Teresa asked.

"More like forty-five," Ali said. "With the humidity, it feels colder."

"Sure does," Becca said, pulling her wool cap down over her ears. "Okay, warm me up. Give me gossip. Start with Maddie in L.A."

"They stayed at a first-class hotel, courtesy of the studio—"

"Which one?"

"Do you know Los Angeles?" Ali asked.

"Well, no."

Because Ali had never been to L.A., the name of the hotel hadn't stuck. "I'm not sure. I doubt it was the Beverly Hills Hotel. But pretty ritzy."

"I thought it was one of the chains near Studio City," Teresa said. "The Sheraton or something."

"Anyway, ritzy," Ali continued. She was feeling calmer now that they were breathing fresh air, gazing up into the towering evergreens. "Kilo was treated like royalty, and by the second night there, he'd been offered a contract."

"Maddie?" Becca prompted.

"She did meet the Makos Brothers. You and I might not have heard of them, but they are the hottest producers in Hollywood right now. I guess Maddie's agent Lola has more clout than you'd think. They just happened to be having an open call for new actresses, with no particular project in mind, as least as far as Maddie knows. She couldn't tell anything from the experience. Said they were more or less respectful, although she did have to parade around naked."

Becca's jaw dropped. "What do they cast, porn?"

"No, no," Ali waved her hands in denial. "Everything has nudity nowadays. Or it's going in that direction. You know, like in *Sex and the City*. Maddie said they even made Kilo strip down to his skivvies. Not that *he* minded. And showing off your pecs is nothing compared to parading around with natural breasts. Maddie seems to think it's different when they're fake. Like they don't really belong to you."

"Can't she get a modesty clause written into her contract?" Becca asked. "I read that Sarah Jessica Parker has one of those."

"Maddie doesn't have enough clout," Teresa said.

"No one messed with her, did they?" Becca asked.

Ali shook her head. "Not that she told me. She detected a leer or two, no surprise. She says the casting couch is real, but there's safety in numbers.

The trick is to avoid being alone with anyone with a reputation. Word gets around."

"Do you think she and Kilo will last?" Becca said.

"Not a chance." Ali stopped to get her bearings. "We're not lost, are we?"

Teresa laughed. "You might be, but I know where we are. Are you ready to go back yet?"

"We should have headed down by the water," Ali said. "It's not as interesting here."

"Next time," Becca said. "What about David? What's up with him?"

"Same old," Ali said. "Except that things have normalized with him and Maddie. He's making a big effort not to be weird around her. We all appreciate it. Oh, and Lorenzo is coming for a visit."

This time Becca brought them to a halt. "*Really?*" she said, eyes wide. "His four-year-old son?"

"More like three and seven months," Ali said, "but precocious for his age. Unfortunately, he'll arrive around St. Patrick's Day, a month and a half before your opening and soon after Joe leaves on the tour." *Ugh*, she did *not* want to think about that. Was David just going to leave Lorenzo with her and May Allen, Susan, and the twins while he went to work? What if the little guy wandered off the bluff?

"What are you thinking?" Becca asked. "Oh, I know. *You're* going to be the one supervising Lorenzo." She smiled. "Maddie's show closes this Sunday. Why not ask her to help? Make it worth her while. She needs the money, I'm sure of it."

Ali grinned. "What a great idea. I know Maddie dreads going back to Seattle. Kilo invited her to come with him to Oahu, but she's not interested."

CHAPTER 23

———•———

Saturday morning, Ali took a deep breath and followed her nose to the kitchen. Liam stood by the stove, presiding over a pan of sizzling bacon. She stood unobserved in the doorway for a moment, appreciating the glorious sight of him, the shiny, straight black hair, appealingly shaggy, the broad chest and long legs. For her money, Liam had it over Kilo in spades. If, after seeing *A Midsummer Night's Dream*, Teresa was carrying a torch for her former flame, Ali hoped it would soon be thoroughly snuffed out. Liam deserved so much better. Kilo was now the fantasy, Liam the reality, whereas before it had been the reverse. She thought of her own situation, where she had fantasized for a year and a half about her silent woodsman, JJ, only to find out he was really a country music star from an old Seattle family. Joe's only competition had been the version concocted in her head—the best listener ever, a man retreating from the world and fully self-sufficient. Joe *was* a good listener, but nothing makes you a better listener than being forbidden to make a sound.

Liam turned around and smiled at her, a lock of hair falling across his forehead. "Your eyes have burned a hole in my back."

She rose on tiptoe to kiss his cheek. "I was just admiring you, thinking how lucky Teresa is." Seeing his smile dim, she said, "Don't think for a moment she doesn't realize what she has in you. I know things have been a little rocky lately. Teresa's still trying to figure out what comes next, and old dreams die hard." His stubborn expression disturbed her. She hoped he understood she meant the music school, not Kilo. Turning on the espresso machine, she said, "Can I make you a latte?"

For several minutes, the loud machine filled the silence. Liam removed the last piece of bacon from the grease and put the plate in the oven to keep it warm. Then he sat next to Ali at the counter.

"I don't care if she buys that damn school," Liam said, sipping his coffee. "It's her money. I'm just sick of hearing about it. If she buys it, she'll get a reality check. Then I'll have to hear about how she can't find teachers or doesn't really like teaching. I told her to buy a piano for the Boys and Girls Club in Sequim, see what it's like to teach a few students first. Is that so unreasonable?"

Oh, he really is sick of this subject, Ali thought. "Women hate to be told how to fix their problems. She just wants a friendly ear." He responded with an angry toss of his head. "I'm not a fan of the school idea either," she said in a soothing voice, "and I think your suggestion is excellent. You've planted the seed. Give it a chance to sprout."

"Every time the subject comes up, we argue." He stared grimly into his cup as if it held the answers. "I don't have to say anything. I'm just worried it's about her dissatisfaction with me, not the school at all. If she thinks marrying me was a mistake."

Ali studied his beautiful face with the faint scars that testified to his courage and saw the frustration written there. Was he thinking about Kilo? "Why don't you ask her? Wouldn't it be better to know now, if that's the case? Before you have children?" She couldn't help but compare her own situation. Did Joe feel trapped? Hadn't life been easier with no family obligations tying him down? But if so, why did he want more children? Maybe it was time to ask him what he really wanted. People with small children did get divorced. Especially celebrities. It happened all the time.

Now Liam was watching her. "Are you worried about Joe?"

She nodded. "I don't like feeling like a ball and chain."

He cocked his head in disbelief. "You?" His laugh was genuine. "Joe adores you. He doesn't want to be free. How could you even think such a thing?" His eyes focused on something in back of her, and she froze, knowing Joe now stood behind her.

Joe's arms snaked around her, and for a long moment he held her in a close embrace. "If I could think of some way to wriggle out of this tour, I would," he told her and kissed her neck. "Please, *please* trust me. It will be over before you know it, and it will be June, with a glorious summer ahead."

The door opened, and Teresa entered. "Mm, bacon!" She took a long sniff, then gave Liam a quick hug from behind. "Is David up? What about Maddie?"

"David left early for the clinic, and I assume Maddie will be with Kilo after their show," Ali said.

Teresa nibbled on a piece of bacon. "David has to work on a Saturday?"

Ali shrugged. "Someone called in sick. I invited him to the party, but when he heard it was a belated Valentine's Day celebration, he made a face. He'll be here, though."

"Unless something comes up," Teresa said. Sitting next to Ali, she asked Joe, who was standing at the espresso machine, "Bro, will you make me a latte?" He gave her a thumbs-up as the machine roared to life again. Liam took that as his cue to finish preparing breakfast, french toast made from bread he had baked the day before.

When they were all seated, Joe said, "Why don't you ladies head into town today, go shopping, have lunch, see a movie?"

"I smell a game afoot," Ali said. "I hope you'll find a way to involve David. I don't want him to drown himself while we party."

"That's not David's style," Joe said, then he paused. Ali expected him to make a joke, because that was what Joe did when faced with an uncomfortable subject. Instead he said, "Although I have to admit, I've never seen him this down in the dumps."

"He's certainly changed his tune when it comes to Maddie," Ali said. "I guess what you said hit home."

"It isn't just that. He's opened up to me about other stuff, and I'm starting to get where he's coming from." They all stared at him with open curiosity. "What? I'm not going to tell you what he said. At some point he'll come clean to the rest of you. I *can* tell you that he's worrying over Lorenzo's visit."

Ali and Teresa were strolling around the pier. "Does Joe ever talk about buying a boat?" Teresa asked. "He knows how to skipper a sailboat. All the boys took the summer sailing classes they offered at the Seattle Yacht Club, and our dad owned a boat for a while."

"No. Does Liam?"

"Sometimes. Just a small sailboat, he says. One more way to take a break from me, I suppose."

Ali gave her a hard stare. "Do you really feel that way?"

"Sometimes."

"Did he do anything for you on the real Valentine's Day?" Ali asked.

"He gave me a bouquet of red roses, and I gave him a new pair of boots."

How much had those boots cost, Ali thought, *a thousand dollars?* A thoughtful, if not particularly romantic gesture. What a mother did for a son.

Or a rich woman for her gigolo. She wondered how Liam had responded. Probably with silent consternation.

Teresa was watching a mother and her young son, who was running circles around the picnic table where she sat. She excused herself to use the restroom, and Ali settled on a nearby bench. She wished she could tell Teresa, *Then why are you driving him away?* Shouldn't she stay out of it? Unless Liam and Teresa were in serious trouble. She wondered what Joe had planned for the evening. Would she be disappointed? Not likely. Joe was great at romantic gestures. Really, she was ashamed of herself. She asked too much of her husband, wanting him to sustain the illusion of the impossibly romantic figure stamped on her imagination at their first meeting. He didn't expect the same of her. All those months of pregnancy, when she'd been bloated and grumpy, he had been patient and cheerful, and he'd never stopped wanting her. So why was she so insecure about the tour?

Her sister-in-law emerged from the restroom pale and hollow-eyed. Wobbly, as if someone had just bopped her on the head.

"Teresa? What is it?"

Teresa gave herself a shake. "Um, do you need to stop?"

"Not really." But seeing Teresa's face, Ali was curious as to whether a ghost was haunting the restroom. "Maybe I should."

The room was unoccupied, not even dirty enough to cause shock. She checked for feet under the stalls. No one there.

* * *

It was one thing to act on stage, Maddie thought, but quite another when you did it in real life. The evening's show had been smooth as ever. Kilo was on fire, and the audience gaga for him. It brought the rest of the performances up a notch too. He was a generous colleague, not the type to steal focus by calling attention to himself when the spotlight wasn't on him. No, he elevated everyone's performance, giving them his rapt attention when they spoke, infecting them with his enthusiasm.

So why was Maddie counting the days until it was over? Was she envious of his future? A little. Mostly she felt his detachment from her, from his present life. He had already moved on. After the show, he had a bottle of champagne on ice waiting for them. Veuve Clicquot, not Cristal, but better than average. After they toasted the show, he carried her into the bedroom and took control, as usual. He never just lay back and let her pleasure him. Afterward, he rested on his side, facing her in bed, playing idly with a loose curl. "I like your hair this way," he said. The director had let her grow it out.

They were playing up the gender ambiguity anyway, and it now fell in soft waves almost to her chin. "Have you thought any more about coming with me to Oahu?" he asked in a low voice.

"It's tempting, though we both know you'll be too busy to spend any real time with me. I'd love to go to Hawaii on vacation, but the idea of keeping myself occupied while you work doesn't appeal."

Kilo didn't reply immediately, just stared into her eyes, no sign of his perpetual air of amusement. "It's okay to admit it," he finally said. She waited. "Admit that this ends with the show." She didn't speak. "I don't want it to," he added.

"Maybe not right now," Maddie said finally, "but you're beginning a new phase in your life. I don't see myself fitting into that." She smiled and rippled her fingers over his smoothly muscled chest. "We'll still be friends, right? You're going to meet so many beautiful women, and they'll all want you. How long do you think you'll resist?"

"No one compares to you," he said in the same light tone, tinged with regret.

CHAPTER 24

———•———

FOR ONCE, THEY ALL SHARED the hot tub, clad in bathing suits. Joe acknowledged that he was the only one comfortable with being nude in front of siblings, especially after Ali reminded him that Liam and she were still coming to terms with their adult friendship. To appease him, she had run the suits through a soapless washing-machine cycle to rid them of residue.

By the time Ali and Teresa returned around four, the men had set the scene with red lights shaped like hearts, stuffed mushrooms and beef pasties, and radishes carved to look like flowers. Dinner was simpler, sauteed scallops and rice and salad, with California strawberries for dessert. No one commented on the fruit's blandness. Berries were a gamble this time of year. Ali and Teresa oohed and awed, and the men confessed that the entire production hadn't taken as long as all that—they'd snuck in lunch at Kelpies between. Ali and Teresa had gone to see *Meet Joe Black*.

"I am, in general, pro Brad Pitt," Ali said, as they all lounged in the hot tub, "but this is one of his less-interesting roles. The pacing is sloooow, in spite of Anthony Hopkins, who elevates any movie he's in."

Teresa raised a hand in protest. "I disagree. It had important things to say about life and death."

Ali gave her a sidelong glance, wondering if Teresa was pulling her leg. "Um, shouldn't a movie make *some* sense? Death, personified by incandescent Brad Pitt, singles out this gorgeous, elegantly dressed, wealthy family after how many millennia to finally see what it's all about?"

Joe laughed. "I don't need to see that. Although, any movie with a hero named Joe can't be all bad."

"It's very romantic," Teresa sighed.

Ali kicked Joe's leg. "We know how you guys feel about romantic weepies."

"I don't mind them," Liam said with a shrug. "It's always interesting to see how women think. A lot of screenplays are written by men. If a woman really responds to a movie, that tells you something about the female brain." He paused. "It's not always pretty, of course. Hey!" He held up his hand to ward off Teresa, who had splashed water in his eyes.

"What do you think, David?" Joe kicked his leg underwater. David had been even more than characteristically silent.

"I don't pretend to understand how women think," David said wearily, though with a hint of levity. "I know they appreciate a man who sings." He nodded in Joe's direction.

"You sing," Joe protested. "If you put some effort into it, you'd sound just like me, only lower, 'cause you're the extra-testosterone, supersized version."

David laughed, a rich, rusty sound. "That's me."

"There must be some attentive female doctors at the clinic, or a nurse …" Teresa probed.

"I get flirted with a lot," David admitted. "I suppose I could lure someone into a supply closet like they do on *Saint Elsewhere*. Although it would be safer, in a legal sense, to let them do the luring."

Teresa laughed. "Not a very current reference. But you're right, those TV doctors are a randy lot."

"In Africa we didn't have much access to TV. Our clinic in Sequim is too tiny for random hookups among the staff. If I were working in a really big hospital, maybe." Now both women splashed him. "Stop!" he laughed. "I'm holding out for more than just a quickie in the supply closet." He lapsed back into silence.

Ooh, he's got it bad, Ali thought, wishing for the umpteenth time that David and Maddie would stop resisting their obvious attraction. Joe had implied that David's sexual escapades with his colleagues in Africa would make the *Playboy* channel subscribers blush. Joe had shrugged it off, saying, "What else do you do with yourself when you're unattached and other entertainment options are limited?" Ali's own sexual past being so tame— until Joe came along, that is—Ali had trouble imagining hot sex with virtual strangers.

Joe stood up and reached for his towel. "Ali, you haven't seen the latest work on the new house. Wanna take a look?"

He was up to something, and her heart began to beat faster. *Joe and his romantic gestures*, she thought fondly as she put on her robe. "I'll go in and change first."

"No need for that."

"But it's freezing out here."

Out of nowhere, he produced their fur-lined winter boots. "You'll stay warm for a few minutes," he said, dropping to one knee and helping her into the boots as if he were Cinderella's prince fitting her with the glass slipper. It reminded her of that first time, at the cabin in the woods, the reverent way he'd removed her hiking boots.

She giggled as he curled an arm about her waist and led her toward the new house.

* * *

David, do you have a minute?" Teresa said as they headed inside to get their clothes. "Liam, can I meet you back at the cabin?"

Liam gave her a strange look, then nodded. Teresa wanted to explain, but she could see he was getting it all wrong, and there was no help for it. "I'll just be a moment." She kissed him on the lips, distressed by his dead-fish response. He stepped into his boots, gathered his clothing, and set out up the hill.

"What's up, Sis?" David said when they were alone in the living room. He pointed his red-stubbled cleft chin in Liam's direction. "Everything okay there?"

"Just give me a second. I don't want the furniture to have water stains. You should probably change too."

"I already took off my bathing suit. I'm naked under my robe. See?" David flashed her, and she laughed, averting her eyes, but not before catching an eyeful of David's considerable assets. "The furniture will remain pristine," he promised and made the sign of the cross, as if blessing it.

She ignored the little dig. Like her mother, she worried about stains and wear and tear in the showplace she'd created. Having changed into her suit in the rec room, she didn't have to fetch her clothes from the cabin. She ran down the stairs to pull on her jeans and cashmere sweater.

"Something really weird happened today," she told David when they were both seated in the parlor.

He leaned forward, brow creased with concern.

"I think I saw Ali and Liam's mother."

She saw David's Adam's apple jump. "That's why you didn't want Liam to hear."

She nodded. "Not until we know more. There was a homeless woman in the bathroom. She had a big backpack, and she was no hiker. All layered up in old clothing with the stench of the unwashed. Her teeth were terrible. I still recognized her. I could see remnants of Ali in her, like Cher after thirty years in a chain gang. But it was also the way she looked at me, as if she knew who I was. She could be seventy, not in her fifties."

She paused, and David urged her on with an impatient gesture.

"I asked Ali if she wanted to use the restroom, thinking that might be the best way for her to confront this, but the woman must have left just after I did." She stood up and started to pace back and forth. "David, I have the weirdest feeling she's been keeping tabs on us, that she's waiting for the right moment to confront Liam and Ali. What happens if she expects them to take care of her? She looks awful, but tough somehow, not like someone with one foot in the grave. More like an old crone looking to cash in."

"You're jumping to some awfully dire conclusions based on one brief encounter," David said. "Shouldn't you tell Liam and Ali as soon as possible?"

"Not tonight," Teresa pleaded. "This is a situation to be confronted by daylight."

"Agreed. How about if I talk to Joe tomorrow? We can come up with a plan. The woman seemed to have realized that the timing wasn't quite right, if indeed she means to reveal herself in the near future. Maybe she just wants to be close to her children, to make sure they're happy."

Teresa gave a derisive snort. "For a guy who's seen a lot of suffering and corruption, you sound like Forrest Gump."

"I know, I haven't exactly been the Bluebird of Happiness lately"—he took her hand—"but Teresa, I'm worried about you. You and Liam. I know he doesn't say much—neither do I, for that matter—but he was quiet tonight, even for him. What's up?"

"It's not him, it's me," Teresa said, guilt washing over her.

"Look, this is none of my business," David said, "so stop me if I overstep. It's got to have been difficult living next door to Kilo after what went down with the two of you when you were kids. You were married, for pity's sake, even if it was for only a minute. Now Kilo's the toast of the town."

Teresa had to tell someone. "Kilo asked me to come with him to Oahu," she blurted out.

He scratched his head. "What, out of the blue?"

"We had a quick drink," Teresa confessed. "He said some stuff … to the tune of, I was the love of his life. He'd drop anything and anyone for me. Before he left me, he said, 'Who knows? My love might last forever. Life is so brief.' I can't get it out of my mind." She put her head in her hands, then looked up, fighting tears. "Ali told me later that he'd asked Maddie to go with him already. She refused."

David was scowling. "Jesus, he's supposed to be Liam's friend. More like a snake in the grass." He leaned forward and grasped her arms too tightly as if tempted to give her a shake. "Teresa, don't you see? He's Anatole."

"Anatole?" The name didn't ring a bell.

"You know, Samuel Barber's opera, *Vanessa*. Anatole has an aria toward the end of the opera. It ends with the lyric, 'Who knows? My love might last forever, Erika. Life is so brief.' Mom used to play the recording when we were growing up. You know what he also says in that song? 'I cannot offer you eternal love.' Kilo left that part out of his pretty little borrowed speech."

Teresa felt a sharp pain deep in the pit of her stomach. Cornish College of the Arts had staged *Vanessa* while Kilo was a ballet scholarship student there. It was Teresa's senior year of high school, and she'd ridden the bus to Cornish on Monday and Thursday afternoons to take piano lessons. They'd met in the hallway and started the secret affair that led to their disastrous elopement. Now Teresa recalled him telling her how much he liked the tenor's aria, how he knew he'd be great in that part, if only he could sing.

Why, oh why had she let Kilo get under her skin? Why pursue her at all? Not because he was in love, surely. Although she had believed him in the moment. The man was the very devil. Revenge? She flashed back to the nightmarish scene when Edward had "rescued" her. He'd yelled at Kilo, called him a "loser punk," left him alone in that hotel room where they'd just made love, thoroughly humiliated. How could it not leave a deep emotional scar? After that, they'd spirited her away to Cape Cod, threatened to disown her, and—she'd since figured out—ensured her letters never made it to Kilo.

"Uh, Teresa?" She realized she'd been silent a long while. "Won't Liam be waiting for you?"

"Oh, yes." She popped up. Liam would assume the worst, whatever that might entail. At the very least that she was avoiding him after he and Joe had gone out of their way to create this romantic atmosphere. She felt a surge of love for her husband and deep regret for the last month's brooding, her moodiness and refusal to listen to reason. He was dead right about the school, and she'd tell him so. Only, what would she do now? Stop blaming Liam, for starters.

"Teresa, one last thing," David said as they trudged up the hill toward their cabins. "Do you remember how Erika reacts after Anatole sings that aria to her?"

"Yes," Teresa said. "She refuses him, even though it means a life of weird solitude." She uttered a brittle laugh. "I always thought she was a fool. Who could resist a beautiful aria like that, at least if it's well sung, no matter how little it promised?"

"Goodnight, Ter-Ter," David said, giving her a big hug. "You'll get through this. I'm here for you."

"I know, D.O." She kissed his cheek.

She thought about Erika and Anatole. She still believed Erika should have taken him up on his offer. Only because the silly woman didn't have a Liam waiting for her.

Other than the nightlight in the bathroom, the cabin was dark. Liam was pretending to sleep. Teresa considered rousing him but was too exhausted to try to make things right. It would have to wait until morning.

She tossed and turned but finally slept soundly. So soundly that she didn't hear Liam leave.

CHAPTER 25

———•———

For the new place, Joe and Ali had chosen an exterior design more in harmony with the forest. Dubbed "The Log Palace," it was a magnificent homage to the primitive log cabin where they'd met. It wasn't significantly smaller than the Sea Captain's House, maybe two-thirds its size. A large patio on stilts took full advantage of the view. Inside, it looked more like a modern ski chalet, with vaulted ceilings, gleaming cedar floors, and a river-rock fireplace. So warm and inviting compared to the cold beauty of Teresa's art deco parlor.

Joe swept Ali into his arms and carried her across the threshold. "You're going to hurt your back!" she insisted as he set her down on the sole piece of furniture purchased so far—a black leather couch positioned in front of the fireplace. After turning on the gas flame, Joe sat beside her, her head lying on his lap. Aesthetically, Ali preferred wood-burning fireplaces, but gas was better for the environment and easier to maintain. In the end, she and Joe were surprisingly practical people. She supposed you had to be when you had children. Now, Liam and Teresa, at least Teresa .... *Don't think about them. They'll sort out their differences.*

Stroking her hair, Joe whispered, "The couch is also a pull-out bed. And it's all made up." The way he spoke, it might have been the most intimate endearment, and she giggled. He kept whispering, which was delightfully silly, considering they couldn't possibly be overheard unless the room was bugged. "I don't know why we got a sofa bed. Unless we have ten children and they each have ten children of their own, we will never host so many visitors that some of them have to sleep in the living room."

She whispered back, "For times like this then, when we're too … *comfortable* to move into the bedroom."

"Or until we buy an actual bed," he said in a normal voice, which made them both laugh.

She sighed extravagantly.

"Was that a sigh of contentment or exhaustion?"

"A little of both, I think."

"Want to talk about it?"

"Not really."

"I think it might be better if we did." He combed his fingers through her hair in a soothing motion that made her want to purr. "Clear the air a little."

She waited.

"I love you," he said. "Nothing is going to change that. Perhaps there will be some young thing hanging around the tour who will publicly make a play for me, but no matter what the tabloids report, she will not succeed. If you doubt that, you are welcome to join me on the tour anytime, with zero notice besides the two weekends we talked about. I promise to welcome you with open arms. In fact, you and the girls and May could just tag along for the entire thing. I don't recommend that, because there will be downtime when I can come home for a few days here and there, and hotels are hard on babies and vice versa. Not to mention travel and late nights. I know three months can feel like forever, but they will fly by if you stay busy." His fingers strayed to her shoulders and breasts, his touch gentle as a breeze. "I love you, my sweetest babe in the woods," he whispered.

Ali laughed. "I do love you, madly, but please, never call me that again except in the song."

With a wicked grin, he stood, untied his robe, and let it fall to the floor.

The next morning, they woke to another unforeseen snowfall. Only one or two inches, but enough to make the path down to the Sea Captain's House treacherous. Fortunately Joe had brought winter clothes for each of them.

Expression grim, Joe pointed at the cars parked at the top of the hill. "Brace yourself. Liam's truck is gone, and there are no tracks in the snow. That means he left in the middle of the night."

"The Harley's still there," Ali said, grasping at straws.

Joe shook his head. "We would have heard him leave."

"Damn," Ali moaned. "What the hell do you think happened?"

Joe punched in the code to the front door but found it already unlocked. Teresa was sitting at the kitchen counter, nursing a latte. Ali could see that she'd been crying, though her sister-in-law was one of those women who carried off tears remarkably well. No red nose and only slightly swollen eyes.

Ali kissed her on the cheek but didn't speak until she'd made Americanos for herself and Joe and they were all seated at the counter. It was latish, around nine, and she supposed David had decided to sleep in on his day off.

"Did he leave a note?" she asked.

"Yes. Said he needs time to get his head straight. If I want to go with Kilo to Oahu, he understands." She sniffed, loudly, and Joe passed her the box of tissues. "What the hell?" she went on. "How does he even know that Kilo offered? He asked, but I told him no."

Ali hadn't realized things had gone this far south. Since when had Teresa and Kilo even been in contact? It had to be after Maddie had turned him down. *Shame on Kilo*. She rubbed Teresa's back. "Someone needs to talk to Liam. Not you. Me."

Teresa was sobbing now, shaking her head. "It's such a shitstorm. I've screwed things up so badly that even if I begged Liam to forgive me, promised to get therapy, and followed all his advice, I doubt he'd take me back."

"No way," Joe said, more confident than Ali. "He's crazy about you. It's a misunderstanding. You'll see. Uh, this might not be the best time to bring it up, but if you're looking for a distraction ...." He waited for permission to continue.

Teresa looked at Ali, a question in her eyes, and Ali shrugged.

"If no one's stopping me," Joe said, "here it is. One of my bandmates saw your, um, *our* living room and asked who designed it. After rehearsing here, he's decided to move to Port Townsend after the tour and needs someone to decorate the house he just bought."

This didn't make sense to Ali. "Really? I mean, the living room is beautiful and all, but it's hardly masculine."

"Neither is he," Joe laughed. "Uh, inwardly. Meeting him, you might assume he's a good ol' boy. In truth, he's gay."

Ali held her breath, waiting for Teresa to respond. It made perfect sense. Teresa was born to be an interior designer. Why had no one thought of it before?

Ali turned to Joe. "Sweetie, do you have any idea where Liam might be?"

Why did he look so guilty? "He's working on his house."

Teresa's eyes widened in shock. "*His* house?"

"An investment," Joe said. "He didn't consult you because he was tired of waiting for you to decide what you wanted. He needed a project of his own. You know how he loves a challenge. This place is a doozie. He figured you'd eighty-six the idea." He wrote down the address and passed it to Ali. "Sweetie, why don't you go talk to him? He might not be ready to confront Teresa. I don't think the snow stuck to the streets, and the temperature is already above freezing, so driving won't be hazardous. Teresa and I will stay here. Matthew's coming over at eleven—the guy who's looking for a decorator. I can introduce him to Teresa before we begin the rehearsal."

Knowing Liam rarely slept in—probably hadn't slept at all—Ali left the house as soon as she'd showered and dressed.

* * *

Teresa wasted no time in telling her brother about the homeless woman. "I told David last night. I should have told Liam at the same time. Here you and he went all out on this romantic evening …. He must have concluded I was putting off being alone with him. After all the arguing we've done lately—the stupid music school, my money—that must have been the final straw. I was bursting with that secret, and I didn't feel like I should reveal it to him or Ali until after I'd conferred with you and David. I know it will be a shock." She slumped onto the counter, resting her hot cheek on the cold marble.

He squeezed her arm. "Don't worry, Sis. Things are weird right now, I know. Try not to panic. He sang softly, 'Gray skies are gonna clear up, put on a happy face.' "

She laughed, in spite of herself. "I can always count on you for a good earworm. First things first. What are we going to do about that woman? She's obviously stalking us."

Joe screwed up his nose. "Is she? If she'd approached the house, the dogs would have alerted us. I agree that her presence in Port Townsend is troubling, but it could be innocent. Perhaps she just wants to be close to Liam and Ali."

"She looked like a long stretch of bad road to me," said Teresa. "Sort of like if you took Ali, hunched her over, made her hair long, matted, and gray, and gave her a Cabbage Patch Doll face. She smells like a sewer. If I had to guess, I'd say she was after money rather than looking to renew family ties. I don't want her to become a burden. You know, start depending on us to keep her in drug money."

Joe shrugged. "Hey, it's not like we can't afford it. We don't want to feed her habit, but obviously we can't just ignore her. Don't you think it's better to confront her before she goes to Ali or Liam? She could be hanging around the house Liam bought."

"What's it like?" Teresa asked in a small voice. She hated that her husband had felt compelled to buy it without consulting her. She knew she'd been inexcusably self-absorbed.

"It's a Victorian," Joe said. "You'll like it, I think, when it's done. It's only a few lots away from the house Matthew bought—the one he'd like you to decorate." He handed her a tissue. "You need to give Liam his space right now. You could use this time to get your shit together too."

She blotted her eyes and wiped her nose. "I don't understand how he knew about that quick drink with Kilo. We were the only ones at the bar."

"He saw you," Joe said, "through the window. He told me about it when he said he was considering leaving." At her narrowed eyes, he added, "He swore me to secrecy. Said he might change his mind. I was counting on that. After you left, he quizzed the bartender—a women he's known for a while. Someone who's flirted with him, I gather, and had a reason to make the conversation sound more damning than it actually was."

"Friggin' small town," Teresa muttered.

Joe threw up his hands. "You said it. I tried to tell him he needed to ask you about it before he rushed to judgment. If it hadn't been for the other stuff, he might have. You know, your dithering over the school, your insistence on paying for everything and calling all the shots. The squabbling."

Teresa hung her head. "What now?"

"Let's see if I can locate that woman. My rehearsal is gonna run late, so I can't do anything today. Tomorrow I'll ask around. I know some folks on the police force. She might have come to their notice."

Teresa reached for another tissue. "What do I do in the meantime?"

"Ali and I are going to make a trip to Seattle. We're taking the rehearsals there because I promised Mom a visit before the tour begins. Less than a week. Come with us. Liam's so high and mighty right now. If he realizes you aren't going to come crawling, he might rethink his passive-aggressive approach."

Teresa's laugh was a humorless bark. "Hah. Liam is not that complicated. He doesn't think, he acts. He's not trying to get me back. He's moving on."

"That's not gonna happen," Joe said, giving Teresa's hand an affectionate squeeze. "Right now, he's too mad to think straight. Give him time to miss you. We'll see how he likes it when *you* move on."

* * *

At ten thirty, Ali drove up to the address Joe had given her and parked. For several minutes she stared at the dilapidated, three-story-high Victorian, which might have been the residence of the Addams Family fallen on hard times. She wasn't sure what color it had been once. Now it was gray. Faded and drab, paint like peeling dead flesh. It needed a new roof—this one was solid moss—but she supposed winter was not the best time to tackle outdoor tasks. The yard was a tangle of blackberry brambles and other weeds, with a large rhododendron fighting for air and sunlight in the center. The tree was gnarly, but until it blossomed and leafed out, it would be difficult to determine its health. An apple tree, judging from the bark.

The door was unlocked. "Liam!" she yelled. She doubted he could hear her over the pounding. She gazed around with trepidation. The interior was also in need of a staggering amount of loving care. Was this house even worth fixing? The layout was kind of cool, she had to admit. If it was a distraction Liam was looking for, he'd found it. The pounding paused, and she called his name again.

"Up here!" he yelled back.

"Is it safe?" she called up the stairs.

"Of course, you nitwit," he called back.

Clearly his mood was foul. Ali called forth all her courage and climbed the stairs, which creaked ominously with every step.

When she arrived, Liam removed his safety glasses and mask. Even covered with dust and holding a sledgehammer, he looked magnificent. Liam, God of Home Renovation, with his mighty sledgehammer. He'd been removing old drywall. "Let's go outside," he said. "There's unhealthy crap in the air and no place to sit. Anyhow, I could use a break."

He brushed dust from his clothing and threw on his old barn coat as they exited the house.

"You've been expecting me," she said.

His laugh was bitter. "Ya think?"

Snow still clung to the grass but had melted on the sidewalks and streets, so there was nothing to impede them.

"How much do you know?" Liam asked.

"It's like I'm on a really depressing treasure hunt. I'm just following the clues. But really, what are you guys playing at? It's obvious you love each other."

"Is it?" he barked out. Ali took a step back at the ferocity in his face and voice. "Or has she always wanted Kilo? Or Reynard. Some other guy with extraordinary creds, be they intellectual or creative? I'm just a handsome, damaged guy with normal-guy skills. Teresa seems to think she was destined for more."

Ali scratched her head. "I'm confused. Why do you think she still likes Kilo?"

"Joe didn't tell you?"

"*You* tell me."

Liam made a disgusted sound. "I was walking by a hotel bar on Water Street, and through the window, I saw them sitting together, knee to knee, holding drinks. The bartender flirts with me a lot, so I stopped by later to find out what they were talking about. She said they were pretty cozy, that he asked her to come with him to Oahu. She said no, but she seemed tempted, didn't absolutely shoot him down. He left it open."

"The bartender's not an impartial observer," Ali said. "She *likes* you."

Liam buttoned up his jacket against the cold and crossed his arms defensively. "It confirms the body language I saw. Face it, Teresa is unhappy. And I am too. I should have known it couldn't work out between us. We're too different."

Seeing a woman approach, Ali waited for her to pass, glad for the interruption. She had no idea how to dissuade Liam. He looked so … resolved. Once he decided to move on, he moved on. Old Liam, anyway. She'd hoped this was Liam 2.0, the new and improved version. Not that she blamed him. Teresa's behavior had been bone-headed. Why had she even consented to the drink with Kilo? That guy was a menace. Puck, in fact, Shakespeare's original creation. The imp who dazzled people with his magic dust, made them doubt their own hearts.

The woman stopped several feet away. Liam had his back to her and so was unaware of her presence. The homeless people in Port Townsend tended to hang out nearer to the tourists or campsites. "Liam, do you have any spare change?" Ali said in a low voice. "I don't have my purse on me."

He turned to stare at the woman. "Uh, Ali, there's something familiar …."

Ali's mind had already raced in that direction.

For a time, the three of them faced each other, speechless.

"I want to say … I'm sorry," the woman said finally. She began to amble away.

"You're our mother," Liam said to her back, and she stopped again.

Without turning around, she said, "Yes."

"Biological mother," Ali said, her tone harsher than Liam's.

"Yes, only that." Ali noted her defeated body language.

"I guess we weren't difficult to find," Ali went on.

"No."

"What do you want from us?" Liam said.

No one had raised their voices. To any passerby, the conversation wouldn't sound friendly, exactly, just normal, as in, not fraught with years of heartache and suffering.

The woman didn't answer.

Liam dug out his wallet. "Eighty bucks. That's all I've got on me. Here you go." He walked up to the woman and handed her the small stack of twenties. She hesitated but ultimately took the money. After several more awkward seconds, she began her slow amble back toward downtown.

Liam was poised to follow, but Ali stopped him. "Let her go. Can't you see what she is? Why waste your pity? What are we going to do, move her into one of the cabins? This woman who left us to the mercy of the world and never bothered to find us till now? She could have reclaimed us any time before we turned eighteen. George and Emily never adopted us. She waited until we were wealthy, quasi-celebrities."

Everything she said was true, Ali knew. What was worse, the woman might walk away this time, but she was their problem now. She was the proverbial bad penny who would keep turning up until they dealt with her, one way or another.

* * *

After Ali left, Liam returned to his Herculean task with a vengeance, taking out his frustration on the wall. He was trying to block out Ali's defense of Teresa, her claim Suzie had skewed what she had overheard because she had the hots for him. He was so used to women wanting him. When was the last time he'd been taken for granted? Never, that's when.

He missed Teresa already—the Teresa he had met in Israel, the Teresa of their honeymoon. Wasn't she still there? He knew he hadn't been supportive of her, and he understood enough about women—intellectually—to hear the truth in Ali's words, that women didn't want to be told how to solve their problems. Men didn't either.

What he really wanted was to apply this jackhammer to Kilo's too-pretty face. He'd never poached another man's woman, and he expected the same of his friends. Kilo was no friend. Maybe he never had been. While Liam was being frank with himself, he might as well admit that he'd only befriended Kilo to defang him, so he'd think twice about making another play for Teresa. "Great plan, you idiot," he mumbled to himself.

And now their *mother* had reappeared? The universe never just knocked you over, it kicked you while you were down, at least in his experience. As if Teresa's betrayal weren't enough to deal with; now he had a sorry excuse for a mother, sorrier than in his wildest imaginings.

He thought back to waking up from the coma, hardly recognizing his own grotesquely swollen face in the mirror. The relentless pain, the long recovery. The brutal training camp, the mission to "rescue" his Israeli "sister." Arriving in Port Townsend, he'd been over the moon. Life would be a bowl of cherries from now on. Forget the bowl of cherries. Once he'd won Teresa, it had been a whole friggin' fruit basket—a horn of plenty with enough bounty to please the gods.

Lesson learned. He'd never stop loving Teresa, but maybe he could stop wanting her. David seemed to have resigned himself to Maddie's rejection, and that couldn't have been easy. Or had he? The last time Liam had stopped by David's cabin, he'd noted the nearly empty bottle of Scotch. David was coping on the outside, barely. Inside, he was a wreck.

He looked around at all the work yet to be done on this rattrap. When he was a kid, hard labor had gotten him through many a slump. Then he'd been resigned to a bleak future. That's what he told the kids at the FOSSP residence: "This too shall pass." For how long, though? Good things passed too. What he should have said: smooth sailing is a myth. There will always be rough spots, the occasional storm. The question was, was this a storm he could ride out? Or should he cut his losses and swim for shore?

Don't think about that now. Don't think about it tomorrow. Don't think at all.

He slammed into the old sheetrock with renewed vigor.

CHAPTER 26

———◆———

By popular demand, the run of the play had been extended.

The studio gave Kilo the extra week but asked that he fly to L.A. early Monday morning and stay through Thursday afternoon. He'd have a costume fitting and a table read with the cast of the *Hawaiian Eye* pilot. This time they'd laid a virtual red carpet for the journey, from the chartered flight out of Port Angeles to the limo into Los Angeles. He'd asked Maddie to come along, an invitation she saw as perfunctory. He had to know she had no real interest in continuing their "relationship," if you could call it that. She sensed he wasn't ready to let go, but his ego forbid him to beg. His lovemaking Sunday night smacked of desperation.

She supposed they'd continue until closing as "friends with benefits." It was the easier path.

On Tuesday morning, as Maddie wandered aimlessly along the beach at Fort Warden, her parka zipped to the chin and a wool beanie pulled low over her head, her cellphone went off. Glancing at the caller ID, she braced herself for a talk with her agent.

She pulled up her hat and pressed the phone to her ear. "Hey, Lola!" The voice was too muffled to hear properly, but the woman's excitement registered. "Hold on a minute." Maddie raced toward the nearest ruined cement fortification that dated back to the world wars. Inside, the howling of the wind lessened just enough that she could hear. "Lola, are you still there?"

"Where are you?" the agent complained. "What's that noise?"

"The wind. I'm walking on the beach."

"You must be freezing your butt off." Lola sounded disgusted, as if questioning why anyone would suffer wind and cold unnecessarily. Lola was a fair-weather person in all matters, including her friendship, which was only gifted to her more successful clients. Today she was way chattier than usual. "Sweetie, I have great news. You're gonna be in a movie!"

"Oh my God!" Maddie screamed, because it was expected. She prayed they weren't going to make her fly out before the play ended. She didn't want to be *that person*, the one who screwed over everyone else when opportunity knocked. This show had no real understudies, though it was understood that one of the shorter male fairies would take over for her if she died or was at death's door. No other catastrophe would warrant bowing out. If she lost her voice, someone else would speak her part as she mimed it. "The show must go on" was even more of a reality in low-budget theater.

She waited with bated breath for details, fighting dread that the project would somehow compromise her. All Lola cared about was money.

It was a small role in a high-profile project produced by the Makos Brothers. The movie was titled *Insanity*. *Hmm*, Makos Brothers—the guys who made her parade around naked—and a title like that. There would definitely be nudity. *Ugh*.

"You're in the opening scene," Lola explained. "You and George Reed Masters. Yeah, I know, George Reed Masters! How exciting is that? He is the 'It' guy right now. He saw your screen test and wanted you in his movie. Can you believe that?"

"You said it was a small role," Maddie said, keeping her voice even. She didn't want hype; she wanted the facts.

"Yeah, you get killed at the end of the scene. You're staying over at his apartment, and he goes out for bagels. You hear knocking, assume he's forgotten his key, and when you approach, shots are fired through the door. Bang! You're dead." Lola paused, waiting for a reaction. Before Maddie could think of a response, she added, "It's a long scene! And you'll be featured in a few flashbacks, from the bar where you meet the night before. Remember Sela Ward in *The Fugitive*? Kind of like that. But better. It's only a two-week commitment, and you'll get to join SAG. The initiation fee will cut into your pay, but hey, it's a start. And it costs less when you're already a member of Equity and AFTRA."

"Lola, it's great and all, but can you specify exactly what that scene entails? Do I have any dialogue, or am I just walking around naked?"

Uncomfortable laughter. "You're not *buck* naked. You'll be wearing his shirt and panties, I promise.

"But my breasts will be exposed."

"Well, *yeah*. But there's dialogue."

"You think it's a good career move?"

"Sweetie, we're talkin' A-list cast. Not some low-budget trash with a lotta unknowns doing degrading things. It could launch you, totally. Don't worry, everyone does nudity these days. With your body, you don't really have a choice. Oh, and they know there isn't time for veneers, but they want someone to work on your teeth. Bonding is cheaper, a lot less drastic, and can be done in one day. It's not like your teeth aren't white, just a little crooked. Still, get 'em whitened while you're at it. And lose five pounds. The camera puts on weight."

After she hung up, Maddie plopped down on a log and shuddered, but not from the cold. She'd known that her first film project—if it ever materialized—would be something like this. She sighed. *Here we go.*

She'd fly to L.A. the same day Kilo flew to Oahu, and their filming dates were remarkably similar. The movie was already in production, which meant she was a last-minute replacement for someone who had dropped out—or been ousted. Two weeks of filming in L.A.; then she'd return to Seattle and see what else materialized. A project like this, even if everything went smoothly, wouldn't translate into instant success. There would be pre-screenings where they solicited audience feedback. The moguls wouldn't come to any conclusions about her performance until their private opinions were seconded by the paying public. She gazed out to sea, dreading the future. Her life was about to take a crazy turn. She thought of George Reed Masters, who'd started his career as an action star but recently was taking on meatier projects, according to the interviews. He was married to another A-list star, Helena Richards, a blonde beauty with an aristocratic air and a Hollywood pedigree. Her father was an Oscar-winning director. Maddie couldn't think of a single nude scene *she'd* done. George Reed Masters didn't have a rep—he wasn't one of those actors, like Omar Shariff or Sean Connery, who were notorious for sleeping with their co-stars. Besides, the marriage was new, and Maddie was a peon, not a co-star. She didn't see him pulling her into his star wagon for a quickie.

Maddie hadn't been back to the O'Connell family compound since the previous Wednesday. Riding in on her Vespa, she noted that David's car stood alone in the driveway. In greeting her, the dogs nearly levitated with happiness, wagging their tails at near-lethal velocities, happier to see her than usual. That meant their favorite humans, Liam and Teresa, were out. Both

Liam's truck and Harley were gone. Joe's car, too. Where was everyone? Not that Maddie was in the loop. Face it, she'd basically been treating her cabin like a crash pad—not checking in or bothering to keep them apprised of where she was. She'd have to remedy that.

No signs of life at the Sea Captain's house. She made a meager meal of leftover chicken and half a baked potato. She couldn't believe she had to lose weight. *Jeez*, she was only ninety-five pounds as it was. Did they want anorexic? Taking advantage of the empty house, she put on her bathing suit and robe and headed for the hot tub. Unless he was in his cabin, David might be lurking nearby, or she'd have risked using the hot tub naked.

As it happened, he was already soaking. He hadn't bothered to follow Joe's feather system and mark his presence, so she opened the gate without expecting company.

"Oh!" She backed up a step. "Hi. I'll just—"

"It's okay," David said. "If I'd known you were coming home, I'd have stuck my feather in the board." She turned to leave. "This is ridiculous. Come on in." He splashed the surface like you might pat the seat beside you.

She was glad she'd worn a suit. She noted his efforts not to react as she took off the robe, gratified that he didn't avert his eyes. She wanted him to want her. She'd figured her defection to the Kilo camp had nixed any chance of winning over David. Maybe she was wrong.

"Where is everyone?" she asked as she eased into the water.

"Ali, Joe, Teresa, May Allen, Susan, and the twins all took off for Seattle."

"Liam stayed behind? I didn't see his truck or his Harley when I came in."

"The jets just timed out," David said, pointing to the control panel. "You're closer. Will you switch them back on?"

As she complied, she realized he was naked. And tracking her every move.

"Liam left Teresa," he said as if the guy had only stepped out to go the grocery store. "He bought a Victorian in town and is renovating it. I'm not sure where he's staying. That house is in rough shape, only fit for rodents. I've been helping out where I can."

"Whoa." Maddie knew things had been rocky of late. Nowhere near the breaking point. Not that she'd been around to notice.

"Don't keep your bathing suit on for my sake," David said. "I won't tell. I'm not wearing one."

"You're serious?" His expression revealed nothing. Her move. She decided to call his bluff and remove the suit, first the straps. She wriggled out of it with deliberately slow, nonchalant movements. All he could really see were her shoulders and the top of her breasts. Tossing the suit aside, she rose out of the water enough to flash him and heard his sharp intake of breath. What the hell was she doing? *He'd* started it.

"I take it you and Kilo are done?" he said, studiously bland.

"Why do you say that?"

"Apparently Kilo invited Teresa to come with him to Oahu."

He'd meant to shock her, even deliver a blow, but he didn't succeed. Maddie had turned Kilo down, hadn't she? The guy needed sex, especially while riding this wave of success. It was his coping mechanism, his valium. He was a bona fide sex addict, and she'd known a lot of them.

"You don't seem surprised," David said.

"Oh? No, I'm not," she said, leaving it at that.

"He told her you'd turned him down."

"Yes."

"What will you do after the play closes?" His eyes burned into her. They were closer together in the water. Who had been the first to move? She wasn't sure. It could have been her.

"I have a minor role in a movie."

A spark of emotion. Surprise? Disappointment? "You don't seem excited."

She shrugged. "I know, I should be. I'm more worried than excited. Imposter Syndrome, maybe."

"That's silly," he said. "You're an excellent actress."

"Stage acting is a lot different from film acting. Although *acting* may not be the main requirement of this role."

He must have detected the bitterness in her voice. "Uh-oh. R-rated, huh?"

"I hope not. More like PG-thirteen. Not that I'm surprised." She didn't bother to elaborate. He clearly got it.

"Are you sure you want to do it?"

For a moment, the words "do it" seemed to apply to the present moment rather than the movie. After a pause longer than some commercials, she said, "It's not porn. It's a legit movie. I'm just worried about what might go wrong."

"Such as …?"

They were almost touching.

"The Makos Brothers are notorious. At least one of them is. I'm not sure how to keep out of his path. George Reed Masters seems like a good guy."

David blew out a breath. "*He's* the star? That *is* an important movie." He appeared to give it some thought. "Can you carry pepper spray with you?"

She snorted. "I wish that were an option. Great way to be out on my ass quickly."

"What's the movie about?"

"They haven't sent me a script yet. Maybe they won't. It's not as if I need to prepare myself as an actor. My character gets shot dead at the end of the first scene. There are some flashbacks to the evening their one-night stand began. At least I'll have a name other than Murdered Girl Number One. Looks better on the résumé."

David grinned. "That doesn't sound like a significant time commitment."

"Two weeks. Given the short notice, I'm fairly certain I'm replacing someone who didn't work out. My agent wasn't clear on that. Could be she carried pepper spray."

"Will you come back here after it's over?" David was whispering, and so close, she could feel his warm, sweet breath on her face.

Their bodies touched, and he reached for her, his hand settling on her waist, where it lingered. He expected her to pull away. She didn't.

"I might," she said in a strained voice. "If I have a reason to."

His hand cupped her breast and gave it a gentle squeeze. He closed his eyes, and his lips parted. He was breathing faster. So was she. He drew her to him until her legs straddled his waist, kissing her mouth softly, then harder. His hands kneaded her breasts.

With a groan, he pushed her away. "We can't do this. Not here. Besides, I need a cold shower." Seeing her confusion, he laughed. "Don't get me wrong. I'm overheated, that's all. And it's unsanitary—or something—to make love in a hot tub. Let's get out of here."

"What about—"

"What? Who's to stop us? Kilo? Sylvia? Unless you go and blab on us, none of our nosy but well-meaning friends or family has to know anything about this."

Did that mean this would be a one-time thing? If so, should she stop him? It did seem too good an opportunity to turn down. Not one her better judgment would deny her. Because she and Kilo had not officially called it quits. The show would run for one more long weekend, and the atmosphere would be awkward once Kilo realized there would be no more post-show sessions at his place.

Lifting her into his powerful arms, David carried her inside the Sea Captain's house with such ease that she might have weighed no more than a log to be tossed on the fire. The dogs greeted them as they left the hot tub enclosure, but sensing their presence was unwanted, headed back down to the rec room.

David carried her into the guest bedroom where she had stayed until after New Year's, laying her on the bed. "Damn," he said, "no condoms. Be right back." He ran to his cabin and returned so quickly that Maddie figured he'd been a blur of movement in the night.

When he reached the bedside, he hesitated. He was breathing hard, so she took the condom—a magnum XL, no surprise—and slipped it on his full erection. "Your cock is a work of art," she whispered, kissing the tip. "Can I have it now? I'm ready for you."

He lay down beside her. "Really?" He slipped two fingers inside, circling her sex with his thumb. "You're so small, and I don't want to hurt you. Ah, you're so wet …." He moved his fingers in a slow circle, and she moaned.

"Yes, really," she said and guided him in. It was a tight fit at first, but he entered her slowly, giving her time to relax around his girth. "Oh!" she cried. "That's feels incredible." He was so large that even the indirect friction was stimulating her to orgasm. She'd never experienced anything like it. He began to move inside her, and the pleasure was so intense she had no choice but to surrender to it, hearing someone—was it her?—murmuring incoherent sounds.

He kept kissing her as they made love—tender, tasting kisses—his strained face telling her that holding off on orgasm required a major force of will. "I'm going to come," he whispered, "is that okay? We have all night."

She nodded, and after he groaned his release, he nearly crushed her with his powerful body. He rolled away and lay on his back, gasping for breath. "God, I'm sorry. I should have lasted longer. I was too excited. I'll make it up to you."

"I didn't mind," she said, smiling. "Your cock is … I don't know how to say it."

"Magic?" He actually blushed. "Please pretend I didn't say that."

"It *is* magic," she said in all seriousness. "I gather you've heard that one before."

"A time or two." After a moment of silence, he went on, "You must think I'm an oaf. When it comes to you, I fall apart." Once his breathing had calmed, he knelt in front of her and draped her legs over his shoulders. His tongue found her most sensitive spot and swirled. She could have come right then and there, but he sensed when she was close and pulled away, returning each time to bring her infinitesimally closer to the edge. By the time he moved in for the final onslaught, her orgasm claimed her with such force that she almost blacked out.

When she recovered enough to speak, she said, "Where did you learn to do *that*?" She stared at him in wonder.

He chuckled. "One of my girlfriends was bisexual. She was a good teacher." Intending her question to be rhetorical, she laughed too. "I've got some other tricks up my sleeve," he promised. "I have a lot to prove after that first time."

"I need a moment," Maddie said. "That last little trick made me get why they call it 'the little death.' "

"Your eyes rolled back in your head," David said with a grin. "I was worried for a second there. Thought I'd killed you literally."

Her laughter was giddy. "*You*, on the other hand, are still very much alive." She wrapped her hand around his enormous erection.

He gave a low chuckle. "Ready when you are."

CHAPTER 27

WHERE AM I? MADDIE THOUGHT, the next morning. As her surroundings came into focus, she remembered. The agony and the ecstasy. Patting the bed next to her, she confirmed that David was gone. It was eight o'clock, which was when his shift started. He hadn't woken her up or left a note. That meant there would be no reassurances until, possibly, tonight, when he returned. They hadn't exchanged cell numbers. It was Wednesday, and the theater was dark. He wouldn't be keeping her in suspense for long.

What had she done? Embarked on another sexual relationship without ending the last one, that's what. Not that she believed for a moment that Kilo, flying solo, wouldn't be capitalizing on his newfound status with the local talent, be they call girls, script girls, co-stars, or Lola herself.

Why had David been so ready to bed her now after professing his profound reluctance Christmas Eve? No headaches last night. Ever since that night, she'd wondered if being sexually aroused triggered his migraines. Obviously not, given that quip about his "magic" cock. Just what had brought on the migraine? He was a doctor. Wouldn't he know?

She recalled all those times she'd made love to Kilo while fantasizing about David. Her main fear was that he'd decided she was someone you could fuck with impunity then abandon when someone more suitable came along. Why had he made a point of saying no one had to know?

They hadn't slept for hours. He had the stamina of an Olympic athlete. She couldn't help but compare this marathon to the one with Kilo. After David had given the term *mouth organ* new meaning, she'd returned the favor with interest and discovered that, unlike Kilo, David didn't always need to be in control. It had felt *mutual*. With Kilo, she might have been the center of a performance-art piece. Then she'd taken the lead, riding David for at least twenty minutes before they both climaxed. She wanted to tell him he was the best ever but was afraid it would confirm his suspicions that she'd done this *a lot*. Being the best might not lessen the sting. She'd learned the hard way not to discuss past lovers with current ones.

She rolled out of bed in search of coffee. Snowflakes were thick in the air again—they'd had more than usual this winter—and was worried David would get stuck in Sequim, leaving her and the dogs alone for the night. As if summoned by her thoughts, the canine buddies appeared at the kitchen door. They knew better than to enter; they wanted her to either come out and play or join them downstairs in the rec room.

"Come on, fellas," she said, throwing on her parka. "If we're going to play ball, we'd better do it now, before the snow traps us all inside."

* * *

Teresa laid down the pack of cards and leaned back on the couch, staring into the gas fireplace. She had been playing solitaire for at least an hour. It bored her silly, and she always lost quickly even when she cheated, which was her custom. However, it was one of the only ways she'd found to mute, or at least turn down, the vicious voices from her conscience telling her all the ways she'd blown it with Liam. They wasted no time in haranguing her again. Joe had been a little too frank with her about his conversation with Liam, mentioning her husband's bitter insistence that he was neither intellectual nor creative enough to keep her interested. She thought of the intellectual and creative men she'd known and scowled. The kind of focus that came with spectacular success in those fields usually left those men stunted emotionally. Thus the revolving door of wives and lovers. No matter what he believed, Liam still fascinated her. She could never get enough of him. His skills were anything but the normal-guy variety. How many normal guys could fix anything just by taking it apart or build a staircase, chair, or table without written plans? How many normal guys—well, American ones—knew French and could charm just about anyone if they set their mind to it? How many normal guys volunteered to help their friends with backbreaking projects, knowing there would be no credit or compensation, maybe even no gratitude? How many could throw knives like a circus performer? So what if he didn't play an instrument or have an Ivy league education? Or a university degree. With the right opportunities, Liam could have been a structural engineer or even a rocket scientist. Why had she never taken the time to tell him how much she appreciated him? Instead, she'd obsessed over her own failure to find an identity other than social butterfly, to do something with her facility at the piano. Her fancy education had left her with zero practical skills because she'd never needed to make a living. She couldn't even cook. Liam could. His hard-luck life had made him totally self-sufficient.

Damn this couch. She looked at the expensive, intricately woven cream-colored fabric and punched the stiff, unyielding cushion. Her mother's living room was not designed for actual living. A showplace. Like the parlor she'd created for Ali and Joe. Why hadn't she accounted for their personalities? As usual, it was all about her. That had to change, even if Liam never took her back.

At least Matthew appreciated her ideas. That meeting at the compound had been the one bright spot of the last *mense horribilis*. Make that, *two* horrible months. Too bad she couldn't just say, "Here, Matthew, take Joe and Ali's living room if you like it so much. No one else other than Mom or Sylvia seems to care for it." Matthew wanted his entire house decorated art deco style. What a great guy. If Joe hadn't told her he was gay, she would never have guessed. He was tall and handsome in a regular-guy way, Rock Hudson, but softer at the edges. Same quiet, confident masculinity. A little like Joe, minus the killer charisma. Plenty of charm, certainly, but not what you'd call star quality. Maybe he didn't want to be a star. He seemed utterly content with his low-key life as a session bassist and guitarist who occasionally toured. He didn't have a romantic partner and claimed he didn't care if he ever did.

Matthew had given her photos depicting each room in his house and a copy of the architectural plans. She'd started collecting samples, researching pieces of art and furniture, and visualizing different rooms. That would be all, for now. Their little group would return to Port Townsend before the tour commenced so she could view the layout in person and take her own photos before Matthew left town. She'd get a glimpse of the home Liam had purchased at the same time. If only she could do it without her husband's knowledge. It occurred to her, briefly, that she could ask Matthew to pretend they were dating. To make Liam jealous. *No, no.* That was the sort of thing that had brought them to this pretty pass. Liam needed to realize he could trust her, not suspect she was moving on to yet another creative genius.

Rain pounded against the windows, and there was an occasional clap of thunder followed by sheet lightning. Joe materialized next to the window as if beamed in, *Star Trek* style.

"Wow, you *are* wallowing," he said with a disappointed shake of his head. "I've been standing here forever."

She narrowed her eyes. "No, you haven't."

A flash of teeth. "Only a minute or two." He plopped down next to her then squirmed with discomfort. "God, I hate this couch. Whenever I sit on it, I can hear it complain." In a squeaky voice, he said, *"Get off me, lard ass!"*

Despite her mood, Teresa laughed. "It's held up well," she said in its defense, giving it a gentle pat.

"That's because it's possessed by the devil, and no one sits on it longer than ten minutes." He scooted over closer and draped an arm over her shoulder. "How are you holding up, T-girl? I see you've been spending the afternoon productively." He indicated the deck of cards.

"Solitaire is meditative for me. What time is it?"

"Almost five. Rostand is making prime rib." He took a deep, appreciative whiff. "Ah, garlic."

"I thought you were rehearsing."

"We're done for now. Tour doesn't start until mid-March. We'll have a few brush-up sessions in Port Townsend before we leave. Ali and I are thinking of heading back the day after tomorrow. Monday. You?"

"The weather sucks in both places," Teresa grumbled.

"Other things do too," Joe said. "I take it you've heard nothing from Liam?" She shook her head. "I haven't, either, but Ali has spoken to him a few times." Teresa perked up. "Nothing about you, I'm afraid. He's talked to their mother—her name is Nancy—a few times. He says she comes by and he gives her money. He has no idea what she does with it, but she doesn't seem high to him. Or drunk. Just disoriented. After talking to her, he's amazed she found her way to Port Townsend. She tells him conflicting stories about her life, as if she made half of it up or just can't recall. She went up to Alaska for a job and stayed. Or she followed a boyfriend to Hawaii."

Teresa frowned. "She could have done both. It's been a while."

"She rambles. She's either mentally ill or her brain is fried."

Teresa felt terrible for Ali and Liam, wished so much she could be there for her husband, who was bearing the brunt of the Nancy problem with such maturity. If only their birth mother could have been like Duncan, the dream parent they might have wished into existence. Instead, she was this sad, broken figure out of their nightmares.

Joe nudged her affectionately. "What are you thinking?"

Tears stained her cheeks. "That she's the mother of their nightmares."

"I wouldn't say that," Joe said. "A 'nightmare' would be a scheming, conniving parent hoping to blackmail us all. She's just a sad homeless woman groping for a lifeline."

Teresa wasn't so sure. The conniving version might be hiding behind the hapless one. Hadn't she detected a greedy gleam in her eye? A neglected mother would make for a dandy tabloid exposé.

"We have to do something," Joe went on. "Liam asked her how he could help, offered to put her up in a motel, only, the motels in town would require her to have better hygiene, and he doesn't know how to get her there short of taking her home with him." Joe frowned. "He's not ready to trust her to that extent."

"Where is *home* for him?" Teresa asked. "From what I hear, the Victorian he's working on isn't habitable."

"He's renting a room in someone's basement. He didn't offer details."

"He didn't just move out on the spur of the moment," Teresa said. "He'd been planning it."

"Not a set plan," Joe said, carefully. "A contingency plan, maybe. After he saw you with Kilo at that bar, he was waiting to see what would happen next. The night he left, he believed he had his answer. That's what he told me."

"Only because I was talking to David about Nancy," Teresa said. "He must have thought I didn't want to come home to him. That I was hoping he'd be asleep."

"Ali explained that to him, but he's still convinced you're both better off."

"*Both*," she repeated. "How *dare* he decide for me."

"Give him time." Joe mussed her strawberry-blonde curls. "He'll come around."

"You think so, do you?" Their Grace Kelly-lookalike mother was standing in the doorway, her blonde weave caught up in a smooth chignon, her makeup flawless, her cream-colored silk pantsuit wrinkle free. "Do you really want him to 'come around,' Teresa?" Her voice was surprisingly gentle. "I know he's exciting. Who wouldn't respond physically to a man like that? But you're young. Admitting that it was a mistake might be best. You are very different people."

Teresa shut her eyes. She did *not* want to hear this. She'd been happy with Liam, *so* happy. It was her fault he'd left. She had pushed him away. Why? Out of fear he'd leave anyway? To test his commitment?

Joe raised a quelling hand and said in a firm voice, "Mom, Teresa doesn't need to hear this right now. And, for the record, I don't agree. You've never taken the time to get to know Liam. There's so much more to him. He's quiet, that's all, so you've taken him at face value."

Their mother had assumed a Wonder Woman stance, hands on hips. "Then why was he so ready to leave?"

Joe looked at her sister. "Could be he thought that's what Teresa wanted."

Teresa covered her face with her hands. "Stop it, the two of you. I'm beating myself up enough as it is."

"One more thing," her mother said, raising a rigid index finger. "You could get an annulment, claim the two of you never intended to have children. That's a valid reason in the eyes of the Church. If indeed the Church even acknowledges your union. You'd still need a legal divorce."

"*Enough*, Mother," Joe told her. "Teresa is all too familiar with annulment, thanks to you and Edward. She also knows Liam wouldn't fight it."

Carrie pursed her lips, the dig having found its mark. "Too bad you didn't get a prenup."

Teresa whipped around to confront her mother. "Liam doesn't want my money."

"No? We'll see. That house he's renovating might prove to be a money pit. And then there's his investment in Jean-Louis's restaurant." Teresa stared at her mother. Why did it still surprise her that she was so well informed? She didn't believe Joe or Ali had shared those tidbits. Unruffled, her mother smiled, pleasantly diabolical. "Cocktails, anyone? Join me when you're ready. I'm going to check on dinner."

As if having waited for the coast to clear, Ali came in carrying an open bottle of wine and two glasses. "Joe can get his own beer," she said, nodding at him. "I am a Saint Bernard with her barrel, responding to an emergency call in the Alps." She winked. "Ruff!"

Teresa accepted the glass gratefully, smiling at Ali's attempt at humor. "No sight was ever more welcome."

Ali toasted her. "Come home with us on Monday. Whatever happens, being away will only make things worse. You have to face your demons." She took a long sip of her own wine. "I also have a demon waiting, a she-devil. Liam thinks she's harmless. I'm not so sure. We'll face our demons together. And perhaps it'll all turn out to be some harmless masquerade."

Teresa pictured a big Mardi Gras party. At midnight they'd remove their masks to reveal … more masks. Or a reality even scarier than the one in her imagination.

CHAPTER 28

MADDIE LAY ON THE BED in her cabin, icing her aching jaw. She'd spent the day at the dentist having her teeth "bonded." A tedious several hours, with the dentist talking her ear off about Los Angeles, the history of cosmetic dentistry, and his reasons for moving his family to Port Townsend. She would pay for the procedure in installments.

After she got home, she stared at her teeth for a good ten minutes. A smile for the ages. The dentist had warned her that bonding could be less reliable than porcelain veneers, and that she should still consider them down the road. They didn't look like her own teeth anymore. Like fake breasts. Perfect, but not hers.

While the dentist worked his magic, she'd only half listened. She'd noticed that dentists didn't expect, or desire, a response beyond vague indications that you're listening … or that your agony wasn't too much to bear. He was entertaining himself. God, that job had to be dull. What about all the patients with low pain thresholds, bad attitudes, and fetid breath? Meanwhile, her thoughts kept straying to David. Did he regret last night?

Ridiculous, this nagging anxiety. She had no interest in her magazines or the book she'd started. Even if the worst happened—however that might manifest itself—she would soon be able to escape. If you could call the looming trip to L.A. an escape. Escape from Kilo and possibly David—if that's what he wanted.

She heard his car come in at six, around the time she expected him. The dogs had kept her occupied, their goofy enthusiasm for the ball never waning. David waved to her as he headed toward his cabin. She wished he'd blown a kiss, done something to acknowledge the change in their—dare she say it—relationship.

"Okay, guys, that's enough," she said to the madly wagging tails. "I'm beat." They whined, but that was the extent of it. Such good boys.

She went into the house to see what she could scare up for a meager dinner. Without Liam to stock the shelves, the cupboard was bare.

"I have takeout," the deep voice behind her said.

She closed the door to the refrigerator slowly, unsure how to react. She needed cues. He'd thought of her enough to provide dinner. "My hero," she said, lightly. "The fridge is a sad, empty shell. As far as I can see, there's nothing but condiments, eggs, and milk. Other than that, cornflakes and canned tuna."

"Blech!" He gave a theatrical little shudder. "Now you'll have to settle for pulled pork, black beans, and collard greens." It sounded wonderful, if not exactly low fat. If an X-rated workout lay ahead, that might not matter.

As soon as she smiled, he noticed her teeth. "Whoa!" he said, raising his palms as if to block the glare. "What did you do?"

He made it sound like a bad thing. "Agent's orders. I had my teeth bonded."

David nodded uncertainly, then said, too late, "You look fabulous. But then, you looked fabulous before."

She joined him at the granite kitchen island, where he was already digging into his dinner. "I'm sorry to be rude," he said, covering his mouth as he chewed, "but I'm starving."

She helped herself to a bite of pork. "I'm also supposed to lose weight." She set down her fork between bites. If she ate as gingerly as, say, a koala bear, she'd be able to stop just short of satiation.

David bridled. "What nonsense. You're already a wraith."

"The camera puts on weight. I only have to watch what I eat for the next week."

"Then you'll gain back twice what you lost," he said in disgust. "Dieting is hell on the body."

"I'm not dieting," she insisted. "I'm just cutting back. I have a fast metabolism."

"If you say so."

He looked like a grumpy teenager.

"This isn't just about my teeth and diet," she said, pushing her half-full plate away. "Do you regret yesterday?"

Now that his own plate was empty, he finished off hers as well. "Do you?"

"No." Her hot gaze never wavered.

He still hadn't answered. "Come back to my cabin?" he asked, extending a hand to help her up. "The dishes can wait."

They fell together onto the bed, which groaned beneath their weight, and tugged at each other's clothing so ineptly that they dissolved into laughter. Finally David stood to undress himself, unbuttoning his slacks and kicking them off. As his dress shirt and T-shirt joined the pile, his eyes roamed her body with fervent admiration. Wearing only boxer briefs, erection straining, he hovered above her while he unbuttoned her blouse and unhooked her bra. He took one nipple in his mouth then the other, sucking and pulling, as he skimmed her jeans and panties over her hips just far enough to give him access. Lowering his head until his tongue found her sex, he swirled and flicked until she bucked against him, her whimpers of pleasure becoming more vocal. Finally, desperate with need, Maddie urged him into position and guided him in. His features went slack as he began to drive into her, slowly withdrawing nearly all the way then thrusting quickly, as if unable to bear being outside her for long. Wriggling voluptuously against him to meet every thrust, she breathed in his clean fragrance with its hints of nautical cologne. On the brink, she heard him gasp and opened her eyes to see that his were closed. Was he in pain? Was another headache coming on? But no, he opened his eyes, and the forest-green of his dilated pupils was all the encouragement she needed to surrender to her own release. His body took over then, and he came apart as if robbed of all will. Afterward he rested on his side, breathing heavily. He blew on the damp skin of her stomach, and she heaved a long, contented sigh.

"Will you be home tomorrow night?"

"Yes, as soon as I can get out of my costume."

"Leave it on. I won't mind."

She laughed. "*You* might not mind, but the dresser surely will. I didn't know you had a fetish for mischievous elves with hokey Southern accents."

"Honey, I'd do you even if you came to me covered in slime."

She rolled onto her back, laughing and holding her stomach. "Thanks for that appetizing image." A minute later, her laughter came to an abrupt stop. "Do you want me to leave now?" She hated how vulnerable she sounded.

He gathered her close. "No, stay." They cuddled for a while, which also felt wonderful. "Were you always this beautiful?" he asked, tracing the curve of her cheek.

She laughed.

"What's so funny?"

"You. In high school I was a drama nerd with coke-bottle glasses, baggy clothes, and an Orphan Annie hairdo. You wouldn't have given me a second look."

His booming laughter sent a thrill through her. "I would have totally done you. If I'd been doing anyone, that is. I was Super Geek, the youngest in my class. Joe had the rockstar thing tied up, even then. Jake was the track star. Edward the mysterious Greek god of handsomeness. I was gawky and too smart for my own good. It never occurred to me that I could get laid. Not until med school." He tweaked her nose. "When did you do the swan transformation thing?"

"Well, my mom worked on my style the summer after I graduated from high school. I was headed for a league drama school, and she convinced me I needed to work on my image. I also, finally, got contact lenses. They got around to inventing a brand I could tolerate."

"Do you still wear contact lenses?" He looked into her eyes with the clinical interest of an optometrist. "I can't see them. Is that why your eyes are such a bright color of green?"

She gently pushed him away. "No, silly. I had laser surgery in 1994. PRK—Photorefractive Keratectomy. Went to Canada to have it done before it was approved by the FDA. My eye color is my own." She batted her eyes at him.

He nodded approvingly. "Nice. I had PRK too. Wore glasses until I graduated college. I was twenty at the time."

She whistled. "You *are* smart. Is that when you became the magic man?"

His startled look confused her.

"You know, the cock of the walk."

His laughter seemed curiously relieved. "Med school was a revelation. I had never been popular before, so I guess I went a little nuts. So to speak. You? When did you discover sex?"

She gave him a long look, trying to discern how much he wanted to hear, if anything. Then she heard herself admit, "I'm ashamed to say, my first time was with a teacher."

David's expression grew solemn. "Oh."

"Yeah, *so* not cool. He was thirty-five, and I wasn't the first student he'd slept with. He didn't force me, and I was eighteen, so, yes, an adult, but in retrospect, it was an abuse of power."

"How long did it last?"

"Oh, a month. I started dating a fellow student and broke it off. He was upset, but he didn't give me a bad grade or anything. I think he worried that I'd expose him as the predator he was. League programs are very competitive, and only the best—or the most commercial—actors make it through the final year. He could have seriously derailed my ambitions, and he didn't. So he wasn't a total asshole." She frowned. "After that, I was super wary of the other teachers and directors. I have to admit, that experience messed with my head."

"I can just imagine," he said with heartfelt sympathy. He gave her a long, soulful kiss. "That's one tough business you're in," he said after he drew back.

She searched his face, wondering if now was the right time to ask him about Africa. But he was already putting on another condom, and she wanted another round just as much as he did.

CHAPTER 29

———◆———

MADDIE LAY ON THE TABLE of the clinic examination room, limp, defeated, and dejected. She was cold, her ankle throbbed, and she had no idea how she was going to get through tonight's performance.

This morning, after seeing David off to work, she'd joined her colleague Jeremy for a hike on Dungeness Spit in Sequim. The road leading to the hike had the head-scratching name of Kitchen-Dick Road. David had told her it was named after two pioneering families who lived across from each other. One of the intersecting streets was also named Woodcock Road. She and Jeremy had a good laugh over the names after they met in the main parking lot. She'd arrived on her Vespa and he, in his sister's old Toyota Camry station wagon. Between his torrid fling with Lysander—Sam—his sister's new baby, and all the turmoil in Maddie's life, they had been too busy to hang out. It being the Saturday before closing, this might be their last chance.

Dungeness Spit was one of your more monotonous hiking experiences. The first half-mile was surrounded by forest, then you entered a long, rocky strip of land that extended out into the Strait of Juan de Fuca—five and a half miles to the lighthouse. Other than rocks of all sizes, it offered a variety of shorebirds, shells, driftwood, and sand. The absence of an actual hiking trail meant uneven ground.

"What do you think?" Jeremy said, about thirty minutes in. "Worth the trouble?"

Maddie blew out a frustrated puff of air. "Are we talking about the hike or the play?"

"You tell me. Drama on stage, drama off. I'd say it was a draw. A draw of drama."

Maddie grinned. "You told me you were hoping for a bit of rest. Did you get it?"

He laughed. "As to the hike, to be determined. Are we doing a debriefing of the play? Because thank *God* that's almost over."

"You broke up with Sam?"

"Yes. He got what he wanted—an introduction to my agent. Then, as if that weren't bad enough, he wanted reassurance that we'd last into the future. I can't do that, can you? Isn't there an unwritten rule that what happens in theatrical productions ends there? Like Vegas? That's the hell of small-town gigs with few professionals. The cats and the kittens. They're wet behind the ears. You and I are well aware that 'Tomorrow' is just a catchy but really bad song. There is no 'Tomorrow' for the likes of us."

She shot him a sidelong glance, unused to so much pessimism from carefree Jeremy. "Ouch. So sorry. I think 'wet behind the ears' refers to calves or colts, not kittens."

"Leave it to Maddie to get technical on me. Horses and cows aren't crafty."

"Sooo … what's next? Leave the childcare to someone else?"

He shrugged. "Yes. Back to L.A. for the end of pilot season. An industrial for general Human Resources use. I'm not clear on the details. Something about how to avoid being accused of sexual harassment."

They shared a hearty laugh.

"Oh, irony, irony, thou art delicious," Jeremy said. "In April I'll do another guest appearance on one of the *Law and Order* shows, *SVU.*"

"Victim or victimizer? Or witness?"

Jeremy's usual air of sardonic humor had returned. "If there's a script, they haven't sent it. I've already been the victim once. Hoping for rapist this time. If I'm lucky, serial killer they don't catch for multiple episodes."

They both knew this was unlikely.

"What about you and the Fairy King?" he went on. "Gonna fly away together?"

"Over." She made as if to slash her throat. "I'm sure you've heard about his big break."

"Yes. He struts around like a peacock on Viagra. He ended it?"

"No, I did."

His eyebrows flew together. "Did someone scramble your brains? Speaking of *Insanity,* I haven't seen *you* strutting around, and from what

I hear, you should be. But baby doll, watch out for Henry Makos." He shuddered. "That creepy bastard eats young actresses for lunch. He'll try to tell you your future depends on your … cooperation." He stopped walking. "Is it just me, or it that lighthouse no closer than it was an hour ago?"

Now that he mentioned it …. "You want to turn back? You're right about the lighthouse. All we've seen so far are Great Blue Herons, coots, and gulls. They're nice and all, but the path is so uneven, it's hard on the feet."

"You convinced me," Jeremy said, doing an abrupt about-face. "So, back to you. How are you going to avoid that powerful bozo's clutches?"

"Any suggestions?"

"Well …. Don't attend any *business* meetings in his hotel room, for one."

"I doubt we'll be staying in the same hotel. Doesn't he have a house in Beverly Hills, Bel Air, or Brentwood?"

"Well, you get the picture. Frankly, I don't know how you can avoid him. Just try not to offend him. Lay it on thick with the compliments as you … demur. He's so *powerful*, or maybe you have your period—I wish I could use that one. You don't want to sully your business relationship."

"A girl can give head any damn time of the month. You've been there, haven't you?"

"Oh, yes. But honey, I just close my eyes and think of England, to quote a literal queen. Those guys get their way or they show you the highway. The high road leads *away* from an acting career, not toward one. Or you can be proactive—glom onto someone else on the set who has the power to protect you. Like the star."

She wrinkled her nose at him. "George Reed Masters? He just got married."

"Weeeell …." He drew the word out. "Nothing surprises me in this business. I haven't heard any specific stories about him, but heck, out of sight, out of mind, as they say, and his bride is making a movie on another continent. I heard he chose you after Jo Beth Brody got canned. That means he's got you in his sights. That wouldn't be so bad, would it? Don't y'all have a sex scene?"

She was shocked. "Jo Beth Brody is the actress I'm replacing? How do you hear these things?"

"My agent knows all," he said, eyebrows dancing.

She pictured the sweet and vulnerable Jo Beth Brody, a rising star with multiple screen credits. She'd even been a regular on a sitcom for a few years.

"Did she reject Henry Makos?"

"Um, maybe. Michael wasn't clear on that. She crossed someone. Or got too hefty. Maybe it was that." He looked Maddie over. "Did they tell you to lose weight? Baby doll, you look a street waif out of Dickens' England."

"Five pounds," she said.

He nodded. "Well, you won't regret it. What looks scary in person usually translates great for the camera. As long as your boobs don't shrink."

"Why would George risk his marriage for a fling with a nobody? From what I've read, he seems like a nice guy."

Jeremy gave an elaborate shrug. "Nice. Huh. Well, he does have a good publicist. As for hanky-panky, there's no risk for him. Not unless you were to kiss and blab, and who would do that? Because who'd believe you? If he were caught, he'd insist *you* came on to *him*. That would be on you." He gave her a gentle nudge. "Maybe he *is* totally whipped by his new wifey. Maybe you'll luck out and she'll finish her own movie early and show up on the set to keep him in line. But then you're dodging Henry Makos again."

"You're not helping to calm my nerves."

"Baby doll, you'll be jus' fine. They're behind schedule and don't have the luxury of recasting unless the replacement is a total disaster. Do what you must. Everyone else does. From what I hear, Makos doesn't insist that anyone put out. He'll just jerk off on you."

"Yuck." She stuck out her tongue. "That's almost worse."

"No diseases," he said with a knowing nod.

That was when she twisted her ankle.

They arrived at the parking lot an hour later, she, leaning on Jeremy and inwardly cursing her rotten luck with every painful step. Leaving her Vespa behind, Jeremy drove her to the clinic and sat by her side, trying to console her as they waited for the nurse to call her in. But they both knew she was screwed. She'd go on tonight, with the help of a walking cast or crutches, but she wouldn't be doing the movie. Her ankle was swollen and tender.

"Baby doll, there will be other opportunities," Jeremy said in a soothing voice, breaking the tense silence that had reigned ever since they'd been shown into the examining room. "Look on the bright side: no need to fight off Henry Makos!"

She shut her eyes and beat her fists against the padding of the examination table.

"Mercy for the poor table!" a deep male voice said.

She shot up from the table and banged her ankle. "Ow!" Pain shot up her leg and she grimaced as she waited for the worst to pass. Then, in dismay, she registered the identity of her doctor. David. Of course. Who else would it be?

There was only one clinic in Sequim, and she'd known he was working today, not that she'd been planning to avail herself of his professional services.

"My God, Maddie!" Dr. O'Connell's voice lost its teasing undercurrent and—for Jeremy's sake, she gathered—assumed the air of a cool professional. "Your ankle then? Okay if I touch it?" He was already leaning over, assessing the swelling and bruising.

Maddie blushed, but so did he. "You need to, right? Touch it, I mean." She painfully extended her leg. She'd aimed for humor but somehow the question came out peevish.

He handled it gently, causing almost no pain, though he did ask at several points, "Does this hurt? What about this?"

She closed her eyes, feeling how his hand moved slightly above the ankle. All proper, of course. But he'd almost managed to distract her from the injury, raising memories of the night before.

"Uh, Maddie?" She opened her eyes. "Who's your friend?" He inclined his head toward Jeremy.

"You don't recognize Titania?" she said, smiling through her misery. "Jeremy Fairewell, meet David O'Connell, Joe's brother."

Jeremy turned on his star glow and beamed at David. "Charmed," he said, shaking his hand.

"Jeremy," David said pleasantly, "it's great to meet you. Would you mind leaving us alone for just a minute?"

He didn't explain further. Visibly disappointed, Jeremy said, "Uh, sure. Maddie, I'll be in the waiting room. Nice to meet you, Doctor O'Connell."

Once he was gone, Maddie joked, "You hurt his feelings. I think he likes you."

"Be still my beating heart," David said, but he was holding her ankle, running a hand up and down.

She wanted to keep up the joking, tell him this was hardly the time or place for shenanigans, but his grave attitude stopped her. He looked up. "You really want to do this movie?"

She nodded, wondering what he was up to. It scared her.

The skin beneath his hands felt hotter, but the pain was receding. She watched in stunned silence as he probed every inch of the affected area. His eyes were closed, and his face held an intense expression of concentration. After a long moment—ten minutes if she trusted the clock—he let go.

He took a step back from the table. "Put weight on it."

Mystified, she slid to her feet. The swelling was gone. So was the pain. She struggled to get a full breath. "What just happened?"

"It wasn't as badly hurt as you thought," he said brightly.

"David—"

"Please," he held up a hand, "it's okay. Don't ask. Sometimes these things are psychological."

"But the swelling—"

"Mind over matter. See you tonight, after the show?"

She nodded, knowing the subject was closed.

"Uh, if I have a migraine, you won't take it personally, right?"

She shot him a look of alarm. What was he saying?

As she walked into the waiting room with no sign of impairment, Jeremy's eyes grew huge. "Um, what—"

She didn't let him finish. "I don't know," she said. "David did some kind of Vulcan Mind-Meld, and my ankle stopped hurting. Please, can this stay between us? If you tell anyone, I won't back you up."

"Of course." He nodded too emphatically. "I'm just so relieved it turned out to be … nothing."

Then he mumbled something under his breath and started humming the tune to "What's going on here?" from *Paint Your Wagon*.

CHAPTER 30

JEREMY WAS AS GOOD AS his word, mentioning that they'd gone for a hike and offering nothing to indicate anything but a pleasant diversion. But Maddie could tell he was freaked out, as if they'd both survived an alien abduction.

Kilo behaved remarkably well under the circumstances. The performance went smoothly, and he was the consummate professional. Afterward, he pulled her aside. "Come home with me for old times' sake?"

She touched his cheek with real affection. "Kilo, that's not a good idea. Of course I'm tempted. But I've already pulled off that bandage. If we keep scratching the itch, it's just going to hurt more in the end."

His doubtful look told her he questioned the appropriateness of her metaphor—or even its logic—but he didn't argue. "Your call. We have one more performance, and I fly out Monday. So do you, I hear, on the same private plane. Can I drive you to Port Angeles?"

"Thanks," she said, "but it's taken care of. I'll see you on the plane." She paused. "Friends, right?"

He uttered a dry little laugh. "Hah! This isn't the end."

She smiled but didn't bother to contradict him. He didn't need to know he'd already been replaced.

* * *

David lay helpless in his motel room bed, breathing through the pain. Excruciating pain like he'd never experienced. This had to be what it felt like to be tortured with a head crusher in medieval times. He couldn't recall the name of the motel or how he'd managed to check in. The pain had started even before Maddie and Jeremy left the parking lot. His shift still had three hours to go, but he was one of two doctors, and foot traffic had been light. His "family emergency" story was bolstered by his haggard appearance. Gritting his teeth against the nails piercing his temples, he headed straight to the nearest motel. Once checked in, he locked the door and ran to the bathroom, where he wretched and wretched. Then he fell into bed and tried to brace himself for the onslaught.

After two hours, the headache showed no signs of abating. Every so often he'd dry-heave into the ice bucket by the bed, but there was little left in his stomach. He thought of the horror movie *Scanners*, with its exploding heads. They would find his brains splattered all over the walls. All to save Maddie's movie career—a career that would steal her away from him.

Finally, he slept, and when he woke, the headache was gone. The clock read two. He dropped the key in the self-checkout box and headed into the dark parking lot toward his black Nissan Pathfinder.

* * *

As she rode her Vespa into the compound, Maddie saw the automatic outdoor light switch on, but no lights in the cabins or houses. David's car wasn't in its usual spot. It was past eleven. She knew he had tomorrow off, but he would hardly have gone out on the town by himself. He had to be seriously short on sleep. With the others gone, they'd been taking full advantage of having the place to themselves. Maddie knew she should be sleeping more, too, or she was going to appear hollow-eyed when she reported for work on Tuesday. If she got too rundown, she might even catch a virus.

If so, David can just heal you, said a giddy voice in her head.

Stop that. Mind over matter, he said so himself.

The comeback, *Yeah*, his *mind over your matter*.

They still hadn't exchanged cell numbers, so she had no way of reaching him. She let herself into the main house and poured a glass of wine from an already open bottle. No choice but to wait and see. Calling Ali or Joe would cause a panic, and they could do nothing from Seattle. The police wouldn't go looking for someone who had been missing for under twenty-four hours. Even the dogs seemed anxious as they followed her down into the rec room. She turned on the TV, looking for mindless entertainment and happened upon *Valley of the Dolls*. After that came *Beyond the Valley of the Dolls*. She fell asleep midway through. Wow, that was one weird movie… and certainly not a sequel. A nightmare vision of the Hollywood party scene and not the reassurance she was looking for. At least *Insanity* wasn't a Russ Meyer movie. Talk about an obsession with breasts....

* * *

David turned off the TV and shushed the excited dogs. "Maddie?" he said in a low voice.

She awoke with a start and sat up on the couch. "David! I thought you were lying dead in a ditch somewhere. Phew! What a relief."

She fell into his arms and held on tight. *Not dead*, he thought, *but too close for comfort.* "I, uh, did have a health crisis of sorts."

She took a step back, hands still clutching his arms, and stared up into his face, her eyes—deep pools of dark green—shimmering. "Are you okay?"

"I am now. Listen, it's late. I had a migraine, and that meant checking into a hotel to ride it out." He leaned in for a long, searching kiss, ending it reluctantly. "Let's go to bed. It's three in the morning." He wanted to sweep her into his arms but didn't have the strength. "We'll use the guest room."

He followed her up the stairs, leaning heavily on the banister.

They shrugged out of their clothing and fell into bed, cuddling but not looking for more. He wasn't aware of drifting off, so sleep must have overtaken him quickly.

He awoke at five. Maddie was asleep beside him, looking positively cherubic. He adjusted the comforter to cover her slender shoulders. He wanted to touch her, wake her, make love to her. He couldn't get enough. But that would be unfair. She needed her rest. In her place, he would have been terrified of what lay ahead in L.A. Like walking into the lion's den knowing for certain you were its favorite food.

David realized, after his rash decision to heal her that afternoon, that he had opened a door that couldn't be shut again. He didn't want Maddie to go to LaLa Land; he also didn't want her to wonder what might have happened if a broken ankle had kept her here.

If they had any chance at a future, sooner or later he'd have to tell her about his "magic" hands. No time like the present. He wondered, as he always did, about unintended consequences. Interfering with the future. In science fiction and horror stories, terrible things happened as the result of such well-intended meddling. If you found a way to raise a beloved cat from the dead, it would return evil. Personally, he didn't believe you had to bow to the vagaries of fate. If you took that idea to the nth degree, you'd never prescribe antibiotics or resuscitate a clinically dead person. He frowned. Not a good example. Most doctors would never choose to be resuscitated themselves.

They knew the unlikelihood of a positive outcome: the person who came back had lost too many brain cells, and their intelligence or personality or physical abilities would never be the same.

Then there were the consequences to his own health. Could he survive another headache like today's?

Sleep, he told himself. *What's done is done. Time will tell.*

He closed his eyes and dreamed of evil cats and the walking dead.

* * *

Teresa sat on the rec room couch, Coogan nestled between her legs, his tiny head heavy on her thigh, and Harry curled up to one side. They were both making soft, contented noises as she stroked them, and she let loose a ragged breath, thoroughly deflated. A fire crackled in the fireplace. A cozy domestic scene, if only her beautiful husband were there to complete it.

It was late Tuesday afternoon. Joe was in the studio, Ali was doing errands, and David was at work. Teresa tried to picture Liam going about his business, whatever that was now. Letting off steam with hard physical labor on the new house she'd only glimpsed from a distance. The next time she visited Matthew's place, she'd bring field glasses. She might be able to see something from the third floor. She'd already done a shameful amount of sneaking around.

She'd spent most of the day at the job site, making notes, taking photographs and measurements, longing for Liam. Matthew was rehearsing with Joe, so she had the house to herself. Maddie was in L.A., making a movie. She couldn't picture that. Maddie and David had been alone all week. If anything had happened between them, David wasn't letting on, though he was so bland on the subject of Maddie that Teresa would bet good money they'd made their peace in bed. Where did that leave Kilo? Out in the cold, if you could call Hawaii "the cold." Consolation would be in rich supply.

There was a certain comfort to be found in Matthew's old Victorian, as if it were a living presence, a benign ancestor cradling her in its hospitality and understanding. *I am long gone, my dear, and you have your whole life ahead of you. Time heals all wounds.* Liam's house looked similar from the outside. According to Ali, the interior was a mess. *The messier the better, as far as Liam is concerned*, she thought. When they'd met, she'd been a mess and in need of his protection. Now she was safe. Had she unwittingly gone back to spoiled-princess mode? She saw how her rich-girl problems must have needled him. If she'd been serious about teaching piano, she'd have followed his advice and taken on at least one student to see how she liked it. But she preferred talking about it to doing. She entertained herself by buying clothes that cost the equivalent of most people's entire wardrobes and sometimes never wore them. She'd paid for everything in their shared life without ever considering the consequences to Liam's ego. She'd acted as if every decision was hers to make. No wonder he'd thrown in the towel. She was hopeless.

Harry sighed blissfully in his sleep. Liam would miss the dogs more than her, but the dogs were part of the security system here, so he couldn't take them away. Besides, there was no place for them to run in the Uptown neighborhood.

The door opened, and Ali walked in. "Hey there. Can I interrupt your doggy therapy session?" Her sister-in-law looked more tired than usual. She had her own problems, such as what was to be done about her trainwreck of a birth mother.

"The more the merrier," Teresa said.

"You don't seem very merry. How did it go at Matthew's today?"

She knew her smile was unconvincing. "It would have been heaven, if only Liam wasn't a hop, skip, and a jump away. Joe's right. Interior design was my calling all along. Only this time, I won't embark on a project by assuming everyone shares my taste."

Ali flopped down next to Teresa. Harry immediately scooted over to her feet and rolled onto his back. "I have some ideas for your website," Ali said as she obliged the big mastiff/German Shepherd mix by leaning over to scratch his belly.

"You're the best," Teresa said, trying to drum up some enthusiasm. "I'm excited to see them."

Ali wagged a finger at her. "You will be. I'll expect some genuine excitement when you actually see my plans in action. In the meantime, I'll tell you about my visit with Liam."

Teresa's long sigh was almost comical. "You said you were running errands. I guess I knew that would be one of them. He was so near today … and yet, so far."

Ali patted her arm. "He asked about you. He couldn't help it. He is back to thinking you are too different to work as a couple, but he's never stopped loving you." She paused. "He has one bathroom in working order, and he installed a washing machine and drier in the basement."

Realization dawned. "Did he actually get Nancy to bathe and wash her clothes?"

"Last week. Technically, Liam washed them. Said they still smelled but it was an improvement. Really, they need to be burned. He was able to get her to move into the new FOSSP residence Joe is funding in Port Townsend. It's within walking distance of Liam's and Matthew's Victorians."

"Did she stop by while you were there?"

"No." Ali's expression turned stony. Unlike Liam, her sister-in-law wanted nothing to do with this broken, selfish woman who had left two small children locked in a car on a hot day while she went in search of drugs. But Liam was a fixer-upper guy, and without Teresa to fuss over, he'd been open to new human projects. Ali continued, "The FOSSP residence plan isn't ideal. Liam says she's not used to rules, and the resident social worker is already complaining about her. Because she's living among young people, I worry she'll be a bad influence. Her brain is off, somehow, and Liam says her color is bad. He's going to see if he can get her to Sequim so David can give her a physical."

"I assume he bought her new clothes."

"*I* did. I picked up several things at Goodwill. I'd have bought them new, but I'd only do that if I had some idea of her taste. Mostly, we just want her to be warm and comfortable. Liam checked the labels of her clothing while he washed it and gave me sizes. I did provide sturdy boots. Her feet are the same size as mine."

Teresa winced. Somehow this little detail had touched a nerve in Ali. "Does she talk to Liam?"

"Not much. When she does speak, he says it's like she's making it up on the spot. Most of it isn't plausible. She seems to have incorporated stuff she's read in books or newspapers into her memory as if it happened to her. She likes to watch him work, and he says it's fine as long as she doesn't object to listening to NPR or that wild jazz he likes. Not when he's doing anything messy, like drywall. Most of that part is finished. The place is starting to shape up. He's installed hardwood flooring."

Teresa sighed. "I wish I could help him decorate."

"If you do get the chance, please treat him like a real client." Ali's voice was gentle. "Find out what he likes and make that happen. I've been giving this a lot of thought." She cleared her throat. "Liam loved—loves—you so much he wanted you to have all your heart's desires. He never considered his own. He has his own taste in décor, if you take the time to find out what that is." Seeing Teresa's stricken face, she added, "I want your marriage to work as much as you do. And since I doubt Liam will agree to go to a counselor or examine his feelings in any depth, you'll have to figure out what he wants without *him* knowing what he wants, if that makes sense."

Teresa smiled. "Perfect sense. Like you did with David's cabin. Maddie told me."

Ali cocked her head. "When did you talk to Maddie?"

"Oh, this was before she left. But I've seen David's cabin, and I love it. It's so … him. Alan Quatermain himself would approve."

"They were alone all week," Ali said.

"Yes, but don't expect David to tell you what went down."

Ali raised her eyebrows. "If anything. I worry about Maddie in Los Angeles, a living sacrifice to Sodom and Gomorrah."

"She'll be fine," Teresa said, not really believing it. "She still thinks an acting career is what she wants. If it isn't, better to find out now, while she's young."

"Like we're so old," Ali scoffed, reading her mind. "Even Schubert was still alive at our age."

Teresa nodded. "He died at thirty-one, and look what he'd accomplished by then?"

"Okay, not a great example. Thirty is the new twenty. And you and I aren't even there yet."

We will be soon enough, Teresa thought. *Oh, Liam, come back to me. This time you'll come first. Cross my heart.*

CHAPTER 31

LATE WEDNESDAY EVENING, ALI LAY in bed, wondering when Joe would come in. The kickoff to his tour was tomorrow night in Des Moines, Iowa. She now understood that the "tour" would not be the uninterrupted bus journey she'd once imagined, but a little like Maddie's play—mostly Thursday through Saturday gigs with time off in between. This first weekend was Des Moines, Omaha, and Fargo. Exhausting for him, with plane trips every day. Then he'd be home on Sunday until the following Thursday, with three more consecutive one-night stands. They'd discussed the possibility of her going with him, leaving the twins at home. She'd never seen him perform live except for one impromptu gig at the Baler Tavern.

She felt his weight on the mattress and opened her eyes, aware that she'd drifted off. "What time is it?"

Joe was pulling off his socks. "Eleven. I didn't mean to wake you."

"It's okay." She sat up and rubbed her eyes. "I want to hear how your day went." She meant the trip to Sequim with her mother and Liam.

He sat on the edge of the bed, silent, radiating weariness. "I wish I'd waited till Monday."

"Why is that?"

"Because I have a long day ahead tomorrow, and what happened today requires a more, uh, in-depth conversation than we should engage in this late at night."

Ali waited, and when the silence thickened, she said, "Go on. You can't stop now."

He let out a long breath and turned around to kiss her lightly on the lips. Then he lay beside her and wrapped her in his arms, speaking low as he stroked her hair. "It wasn't easy convincing Nancy to go with us. As you know, she isn't all there. We told her we were taking a road trip to Port Angeles. A few blocks from the clinic, she panicked, almost like a dog who suddenly senses it's going to the vet. She wouldn't come out of the car, despite Liam's gentle persuasion—he's great with her, by the way. David finally came to her." His hand ran idly along her arm for a moment before he continued, "She liked David instantly, started calling him 'Jack' for some reason, as if he were an old friend. Or rather an old lover, weirdly flirtatious. He played along. Meanwhile he managed to draw blood and examine her as best he could without spooking her."

Ali stiffened. "I'm guessing it's not good."

"It's pretty clearly cirrhosis. He thinks her mental issues might be caused by encephalopathy. But it doesn't take a doctor to see that she's jaundiced. He doesn't give her long." They were spooned together now, and he kissed her neck. "You might want to use the time while I'm gone to get to know her a little, what's left of her. If you can stand it."

It was still dark when Ali woke the next morning. The bed was empty beside her, and the clock read four thirty-five. She slipped on a robe. Halfway down the stairs, she stopped, listening for the source of the voices she heard. It worried her that Joe was up already; he needed to be rested for tonight's performance. Maybe he could nap on the plane.

In the kitchen, Joe and David were speaking in low but urgent voices. Ali stopped to listen. She could only hear a fragment here and there.

"…my vocal cords. Why not…?"

David's voice carried more than Joe's. She heard "unethical" and "unintended consequences."

That was enough.

She stalked into the kitchen, and they both recoiled as if caught plotting a heist. "What's going on?" she demanded, trying to keep the judgment from her voice. "Is this about my mother?"

"Yes," Joe said, "but it's not easy to explain." He turned to David. "She's my wife, and we're discussing her mother. Don't you think it's time we were straight with her?"

Ali put her hands on her hips. "You already told me she was dying. I can't imagine what you have in mind."

Joe's lips thinned. "No, you can't. Imagine, I mean. David?"

David shot him a harsh look. "I told you in confidence. Now you've put me in an untenable position."

Joe was implacable. "Ali and I don't keep secrets from each other. Maybe you can explain it better to her."

Ali looked from one to the other. "I'll make coffee."

Joe pointed at the neglected coffeemaker, superannuated by the espresso machine. "Just make a pot of drip coffee. Extra strong."

They were silent as she filled the tank and ground the beans. After she pressed the start button, she sat on a stool at the kitchen island, folded her hands, and gave David her full attention. Privately, she thought everyone was wide awake enough already. She should have made a pot of herbal tea instead.

"When I was in the Congo, our Jeep swerved to avoid an animal and crashed. The driver was killed. I had a mild concussion, some bumps and bruises. Then, though it made no medical sense, I slipped into a coma. They were afraid I wouldn't make it, but I did—somewhat miraculously. A week later, I woke up and recovered. Or so it seemed."

He lapsed into silence. No one spoke as Ali filled their cups.

"I had headaches, trouble concentrating. And then came the weirdest symptom of all. I was treating a small boy for Sleeping Sickness, quite advanced. My hands started to get hot, and as I touched him, the swelling in his lymph nodes began to disappear. The disease is caused by a fly bite, and there's always a nodule at the infection site. I made that go away too."

Ali rubbed her forehead. "What are you saying?"

"He's saying he can cure people," Joe said. "He cured my vocal cords. No swelling or nodules on them now."

"I can *sometimes* cure people," David amended. "It isn't reliable. And if people detect me doing it, things get weird in a hurry. Now you know why I came home. I couldn't function normally there anymore. I was trying to explain to Joe; there are consequences. The boy I cured that first time recovered, but then no one believed my explanation, and rumors spread that I was a witch doctor. We had to move on quickly, but you can imagine my inept efforts to explain what happened. Recoveries that seem miraculous *do* happen without a shaman's or a doctor's intervention, you know, but everyone was spooked."

"Now Joe wants you to cure my mother." She looked at Joe.

"It would give you a chance to get to know her," he said.

"I can't cure her mind," David almost pleaded with Joe. "I might be able to stop the progress of the physical disease, but there's a lot of damage.

I hate the playing-God thing. When I left Africa, I swore not to use my, uh, *knack* anymore, but I couldn't help myself when Joe told me he was fighting hoarseness again. I thought I could do it without his knowledge."

Ali stared at Joe, shocked. "It was?"

Joe slumped. "You couldn't hear it in my speaking voice?"

"How did you know he'd cured you?" Ali asked him.

"It was too much of a coincidence. He said he wanted to 'examine me' and spent some time touching my throat. When I felt the heat in his hands and the results were so instantaneous, I hounded him until he came clean."

David sat completely still as if time had stopped. "Ali and Joe, let's *please* not decide anything, er, this morning. Joe, you're going to be dead on your feet tonight."

Ali poured herself another cup of coffee, shaking her head slowly, a cynical smile on her face.

"What is it?" Joe asked. "Still a skeptic?"

"Not at all. It's only …. Do you remember, in the woods that first time, when you asked me about my degree in Comparative Religion and it was like you'd pressed my religion button?"

Despite the early hour and serious subject, Joe grinned. "Who could forget anything about those few days?"

"I told you why I couldn't believe in organized religion, that there were too many common mythologies among religions with different deities or prophets. Things like the virgin birth. Spontaneous healing." She looked at David. "You don't think this is a gift from God, do you?"

David shook his head, bone weary. "Never occurred to me. Prayer has nothing to do with it."

If there is a God, she thought, *he wouldn't be happy with any of us.* "By the way, why are you continuing this discussion so early in the morning? Why weren't you sleeping in your cabin?"

"That's my fault," Joe said. "I was up, and I saw the light in his cabin. Now I have to get ready to go." He looked at his watch. "Matthew's going to pick me up in an hour to drive us to Port Angeles. I have to shower and shave."

Joe would travel by charter plane to Boeing Field, where he'd board the private jet that would fly them and their crew and equipment to their first venue.

Joe gave his older brother a hug. "David, I'm sorry. The timing for all this stinks. I'm not usually such an inconsiderate bastard. I don't want you to compromise your principles …. Hell, that's too mild a way of putting it.

I don't want you to sacrifice your soul for a woman who spent a lifetime squandering hers." He gave Ali a slow kiss. "I love ya, darlin'. If the twins do anything interesting while I'm gone, I wanna see a video."

After he left to go upstairs, Ali said, "I don't expect you to cure her, David. Joe and I are the only ones who know about this, right? We won't tell, and if I were you, I wouldn't tell anyone else." Something about his expression made her add, "Who else did you tell, Sylvia?"

"No, not Sylvia." She stared him down. "Okay, okay. Maddie may know."

"*May* know?"

"Uh, she was hiking a few days before she left for L.A., and she, uh, broke her ankle."

"You *didn't*."

"How could I let her miss that opportunity?"

Ali realized then just how much David loved Maddie. Enough to risk everything, to let the big cat with an unpredictably dangerous streak out of his doctor's bag. *What a mess.* She thought about Joe's vocal cords, and what might have happened if he'd had to cancel the tour. He'd have been disappointed, but it might have been better for their marriage. *Unintended consequences, indeed.*

CHAPTER 32

———◆———

ON THURSDAY MORNING THE FOLLOWING week, Teresa sat in Matthew's living room, sorting through her notes and drawings. The last owner of the place had decorated in a style she privately referred to as Manly Man Modern. Black Naugahyde couch and chairs, heavy, graceless, dark utilitarian furniture—mostly constructed of laminated particle board. A moose head, for God's sake. Matthew had bought the house fully furnished. So wrong for a man who, like her, had left his heart in fin-de-siècle Paris. She did like the burgundy walls, though they wouldn't work with her City of Light concept. The moose head would go to Jean-Louis for his new restaurant, though it would be the only actual trophy head.

She heard the junk truck arriving outside and went to greet the two men. The painters would complete the interior over the next few days. Matthew would be home Sunday night, and by then some of the furniture would be in place. He would have a mostly complete bedroom and remodeled bathroom until he left town again. Teresa stood on the opposite side of the street while the men worked, after making sure they knew where to deliver the moose head. From here, she could see Liam's Folly, which looked exactly the same as it had two weeks ago. She felt like a government agent doing a stakeout, only with total ineptitude. Liam had to know by now that she lurked a few houses away. Joe or Ali would have told him. She didn't dare ask.

After the junk truck left, she skulked a little closer to Liam's house, trying to stay out of sight. A few goats could make quick work of that jungle of a yard, but they might eat the rhodie. She hoped for a glimpse of the interior, but she never caught Liam leaving so she could be sure of escaping detection. She didn't think he was around. It was already noon. His red truck was parked in front, but Kelpies was a short walk away, and it was nice out, in the sixties. He might have taken his Harley—she didn't see it anywhere. Surely she would have heard it.

Only one house away now, she couldn't hear noise from inside, no machinery or pounding. Emboldened, she crept up to the window and peered in. The oak flooring gleamed like new. The original flooring must have been too thin to refinish. The walls were painted burgundy, a color similar to Matthew's living room. Was Liam going for Manly Man Modern too? It was impossible to tell, there being no furniture in the room at present. It did have an impressive fireplace with an elaborate wrought-iron grate. Did she even know what style Liam preferred? Another wave of shame washed over her. How stupid she'd been to assume her taste would suit everyone without even bothering to ask. For Matthew's décor, she'd run every idea past him and readily accepted his few modifications.

"Uh, Teresa?" Liam said quietly, nearly stopping her heart. As if cornered by a tiger, she turned to face him, breathing hard. He was wearing his grubbies—weathered jeans, worn work boots, and a ratty old T-shirt, everything speckled with paint and plaster. He looked glorious.

One hand on her thumping heart, she said in an even huskier than usual voice, "Give me a second." She took a long, calming breath and blew it out. "I was only a few houses away. I'm sorry, I shouldn't have—"

"Why not?" he broke in.

"Why not what?"

"Why shouldn't you come over? Everyone else has." He grinned. "All the visits from Ali and Joe, not to mention my, uh, mother, have really cut into my work time."

Her answering smile was tentative. "Plus the obligatory lunches at Kelpies."

"Those too."

"How's it coming along?" She nodded at the house.

"As you can see for yourself, not bad. Most of the basic work is done. I still haven't decided which way to go with the interior style. I'm tackling the exterior sanding and painting next, now that the weather's better, and I'll have to replace the roof. If I sell, I won't have to decide on décor."

If he sells, she thought. "You're really doing the roof yourself? It's high and steep. Isn't that dangerous?"

"Not if you're careful. Afraid for me?"

"Always." She moved in a step, and he countered her by stepping backward. So much for détente. Her heart sank. "Well, I guess I'll be moseying along." She tried to sound casual.

"Set a spell," he joked, lightly mocking her folksiness. He pointed at the window. "The kitchen is a work in progress, but I have a marble counter and a hotpot. I could make tea."

"Okay." A ray of hope slipped through as she trailed him into the house.

As he filled and plugged in the hotpot, he said, "Have a look around. You don't need me as a guide. You might have some suggestions."

Hah, that'll be the day, she thought. "If it's all the same to you, I think you should please yourself. I'm ashamed to say I don't know your taste in décor."

His lips twitched in a suggestion of a smile. "I guess we don't know each other very well. We should have thought before we leapt."

Her answer was fierce. "I gave it plenty of thought, believe me. I don't regret marrying you, not for one minute. But I can tell you do. I'm sorry you feel that way."

His features hardened. "How can you presume to understand how I feel about anything?"

The words stung. "I'm sorry. I should know better."

"You apologize a lot," he said.

She wanted to tell him she owed him a lot more apologies, but because he didn't want to hear them, she kept quiet. She backed away. "I'm going to accept your offer and give myself a quick tour."

He'd replaced all the flooring, even on the stairs. Not that she was surprised, but all the details were perfect. If only she knew someone half so skilled to do the work on Matthew's house …. He'd chosen different colors for the walls, depending on the rooms. A blue kitchen, a honey-brown master bedroom. Visions of what she'd do with the space scrolled through her head. Claw-footed dressers, a canopy bed. Or maybe the clean lines of Shaker furniture. When she rejoined him in the kitchen, he was pouring tea. He knew what she liked, an herbal blend called Springtime, and she was surprised he had it on hand. He'd always wrinkled his nose at the smell.

"Will you go with Victorian?" she asked.

"Too fussy." He handed her the cup of tea, preferring English Breakfast for himself. "I was thinking Urban Modern or Industrial Modern. You know, maybe reclaim some pieces from old factories." Seeing her face fall, he laughed. "Just kidding. Still gullible as ever, I see."

It was a fraction of their old rapport, but she'd take it. "How do you feel about Shaker furniture?"

To her surprise, he didn't ask her to describe it. "I like the idea." He cocked his head. "So … I hear Maddie's in Hollywood. Any news?"

"Well, she's still there, so they didn't fire her like her predecessor."

"She replaced someone?"

"Yes. Maddie said she was afraid the actress didn't put out and then made waves. The producers are notorious, at least one of them is."

Liam sipped his tea with all the decorum of a British aristocrat. "Does that mean she was prepared to do just that? You couldn't really blame her, I suppose."

"She said Jeremy gave her some ideas about how to dodge any passes. She seems to think the acting required off the set would be more challenging than the performance they're paying for."

He chuckled. "I look forward to hearing her account. She's a pistol."

Teresa laughed too. "*If* she comes back. Ali's counting on her to help with Lorenzo. She left an invitation on her voicemail. So far, no reply."

"We can't suck Maddie into our Hotel Port Townsend forever, you know," he said with a weariness that caught her off guard. "Like the Eagles' 'Hotel California'—you can check out, but you can never escape, or something like that. We're all weirdly trapped in our little drawing room hell. *L'enfer, c'est les autres.*"

She didn't know what to say to that. Why was he quoting Sartre's *No Exit*, where a locked drawing room was the punishment for three lost souls? "Hell is other people." The word "*L'enfer*" echoed between them. So it had been hell, had it? All of it? What was the point of all this, then? She put down her cup.

"No more school," she said.

"Huh?" It was his turn to look mystified.

"I'll never be a teacher."

He nodded, unsurprised. "A decorator, then. Perfect."

Was that sarcasm she detected? She didn't think so. "Do you approve, or are you being snarky?" She kept her voice even. "That Saturday night …." He waited, incurious. "I'd seen your mother that day. I didn't know if I should tell you. That's why I wanted to talk to David, why I didn't come to bed right away."

She wasn't telling him anything he didn't know already. In a gentle voice, he said, "I'd already decided to leave."

Silence. He appeared to wait for her next move, and she imagined she felt the old heat between them. But his words had formed a barrier.

"I've missed you," she said, taking a chance. "I'm sorry I drove you away."

In the silence that followed, she imagined her words landing but not sinking in, like raindrops on parched soil. What he said was, "You know, I really prefer coffee. Maybe my next purchase will be an espresso machine." He put down his cup.

She spoke carefully. "I can't ask you to return to hell after your narrow escape."

Elbows on the table, he rested his chin in his hands as if the whole conversation oppressed him. "I shouldn't have said that. I didn't mean you and me. You can't deny that we all had cabin fever. You and I especially were driving each other nuts. We're too different."

"Oh, we're back to *that* old argument." She hadn't meant to sound so bitter. "Tell me, what type of woman do you see yourself married to?" There was no denying it now. His eyes burned with the old hunger. She knew he couldn't picture himself with anyone but her.

He took her hand. "I don't want to live there again."

"All right." She'd miss Ali's constant proximity, since Liam and Joe were so good at keeping themselves occupied, but they wouldn't be *that* far away. Teresa didn't ask about the dogs. Their home was the compound. Who would live in the Sea Captain's House?

"What about the piano?" he asked. "Could you be truly happy in a life that didn't center around music? I thought that was your dream."

"Matthew, the guy whose house I'm decorating … he's a session guitarist and bass player, but he was trained classically. He wants to start sponsoring house concerts—once he moves into his new place. He said we could do it together, and that I could perform. That will be enough. He bought a piano and said I could play it anytime I like, even if he's home." The wariness on his face made her add, "He's gay."

Liam drew her in for a soft kiss, which quickly deepened. When he pulled away, she saw the love and longing in his eyes. "The bed and mattress will be delivered tomorrow."

"Ah," she said, her heart leaping in her chest. "What does it look like?"

He grinned. "It's a Shaker design, as it happens. Simple, clean lines. Maybe you'll stay over?"

Her laugh was giddy. "What if the ghosts try to drive me away? This place looks totally haunted."

Expression solemn, he laid a hand on his heart. "You know I'll always protect you."

CHAPTER 33

———◦———

After a short visit with Laurie and Duncan in Seattle, Maddie traveled by bus to Port Townsend. Ali picked her up at five. She and David hardly spoke at dinner, much less kissed. She caught him watching her as they all lounged in the rec room before bed but couldn't read his expression. Joe was on the road, and Teresa and Liam were in Liam's new place, so it was just Ali, David, May Allen the nanny, May's sister Susan, the twins, and little Lorenzo. They were all focused on the twins, whose favorite toys seemed to be a pair of wooden salad tongs, as they debated what they were saying, beyond "Yes!" "No!" "Mama!" "May May" and "Doggy!" (to either dog). They had skipped the crawling stage and were walking unsteadily, usually falling back onto heavily diapered bottoms and screeching with excitement. When you played a game of Peekaboo with one, the other wanted in too. It was clear to Maddie why Ali needed all hands on deck. It was exhausting.

Lorenzo did not contribute to the chaos. A solemn child, he watched the twins with round eyes and pursed mouth as if he were a grumpy, seventy-year-old bachelor uncle. Tall for his three years and eight months, he had bristly, bright-orange hair with features that were a softer version of his father's. The chin dimple, the bright-green eyes, and the hair all left no doubt as to his parentage.

In the few minutes of private conversation they'd managed to exchange since her return, Ali had told her that, since his arrival on St. Patrick's Day, the little boy had spoken only when spoken to. He was most definitely not made of "slugs and snails and puppy-dogs' tails," like the nursery rhyme said, and liked everything in its place. But he had taken one look at Maddie and thrown his arms around her. She wondered if she resembled someone he knew in Portland. David had said he was simply a red-blooded male responding to a beautiful woman.

She'd seen the way Ali and David had taken in her changed appearance when she came in, as if Hollywood had transformed her into someone they didn't recognize and might not like much. The studio had lightened her hair and given her extensions. The color suited her complexion, but the upkeep wasn't worth the trouble. She didn't know what she'd do when the roots started appearing, maybe just cut it short to avoid doing a reverse color. The Disney-princess look was probably what drew Lorenzo to her.

Maddie missed Teresa but was glad she and Liam were back together, even if it meant their living elsewhere. Liam was helping Teresa with her first paid remodeling/decorating project. For a time Ali and Maddie laughed over the twins' latest antics and praised a silent Lorenzo's progress on the elephant-family puzzle. Then Ali filled her in on Joe's tour—glowing reviews, sold-out houses, a refreshing dearth of rumors. Ali had tagged along for one three-day weekend, leaving the twins at home. As much as she loved seeing Joe in his element, she'd been relieved to be home again. She was glad to have witnessed firsthand how much energy Joe got from being onstage and performing for sold-out houses of adoring fans. That and his budding friendship with Matthew made the tour's punishing pace bearable.

Liam and Ali's mother appeared to be improving, despite a dire diagnosis. David had little to contribute and appeared distracted—no surprise.

"I know it's getting late," Ali said, "but you haven't told us a thing about your Hollywood experience."

Maddie avoided their eyes. "It was okay, overall. I'm not going to win any acting awards for this part, but I think they were pleased with my work."

David excused himself to tuck Lorenzo into bed and read him a story. As the little boy followed him out of the room, he stared up at his tall father, clearly awestruck. Maddie wondered why he'd chosen that moment to make his exit. Fear of what she might say? Perhaps it was as simple as wanting to spare Lorenzo more grownup talk.

"I think he likes you," Ali said after David's abrupt exit, hastening to add, "Lorenzo, I mean. Now, as eager as I am to hear your story, I should help May Allen put the twins down. They are a two-person job, and I like to read to them too, even though I doubt they understand much. Talk tomorrow?"

With David fully occupied, Maddie thought she might as well retire early. She had expected to drop off easily; instead, she kept thinking about David, a stone's throw away. She'd heard him return to his cabin. Should she knock?

During their clandestine week together, he'd told her no one needed to know about them. Maybe now that Ali, May Allen, and the girls were back, with Joe visiting between concert dates, he didn't intend for there to be a "them." Even though he'd driven her to Port Angeles and kissed her soundly before letting her go. Ali was the one who'd asked for help with Lorenzo, not David. But … even if they weren't going to keep *seeing* each other, shouldn't they clear the air, establish some ground rules? Tonight had been too awkward. Maddie read for a while, a less-than-thrilling thriller she'd started on the plane. Wondering why it was a best seller, she turned out the light, willing David to knock on her door. He never did.

In case Lorenzo was an early riser too, Maddie came down at seven the next morning and found David putting his plate and mug in the dishwasher. They had a moment, then, with no one else around. He took a step toward her as if to steal a kiss. Then he didn't. With a harried, "I'll see you later," he rushed out the door, leaving her more flummoxed than ever.

Ali appeared soon after. "Latte?" she asked.

Once they'd settled at the granite counter, Maddie asked, "Where's Lorenzo?"

"Oh, he's already downstairs in the rec room playing with his wooden train. I fed him breakfast earlier. The twins are awake too. May and Susan are supervising."

Maddie smiled. "You don't really need me here."

Ali's laugh was ragged. "Oh, I need you, believe me. I need you psychologically. I know I put a good face on things, but I'm torn in multiple directions right now. I'm helping Teresa with her website and overseeing problems at the FOSSP residences while Joe gallivants around the other side of the country. When he appears again, he's totally beat. Now that everyone is gone, we have an extra house and several extra cabins. We might as well open a hotel. Teresa is on pins and needles, bending over backward trying to convince Liam their marriage works, and Becca and Jean-Louis are at each other's throats." She paused, bemused. "Really, they have nothing to worry about. The restaurant is almost ready. They could open next week, and the May-first grand opening is almost a month away." She sipped her Americano.

"I get it," Maddie said. "You built the house so that Teresa and Liam would live here permanently—or maybe you wanted them to take over the Sea Captain's house—but they opted to go their own way. At least Liam did." *The chicks have flown the coup*, she thought. Personally, Maddie found the confines of the O'Connell compound comforting, but she could see how a man might feel otherwise. She privately believed Joe would have put off touring longer if he hadn't become restless, and Liam's love for Port Townsend was about the beauty of the area, the town, and the friends he'd made. Wolflike, he needed to roam his territory, revisiting the places he'd marked. He didn't appreciate being isolated. Ali was an introvert, as was Teresa, when you came right down to it, although she faked it better than most. Becca was a city girl, and Maddie didn't see her settling down here permanently, much as Ali would have liked that. She guessed part of the tension with Jean-Louis was missing Becca's large, close family and the hustle and bustle of Seattle and Bellevue.

She shook herself out of her thoughts to find Ali watching her.

"How did it really go? I've been dying to know."

Maddie had given her own mother the sanitized version, but with Ali she could come clean. Minus her feelings for David, which seemed like his secret.

"Okay, well, here goes." She finished off her latte and poured herself a tall glass of water. "There was a car waiting for me at the airport Monday night, and it drove me to the hotel. Not as fancy as the Sheraton, where Kilo and I stayed that first visit, but not a dive, either. A few other supporting actors and crew—the ones who didn't already live in Los Angeles—were staying there too. Not the stars, of course. The next day was mostly costume fittings, a mani-pedi, and hair." She fingered her extensions as if they were invasive ivy. "Then they finally gave me a script. The primping was fun, and I liked all the people I met. The weather was warm and sunny, the air not too hazy. So far, so good. The director checked in, briefly. He was a silver fox in his sixties, still a working actor himself. His attitude was paternal, so no problem there. Told me they'd be filming the bar scene over the next few days—I knew he was implying I'd have my clothes on—and wouldn't get to the scenes in Josh's bedroom until later in the week, if then." Seeing the question in Ali's eyes, she said, "Josh is the main character, the one played by George Reed Masters."

As Maddie talked, she traveled back in her mind to that first day of filming, less intimidating than she'd anticipated. With so few lines, she had no trouble memorizing them the evening before. She could have memorized them in ten minutes. She spent the morning in makeup, then waited in one of the trailers to be called. She was costumed in a ridiculously revealing red cocktail dress and stiletto heels. Her working-girl character never could have afforded such an outfit. The front of the dress had to be taped into place so she wouldn't flash the rest of the bar patrons. No bra, naturally. There was a knock on the door, and George Reed Masters came in. She'd thought it was locked. She hopped up, wondering if she was supposed to bow or genuflect or something, but he was cool. He shook her hand.

"Hey, welcome to *Insanity*." He chuckled. "I like saying that. You're every bit as pretty as your screentest. Prettier."

She was still standing, waiting for him to say "At ease" or the equivalent. "It's an honor to meet you, Mr. Masters. Congratulations on your marriage."

"Thanks." He appeared amused by her formality and awkwardness. He wasn't quite what she expected. Handsome, of course, but shorter, and his features were sharper than they appeared on screen. He had coarse black hair and an easy, aw-shucks smile that lit up his face. His eyebrows were dramatic slashes that drew attention to intense, dark-blue eyes. Grinning, he said, "Please sit down. You're not at a job interview."

"I'm not?" she quipped before wishing she'd kept her snarky side under wraps.

His grin grew wider. "Ever done a sex scene before?" he said easily as he sank into the couch and patted the space next to him. She was pretty sure he knew she hadn't.

"Not on film." She sat on the couch next to him, back ramrod straight, putting the greatest possible distance between them. Her mind raced as she tried to come up with a way to deflect what she feared was coming.

"Well, sometimes it helps your nerves to mess around a little first."

Yeah, I can see what you're proposing, she thought. *You're just not calling it sex.*

She narrowed her eyes. "You're not seriously proposing messing around now, in full makeup and costumes?"

"Of course not." He looked down at his own club outfit—jeans, fancy cowboy boots, and a crisp button-down shirt. "I thought we could meet for drinks after the rushes."

She tilted her head as if confused. "The script says it's a one-night stand, right?"

"Well, yeah …."

"So, wouldn't it actually help our performances if we were really getting intimate for the first time? I mean, in the bar and all."

There was a knock at the door. George got up to answer it. "Uh, Henry, what can I do for you?" he asked, all solicitude. Although she couldn't see much of him, she knew Henry Makos stood there. He was almost as wide as he was tall. He stuck his head in, and she recognized the doughy, pockmarked face. Thank God George was there. The lesser of two evils. Her eyes darted to the wall clock. Two PM. When would they start filming?

"How you doin', Ms. Leftwood?" Henry asked. "Just makin' sure you're comfortable. You're lookin' good. I see you lost the baby fat."

Baby fat? What a jerk. "Uh, thanks, Mr. Makos!" she said brightly. She sounded like the bimbo he thought she was. "This is all so exciting!"

"Yeah, sure." George could hardly miss the dirty look Henry gave him. "Well, later." He practically slammed the door of the trailer.

George widened his eyes in mock dismay. "I wonder what he wanted?" He chuckled. "Excellent timing on my part."

She folded her arms across her chest. "Isn't filming going to start soon? How am I going to keep out of his way?"

George sat down again. "I see you've been warned."

"Are you kidding? He's notorious. You, on the other hand, are not." She gave him a puzzled look. "Your wife is so incredible looking. Why would you bother with someone like me?"

"Direct, I like that." His tone belied his words. A little forlorn, he said, "Don't you like me?"

Leaning toward him, she said in her warmest, most sincere voice, "George, how can I help but like you? You're every woman's fantasy. I've seen all your movies," she lied. "But this heat between us? I'd like to keep it for the movie."

"Good one!" He slapped his thigh, genuinely amused. "Peter Coyote in *Heartbreakers*, right? I loved that movie." His laughter was so infectious that she joined in, unsure if she hadn't just raised the stakes rather than dissuaded him. "Don't worry, Miz Leftwood. Your virtue is safe with me. But I don't guarantee not to get a hard-on while we're filming. Try not to let it shock you too much."

As he opened the door, she said, "Uh, George?"

"Yeah?"

"If the opportunity, uh, arises, would you try to imply to Henry that he shouldn't horn in on your, uh, territory?"

"Ah, you want me to run interference." He let loose a merry peal of laughter she had never heard from one of his screen characters. "Listen, honey, if I can help you there, I most certainly will. 'Master Bait' is one creepy dude. You know I can't do anything that might result in Helena reading about it, right?"

"I wouldn't expect that. And … George? You really are pretty irresistible.

It's just that I'm in love right now myself. It wouldn't feel right, even for what I'm sure would be a truly unforgettable experience."

He patted her knee. "How refreshing. It might just be that you're a good actress, but I believe you. Or my ego wants to, anyway. Good luck with that in Hollywood."

The rapport they'd established made the bar scene infinitely easier. There was almost no dialogue because the music was so loud. He bought her a drink, then pulled her onto the dance floor. Here George reminded her of Kilo. She thought she recalled reading that he came from a musical theater background. Allowing herself the freedom of her reckless character, she became fully immersed in the heady atmosphere of music and sex, almost forgetting that the cameras were rolling. He spun her around, and she tripped, finding herself pinned against the wall. She expected to hear "Cut!" but the camera kept rolling. George was kissing her with what she hoped was cinematic fervor, and she kissed him back, surrendering fully to the moment. Then he drew back and stared into her eyes as if she were the most delicious thing he'd ever seen.

"Cut!" The director walked up to them and slapped George on the back. Then he kissed her hand. "Nice work, guys. We'll do it once more, just in case. Makeup!"

After they fixed her face, they repeated the same sequence, and by the time it was over, she almost *did* want to sleep with George. At least her character and her body did. She knew from experience that it was a little like being drunk. As soon as the pheromones produced by the imaginary scenario and the physical stimulation had receded, she would come to her senses. Next they filmed the two of them leaving the club together. His hands were all over her. It had to be dark outside to film the scene of them making out in the cab, so they broke for dinner, a catered buffet on the set.

"How're you doin'?" George said. In her ear, he whispered, "Let's see how well you hold out after tomorrow. Those were real kisses you gave me." Anyone watching would assume they were joking around. He didn't touch her. She wasn't particularly hungry, and she was worried about gaining back those few extra pounds, so she limited herself to one piece of roast chicken and a few bites of coleslaw, then brushed her teeth and flossed.

They called her around eight for the taxi scene. The car was mounted on what they called a process trailer, so no one was actually driving. The scene involved nothing but hot and heavy kissing, with the driver taking peeks in his rearview mirror. They did four takes. When it was over, she felt wrung out. As they helped her out of her costume in the trailer, she was told to be ready in an hour if she wanted to watch the dailies. They gave her the option to skip them and go back to the hotel, and after about a minute's reflection, she decided that was best. Otherwise she was going to worry about what she looked like during the sex scene, and she didn't want to go there. Besides, what if they didn't like what they saw? She didn't want to witness their disappointment. She figured seasoned actors enjoyed reviewing their own work, but today hadn't been acting, not as she knew it; it had felt more like softcore porn. She didn't want to see herself with her hands and mouth all over George.

Why did they need her here for over three weeks? Her character was about to be murdered. If they stuck with the script, she had only the bar scene, the taxi scene, the love scene, and the murder scene. Unless reshoots were needed.

CHAPTER 34

BACK AT THE HOTEL, MADDIE was too wired to sleep. No one had told her what was happening the next day. Maybe they didn't know. It depended on the dailies. A car was supposed to pick her up at five in the morning. From there, she'd just have to wing it. Finally she took an allergy pill and slept.

The phone rang at eight. Though groggy from the allergy pill, she quickly realized no driver had arrived and she had slept in. *Oh no*, she thought, *that's it. I'm out of here*. Instead, the woman on the phone said, "Is this Maddie? This is Jules' secretary." Jules was the director. "He is very happy with your performance—congrats!—but they aren't ready to film your other scenes today, so … lucky you! You have the day off. Enjoy."

Maddie considered a sightseeing tour but they all seemed too cheesy. Homes of the Stars sounded interesting, if only for the architecture. It might be fun to wander around the cemetery where so many stars were buried. First things first: caffeine.

She found a coffeeshop, where she sat for a while. Back at the hotel, she watched Turner Classic Movies until four, when she heard a knock at her door. Through the peephole, she saw Henry Makos. Could he hear the TV? If she turned it off, he'd know for sure she was there. She'd just pretend she wasn't. The knocking grew more insistent, but after about ten minutes, he gave up and went away. She waited until six to order room service, then took a bath and went to bed early.

The next day, they filmed the sex scene. Makeup was different this time. They left her face alone, mostly, but they combed her body for flaws. They found the last traces of the Christmas Eve scrape, which didn't require much coverage. The makeup artist explained that she would have a patch for her pubic area, and George would have a sock, reassuring her that everyone knew this was awkward and would be sensitive to that. For about an hour, she sat alone in her trailer wearing a thin robe and slippers, idly flipping through a *People* magazine someone had left behind. When they finally called her, she was skittish as hell, ready to jump out of her skin.

The director had them sit in comfortable chairs and offered Maddie a large glass of chardonnay, which she gratefully accepted. George, who was given what looked like a Scotch on ice, toasted her. "I thought you might like a Sex on the Beach," he joked, "but Jules says you're not a cocktail girl, that you prefer chardonnay. Relax, kiddo. It's a small crew, we have our protective barriers, and everyone's a grownup here." His words helped, as did the wine, and she relaxed.

First, dancers in bodysuits performed the choreography. It was the strangest dance sequence, ever—not the least bit erotic, like two aliens gyrating together. Or robots. The director explained that he expected them to improvise when "inspiration" struck—the word jangled her nerves—but this was the framework. Three cameras were set up aside from a handheld. When the time came, she walked to the bed as if in a dream state, trying not to astral project. She handed her robe to the assistant and faced George, who to his credit looked way more on edge than she'd expected.

"Okay, you understand that this is acting, right? You're not going to worry that I'm, uh, taking liberties? 'Cause I know you've got the jitters and all, but I'd rather not worry about that."

She gave him a stern look. "Of course not."

"God, you look like a lamb going to slaughter," he whispered, "a really pretty one. They told me you were wearing almost no makeup. Jeez, I need more beautification than you."

They did a practice run, which was also filmed. It was a waking-up-in-the-morning scene, so they began by feigning sleep. They positioned her on her side. He woke up first, uncovered her, ran his hand down her body. She opened her eyes and smiled. The director shouted directions as they moved, and soft jazz played in the background. Although she kept her attention on George—imagining David's stronger, more masculine face all the while— she let her body take over. Like an erotic dance. In the end she had a hard time recalling what they actually did. There was more improvisation in the second take, and she felt George's erection through his sock, but she went with the flow. He was a sensitive kisser, and nothing he did felt overly invasive, considering the process.

Finally it was over. They were handed their robes and another drink as they waited for the director to decide what else needed to be done.

"You have the most beautiful breasts I've ever seen," George whispered. There was nothing lascivious in his tone.

"Great job, you two," Jules said. "I know that was difficult. Maddie, you're a natural. I think we're done here. Tomorrow we'll shoot the murder scene. We have a double for you when the bullets fly, so it's fairly simple. George goes out to get bagels; you're wearing his shirt. The doorbell rings, and you walk to the door, look through the peephole, and yell, 'Who's there?' Then we switch you with the double, who flies backward as if blasted to the floor. They cover you with fake blood, we arrange you on the floor, and you hold your breath, eyes open."

Which was exactly how it went.

"I could have done without walking to the door wearing just panties and his unbuttoned shirt," Maddie told Ali. "They wanted my breasts exposed. Come on, what woman would put on a man's shirt and leave it unbuttoned? What's the point? Beyond titillation."

They both laughed. "What about Henry?" Ali asked. "He left you alone after that?"

"Oh, we had our run-in. He called and asked me to come to his office for a meeting, where he was wearing only a robe. I knew what I was up against, but that didn't make it any easier. Henry wanted me to be 'nice' to him and let his robe gape open. I backed away, but I didn't overreact. I told him I was a lesbian, though I think he'd heard that one before. That's the nice thing about being an unknown actress. No inside scoop on your love life or sexual preferences. He was angry, told me I'd never work on another movie of his. Maybe that's so. Frankly, I'm not so sure I care."

Ali's concern touched her. "Are you sure? You said the Mako brothers are powerful."

"The director was pleased. I never saw the dailies—couldn't bear it— but he got what he wanted. I wish I'd taken the time to see more of Los Angeles. I did sight-see a bit at the end because we finished way ahead of schedule. Walked around Forest Lawn cemetery and hung out at Venice Beach. Shopped some."

"George Reed Masters didn't make another pass?"

Maddie laughed. "Well, sort of. He showed up at my hotel room. I knew he wouldn't attack me, so I let him in. He expected me to make the first move, which I didn't. Finally he asked me outright if I wanted to 'mess around.' I said I was tempted but wanted to stay friends. He said friendship didn't preclude a roll in the hay. In the end I talked him out of it."

"What does your agent say?"

"She was ecstatic," Maddie replied. "Heard only nice things, or so she claimed. If she knows I've been blacklisted by the Makos brothers, she didn't pass it on. But at the moment I'm unemployed."

"Except by us."

Maddie got off the stool and stretched. "I can't accept your money. I have no formal duties."

"Sure you do. Cheer me up, work your magic on Lorenzo, break through David's emotional armor."

Maddie hadn't mentioned the part about seeing David's face while pretending to make love to George. "David's going to have to take responsibility for his own emotional armor," she told Ali.

* * *

The next day, Ali was reading about Joe DiMaggio's ill-fated marriage to Marilyn Monroe aloud to the twins using her baby voice. It was a magazine article that interested her, and they seemed fully engrossed, so why not? Even if they did understand, there was nothing scandalous. Marilyn was a notorious sex kitten, and Joe was too jealous. Sort of like if Rina had married Joe O'Connell. That didn't bear thinking about.

Her cell phone rang, and she saw that it was Liam.

"Hey," she said, "what's up?"

The strain in his voice was immediately apparent. "Ali, Nancy is gone."

Ali was silent. Unlike Liam, she'd remained aloof from their birth mother. Now she was sorry she hadn't let her guard down, attempted to connect with her, if only for a moment. There might not be another chance.

"Ali? Are you there?"

"How do you know she's gone?"

"I deposited a thousand dollars in a bank account for her so she could function more independently. Too much temptation, clearly. She withdrew it all at once and left a note in my mailbox."

"What did it say?"

He read, " 'Sorry, honey. Thanks for the leg up. Glad you and Ali are doing so great. But you don't need me in your lives, and I got things to do.' That was it."

"Damn it!" Ali muttered. "She was doing so much better! She made that miraculous recovery and everything."

"Yeah, I know." Liam sounded bitter. "I guess she's just a ramblin' gal. At least the mystery is solved."

Ali felt an instant throbbing at her temples and pressed them with her thumb and middle finger. "We'd have been better off if she'd stayed gone."

"I don't buy that." Liam sounded implacable, betrayed, the embodiment of justice scorned. "We'd always have wondered. Thank God we take after our father in every important way."

"Should we try to track her?"

"Nah," Liam said. "If she's bent on self-destruction, I don't want to witness it. Especially knowing I financed it. I genuinely thought she wanted to turn over a new leaf."

"You can't blame yourself." Ali was confused by the desolation that weighed her down, making even the effort to sit up straight a trial. She was thinking of David and the law of unintended consequences.

When she ended the call, the twins were staring at her, wide-eyed, their lips quivering. She immediately set about reassuring them, passing them their blankies. She must have done a convincing job because they suddenly lay down and slept, as if their batteries ran out at the same time. This kind of thing wasn't unusual. They often acted in tandem. With a heavy sigh, Ali reclined on the couch, unable to move, but she didn't sleep. That was where Maddie found her at lunchtime.

"Ali?"

She lifted her head.

"Are you okay?"

She told Maddie about the phone call. "I never trusted her," Ali said in a low voice so as not to wake the twins, "but I wish I'd at least *tried* to connect. Now I might never get the chance. I wonder …." She stopped herself, but Maddie had already read her mind.

"Her recovery," Maddie said. She was perched next to her on the couch, a reassuring hand on her arm. "Maybe it wasn't meant to be. Maybe David should have left it alone."

"That's what I told Joe," Ali said. "Joe's vocal cords …." It was as if neither of them wanted to acknowledge David's gift in plain language. What he'd done for them, against his better judgment.

Maddie nodded. "And my ankle. Also my hip on Christmas Eve, though I didn't know it at the time."

Ali's eyes widened. Of course. She recalled the story of the natives who couldn't see Magellan's ships until the medicine man pointed them out. Because the ship was beyond the scope of their imaginations, their brains didn't register the sight. Whether or not the story was true, what it said about human nature was valid.

"Have you spoken with David since you returned?" Ali asked. "It might help him to know that at least one of his … *efforts* worked out. That the experience didn't damage your psyche, as we feared it might."

Maddie nodded slowly. "What about Joe?"

"I wonder," Ali said with a weak attempt at a smile. "Is he enjoying the tour? When he's home, he sleeps a lot. It's like he's drained his life force for the sake of his performances and can do nothing here but recuperate. Those few days I tagged along were fun, quite the whirlwind. Joe just blows me away. I was so proud of him …. The fans seem ecstatic. The older singer he's touring with? His daughter is part of his band. I met her. She's kind of a pocket-sized Rina. About five feet tall with a bubbly personality and milkmaid prettiness. Joe told me she's a terrible flirt, and that I shouldn't be surprised if the tabloids start speculating."

"You're not worried, are you?"

"Not about Joe. I just hate that aspect of it. When you're a public figure, anyone is free to speculate about your life, come to crazy conclusions. Now what? The demand will continue. His album has already gone gold. Award season doesn't start until November, but I expect a song—maybe the whole album—will be nominated. We were happier when he was in semi-retirement." She blew out a disgusted breath. "At least I was."

"Don't be so hard on yourself," Maddie said in a soothing voice. "I think about that movie, dread the idea of everyone seeing me waltz around in my thinly veiled birthday suit. And I wonder, will my career be all about exposing myself until no one wants to see me naked anymore? Everyone was nice. Overall, it was a positive experience. But being a woman in Hollywood …." She sighed.

"Can you go in a different direction, ask to be in G- or PG-rated movies even if they don't feature A-list stars?"

Maddie snorted. "Not with Lola as my agent."

"Maybe it's time for a different agent," Ali said.

CHAPTER 35

AT DINNER THAT NIGHT, MADDIE mostly stayed silent as Ali told David about Nancy's "departure." She didn't call it a betrayal, which is how it appeared to Maddie. She couldn't help but think of her own father and the damage his alcoholism had wrought. Nancy's weakness seemed to be for drugs, meth in particular. What if someone had "cured" Maddie's father? Would he have grabbed the second chance, tried to make it up to her and her mother? He'd been so regretful, so penitent at the end. Perhaps there could have been another chapter.

With an air of martyred calm, David listened to the story of Nancy's disappearance. Finally, he said, "Where's Lorenzo?"

Ali explained that he'd had an early dinner—had requested a frozen chicken pot pie. This triggered laughter and childhood memories of macaroni and cheese, Beefaroni, and TV dinners. Comfort food for children. "He's probably sensed a shift in the Force," Ali said. "He's downstairs in the rec room with May, Susan, and the twins. He loves that wooden train, says he wants to be a conductor when he grows up. Well, that's not quite what he said. 'Drive trains' were the actual words. I think he'd welcome some playtime with his dad and a bedtime story."

David stood and nodded at them. "See you both tomorrow."

Tomorrow was Monday, and David had mentioned a day off. So far he'd avoided being alone with Maddie. Was he afraid to talk to her, afraid of what might have happened in Hollywood? Since the conversation with Ali, the thought had occurred to her. At first Maddie had assumed he was determined not to continue their affair. Now she wasn't so sure. As she lay in bed, reading, she stayed on the alert for David, knowing he would appear on the lighted pathway between nine and nine thirty. When he did, she was ready. Before she could chicken out, she sprinted over and knocked on his door.

In the entire minute it took him to answer, she started to second-guess herself again. But then he opened the door and stood aside for her to enter. No greeting.

"David?" His expression was guarded. "Is this okay, or do you want me to go?"

He answered quickly, "Don't go," and she relaxed. He sat on the couch and waited for her to join him.

Sitting alongside a man you wanted but who might not want you was a tricky business. She thought of George and how she had sat as far away from him as possible. This item of furniture was more love seat than couch. Even sitting on the far end, David could easily reach over and touch her.

"Miss me?" she said, inanely.

He arched his eyebrows. "What do you think?"

"Honestly? I have no idea. Ali thinks you're worried about what might have happened to me in Hollywood."

Did she imagine the change in his expression?

"Why don't you tell me?"

She recounted the story, leaving little out. "I honestly didn't know if I'd have the strength to stop what I saw as the inevitable," she confessed. "The path of least resistance is how most actors do it. Me too, usually."

David grimaced. "Let me get this straight: I'm going to have to endure watching you make love to another man on a huge screen then see you shot to death."

She didn't blush often, but she could feel the heat in her cheeks now. "The person you'll see riddled with bullets will be a stunt woman. It *is* me lying on the floor, covered in fake blood. So, uh, yes."

He reached for her then, at long last, and just held her. She relaxed in the firm embrace of his strong arms and the delicious scent of his warm body that enveloped them both.

"I've thought a lot about gifts," she said, her cheek pressed against his chest. "Gifts, as in talents. After one of my performances, a director told me, 'You have a gift. It would be a crime not to use it.' What if that gift doesn't come with the right psychological makeup? The successful actors I know— and I have a loose definition, I just mean they don't need a day job—are hungrier than me. They have no boundaries. For me it all takes too much of a toll."

"Gifts," he repeated, "like mine."

He told her the story of his car accident then, how every time he "healed" someone—sometimes it was incomplete, sometimes total—it had backfired. Especially in Africa, where they thought he was a witchdoctor. "I swore that when I came home, I wouldn't use it, but when I see people I love in pain …." He stopped himself.

She turned to look at him. "Like Joe, for example?"

His smile was pained. "For example. Is Joe happier now that his vocal cords are clear? I can't guarantee they will stay that way. And now, will he expect me to heal them again, no matter what he does? Teresa's voice is rough too. My guess would be a combination of genetic weakness, acid reflux, and overuse. Some vocal cords can take anything. That will never be true of Joe. During his short visits between gigs, I haven't observed that he is happier. Ali certainly isn't."

"You gave Joe a second chance. Ali says he's terrific on stage, gets so much energy from it. If you can't have something, you want it more than ever. Perhaps this tour will be enough. He'll realize that staying home wasn't as much of a sacrifice as he thought."

He gathered her to him in a slower, less innocent hug, pressing her against his hard chest. Over the top of her head, he said, "Human beings are slow learners. And their memories are short."

Reluctantly, she pushed him gently away. "David, did healing Joe and Nancy also leave you with a blinding headache?"

He didn't answer immediately.

"After that first time," she went on, "I didn't suspect anything. After you fixed my ankle, when you had to check into a motel, the cause and effect were obvious. Joe doesn't realize that healing is so hard on you. Why don't you tell him? He might not be so ready to ask that particular favor again."

David took a minute to consider her words. "For some reason, after healing Nancy, I was fine. I had a slight headache with Joe, but nothing like I did with you. I wish I understood it better. Hell, I wish I understood it at all. Maybe being motivated by self-interest sets off a painful guilt response."

Maddie felt terrible. "Oh, David, if I'd known—"

"It was my choice," he broke in. "I knew how much you wanted and needed that opportunity."

Maddie took his hand and kissed the palm. "David, where do we stand? I thought about you the entire time I was gone."

He kissed her on the forehead. "I've never stopped thinking of you—not since the day we met. The jealousy is almost unbearable. Of Kilo, of your costars. How do people manage relationships with actors?"

Not well, she thought, unable to think of a single positive example other than Paul Newman and Joanne Woodward—and they must have had their ups and downs. She wanted to protest that David had insisted they wouldn't work as a couple, that Kilo …. But she couldn't explain Kilo away without admitting it had been a relationship of convenience. That wouldn't help matters.

"I could give it up."

He gave an emphatic shake of his head. "I would *never* ask that. I will learn to deal with it. I love you."

"You do?" She grinned. "Well, I definitely love you."

"Um, I *don't* love these." He fingered one of her hair extensions as if it might bite.

She laughed. "If you don't mind me looking like a punk rocker, I was planning on cutting everything off so I could go back to my natural color."

David broke into that rich, baritone guffaw she loved so much. "Lorenzo will be disappointed. They make you look like a fairy princess."

"You're not into fairy princesses?"

"I'm as susceptible as the next man. But I prefer the real you. You'd be my fairy princess if you were bald as a cue ball."

She unzipped a few inches of his cardigan sweater. "Do you mind? You look, uh, hot." When he didn't stop her, she kept going until it was completely unzipped. His lips were twitching, and relief had made her giddy.

He reached for her T-shirt. "You look *hot* too."

She batted his hand away. "You first." She helped him shrug out of his sweater and pull the T-shirt over his head. She thrummed her fingers down his chest, then planted wet kisses on each nipple. "How is your chest so smooth?" she whispered. "You don't shave, do you?"

His deep laugh rumbled through her. "I've never had much body hair." He reached for her, but she gently slapped his hand away.

"Not yet. I've been dreaming of this." She unbuttoned his jeans, feeling the daunting bulge poke through his briefs and hearing his breath quicken. She freed his enormous erection and licked the head, enjoying the way it bucked against her. When he tried to pull her up, she resisted at first. Finally she acquiesced, falling back on the couch with a sigh of pleasure.

Then the tables turned. Without warning, he reached under her arms and lifted her onto his lap, kicking off his jeans as she squirmed on top of him, still fully clothed. "I hate to end this sweet torture," he rasped, "but it's been too long, and I need to be inside you … *now*." Despite his words and flagrant arousal, he took his time undressing her. He skimmed her T-shirt lightly over her breasts, unclasped her bra, and ran his tongue over her hard nipples. Unzipping her jeans, he pulled them down, his palms massaging her bottom as she straddled his lap. Still holding her close, he reached into the nightstand drawer for a condom. He stood—her legs wrapped around his waist—and reversed their positions so that he was the one straddling her. Slipping on the condom, he eased himself slowly inside her, making them both sigh with pleasure. Gradually his thrusting became more urgent, bringing them both to the brink. She'd never been with a man large enough to make her orgasm this way. She could hardly believe it was happening.

"You like this," he gasped, but she was beyond speaking. She was moaning, shuddering, liquifying, floating away. With a mighty groan, he surrendered to his own need. When it was over, he pulled out and fell back on the couch. She nuzzled against his chest, wanting to ask him for reassurances, for forgiveness, wanting to know if he still intended to keep their relationship—if she dared call it that—a secret.

In the morning Maddie awoke to find an arm clamped possessively across her chest by a lightly snoring giant, his lips curved in a beatific smile. They had spent the night together only a few times. She thought of the unanswered questions, then the declarations of love. Even if he meant them, was he serious about her? Now that she knew his secret, she understood his reluctance to trust, to give a woman his heart.

He stirred next to her, and his fingertips skimmed over her breast as he opened one eye. "Good morning."

"Good morning." She kissed him lightly on the lips, and he pulled her in for an embrace that demonstrated exactly how excited he was to wake up next to her.

After they were both sated by another mind-blowing bout of lovemaking, she remarked, "You have a pile of condoms on your bedstand."

He laughed. "All for you. I wanted to be prepared for your visit. I know you wear an IUD, but one unplanned pregnancy was enough. Since Lorenzo, I can't be too careful."

"I get it." Maddie peeked at the clock, which read nine. "I'm usually in the kitchen by eight. Ali's going to be knocking on the door any minute just to make sure I'm still alive."

David chuckled as he ran a finger along the curve of her waist and hips.

"Um, give her credit. She can connect the dots. We're both missing in, uh, action."

She laughed, then said, trying to keep her tone light, "So … we're not a secret anymore?"

He gave her a long look. "I told you I love you, remember? Unless I had an auditory hallucination, you said you love me too. I don't speak those words lightly. I want you to marry me as soon as humanly possible."

Her jaw dropped.

When she didn't speak, he said, "Too soon?"

She touched a finger to his lips. "It's not that. There's so much to work out."

He rose and sat on the edge of the bed. "I know. Your career, my career, where will we live? It will be an adventure. I'll never stand in your way as long as I know you're committed to *us*. Maybe I'll start a private practice in Port Townsend. Or we can move back to Seattle. I'm open to anything. Except that we have to consider Lorenzo too. I'm investigating the legal angles. Sylvia's sister and her husband don't have a valid claim, and Sylvia doesn't want him. But I also have to consider Lorenzo's wishes. Young as he is, he's old enough to weigh in."

Maddie ran a hand along his powerful thigh, avoiding his eyes, unsure of how to respond.

"Just say yes," he urged her. "The rest will work itself out."

"Yes."

CHAPTER 36

———◆———

On a Friday afternoon in mid-May, Ali was sitting on the flagstone terrace in the shade. She faced the spectacular view of the Strait of Juan de Fuca, a book in her lap, but her thoughts were elsewhere.

"Ali?"

"Becca!" She hopped up to hug her friend, and the book fell from her lap.

"We said I'd come over around four, right? I didn't mean to startle you. I'm surprised the dogs didn't bark." Becca was wearing a peasant blouse and flouncy skirt in yellow and orange that fanned out as she spun around to survey the premises. "Come to think of it, where are the dogs?"

"Oh," Ali made a face, "shared custody."

Becca took a chair in the sun. "It's coolish out here. Could we turn on a heat lamp?"

"Oh? Sure." In her jeans, fleece, and down vest, Ali hadn't noticed the temperature drop. She fiddled with the mechanism, turning on the gas and flipping the switch. She lit the firepit as well.

Becca moved her chair closer to the lamp. "So, it's come to that."

"Huh?"

"The dogs. Like a divorce."

Ali laughed and waved away Becca's words. "Nah. Liam's taken them for a run. He knows they're happier with room to run free, and we need them for security, especially now that Joe is hot property again. Harry likes to chase sticks in the water. I told Liam that's okay as long as he hoses that big boy down when they're done. He'll bring them back when he and Teresa come over for dinner."

"I'm sorry Jean-Louis can't make it. The restaurant has only been open a few weeks, and Friday night, you know …."

"Of course. Everything's okay with you two?" She was relieved to see that her friend's aspect didn't darken. Becca hated pity and so tended to underplay her own problems, but her expression didn't lie.

"Sure. We've had our tense moments, but it's all good now that the restaurant is a success. No primetime reservations available until January. Of course, you can come early or after eight."

"Jean-Louis isn't driving you nuts? I got the impression his ebullience could be a bit much at times. You know, Snagglepuss."

"Marriage is an adjustment, right? I knew I was marrying Snagglepuss. I wasn't quite prepared for Snagglepuss with the dial turned up to ten. In North Bend he handles stress really well, as if he's more in his element. We're both a little at sea here, frankly. But he's hired a manager he trusts, and he's been training a talented young chef who is blessedly free of ego. Which means we can go home soon." Seeing Ali's obvious disappointment, she said, "Don't look like that. Like you've lost your best friend. I won't be around as much, but I'll be around. You might also consider visiting us more often. How are the twins?"

Ali pointed at the baby monitor. "Down for the count. I haven't heard anything to the contrary, though May is looking in on them. They are like little whirling dervishes when they're awake."

Becca cocked her head, taking in Ali's appearance. "You do look tired. Beautiful as ever, though. How's Joe?"

Ali shrugged, unsure how much to share. Her husband was much on her mind. "Oh, uh, the tour was a success. A triumph, really. The fans are clamoring for more."

"And you seem *totally* psyched about it." She raised her fist in the air with an anemic, "Yay."

"Okay, you got me. I'm torn. Of course I'm happy for him. If only *he* were happier. I enjoyed seeing him do his thing. Maybe next time I'll go along for the whole tour."

"They'll be a next time?" Becca sounded worried.

"Who knows? He sounds froggy to me."

"Uh-oh."

"Yeah. And the studio might as well be radioactive. He goes out of his way to avoid even the sight of it."

"It's only been just over a week," Becca said. "Obviously he needs a break. Where is he now?" She looked around warily, as if Joe might be listening in.

"With David. They went on a hike somewhere. It's too early in the season for anything in the upper elevations, so I'm not sure where. They might just be walking around Fort Worden. David has a … calming effect on him." She hoped Joe wasn't pushing for a refresher treatment on his vocal cords. David had made it clear how reluctant he was to use his gift.

"David's not at the clinic? I thought he worked Fridays."

"He quit. I believe the doctor who was on pregnancy leave is ready to come back anyway. Then there's the wedding on May thirty-first to prepare for."

Becca brightened. "Jean-Louis is *so* excited. He's got a killer feast planned and the special-events room reserved for the rehearsal dinner. I gather the actual ceremony will be low key."

"Yes. Maddie and David said they don't want a big romantic to-do. No bells and whistles. No rain-forest bowers, though between you and me, Joe has one planned anyway. Simpler than the one he made for Teresa and Liam. Teresa insisted on buying her a dress. I haven't seen it yet."

"What about Maddie's career?"

"When she was offered another role like that—you know, big-budget but with a lot of nudity, minimal dialog, and a bloody end—she turned it down. Her agent threatened to drop her, and she called her bluff. Which is how she got out of her contract. David had nothing to do with her decision to turn the role down. She wants to hold out for parts that challenge her as an actress."

"Amen, baby," Becca said. "Will David look for another job after the wedding?"

"Probably not. He was pretty bored at the clinic. No challenges there. Stasis. Or staleness. Not sure of the word. Maybe I mean 'stifled.' And he says the temptation to use his gift is simply too great. Especially when children come in."

Ali knew she shouldn't have told Becca, but there was no keeping secrets from her best friend in all the world.

Becca nodded. "I get it. So, what's he gonna do?"

"Take a break, I guess." Ali gave a helpless shrug. She hoped David and Maddie knew what they were doing. "They're going to embark on an extended honeymoon on the Peninsula."

Becca hugged herself and moved closer to the heat lamp. "Is that what

Maddie wants? She's never been outside the country. They could at least go to another state. Hawaii, maybe."

Ali flapped her arms around. "I'm staying out of it. They have reservations at Lake Crescent and Lake Quinault."

"How'd they manage that? Those places book up months in advance."

"Don't underestimate Joe's connections. Actually, I think the reservations are a wedding gift from his manager Linc. He always reserves a couple of rooms for VIPs. Clients or other business contacts he wants to butter up. You never know when you need someone to owe you. If they're not spoken for, he uses them himself or gives them away to friends or relatives."

Becca looked doubtful. "Um, okay. Makes sense. All you have to do is put down a deposit, right? Linc's not hurting for money."

"David will pay the balance. None of those O'Connell kids needs to work a day in their lives, thanks to their grandmother's will."

"Huh." Ali caught a whiff of envy from Becca.

"Yes, I know," Ali said. "It's a mixed blessing, though, don't you think? Your parents raised you with an excellent work ethic, but where would I have been if money were no object? The master's degree in Communication was supposed to lead to our dream jobs. But neither of us found a way to capitalize on it and still be happy. You do PR for Jean-Louis, of course, but no degree was required for that. I still haven't found a way to monetize my drawings. Then Joe came along and I never had to figure it out. Without work, it's easy to get depressed."

"Are you depressed now?" Becca asked. "Don't sell yourself short. What about the FOSSP kids? You have a purpose, clearly."

Ali wasn't quite convincing when she replied, "Only sometimes. Depression is complicated. Maybe it's chemical, or perhaps some of the past still weighs on me. I have a lot on my plate."

"You've hired therapists for the FOSSP kids," Becca said. "Ever consider seeing one of them yourself?"

When would I fit that in? Ali thought.

"Don't worry, sweetie," Becca went on. "Joe will rally, the twins are amazing. David and Maddie are madly in love. All will be well." She shook her friend's hand. "You and I need to hike more! Now that the guys are using their hikes for male bonding."

Ali smiled at the thought. "I would love that. Let's make it a regular thing until you return to North Bend. Although our options are limited, it being so early in the season."

Becca looked toward the house. "What about Lorenzo?"

"He's back in Portland, for now. At his request. I did notice that he hugged both David and Maddie awfully tight when they said goodbye. Sylvia's sister and her husband get that they have to figure out how to share him—at the very least. Fortunately he isn't school age, which would mean taking that schedule into account. David didn't want to uproot him while they themselves were so rootless."

Becca pointed at her book. "How do you like *The Hours*?"

"It's okay." Ali picked up the hardcover book. "It's an interesting concept. A riff on Virginia Woolf's *Mrs. Dalloway*. The women's lives are so depressing, I might not finish it."

Becca looked taken aback. "Why *would* you? Stick to happy books, for pity's sake. Save the angsty stuff for when you're happier." Becca paused, biting her lower lip. "Other than the family unit, who have you met here?"

"Almost no one," Ali admitted, "but that will change now that Joe is home. Joe's bandmate and friend Matthew just bought a house here, and he's way more extroverted than us. Maybe he'll expand our horizons. It takes time to feel at home in a community. And I need to make more of an effort."

"I can't imagine there are a lot of mom/baby groups here," Becca said. "Mostly retirees." She smiled, leaned forward, and made a come-to-mama gesture with her fingers. "What about Teresa and Liam? Still talking?"

"As far as I can tell—I haven't seen much of either of them lately— everything is hunky-dory. They're living together in Liam's Victorian. Liam finished the roof, and now he's putting on new cedar siding. Teresa's expanding her decorating business, thanks to Matthew."

"*Liam's* Victorian," Becca repeated. "I guess he's got the upper hand now. Teresa's not worried he'll leave her again? That's what I'd be thinking. 'Whenever things get tough, he leaves.' That threat would hang over my head like the sword of Damocles. I'd be afraid to speak my mind at all."

Ali gave a wave of denial. "It's not like that. Liam didn't know what to do. He was desperate to break the stalemate. He never intended for them to divorce."

Becca blew out a disgusted breath. "Yeah, right."

"Between you and me," Ali went on, "Liam always believed Teresa was too good for him. And when he saw Teresa supposedly falling for Kilo's schtick again, it triggered something. The jealousy was overwhelming."

"Men will never understand the appeal of a Kilo," Becca said.

Ali laughed. "Nope. Reminds me of something Carrie once said, referring to Joe's ex-girlfriend, Rina. That men overlook a lot of faults when a woman is spectacularly beautiful. And in Rina's case, crazy talented."

"For women, same goes with men like Kilo," Becca said. "Even knowing they're trouble, they can't stay away."

"Not you and me," Ali said.

Becca stared at her manicure as if inspecting it for flaws. "I had my share of Kilos. Got them out of my system. You survived a couple of bad-news men as well."

Ali snorted. "Luis was like Kilo without the charm or finesse."

"Oi! I'm sorry I wasn't around to support you through that."

Becca had gone to Princeton while Ali attended the UW. Ali had been accepted into Princeton, but even with the generous scholarship, those four years would have left her deeply in debt. As it was, her school loans had been daunting, until Joe had come along and made them disappear, just like magic. Becca's parents had paid for all their children's educations without breaking a sweat. Time to change the subject.

"Speaking of bad news, any developments in the Nancy case?"

Ali sighed. "No sign of her. Joe hired a detective, but it's like she vanished from the face of the earth."

"She's good at that, I guess. I'm so sorry."

Ali sat back in her chair. "We were lucky with Duncan. Most stories like that don't end happily." Ali couldn't help but think, *What if David had refused to help her?*

"When's the premiere of *Insanity*?" Becca asked.

"Sometime around Thanksgiving. Maybe Thanksgiving Day. Maddie's dreading it."

Becca made a face. "No kidding. I wouldn't be in any hurry to see my business blown up to the size of the Goodyear Blimp and jiggling around for all the world to see."

Ali shrugged. "Who knows? The role might make her a star. With movies, it's all about that on-screen magic. You either have it or you don't."

"Even if you don't care."

Ali laughed. "*Especially* if you don't care."

EPILOGUE

———•———

In Teresa's opinion, Jean-Louis's newest Fête Sauvage was a perfect fit for Port Townsend—the sort of restaurant you imagined some nineteenth-century British explorer like Sir Richard Burton would frequent between expeditions. Or maybe the setting of an H.G. Wells novel. The side room Jean-Louis had reserved for them contained three round tables, occupied by the usual suspects.

"This is the perfect venue for David and Maddie's rehearsal dinner," Teresa told Liam as they entered. "You know how he used to love adventures set in Colonial Africa. Even if Jean-Louis and Becca weren't Ali's dearest friends, he'd have chosen this place."

"I preferred those Rafael Sabatini books," Liam said. "You know, *Scaramouche, Captain Blood, The Sea Hawk.* Even though most boys my age were into more contemporary stuff. Our foster father was raised on them. Maybe he joined the Peace Corps in search of adventure." He grimaced. "Clearly being at home didn't do the trick."

Seeing a shadow cross her husband's face, Teresa wondered if he was thinking about the motorcycle accident that had killed them in Botswana, while Liam was struggling to recover from his own brush with death in Jerusalem. She wished he'd sell his Harley, though he only drove it around town.

"Where did they get the paintings?" Liam asked, his gaze traveling along the walls. "I don't think Delacroix ever painted wild boars. I thought they were going with reproductions."

"He did," Teresa said without thinking. "*The Wild Boar Hunt, After a Painting by Rubens*, it's called." She instantly wished she could have left it alone. The last thing she wanted right now was to lord her knowledge of art over Liam. "That isn't this painting, though," she rushed to add. "They found someone who did Delacroix *hommages*," she said. "Becca has a good eye for design. I'm impressed."

Fortunately Liam didn't take issue with being corrected. He gave her an affectionate nudge. "Really? So says the hottest interior designer in Port Townsend? Today, Port Townsend, tomorrow, the world."

"Don't tease me," she pretended to pout. "I don't want to conquer the world."

"I know. You just want to cultivate your garden, like Candide. Maybe that's all I want too. I just didn't want to cultivate Joe's garden. I wanted my own."

She gave him a worried look. "In the future you'll tell me what you want? You won't let me assume I know? I never meant for that to happen."

Liam gave her a long, appreciative onceover. "You look amazing. God, you're a stunningly beautiful woman. How did I get so lucky? I love this dress." He touched the silky fabric and purposely let his hand wander past the hem to her leg. "And what's under it."

She gave his hand a little swat. "Behave!" She'd worried he wouldn't approve of the dress, which by his standards was obscenely expensive. The shimmery blue-silk spaghetti-strap underdress skimmed her body and was layered with a filmy sheer fabric. Though it was too fancy for casual Port Townsend, she couldn't resist. She and Liam had discussed their issues, and it turned out her wardrobe wasn't one of them. He wasn't worried about how she spent her money, as long as she didn't use it to control him. She assured him she'd never meant to do that. She spent money on him because she loved him and wanted to please him. Perhaps too much. He didn't want to feel like her kept man, and for that she couldn't blame him. She marveled at his appearance tonight, the tailored suit and crisp linen shirt he'd purchased in Paris without her knowledge. It was an outfit any Parisian dandy would be proud to be seen in. On him it was supremely masculine, naturally, because on Liam, even clothing off the rack appeared made to order. He had the sartorial taste of a French aristocrat, but no matter how shabbily he dressed, he had the look of a prince in disguise.

They turned to find Becca right behind them. The red wraparound dress with matching pumps made her look like the human equivalent of an American Beauty Rose. "What do you think?" Becca said, indicating the interior of the restaurant with a broad sweep of her arm. "Does it work?"

Teresa gave her a warm hug. "You know it does."

"That means everything, coming from you. Even the gilded antler chandeliers and the gold-leaf wallpaper?"

"Oh, definitely. I'd love to see that wallpaper in Liam's—um, *our* house—but I don't think he'd go for it." Liam gave her a warning look that she guessed was meant to be humorous.

"Do you like the mushroom ragout appetizer?" Teresa had never seen Becca so antsy. She was practically dancing around the small room.

"Divine," Ali said from behind Becca, wrapping an arm around her waist. "Everything is divine. You needn't worry at all. I hope you'll relax and enjoy your role as guest. You know it wouldn't matter to any of us if some dish didn't rise to the Michelin-star standard—though with Jean-Louis at the helm, that's hardly likely."

Ali was dressed in a sequined off-white sheath with a plunging neckline that Teresa happened to know was Chanel couture. Joe's birthday gift—the sapphire necklace—made her eyes appear impossibly blue. Joe had asked Teresa to buy her something special. The rest of the guests were trickling in from the outdoor tent. Teresa's beloved brothers, Joe and David, wore bespoke suits with identical European cuts as if they'd gone to the tailor together, which they probably had. Suppressing a giggle, Teresa imagined them in a new spy series featuring James Bond and his lesser-known and somewhat less suave giant of a brother. David's discomfort with being in the spotlight made him all the more lovable, along with his obvious devotion to Maddie.

Joe walked up behind Ali and kissed her neck. After everything they'd been through—Joe's vocal woes, the lustful nanny, the tabloids' willful disregard for the truth, their emotional investment in every stray who came into their orbit—their love never wavered. Teresa hoped Liam and she would make it to that place of security someday.

Joe and Ali took their places at the table as the duck à l'orange with polenta was served. Their other table mates included Joe's manager Linc and his bandmate Matthew, now also on Linc's client roster. They were hitting it off so well, Teresa thought, it was a shame Linc wasn't gay. But then again, maybe he was. He'd never brought a date to any of the family events he'd attended. *Nah.* She didn't get that vibe. The rapport between them wasn't flirtation. She looked over at Maddie's friend and fellow actor Jeremy, sitting with Maddie and David. Jeremy was a knockout, but she couldn't picture him with Matthew either. Though equally talented, Jeremy sought the limelight and Matthew was content to fade into the woodwork.

"So, Joe, what's next?" she was dismayed to hear Liam say. Didn't he hear the huskiness in her brother's voice?

Joe took it in stride. "I'm going to enjoy summer on the Peninsula." He leaned back in his chair, drumming his fingers on the table as if hearing a new song in his head. Teresa knew better; it was a nervous gesture. "Also, the company of my beautiful wife and my rambunctious daughters. I'll start my memoirs and decide which American standards to record on my next album." Seeing the look on Linc's face, he added, "Kidding. Don't count me out yet."

"No one's counting you out," Linc said in the stentorian voice that made you expect him to say something quotable. He'd shaved off his mustache, but he still looked like Mark Twain. His shaggy hair and older-style suit also didn't jibe with her gay theory.

Joe was refilling their wine glasses. "Speaking of careers, how's Kilo doing?" Liam bristled, which made Joe add, "Liam, don't get your hackles up. I'm personally rooting for Kilo to be a star and never return to Port Townsend. His name should be Loki. Wherever he goes, trouble follows."

"Huh," Matthew said. "It's even an anagram."

"Is anyone in touch with him?" Ali asked.

"According to the industry gossip," Linc said, "he's in L.A., shooting a commercial. The pilot for *Hawaiian Eye* is getting a lot of buzz. Word is, he has a bright future."

"So glad to hear that," Liam said dryly.

Teresa squirmed.

Becca came to the rescue. "What about Lorenzo?"

Ali replied, "He's home with May, Susan, and the twins. He came with Sylvia's sister Chiara, who's going to stay on for a week or so. He'll be the ring-bearer at the wedding tomorrow."

Becca whistled. "No kidding? Sylvia's sister?"

Ali laughed at her friend's expression of mock horror. "She's quiet and kind, nothing like her sister. I have no idea how two such different women could come from the same parents. She told me she's here for Lorenzo, not for rubbing noses with the glitterati." She rolled her eyes. "Or whatever Sylvia imagined us to be. She thought she'd be out of place at the party, much as I tried to reassure her. Said she didn't bring a party dress, didn't want to make anyone uncomfortable by introducing a stranger into their midst."

Becca broke into a mischievous grin. "You're right! She's nothing like Sylvia."

* * *

At eleven that evening, David and Maddie stood arm in arm at the entrance to the art deco living room.

David looked down in wonder at the spectacularly beautiful woman who, tomorrow, would be his bride. Her golden-blonde hair was curled in a sleek bob that framed her elfin features, and she was wearing a dress Teresa had bought for her, a shimmering gold-lamé cocktail number that settled into flattering folds as it skimmed her body, ending just above the knee. Maddie described it as "ruched."

"What do you think?" he asked her.

"Delicious," she said, taking in his white linen shirt and black suit. "The cut of your clothing is much more European than I'm used to seeing on you. That Liam does have great taste."

They laughed. They'd joked that Liam and Teresa had made them their fashion protégés. They didn't mind. Neither had had much call to dress up in their former lives.

David did a clear-eyed assessment of the room. "I wasn't asking what you think of my fancy duds. I mean, the décor. Are we going to preserve Somerset Maugham's drawing room?"

Maddie wrinkled her nose. "Nah. Too uncomfortable. I don't think Teresa will mind … much. She can repurpose a lot of it or recreate it for someone who'll appreciate it."

"You're really okay with me buying the house? We might end up in Seattle."

Teresa shrugged, pulled him with her onto the couch. She bounced a little on the unyielding cushions. "Yep, still feels like sitting on an ironing board. Who else is going to live in it? Ali and Joe have already moved in to the Log Palace. Liam and Teresa have flown the coup. We can keep this house for vacations and get something more modest in downtown Seattle, a condo maybe. You're rich, right?"

He looked at her askance.

"Sorry," she went on quickly. "I don't mean to sound flippant. All this takes some getting used to, that's all. I was fully prepared to live in genteel poverty for the rest of my life."

David pulled her into his lap. "More comfortable?"

She laughed. "I don't know. Your lap is also quite … hard." He bounced her a few times, and she wiggled her bottom in response, nuzzling his neck.

He grinned. "Shall we check out the master bedroom?"

She kicked off her gold sandals. "I think you should make love to me right here on this godawful showpiece couch." She ran a finger along the arm. "On second thought, I'm not sure it's built for … that sort of thing. This fabric looks like a silk blend. We could ruin it."

He took a closer look. "Expensive. But really, no matter how much a couch costs, don't they all end up as landfill or on a street corner with a 'free' sign? No one wants someone else's old couch."

"It's not old," Maddie protested. "No one has eaten Cheetos on it or done anything like what we're contemplating. Do you want to answer to Teresa when she comes to dismantle the room and notices its desecration?"

David stood up. "You convinced me." He picked her up and tossed her over his shoulder like a sack of potatoes—high-priced potatoes you didn't want to bruise. She laughed and kicked a few times in a token show of resistance as he carried her to the master bedroom and gently stood her on her feet.

He unzipped the dress with the same care he'd apply with a tricky incision—*Jesus*, the label said Dolce & Gabbana. If he damaged it, he'd have to answer to Teresa there too. Once unzipped, it skimmed sensuously over Maddie's beautiful breasts, past her tiny waist and wide hips until it puddled on the floor with a sigh, like a pool of molten gold. He watched the dress' progress, mesmerized, thinking it appeared to be savoring Maddie's body too, leaving its exalted position with extreme reluctance. Underneath she wore nothing but thong panties. He took a moment to ogle her body in appreciation—make that worship. Few women her size could do without a bra so successfully.

He picked up the dress and draped it over the chair. Then it was her turn to watch as he carefully removed his own obscenely expensive getup. She lay back on the bed, watching him with rapt attention.

When she chuckled again, his hand froze on a shirt button. "What?" he said, miffed. "I amuse you?"

She clapped a hand over her mouth. "Sorry! It's not you. You're … I don't know, magic."

He was taken aback, wishing he'd never mentioned his "magic" cock. He hoped she wouldn't push for numbers or details. Nor did he wish to know any more about her sexual past.

"Don't stop!" she urged him. "I was just thinking, I don't want to make a habit of letting Teresa and Liam dress us, but it does make the undressing part quite … interesting."

He was laughing, too, as he removed his clothing at a brisker pace. After carefully hanging his suit and shirt in the closet, he realized she had moved right behind him. She pressed her breasts against his back, and he hoisted her up, earning a little screech of delight, and gave her a piggyback ride back to the bed.

AUTHOR'S NOTE

MY HEARTFELT THANKS TO MY amazing sister Laura and my dear friend Karin, who have read several drafts of this book and provided invaluable feedback.

When I lived in New York in the 1980s, I thought, briefly, that I would be an actress. I was "discovered" by a manager who, after my close friend Tina and I moved on, scored some famous clients and moved to Hollywood. He was seriously "You Too'd" a few years back, deservedly so. Through this manager and while cast in various plays, musicals, and operas, I met some wonderful friends, including Tina and Charles, Paula and Alison. Doing small-time opera, I met Bill, Tim, Ramona, and Ellen. I've kept in touch with several friends from summer stock days, some who had (or have) actual careers: Karen H., Jeanmarie, Chris, Patti, Gregg, another Bill. In Seattle, during various singing gigs, I met Deeji and Bob, Ellen and John, Nancy, Fred, Karin, Katie, and others. All had stories to tell, many stranger than fiction. Charles and Ramona died young and are sorely missed. Thank goodness for Facebook—for all its faults—and Zoom. The pandemic and my husband Jeff's stroke ruined many of our plans for keeping in touch in person.

Some actors insist love scenes are just another day at the office. Not in my experience. Though most of my stage work was in small opera companies and musical theater, I often got a crush on my romantic interest, even when the actor was gay, and occasionally dated them. I saw a lot of ill-advised flings happen between people you'd never expect to stray. For some of us, I suppose, it is more difficult to separate fiction from reality, especially when lips and body contact are involved. I wasn't destined to make it as an actor or an opera singer, though I did get my Actors' Equity card and was certified in stage combat after one bug-infested summer doing outdoor drama in Ohio. I wasted a lot of my precious youth dreaming of that elusive Big Break, but I had a blast.

I tried as best I could—from my own experiences, those of my friends, and Google searches—to get Maddie's career right. As I explained in my foreword to *The Guardsman*, my Port Townsend is more removed from reality than I'd like. Jeff and I are spending our winters in Arizona now. Originally I planned to retire to Port Townsend, but now I'm lucky to spend a few days there once or twice a year. When last we visited, I realized how much I'd deviated from the real place. For starters, the O'Connell Compound, with its beach access and view of the Strait of Juan de Fuca, would have to be located in Sequim.

I wrote this saga as an escape from my own troubles. I hope you can fall into it and let it take you away to a place where all roads, even the semi-rocky ones, lead to Happily Ever After. In Books Four and Five, you'll meet the real Jake—not Ali's and Joe's perceptions of the man—and Edward, the (former) priest. Their stories are already written and will be released as I complete the audiobooks. In every book, you'll revisit most of the characters you've met so far—even the troublemakers.

Maybe someday Reynard, Kilo, and George will get their own books. It's way easier to redeem a bad boy in fiction than it is in real life.

Feel free to read the books out of order. I've worked hard to make that possible.

I am so grateful for you, my readers. If you're enjoying these books, please leave a review on GoodReads or Amazon and help me spread the word on social media. You'll find the links and updates on future books at www.CatTreadgold.com.

Photo by Claudia Meyer-Newman

Cat Treadgold has been a publisher and editor, a classical singer, an Equity actress, a coordinator in *Newsweek*'s External Relations Department, a secretary at Siemens AG, a voice teacher at Shoreline Community College, a receptionist at a major recording studio, a cater-waiter with Glorious Foods, a restaurant hostess, and a coat-check girl at a fancy New York nightclub.

Cat has an AB *cum laude* in German Literature from Princeton University, a Master of Music in Vocal Performance from the University of Washington, and a certificate in Technical Writing and Editing from the University of Washington.

She was once semi-fluent in French, German, and Italian and occasionally attempts to revive those languages.

Thank goodness she's good with computers (for a digital immigrant) and learned to touch type in high school.

Two of her unpublished novels, including *The Silent Woodsman*, made it to the finals in their categories (mystery and romance) in the Pacific Northwest Writers Association Annual Contest.

Three of her one-hour adaptations of operas (original translations and dialogue) were performed by Shoreline students while she was a teacher there.

She and her husband Jeff reside in Washington during its drier months and Arizona during its cooler ones.

Cat loves to hike and walk, ride her bike, hula hoop, play golf, listen to audiobooks, cook dishes with lots of leftovers, play piano (she used to be good at it), and play accordion (she will never be good at it). She sings in the occasional concert with Ladies Musical Club, but never in the shower. Her favorite classical composers are Ravel, Debussy, and Brahms. She prefers pop music from the '60s and '70s, particularly Steely Dan and the Rolling Stones.

One hot, humid summer in Ohio, while playing a Shawnee Indian in an outdoor drama during the week and Anne in the musical *Shenandoah* on the weekends, she became certified in stage fighting. That skill later helped her win the role of a broadsword-wielding Maid Marion in a Theater for Young Audiences musical titled *Maid Marion (and Robin Too)*. She always wanted to sing the role of Carmen, but only did it in Seattle Opera previews. She has played Edwin Drood in *The Mystery of Edwin Drood*, Maria in *The Sound of Music*, Julie Jordan in *Carousel,* Cherubino in *The Marriage of Figaro*, Prince Orlofsky in *Die Fledermaus*, Maddalena in *Rigoletto*, Julius Caesar in Handel's *Julius Caesar in Egypt*, and Rosina in *The Barber of Seville*. Along with other fun gigs (including a few at Port Townsend's UpStage), her opera quartet (The Operatic Four Players) performed regularly on Friday nights for about a year at an Italian restaurant. For three years, she toured with NOISE (Northwest Opera in Schools Etcetera).

Videos of her vocal performances can be found on the Cattread channel (www.youtube.com/@cattread),

For more information, go to www.CatTreadgold.com.